MARKED BY FATE

THE CELESTIAL SERIES BOOK 4

LILLITH CARRIE

LILLITH CARRIE PUBLISHING

First paperback edition April 2023

Book Cover designs by Natasha Designs

ISBN 979-8-88862-944-4

Published by Lillith Carrie Publishing

www.lillithcarriepublishing.com

To everyone who has stayed with me on this journey, thank you.
None of this would be possible without you.

Chapter One

Cassie

Three months. It had been three months since the day I died, and every single day I spent in Asgard in this new form, I realized my life, though was said to be my own, wasn't. I was no longer the Lycan beast I once was. Instead, I was a celestial goddess with powers no one could comprehend.

I had no clue how I was going to do this, and when I sacrificed my mundane existence to save my brother and my friends, I hadn't considered what might happen afterward.

However, now with my brother having given me his powers, I was almost as powerful as my grandfather, or so some have said.

"Cassie, are you in here?" Trixie's voice trailed through the open balcony doors, and turning, I met her hypnotic green eyes and smiled. "Oh, there you are."

"Yeah, I'm just out here trying to clear my head. Is everything okay?"

I knew very well what today was. My brother and Trixie were both leaving to head back to my parents' home. Considering my brother had given me every bit of celestial soul he had, it made him just a regular shifter, the Lycan no longer alive in him, and because of that, he was not able to stay in Asgard.

At first, my brother had resented me for what had happened to him, but over the past few weeks, we had talked and things had gotten better, which I was grateful for because if it wasn't for my brother, I would cease to exist.

Honestly, I felt like a lot of it had to do with Trixie. She had changed him completely. The man he was when we first came here was not the same man leaving. I knew without a doubt my parents would be proud of who he had become, and for that, I was proud of him as well.

"Yeah, everything's OK. We're just getting ready to leave," she replied, pushing a strand of her blue hair behind her ear. "I actually wanted to talk to you about something though."

I wasn't quite sure what she wanted to talk to me about, but gesturing for her to follow me into the room and take a seat, she did just that. We sat down and I waited to hear what she had on her mind. "What's going on? You guys aren't having second thoughts, are you?"

"No." She laughed. "I actually spoke with Odin and a few of the others and asked them if it would be possible for you to be able to visit your family one last time. That's if you want to go, of course."

I was shocked to hear Trixie had spoken to the Celestials on my behalf and approached my grandfather about this. To hear they agreed for me to be able to go back one last time if I wanted was something I never thought would be possible.

"My grandfather said that I could go back?" I asked softly as I spoke under my breath, trying to wrap my head around all of it. "I didn't ever think that I would get a chance to see my parents again."

Laying her hand upon my knee, Trixie smiled at me, nodding her head in understanding. There was a lot that had been going on, and I was going to be managing all of this without them, something I wasn't sure I would be able to do.

Granted, I would have Sansa here to help me when I needed it, and according to Trixie, she was sure I would make a few new friends and that she could always pop back if I really needed her. But I just wasn't sure if it would be the same without my brother and Trixie partaking in my future.

"Your grandfather said that if you wanted to go, that was up to you. He understands what you need more than you think he does, and just because he's

Odin doesn't mean that he's any less of a grandfather to you. Perhaps you should take these next few months to really get to know him."

A scoff of annoyance left me as I rolled my eyes. Getting to know my grandfather was at the very bottom of my list of shit I needed to get done. And perhaps that was the stubborn side of me refusing to back down. But it was clear my grandfather had never taken the opportunity to get to know us before. So why should I do that now?

"We'll see," I replied, watching a stern expression cross her face before she smiled. "When are we supposed to be leaving?"

"In like ten minutes," she said excitedly. "No need to pack anything, though. It's only for 24 hours, so get your ass up and let's get going. I'm excited to meet my new mother- and father-in-laws. That is what you guys call them, isn't it?"

Amusement filled me at her lack of how our world worked, and I knew she was going to have one hell of a time learning how to regain her sense of living when it came to living in the world I came from. The human realm. We didn't express our magic or anything like that freely, because the human beings of the world did not know such things existed.

That was going to be problematic in the end. But as I stood to my feet, Trixie took my hand and quickly walked me out of my room and down the hallway towards the portal my grandfather was waiting at with Pollux.

Trixie was quick to let go of my hand as she ran to my brother, wrapping her arms around his neck and kissing his lips gently. Seeing such things made me yearn for what I had lost. The moment I became a celestial being and the other half of me had died away, I felt the bond between Lucas and I break.

The pain of losing a mate was something I would ever wish upon anybody.

It was as if my heart had been ripped from my chest, and though when it happened I was protecting my brother, I couldn't help but relive it every time I closed my eyes at night.

It had been months since I had seen Lucas or Silas, both of them steering clear of me, and honestly, I couldn't blame them. After everything that had happened, I had been a spoiled, rebellious bitch, completely lost about everything that I wanted, searching for the wrong things instead of appreciating what was in front of me.

It took me dying to realize what it was I wanted, and now more than ever, I wished I could have with my brother and Trixie have. I wished more than anything I could go back to the day I found Lucas as my mate and instead of rejecting him by running away, appreciate him and accept him as I should have done from the beginning.

Maybe our futures here would have changed for the better instead of going down the rabbit hole in the dark and dangerous way that ended up causing me to lose part of my life.

As Odin's eyes met mine, I calmly gave him a smile before glancing towards the portal and back at him. "Are you ready to go?"

Hesitating for about a moment, I tried to push back the tears that threatened to fall over the fact that this was going to be my farewell visit. My good bye to the realm I desired to be in.

"Yeah, I'm ready."

Nodding his head, he gestured for all of us to step forward, and as we did, he waved his hand and opened it. The soft, shimmering lights I had seen before filled my vision in front of me and as the three of us stepped within it. We came into a clearing that was dark as night.

The smell of the fresh, clean air of my home filled my nostrils and my heart swelled with joy. Things looked so much different now. The area we walked into was the same one I had left from, and though we used to always have bonfires here, it looked like it hadn't been used in years.

"Do they know that we're coming?" I asked my brother and Trixie, who gave me a slight glance before shaking their head. No.

"Of course not. You know, I like to make an entrance."

Pollux's remark caused me to chuckle as we continued walking across the grassy field, through the tree line, towards the direction remembered to our pack house. As I looked around, I noticed how different everything was. There were new homes that looked to only be a few days old, perhaps, and then there were older ones that, at one point, had been new but now were dilapidated in some way. All of which was so confusing considering we had only been gone a year.

"Why does it look like it's been years since we've been here?" I muttered under my breath. Trixie's hand reached out to stop my wrist, which stopped me in my tracks.

"Did nobody tell you how time worked between those two realms?"

It only dawned on me that whatever answer she was about to give me, I wasn't going to like. I quickly shook my head no, and before I could open my mouth, I heard a howl that was all too familiar.

All grew closer as the rest rustling in the tree lines grew near. Pollux, of course, instinctively stood on edge as he pulled Trixie behind him, his eyes warily glancing around the area as a smile rushed across my face. "Daddy."

Bursting through the tree line, a black wolf stood on edge, snarling his teeth bared, his eyes narrowed, and then suddenly his glance softened. And with the cracking of bones, he quickly shifted back into his human form.

Before me stood Talon, my father, the one who I was closest with. He looked far different than how I had left him, between his graying hair and the crows feeds at the corner of his eyes, I was glad to see him. "Oh my God, you're back."

Rushing towards him, I threw my arms around his neck, his arms grasping around my waist as he spun me around. I didn't care that he was naked. Granted, he was my father, and it really wasn't something I wanted to see, but we were shifters, and this was normal for us.

He inhaled my scent deeply before setting me on my feet. His brows furrowed and confusion as he looked at me over. "Something's different. What's wrong with you?"

"That's a long conversation. Perhaps not tell Mom we're here yet. I kind of wanted to surprise her," Pollux intervened, my father's eyes glancing over him as his smile widened and he quickly hugged my brother, patting his back.

"My boy, you've grown so big and this..." he paused, sniffing Trixie, "is she your mate?"

Trixie glanced over at me with a wide eyed expression as she leaned in close. "Your dad just smelt me. What the fuck was that about?"

Shaking my head, I laughed, finding her response to what my father did amusing. "Don't worry, I will explain later."

All of us began walking back towards the pack house after our reunion, my father explaining to my brother everything that had changed since we had been gone. Come to find out, we may have only been in Asgard for about a few months, but here we had been gone for two years.

The moment my parent's home came into view, my breath caught in my throat. I never thought I would miss this place as much as I did right now, and as the front door opened and my mother stood there staring down the driveway at us and disbelief, I couldn't help but run to her.

She met me halfway, her arms wrapping around my body as she pulled me close with tears streaming down her face as a sob racked in the back of her throat. "Oh my God, you're back. Both of you are back. I have missed you so much."

I didn't have the heart to tell her yet that this wasn't the case, and though my brother and Trixie were staying, I was not. But it was something I would end up having to tell all my parents eventually. For now, though, I would relish in the 24 hours I had with my family.

Because I had no doubt when my parents found out what had happened, they were going to be furious with the gods. The same gods I looked up to and one day would become.

My mother wasn't a forgiving person and I pray for their souls she would go through in order to seek revenge on losing me.

Chapter Two

I had dreamed of this day. The day I would end up returning home, and the moment I stepped through the door, the chaos that was my siblings came rushing towards me. They hugged both me and Pollux and even welcomed Trixie with open arms. My mother had grayed over the last two years and was more pale than I had remembered her being.

I wasn't sure what had happened while I was gone, but it was clear that whatever had happened, had taken a toll on all of our parents. I was shocked to see how grown my siblings had become. No longer were my little brothers, Zach, Dillon and Tatum the little boys I had left. Zach was now 16, Dylan was fourteen, and little Tatum, no longer looking sick, was now 11.

The moment my eyes locked with my little brother Tatum, they began to fill with tears.

"You look so much better," I whispered as I quickly wrapped my arms around him and gave him a hug.

He chuckled softly as he pulled away from me and shrugged his shoulders. "It's weird. One day, I just woke up, and it was gone."

Glancing over at my brother and Trixie, they gave me a knowing look, knowing full well what had happened and how my brother had gotten better. However, I quickly shook my head, telling them not to say anything because it wasn't something I wanted my parents or my family to know.

What I had done for my little brother was out of the goodness of my heart, and perhaps one day, I would tell him. But for now, I didn't want it to be known.

"Are you guys hungry? Shall I cook some food?" James said as he came from the kitchen, wiping his hands on a towel. "I could grill some steaks on the stove just like you guys used to like."

"It's okay, Dad," Pollux chuckled, not wanting our father to go out of his way. "We ate before we came, but I do look forward to having one of your famous breakfast in the morning."

At first James had looked slightly disappointed, but with my brother proclaiming he wanted his famous breakfasts, he easily became happy and pointed at my brother before turning and running into the kitchen.

Knowing him, he was going to be going in there to defrost the meat for the morning because these breakfasts happened to contain a lot of meat.

For a few hours we talked through old memories, laughing, sitting with each other in the living room, talking about everything that had happened. And eventually my siblings were told that they had to go to bed and they could continue to spend time with us tomorrow.

Even though I would be away for a good part of the day, and then I'd disappear come night time.

"Cassie, are you okay?" Mom asked, pulling me from my thoughts. My eyes cast toward her to take in the aged expression upon her face that showed all the trouble she had been through over the years.

"Yeah, I'm fine. But there is something I really do need to talk to you guys about."

My father's James, Talon, Damian, and Hale all sat around my mother Ivy, watching me with much intent as I cast my glance toward Pollux, who nodded his head for me to continue. I had dreaded having to have this conversation with them to tell them I wasn't going to be staying permanently as my brother was.

I knew it was going to be hard on them and I was trying to come to terms with what my future had in store for me. It still wasn't easy to say goodbye.

"What's wrong? Why does it feel like you're going to tell me something I'm not going to like?" My mother's question caught me off guard. I tried to push back the emotions that threatened to fall down my face. I knew I had to do this.

"There were some issues in Asgard, some things happened and because of it, I had to change..." I replied, trailing off as I tried to find the words to express what had happened.

"You are not a Lycan anymore, are you?" Talon said, catching both Hale and Damian's attention. They furrowed their brows in confusion as they glanced back at me, and my mother quickly gripped James's hand as she held her breath for what I was about to tell her.

"No, I'm not," I replied softly. "There was a battle in Asgard and I got hurt. When the battle was going on, Pollux and Trixie, as well as a few others, were in danger. In order to protect them, I sacrificed myself and touched a part of my power I had never tapped into before."

My mother's face looked at me, horrified by what I was saying. I left out the part where Lucas had caused a lot of the issues. The last thing I wanted was for him to ever come back here and for some reason, my fathers to take out their aggression on him over losing me.

He was my mate and at the end of the day, I would do what I needed to do to protect him. I didn't regret my choice in saving them all. I sometimes wished that things could have gone differently, but it simply was what it was.

"This can't be right. How could Odin have allowed this to happen?" Damian exclaimed as his face contorted into an angry expression and he clenched his fists at his side as if preparing to punch somebody.

"Don't blame him. It wasn't his fault that this happened. Just like it wasn't any of your faults what happened with Loki... I don't hold any grudges and I don't regret what I did. My brother and my friends are safe, and that's all that matters."

Shaking her head, my mother refused to listen to what I was saying and as she stood to her feet, I knew that it was going to be an emotional mess by the time we got done with this conversation.

"So what? You're different now. What does that mean for your life here—"

She seemed to realize what exactly it meant as I opened and closed my mouth, frowning in sadness as I tried to find a way to tell her that I wasn't staying. "Mom, it's not that easy."

"You're not staying, are you?" Hale asked as he stepped around from where he had been silently listening and made his way towards me. Hale was the diplomatic one. Once he just simply wanted to be amongst his books, going to school, bettering himself. But then, when Damien fell from his grace, Hale stepped in to be the alpha of this pack needed.

He had changed so much from how I had remembered him, and as he made his way in front of me, I couldn't help but sigh, shaking my head. "Unfortunately, I can't stay. I'm only here for a few hours to spend time with you all to say my goodbyes. I don't know if I'll be able to come back in the future. But one day, when you go to Asgard yourself, we'll be reunited again."

"No!" my mother shouted as she jumped to her feet, "I refuse to lose you again. You are not leaving me. I will not have my children leaving me. You didn't die. You're right here in front of me."

No longer able to hold back the tears that had filled my eyes, they fell down my cheeks in silence. I couldn't do this, and as Trixie slid over in the seat next to me, wrapping her arms around me, and she laid her head upon my shoulder, I could feel her sorrow in it as well.

She and I had talked so much about all of this. And it was hard for me to say goodbye to my family. Once upon a time, I thought the idea of being an only child or moving away was great. However, now that I'm an adult, the only thing I wish I could do was spend more time with my family.

"I'm sorry. Mama, I'm so sorry."

My soft sobs of sorrow were enough to cause my mother to quickly be across the room in front of me, pulling me tight against her chest as we both cried. My mother's oldest daughter, the one who had pulled her from her coma. Once upon a time, the power that radiated through her was mine. We were closer than most people would realize. And even though we had our differences, I would forever be grateful for the person she made me be.

After the small conversation over everything that had happened and coming to the conclusion that I would not be able to stay with them, my parents had drifted off to bed and I was left in silence. The room that had once been mine was now my younger sisters.

It was the largest of the rooms next to my parents' room and it was of no surprise to me she would want it for herself. So instead of arguing, I took up the guest room. It was small, but it was cozy and as I laid there in the bed, staring at the ceiling, I couldn't help but wonder why it was that I had wanted to come home in the first place.

The only thing coming home did was bring me pain and hurt and maybe this is what I needed to help get over what it was that I had. But in order for me to move forward, I had to come to terms with what my life was going to be like.

The crack of the door caught my attention, and as I glanced over, I saw my mother enter the room. A smile upon her face as she made her way towards the bed, she climbed upon it, wrapping her arms around me as she pulled me to her chest.

"I'm sorry that I wasn't there to protect you," she whispered in my ear, causing the tears to brim my eyes once more. "It should have been me protecting you all."

"Don't say that. Your job is to stay here and protect everybody. Trixie's a good girl and she loves Pollux very much. Help her get used to this place, and show her the ropes. I know she won't replace me in your heart, but she understands more about everything than you think, and she and I are very good friends."

My mother sighed at my response. "I will help her."

As she ran her hand through my hair, I couldn't help but remember how she did this when I was younger. The scent of her perfume wrapped around me, lulling me into a deep sleep.

"I don't want to go to sleep, mom," I whispered, not wanting the moment to end.

Hushing me, she pulled me closer. "It's okay... I'll be here when you wake up."

Even though she said this, I had a feeling deep inside me that told me that wouldn't be accurate. However, I looked forward to the morning so I could spend more time with my family. It was the only time I would have to say everything I needed to say before I was forced to leave them again.

Letting the darkness of sleep wash over me, I dreamed of a reunion with my family that didn't end in tears, and looked forward to conquering a future I was made for.

Chapter Three

As the sun filtered through the open window of the room I was staying in, I stretched my arms above my head and realized I was lying in bed alone. Glancing around with groggy vision, I realized I was no longer at my parent's home but back in a room in Asgard where I had been before.

Bolting from the bed with panic setting in my heart, I looked around, trying to understand how it was. I was back. I shouldn't have been back. I still had more time with them, and though I had more time, my body, for some reason, had been cast back into Asgard without notice.

Without me even getting to say goodbye.

Quickly jumping from the bed, I ran towards the door, throwing it open as I made my way down to Odin's hall. I wasn't sure what I was going to do, but I knew one thing. I wasn't going to tolerate this. He couldn't just give me time and then suddenly take it away from me.

The moment I stepped foot into the hall, slamming the doors open, all eyes turned to me, my grandfather sitting ahead of me in his large chair, his brows furrowed in confusion.

"Cassie, what are you doing back so soon? You still had a few hours."

He looked just as confused as I was, and as I glanced at the others, I realized I had made an entrance and a spectacle of myself when I probably shouldn't have. "I don't know how I got back here. I still had time with them. I need to go back. I didn't even get to say goodbye."

Opening and closing his mouth, he gave me a sorrowful look and shook his head.

"Unfortunately, I can't send you back. You must have projected yourself back here for some reason. We only get to visit Earth once a year, Cassie. At least until you're stronger and you can take yourself."

I wasn't sure what to make of all of it, but as I turned, making my way out of the hall and back towards my room, a voice called behind me that I hadn't been expecting. "Cassie, please wait."

Turning and looking over my shoulder, I saw Freya standing there, staring at me with concern. "I know that all of this is a lot for you, and I'm so sorry that you ended up back here so soon. There's still a lot that we don't know about your condition. There's never been anything like it before. Give us some time, and we'll see if we can fix this for you."

If Odin couldn't send me back, then there was no fixing anything for me. Perhaps I was different, but now I was supposed to be like them. And if they didn't know what to make of me, then what was I, honestly? Was I like them, or was it something else?

Refusing to listen to what she had to say, I remained silent and made my way back to my room. One day, I would be able to be reunited with my family. Until then, I would simply have to play my part here and figure out exactly what I was supposed to be doing.

My mother's words rattled through my mind, and the moment I reached my room, I found a small brown-haired, blue eyed girl standing there before me in a servant's outfit, her eyes cast to the floor as if she was unsure of what to say. "Who are you?"

"My name is Ansley. I will be your servant through the trials."

"What trials? What are you talking about?" I asked, slightly confused as to what she was referring to. There were no trials that I knew of, but according to her, as her eyes looked up at me, she was almost perplexed as to why I wasn't aware of them.

Hesitating for a moment, she stared at me as if unsure of what to say. I didn't mean to make her feel uncomfortable, but with the way she fidgeted with her hands as she kept staring at the floor, I knew that I had. "The Solstice Games, ma'am."

The girl stuttered over her words. I felt bad about what I had done until I realized she was in the same situation I was at the moment. She had to do things she didn't really want to do in order to get by with no way to leave this place.

Or at least that's what I imagined when I thought of what this girl was going through.

"Oh, I understand. It's okay. I'm just a little flustered this morning."

"Would you like something to eat for breakfast before your meeting this afternoon?" Again, she was giving me information about stuff that I had no idea what she was talking about. Yes, I was hungry, but now I didn't know I had a meeting.

"Let's just say I'm unaware of whatever meeting it is that I have supposedly going on. Do you think you might be able to fill me in on this?"

Ansley hesitated for a moment, and slowly, her head lifted, her eyes locking with mine as she furrowed her brows with confusion, opening her mouth before slowly closing it. "Uhhh—you're supposed to be meeting with Odin in an hour to meet a few people. I don't really know anything else. I'm not privy to that information."

Running my hand over my face, I closed my eyes in frustration as I let out a groan of irritation. "I see. Some breakfast actually does sound good. Just something light and refreshing, maybe. I don't know. Oh—and coffee. Lots and lots of coffee."

I felt guilty having this girl wait on me hand and foot as if I was incapable of doing so myself. But as soon as I gave her a command, a smile crossed her face, and she quickly exited my room, obviously in search of the coffee that I desperately needed.

With Ansley gone, I was left to my own devices once more, and with the realization I had to get ready for a meeting with people I had no knowledge of, I made my way toward the bathroom to get ready.

Twenty minutes later and a wonderfully magnificent hot shower, I had cried out all my frustration and prepared myself for whatever it was that I was going to be faced with. If my mother was able to get through everything that she went through with my father's, then I had to be able to get through whatever it was that they expected of me here.

It was clear the more I learned about myself, the more I would possibly be able to go back home. And that was something I really wanted. Even if I was only allowed to go once a year, it was better than not going at all.

In the corner out to my bedroom, I ran into Ansley, a scream escaping my throat as we both jumped and she quickly spilt some of the coffee onto the floor. "Oh my gosh, I'm so sorry! I'm such a klutz."

I watched as the girl put the cup down on the desk and knelt on the floor using a rag attached to her apron to clean up the mess. I didn't even have a chance to acknowledge what had happened before she was in action. The girl was faster than I had ever seen anybody, and I was slightly curious as to why she was so overwhelmed with the fact she spilled coffee on the floor.

"Hey it's okay, I ran into you. Why are you freaking out?" I replied as I knelt down beside her, my hand laying upon hers as she looked at me in fear.

"I'm so sorry. I understand if you want to punish me, I should be more careful–"

"Whoa, whoa, whoa. I'm going to stop you right there," I replied quickly, standing to my feet with my arms crossed over my chest. "First of all, I would never punish you. And second of all, if you're going to be working with me, you gotta calm down. It's okay. I'm not like the other people. I will not get upset over you doing some shit like this. I ran into you. It's not the end of the world."

"I don't understand," she muttered softly. "You're so nice. That's not how things work here."

It was clear I didn't know this place as well as I thought I did, and that frustrated me even more. This girl was fearful of me, worried she was going to get in trouble for spilling something as stupid as a little bit of coffee on the floor and acting as if I was going to beat her to death for it.

"Who the hell were you serving before you came to me?" I laughed with concern edged at the forefront of my mind. "Did someone hit you?"

I hadn't meant to be blunt, and the girl was taken aback by my very forward questioning. She again hesitated as if she wasn't sure she wanted to say anything, but I stepped forward, taking my hand, and lifted her chin to lock eyes with me once more.

"It's okay. What you say to me stays between us. Just tell me what happened."

Tears filled her eyes, she nodded her head. It was clear she was uncomfortable, but if I was ever going to make sure she was okay, I needed to know who it was that had hurt her. "Solina, she was my mistress before I was given to you."

I didn't know anyone named Solina, and as I watched Ansley stare at me with so much fear in her eyes, I couldn't help but wonder what this Solina girl had done to her.

"Look," I sighed, shaking my head. "I'm not like that girl, okay... just work with me. You will see how different being around me will be."

Taking in everything I said, she slowly nodded. "Okay... do you want to get dressed while you eat?"

I had almost completely forgotten I was supposed to be meeting with Odin shortly. My mind swirling over what I was going to have to do, and the people I was going to meet. I wasn't a girl brought up in this kind of world, and because of that I didn't have the slightest clue how I should dress.

"Yeah, actually that sounds good... but uh—what should I wear?"

Ansley snapped her gaze to me as she raised a brow, and a small smile crossed the corner of her lips. "You want my opinion? I'm just a servant."

"So?" I shrugged in response, "do you not know?"

"Well, of course I do... I have helped others get dressed multiple times," she replied with a sigh as she made her way towards my closet, disappearing into the array of colors and fabric that lined the closet walls.

I wasn't quite sure what I was getting myself into by asking Ansley to help me, but when she came back with a royal blue dress dripping in crystals down one side, I had to admit the girl had taste. "Are you sure this isn't too much for a meeting?"

Glancing down at the dress, she ran her hand over the fabric with a smile upon her lips before glancing back up to me. "Nope... you will definitely make an entrance."

And that was what I wanted... if they wanted me to be this heir apparent, then I needed to make them realize I was worthy of the title.

After all, I was an outsider in this world. The last thing I wanted to do was to be eaten alive.

Chapter Four

To say the dress looked amazing on me would be an understatement. I fucking rocked this damn dress, and I knew it. "Damn... I look sexy as fuck."

The high slits on the side of the navy blue dress did wonders for my legs, and the way the bust perked up my boobs made them look like I had a five-thousand dollar boob job which made me smile. Even with me being young, my boobs didn't honestly sit perky like most would think. I was heavy-chested, and these girls—though they sat nicely—weren't porn star tits.

Turning from side to side in the mirror, I smiled at my reflection. "What do you think?"

Ansley stood beside me, quiet as always, her eyes gazing over my figure before a smile played across her lips, and she shrugged her shoulders. "I think it looks like perfection. You definitely fit in with the royals around here."

"Royals?" I laughed, shaking my head. "I don't know if you want to call us royals, by all means. I'm just as normal as you or anybody else. I don't sit on a high pedestal like some of these people may do, but I do plan to try and make everybody proud in the position I'm being given."

At that, Ansley got quiet and stared at the floor once more. She let out a small sigh. "I know it's out of place for me, but could I give you a piece of advice?"

Considering how she was when she first walked in here and started dealing with me freaking out over the smallest of incidents, I was honestly shocked she wanted to give me advice, but I was more than happy to receive it.

"By all means, anything that you can tell me that I might need to use would be wonderful."

Taking a moment, she seemed to ponder over whatever it was that she had to say before her eyes met mine, and she let out another heavy breath. "Be careful of Solina and her brother. They're pretty upset that you're being called the heir apparent when they think that it should have been them."

I wasn't all that surprised she said they would be upset. In all honesty, I expected there to be a few people who weren't happy, considering I was new, had just arrived, hadn't really earned my way around this place, and now I was being cast ahead of all of them and supposed to rule over everybody. Or that was the idea I had in mind for being an heir apparent.

"Thank you for letting me know, but you don't need to worry about them. You're with me now, and you're safe. And if for any reason they give you any kind of trouble, make sure you let me know, I'll handle them accordingly."

Reassuring her the best I could that I would take care of her was a step I didn't think I would ever take for anybody else. Granted, I had a big heart, and I was always there for my friends, but dealing with the levels of hierarchy in this place wasn't something I was exactly comfortable with yet.

I was a rebel at one point in time, a badass with a name that people made sure they knew. However, coming here, I was just like anybody else. I was a nobody. My name was big now. After Odin, my grandfather, proclaimed me the heir apparent, I hadn't shown anybody what I could really do.

At least not in a normal sense.

Giving myself another glance over into the mirror, I nodded my head in approval, ready to go meet whoever it was I was supposed to be meeting in the Grand Hall with Odin.

Leaving my room, I made haste as I headed down the hallway toward where I was supposed to be meeting everyone. I would have expected someone to come get me, but according to Ansley, she was informed I was supposed to be arriving there on my own.

Not that I cared, but it would have been nice had someone told me what I needed to do.

The moment I got close to the Grand Hall doors, I could hear the murmured sounds of voices and laughter coming from the other side. No one waited outside the doors to greet me, and for the first time, I felt the nerves about what I was about to do flow through me.

Taking a deep breath, I pushed on the massive wooden doors with gold ornate handles and set my eyes on the hall and everyone in it. There were various people before me I didn't recognize, but some that I did. Freya, Frigg, and Odin were all present.

Yet, as I stepped forth into the hall with everyone's eyes on me, I felt like I was the outsider among them all. Even the ones I knew.

"There she is!" Odin bellowed with a smile on his face as he stood from his throne in furs and with a horn in his hand. "Everyone, this is Castor, the heir to my reign."

The announcement he made caused whispers to flow around me as he gestured for me to come forth toward him. There was no way I would reject such an offer, and stepping forward towards the throne, my stomach fluttered from the anxiety flowing through me.

"You asked for me to come," I replied softly as I held my head high, taking my grandfather's hand as he helped me up to the last of the steps to stand at his side.

The moment I turned at his side to face the people in front of me, uneasiness washed over my body that kicked in my flight response, urging me to escape. There had to have been at least one hundred people in front of me of all sizes and races. The colored eyes of creatures watching me as if they were looking for me to make some sort of mistake.

"Yes, Cassie..." he chuckled before turning back to the crowd. "Today, I have gathered you all here to introduce Castor, or Cassie, as she prefers to be called, to talk about the upcoming Solstice games that will happen in a few weeks' time.

As per tradition, Cassie will be required to take a suitor and select those who will be part of her reign..."

My heart dropped into my stomach as I turned to him, trying to understand why he was telling these people this. Of course, I was told about finding a mate or two... but I didn't think the games were honestly about that.

"I know your sons will make fine warriors in the games, and the winner will win the right to marry my granddaughter, as tradition dictates."

The crowd cheered as smiles crossed their faces. I didn't know what tradition he was talking about because the last time I checked in the history books back home, Odin had always been in charge. Then again, the human history books did have his entire persona completely wrong.

"What do you mean, the winner will marry me?" I asked as I turned to him with confusion, trying to understand why he hadn't thoroughly explained the games to me before throwing me to the wolves in this room.

"It's not that big of a deal. Didn't you learn any of that while you were at the school?"

Opening and closing my mouth, I stared at him wide-eyed. "No... I literally have been here for a few weeks. How was that supposed to have been taught to me?"

Odin seemed a bit lost for words at my comment, and after a moment, he slightly narrowed his gaze and leaned in. "Don't make this difficult, Cassie. You agreed to this, don't forget that."

I hadn't forgotten that, and in fact, I had thought about it multiple times since I had allowed my brother to agree to giving me his powers. It was because of what he did that I was allowed to reside where I was instead of being in limbo, but at the same time, limbo sounded better than before, forced to marry someone I didn't want to be married to.

As Odin cast his gaze to the approaching figures, seemingly satisfied with my silence, I decided to play along. Even if deep inside me, I was angrier than a viper whose nest had been disturbed.

"Odin, it's good to see you again," a young man not much older than me said as he approached.

His blonde hair and blue eyes were styled to perfection in loose waves down to his shoulders. While his bare, unmarked chest glistened in the light, highlighting each and every curve of his well-defined muscles. Something about him didn't sit right with me, and the woman at his side made the feeling even worse.

She was just as beautiful as he was with long blonde hair braided in sections going straight down her back, while the white, tight-fitting dress hugged her small breasts and flowed down over her body towards the floor.

"It's good to see you as well, Mani, and Solina... my you grow more beautiful every time I see you," Odin replied with so much confidence I almost forgot he once had a normal conversation with me. Right now, he wasn't a grandfather showing off his granddaughter. He was a god showing off his reign.

When Mani's gaze turned towards me, he seemed pleased to be in my presence yet, behind that warm gaze was nothing but irritation. I could almost feel it pouring off his entire persona.

"Cassie, you're as beautiful as I dreamed you would be."

"You dreamed of me?" I asked with a small smirk on the corner of my lips. "I didn't think I was that well known yet, as this is my coming out party."

Odin laughed at my comment while Mani's happy gaze quickly narrowed and his sister stepped forward, trying to obviously diffuse the growing issue. "I think that what my brother means is we look forward to being the best of friends... especially since we will end up being family."

Family...this man was bold. I will give him that.

"I didn't realize we were going to be that close... I take it you're entering the contest?" I asked with sarcasm.

"Enter?" he replied with a twinkle of amusement in his eyes. "I plan to win, Cassie. I mean, the reign needs a male to sit upon the throne, and I have plenty of knowledge to help you lead in ruling the kingdom as needed."

Again, the man was confident in his thoughts of winning the battle for my hand and the games hadn't even started yet. "I guess we shall see if you're really up to the standards I expect in my match. The games won't be easy for you to accomplish."

"What are you talking about?" he scoffed as he stood just a bit taller.

"I mean, if the games are going to be for my hand, then I want to help in their creation. It's only right that with new generations coming along, I get a say in certain things. Is that right... grandfather?"

My comments seemed to surprise Odin as he stared at me for a moment, as if contemplating what he wanted to say. I'd expected him to say no and that it wasn't how things work, but instead he smiled at me. "If you'd like to help design the games, by all means you can. I'm actually intrigued to see what you come up with."

Mani didn't seem very happy that my grandfather had agreed, and though he wasn't happy, he couldn't say anything. This was Odin. When Odin said something, it was final and his word was law, or at least that was what I had learned since being here.

With Solina and Mani put in their place, there was nothing else for them to say. They casually nodded their heads, bowing their respects before turning away, whispering to each other as they walked to the far side of the room.

The event was in full swing and as more people approached, I found myself slightly overwhelmed with it all, but if I was going to end up being the heir apparent, it was something I was going to have to get over.

Through all of it, though, I knew one thing was for sure. Mani and Solina were people I would have to watch out for, especially since Ansley had explained to me what Solina had done to her.

Chapter Five

By the time I got back to my room, I was beyond exhausted over having to deal with people in general. The sun had set long ago, and as the moons rose up within the sky, I had a feeling my night was far from over. As soon as I walk through my door to my bedroom, Freya stood there waiting for me. And honestly, I was surprised how she had moved so quickly from the Grand Hall to my room without me even noticing.

"Freya, did you need something?" I asked her, watching as her cool eyes turned towards me with a smile on her face as she looked at a photo within a white frame I had set upon my dresser.

The photo was of me and my mother from just before graduation. I hadn't wanted to take the picture with her, however, she had coerced me into doing so. And because of it, I was grateful, because it was a part of her I got to keep.

"You didn't seem too pleased to take this photo with your mother," Freya said, catching me slightly off guard as I moved within the room closer to where she was standing. I knew the woman wouldn't cause me any harm, but after all of the issues I had with Inanna and Loki, I wasn't going to take any risks of trusting people so easily.

"Yeah, that was before my mother and I kind of fixed things with each other. I was rebellious when I lived there. And my mother got on my nerves, as every mother typically does with their daughters."

"Yet you miss her dearly," she replied in a very awkward kind of sense, as if she was trying to understand what the connection with my mother and I was.

"Well, of course I do. Don't you miss your mother?" My question was hesitant, and as I stared at her, I watched her gaze slightly furrow before she placed the picture back upon the dresser and turned to me completely.

"That isn't important, but what is important is I have a surprise for you."

Not sure what the surprise was going to be, but as she took my hand and pulled me along back outside of my room and down the hallway in a different direction than I had ever been. I couldn't help but wonder why the surprise couldn't have waited until morning.

The last thing I wanted to do was go gallivanting around this damn place. All I wanted to do was crawl into bed in PJ's and possibly read a book or something, considering there was no damn TV.

"Freya, where are you taking me? It's late and I want to go to bed," I whined slightly, not happy with the fact she was taking me halfway across this massive palace of Odin toward a wing that was explained as being restricted.

"Well, since you've taken to your new position so well, there's no reason for you to stay in the room that you had. All of your stuff is going to be moved over in the morning, but for the time being, you're being placed in a different wing of the building."

She was literally moving me in the middle of the night to a new bedroom instead of just waiting for me to wake up in the morning refreshed after having spent a long period of time speaking with people I had no interest in actually speaking with!

Freya was a bit of an extraordinary person, and though I had gotten to know her slightly in passing since I had been here, and I had heard stories of her from my mother when I was growing up, I still couldn't understand why it was that she did things she did.

Freya always seemed to ask the most questions, and she watched everybody carefully, as if trying to mimic or understand why they did what they did, whether it be from eating to simple conversations or even the way that I would dress. I could remember right after I had come here she had made a comment on why I was wearing leggings because she found them most extraordinary. Or so that was the wording she used.

Someone would think for a goddess who's been around for a very long time, she would at least have been able to understand what comfortable clothing was.

A few moments later, we finally arrived outside a set of white and gold double doors. I wasn't exactly sure what was beyond it, other than the room she supposedly had said was for me, but as she opened the door, my breath was literally taken away.

This room looked to be the size of an entire house. The moment I stepped in, I took in the white and lilac decor, the king-size bed that sat within its center, rounded edges with draped sheer curtains and canopies that billowed down the sides of it.

Of that there were photos upon the walls of floral designs and different abstract pieces of colors, some shades I didn't even know existed. "Holy shit, is this all for me?"

Freya laughed and as I glanced over my shoulder at her moving around the room, I couldn't understand why they would give me something so massive an entire family could live in the size of this room.

"Of course it's for you. If you're going to be a leader one day, you need a proper room."

Her question paused me in my steps, and as I spun to look at her, I couldn't help but frown. "What does a room have to do with me leading people? I don't even know if I can do this, Freya."

Opening and closing her mouth, she stared at me as if I had grown a second head. "You can, Cassie. It's in your blood."

"I don't know about that," I muttered in reply as I turned from her and continued making my way around the room.

More white accented furniture was decorated with crystal vases and a variety of flowers in different colors. It was magical and all, but the taste of the room was far from who I really was. Something I would have to fix if this was going to be my permanent situation.

"You can do it, you just need to give it time," Freya replied with hope in her voice. "Perhaps meeting with some of your friends will help to clear your mind. I let the guards know Sansa would be a frequent visitor."

Guards? What guards... I had never seen a single guard around this place since I had been here, but as I looked at Freya once more over my shoulder, I could see how serious she was about what she had said. "What guards?"

"The valkyrie. They protect us... certainly you knew this."

I did. I remembered the woman who came to check on us various times over the years of growing up, but I hadn't really thought of them as guards. They were warriors, but I guess to these gods, maybe they had multiple purposes.

"Yeah. I just wanted to verify," I replied, trying to play it off, "this room is beautiful, but I'm really tired..."

Freya's eyes widened slightly as she smiled, nodding her head. "How silly of me. You have had a really busy day, and tomorrow is going to be even more fun."

"Fun..." The flat tone of my response amused Freya, and as she turned without giving further explanation, I had little hope whatever I was going to do was actually fun. If it was anything like I had gone through today... it would be zero fun.

As soon as Freya left, and I was left alone again, I took the opportunity to wander around my new room—or large apartment—to see what else it had to offer. Which was a lot.

A separate room held a small living area with navy blue sofas and a white coffee table and what took my breath away was an actual fucking TV in the room. "No fucking way..."

"I thought you would like it..." the sound of a woman's voice made me jump out of my skin as I screamed and spun around to find Trixie leaning against the door frame to another room with a wide smile on her face.

I had never been so happy to see her, and as I ran to her throwing my arms around her, I tried to understand how she had even gotten here. "What the hell are you doing here?"

"Well, I kind of needed a small break from your...parental units, and figured you may want some more reminders from home."

Hearing she was already tired of my parents worried me, and as I pulled away staring at her with a look of concern, she let out a small laugh. "It's fine...really."

"What's fine? What have my parents done?"

Shrugging her shoulders, she moved towards the sofa in the center of the living room, and plopped down upon it. "Well, when you disappeared your mother went into full on panic mode, and took it out on everyone. Of course, your father's Hale and James were able to sort of get her calmed down, but when she found out I can still come and go between realms, she was on me like... what was that term your brother used..." she replied while thinking to herself, "oh yeah... she was on me like white on rice... or something like that."

A snort of laughter echoed from me hearing Trixie try to speak in normal terms, considering she came from a culture that didn't speak like that. "I'm sorry she acted that way towards you. She can be a little dramatic at times."

"A little?" Trixie scoffed with a smile. "She was the one who made me bring you tons of shit... including the TV which I told her wouldn't work because we don't have television... so she gave me the dvd player in the living room to give you as well as the collection of dvds... which your brother Dillon was pretty upset about."

Hearing the stuff going on back at home made me want to cry. I missed my family, and hearing the usual dilemmas from Trixies' mouth while not being able to experience it was heart wrenching. "Thank you for bringing that stuff. It means a lot."

There was a moment of silence until Trixie sighed, pulling me from my own thoughts of what my family was up to. As I let my gaze meet hers once more, I found her looking around the room, taking in all the decor and extras it had to offer.

"Freya didn't waste any time in having Odin put you on a pedestal, did she?"

"I wouldn't call it a pedestal," I replied, "but it's really nice."

"That's good... so Ansley said you had to meet with the council today. Played nice and whatnot so everyone liked you," she replied, completely disregarding what she had said before.

"Yeah... but how do you know Ansley?" Trixie looked at me for a moment before smiling and shrugging her shoulders. "I know everyone..."

"So I see..." Shaking my head, I took a moment thinking over the event, and my mind quickly drifted back to Solina and her brother. "I did meet the children of Thor... Mani is something else."

Sitting up straight, she leaned forward with wide-eyes. "Oh, shit... those two are back?"

"What do you mean back?" I asked, now worried about them seeing as Trixie wasn't one for explaining shit very well and from the gaze in her eyes, I could tell she didn't mean to say what she had.

"Well—" she sighed, "let's just say that Mani was supposed to have your title, and you came and took it from him without him being able to fight to keep it. Not to mention you're a girl and outside of his sister, he is completely sexiest."

Great... just fucking great.

Chapter Six

After spending the evenings staying up late talking with Trixie, I felt refreshed when I woke the next morning. Granted, I was still nervous about how things were going to go, but at least I had a clearer mind going into it. I wasn't as stressed out about my position, and though I felt like I had to impress certain people, I would do it on my own terms.

I climbed out of bed, stretched my arms over my head, and made my way to the bathroom to get dressed. Determination surged through me to prove to myself I could be the person I was supposed to be. But first of all, I was going to need a lot of caffeine in my system in order to be able to accomplish what I needed to get done.

Heading out of my room, fully dressed and prepared for the day, I made my way down the corridors trying to follow the steps I had taken with Freya from the night before. Sansa was supposed to be meeting me, and the two of us were going to go up to the local cafe to get a bit of coffee and catch up on what had been going on.

I was informed by Trixie last night with my position, I was no longer going to be allowed to attend the school, which is a bit shocking because I was hoping to catch up with people. Even though there were a lot of people there that didn't care for me.

There were still some I did enjoy speaking with on a daily basis, like Kathy from my magic class.

Letting out a heavy sigh, I tried not to let everything bother me and instead continued on my path, out the front doors of the building and down the street towards the cafe where I knew Sansa would be waiting for me.

It was beautiful outside, as it always was, but the more I walked down the street, the more I realized people were stopping and staring at me. Hushed whispers, excited faces, even smiles, while other people seem to be slightly concerned.

I wasn't quite sure why they were looking at me like this. I mean, granted, Odin did come before everybody to say I was the new heir apparent, a word I couldn't stand hearing, but I was just like anybody else. I wasn't going to be like these other gods and goddesses who thought they were better than everybody, although there were a select few who didn't.

I closed in on the cafe and was excited at having the coffee I needed this morning. As the doorbell chimed above me, people meandered around the cafe with a variety of different caffeinated beverages, I couldn't help but feel finally at home and safe amongst the walls.

Letting my eyes scan over the surrounding tables, I finally landed upon Sansa, who stood sat with her eyes on her phone and a frustrated look on her face.

"Are you okay?" I asked as I approached the table, her eyes lifting to mine before she let out a frustrated groan of disapproval and placed her phone on the table.

"Yeah, I'm fine. My brothers are just pissing me off this morning."

Taking my seat across from her, I noticed she had already gotten my coffee, and as I lifted the cup to my lips, taking a deep breath in of the beautiful aroma it created, I sipped it, enjoying the flavors that bubbled over my tongue. "Oh my God, you have no idea how much I needed this coffee."

"I bet." She laughed as she eyed me up and down. "What's with the new get-up? I don't think I've ever seen you dressed so well before."

"Hey, I take that offensive. There's nothing wrong with the way I dress," I replied as I used my hand to gesture up and down my body, causing her to laugh even more.

She wasn't wrong, though. None of my stuff from my old room had been transferred over to the new room yet, so I was forced to get dressed in the attire provided for me in the closet of my new room, which consisted of more formal clothing and not the typical leggings and a sweatshirt I would have rather have been in.

Still, I was able to find a cute pair of black tights that almost resembled leggings and matched it with a black skirt and red sweater, as well as the closest thing I could find to normal boots.

"Okay, I'll admit it isn't that bad. But still, it's weird seeing you out of sight of your leggings and sweatshirts..."

The more we continued to banter, the more I was glad I had come to see her. I had almost decided to cancel the entire thing when I woke up and realized I had to stop being my normal self and start being more... professional, I suppose. Yet, sitting here with Sansa now, I realized I could face everything I had to do.

I simply needed a force of people at my side. That way, I was able to get through this.

"So I was thinking I might be able to get you to help me with some of this stuff..." I said in a very nonchalant kind of way that made her brow quirk with interest.

"What stuff?" Sipping on her coffee, I took a moment to think over what exactly I was going to say and how I was going to put it across to her. Sansa was cool as shit, but she was the kind of girl who enjoyed blending into the background. Even when things went down with Loki, and we needed her help... she wasn't one who really wanted to be part of it.

"Well, I got Odin to agree to let me help with designing the games that the men would have to go through... or something like that, and I thought maybe you could be by my side through all of it and keep me sane from the mass of socialites who want to sweep me up."

Sansa paused, staring at me before she broke out into a fit of laughter as if what I had suggested was the most amusing thing she had ever heard "Oh. You were being serious?"

"Yes—" I replied, rolling my eyes with a groan, "I have no idea what the hell I'm doing, Sansa. You know this place and the people better than I do."

Shaking her head, she scoffed. "No... that was Trixie's department, not mine."

"Yeah, and she can't be here." I reminded her, causing her to sigh.

"I know she can't, but I'm not sure I'm the best one for this task. I mean I can't even get shit right when dealing with my brother and his friends, and you want me to take on the whole elite socialite department of this realm?"

I could tell by the look on Sansa's face she didn't really like the idea of having to do this, and I hated asking her but I didn't have anyone else to really ask that wasn't a goddess already or someone who didn't like me. "So I'll take that as a no?"

Setting her coffee cup down, she glared at me before crossing her arms of her chest in anger. "Well, of course I'm going to fucking help you, Dum-Dum... I'm just saying I don't know shit about this crap and we need someone who does."

A victorious squeal escaped me as I jumped from my seat and about knocked the drinks over on the coffee table in front of us in an attempt to hug her. "Oh, thank you, thank you, thank you!"

"Calm down, woman!" she gasped as I pulled away laughing and took my seat watching the shock settle in her facial expressions. "Jesus, you spill my coffee and you're buying me a new one."

"Deal," I muttered with a smile as approaching footsteps caused us both to look over to see Solina walking towards us with her own coffee in her hand. Her eyes gazed between Sansa and I with amusement.

"Cassie, it's good to see you again."

My demeanor completely changed the moment this girl spoke to me, and sitting a little bit straighter, I held my chin high and gave her a blank expression. "You as well, Solina."

I wasn't looking to carry on conversation with her after the things I had heard she had done to quite a few of the staff–besides Ansley—over her time in staying in this place. Not to mention the introduction we had yesterday was enough to last me a lifetime.

"So, if I overheard correctly... you're looking for help? I'd love to offer my services. I know all about this kind of stuff."

If she thought for one moment her smooth talk was going to get her anywhere with me she was sadly mistaken. "Thanks for the offer, but Sansa and I have this covered."

Solina's eyes gazed over at Sansa again before she sneered slightly in disgust before looking at me once more. "But she is just a witch... surely you need someone with a better understanding."

I couldn't believe Solina had enough balls to take shit to me in front of Sansa. She didn't even know the girl and from the looks of it, Sansa was glad she didn't have to know Solina.

"She said we got it," Sansa said as she leaned forward in her chair. Her elbows rested on her knees as she stared at Solina. "Thank you, though... you can go find a new victim—I mean, best friend to play with."

It was clear to anyone in or out of the conversation that Solina and Sansa did not get a long. Part of me wondered if it was something to have been done in their past, but the other part of me wondered if it was just because they were stubborn and didn't want to relinquish the idea of us all being friends.

Not that I wanted to be friends with Solina.

She was too wicked for her own good.

"Fine, suit yourself," Solina said, finally turning towards the door of the cafe without another single word said to either of us.

"For some reason I have a feeling this isn't the last we see of her..." Sansa muttered, picking up her phone again, "what about reaching out to Silas or Lucas to help?"

"What?" No way... Lucas hates me and Silas was MIA... and for a dragon, that's nearly impossible.

"Why not?" she shrugged, gesturing towards me with knitted brows and a look of confusion.

I wasn't sure what exactly to tell her when it came to Silas and Lucas. She knew the gist of it but at the same time shit was a little more complicated with them than I had initially told her and Trixie. "I—I can't use them."

"And why would that be? Both boys are fucking in love with you."

"Yeah, but neither of them are my mates... Well, Lucas isn't anymore. Plus, I haven't spoken to them since the day everything happened," I countered in frustration, hoping that she wouldn't get on to me like a few others had.

Opening and closing her mouth, she hesitated before she began to laugh. "No communication like... at all?"

"Yeah, no. They are avoiding me like the plague."

"Well then, you need to fix that," she commanded as she stood to her feet. "If we are going to make shit happen, then you have to fix things with them. That's your task. In the meantime, I'll hit up the school and see if I can find trustworthy people there."

There was no point in arguing with Sansa when she said something, and leaning in to hug her goodbye, the feeling of easiness washed over me realizing I didn't have to do this alone.

The only other problem to deal with now... was making sure Silas and Lucas were talking to me and ready to help with my crazy ass bullshit.

Chapter Seven

Telling Solina off ended up being the beginning of a great day. Sansa had made it her personal objective to guide me through how to make an eventful Solstice game and according to her, this was something they usually did every few years, but this time... it was going to be epic.

Why was it going to be epic? Because she said she was helping me plan.

The laughter that escaped me upon this proclamation was uncontrollable, but I loved her for that. She had turned my worries and fears around and made me realize I was freaking out for nothing. Not to mention pointing out that if Trixie happened to pop back once... she was definitely bound to do it again.

The girl was notorious for doing things spontaneously.

"So, where are we going?" My question followed a twenty-minute walk uptown, and when the arena came into view, I found myself growing more confused as to where we were headed.

Turning her gaze to me, Sansa scoffed, "I figured the giant arena ahead of us was a dead giveaway, Cassie."

She was annoyed with me asking questions, and that made it all the more amusing when I did ask them. Yet, nudging her shoulder with mine, I was able to get her to smile quite easily. "You know I just enjoy teasing you... but for real though... Why are we going to the arena?"

"Because that's where the shit's taking place. I figured our first stop would be to the arena to get a good look at the area and maybe get some ideas."

"Sure it wasn't because you wanted to watch the guys sparring?" The smirk that blessed the corner of my lips made Sansa roll her eyes.

"Shut the hell up…" she muttered, smiling back at me. "I can't help it. They are gorgeous to look at."

She wasn't wrong, and as we made our way through the tunnel, the view of the field came into view as well as the many half-naked bodies upon it. "Maybe this was a good idea…"

"See, I told you," she mumbled back as we made our way down the steps towards the concert seating towards the front. "I think sitting close would be better. Helps to get a good view of the competitors."

I wasn't sure what she meant by that. I knew that it was a competition, but I didn't think it was open to everyone. I had figured it was just all those high socialites I had met the other day. "Wait… can anyone join?"

Looking over at me as we took our seats, she raised a brow in confusion. "Uh, yeah, of course. Didn't they tell you anything about this shit?"

"Obviously not."

The fact I was walking into this whole competition blind was beyond aggravating. I had told Sansa I didn't know anything about this crap, but I suppose it would make sense that they at least would give me the basic rundown. I mean, I hadn't even been told what my job title was going to entail once the competition was over… if I had a job title or whatever it was.

"Look, I'm blind with this crap. That's why I need you to help me because I literally know nothing." Sansa nodded in understanding as she pointed towards the field.

"You see those guys right there with the blue shorts on?"

Following the direction she was pointing to, I spotted four guys who were overly chiseled and dripping in sweat. Their toned bodies in various shades of bronze glistened underneath the sun as they messed around with each other, pretending to spar and wrapping each other in headlocks. "You mean the oversized children?"

"Yeah," she snorted in laughter. "Those are wolf half-breeds. They are typical jocks you would see on earth, but they love a good challenge. Last tournament, the tall one with the golden brown hair lost by half a point and has kept that grudge for a very long time."

"So, in other words, he needs to be watched out for?"

Nodding her head, she sighed. "Yeah... and he is a complete asshole. However, since you're the prize, he may try to approach you. Just don't fall for his bullshit... It's all a lie. He has never been nice with a single girl he has been with, and that has been a lot."

The longer we sat there, the more Sansa explained to me about the different people on the field who would end up signing up to compete. Most wouldn't as they weren't interested, but there were a lot who would, and they were all ones to watch out for.

As I took in the competition, I didn't miss the dark-haired figure of a man I knew all too well walking across the field to spar. Lucas looked as gorgeous as he did the day I met him, and from the looks of his bulked-out muscles, he had spent a lot of his time on this training field changing.

"He looks good, doesn't he?" Sansa asked, pulling me from the dazed thoughts I had. As much as I didn't want to admit that he did look good, I couldn't.

He was a walking sex machine, and even with our bond broken, I still yearned for him.

"I wonder if he is entering..." I muttered, "he won't talk to me, and I hate it."

Thinking about Lucas only put a damper on my mood, and as I tried to focus my attention away from him, I couldn't. He stood across the field, his body shining in the setting sun and as if he knew that I was watching him, he turned to face me, narrowing his gaze.

Was he mad at me? I had no fucking clue, but I was tired of playing games.

I wanted answers. "I'm going to go talk to him."

"What?" Sansa replied wide-eyed, "didn't that end up badly last time?"

Thinking of last time and the way he looked at me when he realized what he had done was heartbreaking. The moment he realized he was the reason I wasn't alive, he wanted to die. The scream that left his throat wasn't something

I wanted to remember, and his anger had been so intense he even begged Pollux to kill him for what he had done.

Of course, I didn't allow that. It wasn't his fault entirely. Inanna had been poisoning his mind.

"Yeah... well, kind of. Still, look at him... he looks so angry," I replied, still staring at where he stood, no longer looking at me but instead working out with weights as he waited for his turn on the field.

"He does look like he has spent most of his time out here working out, doesn't he? Damn, that man got bigger..."

"Sansa!" The laughter that broke out between us was refreshing as always, and as she nudged me with her shoulder, she urged me to go and speak to him.

Standing to my feet, I made my way down the concrete steps towards the field and directly across the green grass towards where Lucas was. All eyes were on me for the most part as I made my way towards Lucas, and with the hoots and hollers of the men on the sidelines of the field, it perked Lucas's attention, who turned his gaze towards me with a raised brow.

"What are you doing?" he murmured the moment I approached him. "I have nothing to say to you, Cassie."

"Well, I have a lot to say to you..." The stern tone of my comment caught his attention, and turning to face me, he sighed with what seemed like aggravation.

"I don't know why. I thought we already made it clear I was not someone you needed to be around."

Rolling my eyes, I stared at his chiseled jawline and deep dark eyes that made my core ache with the longing he had created in me. No matter how much time had gone by with us and even with a broken bond, I wanted him. Yet, he refused to see that.

"That wasn't you, Lucas. It was Inanna—"

"Stop it!" he snapped at me in a low and hushed tone, trying not to drag the attention of others who stood nearby. "I was the cause... had I been stronger, you wouldn't have gotten hurt. Not that any of that matters now. You're going to be getting married to one of these pricks anyway."

"One of those pricks? I'd wish you would come to your senses and be the man I want you to be."

The anger that poured off of him was not expected, and as he slammed the weight down upon the ground, the metal clanged against the others. I couldn't help but jump slightly, and the moment I did, remorse crossed his face. "Can't you see I'm nothing but bad for you?"

The fear lingered in his eyes as they searched mine, trying to find some sense of understanding, but I couldn't give up on him. Lucas may have given up on me and everyone else, but I couldn't give up on him. "We were mated, Lucas... those feelings don't go away."

"Yet, they do," he snapped once more. "How many times do I have to tell you we're not mates anymore."

Tears pricked my eyes as a calming flow of energy washed over me, and looking over my shoulder, I watched Sansa approach. Her eyes glowed a slight silver as the powers she used on me kept me in check. "I could feel you getting worked up from all the way over there. Remember what we have talked about."

I knew exactly what she meant. She didn't want me to show my emotions too much to the people out here on the field or in general, period. They could use the emotions and situations to create problems for me that I may not be able to come back from. It was a weakness I couldn't afford, or so that was what Sansa had proclaimed.

As she stood beside me, staring at Lucas, his narrowed gaze darting from me to Sansa and back, I wanted more than anything to reach out to him. To hug him and tell him I forgive him. Yet, that was the kind of emotion I couldn't show.

"If that's how you feel... just remember, it's only your opinion, Lucas."

My feet couldn't carry me any faster as I darted towards a side exit and hastily made my way back towards my suite. The green grass flew by me as I sped towards the elegant white-marbled building in search of the solace I needed.

I wanted to cry... to scream, and yell. To tell him how stupid he was, and I couldn't.

Doing something immature like that in public was just going to make questions arise. Never in my life had I felt so conflicted over my emotions. I was a girl who said it how it was and showed full well that she wasn't someone to be fucked with, and now... I had to be reserved.

It was bullshit, and I hated it more than anything.

If Odin and the other gods thought I was going to be a prim and proper girl...

They were fucking wrong.

Chapter Eight

Lucas

I hated myself for how I was treating Cassie, but it was for the best. It was the only way I could keep her safe from the person I had become. From the person who had done nothing but cause her pain. I was supposed to have been her mate, and instead, I allowed myself to fall prey to a greater power. One able to manipulate my mind.

Watching her walk away from me hurt, and the moment she disappeared from my sight, I was left with Sansa's angry glare and look of disapproval. "You're a fucking idiot, Lucas."

"Whatever," I scoffed, rolling my eyes, trying to rationalize what I was doing. "What did you expect me to fucking do? You know the fucking risks of me being around her."

"Risks, Lucas? Please tell me you're joking right now."

There was no point in talking to Sansa about this. She had been telling me for weeks to stop acting the way I was, and I doubted that Cassie knew of my and Sansa's conversations. Not that there was much to tell. Usually, it was a bunch of scolding and my refusal to admit I was being stupid. As much as part of me yearned to be with her, I couldn't. I couldn't run the risk of me falling back on old ways and hurting her again.

Cassie was important to everyone here, and I cared too much about her to let her fall hurt because of me. I didn't care what anyone had to say about that... it was my choice, and I would do what I wanted to in regards to Cassie. "I'm done discussing this, Sansa."

"Well, I'm not," she replied, grabbing my arm to stop me from turning away from her. "Cassie is going through this without anyone to really be by her side, and out of all the men she could be paired with, she wants you to be there. Even though I think she is stupid for wanting that because you don't deserve her when you're acting like this."

Sansa had said many things to me in the past, but she had never been this forward before. I was honestly shocked to hear her comment, and also to learn that no matter how mean I had been to Cassie and all the shit I had done to her, she still wanted me to be with her.

"Even if I wanted to... they won't let me participate."

Laughing, Sansa shook her head. "And why not? What could possibly stop you from doing so?"

No matter what I said, Sansa wasn't going to let this go, and with a groan of frustration, I threw my hands in the air and sneered at her. "Because I'm the reason she died to begin with. Not to mention, I'm not like the rest of them. My bloodline makes me defective."

Sansa stood there for a moment, surprisingly quiet as she stared at me, and then glanced towards the arena where multiple men stood glancing over at us, obviously having heard my outburst. The dirty looks of some and amused glares of others only further irritated me, but what did I expect after what I had fucking done?

I had made things worse for myself by listening to that stupid bitch Inanna.

Tired of dealing with Sansa, I bent down and grabbed my shirt off the ground, tossing it over my shoulder as I stormed off toward the exit. I was still staying in the same room I had been before, and it was clear when they moved Cassie to a more private wing, I wasn't welcome.

I wanted more than anything to go back home to Earth and live my life out there away from Cassie, but the private conversation Odin had with me after the incident made it clear I was never going to be allowed to go back home.

My place would be here permanently, and as long as I stayed in line and did what I was asked to do, then I wouldn't be a prisoner. Even though, essentially, I fucking was.

"Lucas, wait!" Sansa called out as I stopped in my tracks, looking over my shoulder to see her running across the green, the arena looming in the background.

"What do you want, Sansa? I'm done with the scolding bullshit you constantly throw my way."

Out of breath, her curly black hair bounced off her shoulders as she bent over, huffing and puffing, she held up a finger, telling me to give her a minute.

"Fuck, I really need to start working out... my cardio fucking sucks," she panted, causing me to snort with laughter as I watched her.

"Well, I'm surprised you don't work out, seeing as your brother is addicted to it."

Standing straight, she raised a brow glaring at me before quickly shaking it away. "Look... all I was going to say was that you shouldn't give up. She refuses to give up on you, so instead of acting like you are, why don't you prove to her that you want to change... or better yet, prove to yourself and everyone else what you're actually capable of."

Stunned and slightly speechless, I tried to process what she was saying, yet before I could even get a word out, she turned and made her way back towards the school without so much as a goodbye.

I had tried for weeks to stay away from Cassie, and as much as I thought that was the best idea, I couldn't help but wonder if I was making a mistake.

Maybe everything that happened did happen for a reason, like Freya had told me.

Maybe the steps taken were setting up a future I needed to be prepared for.

Cassie

I couldn't believe how idiotic I had sounded trying to explain myself to Lucas on the field. I had really hoped after all this time, he would have seen I was trying to be the bigger person. That I was trying to fix this relationship between us.

Pacing around my small living room, I ran my hands through my hair, trying to let go of the negative anger currently coursing through me. I was pissed, but most of all, I was hurt.

I couldn't understand why he didn't want to just try and make things work.

It was as if the thought of trying was too hard for him to imagine, and perhaps it was time I started accepting that. The roles were reversed for once, and I had to figure out how to do what I was expected to do. I didn't have the luxury of messing around with love when I had a festival to plan.

A knock at my door caught my attention, and stopping in my tracks, I turned to the large double doors and contemplated telling whoever it was to get fucking lost because I wasn't in the mood.

Yet as the door opened, revealing Ansley, the anger subsided.

"Ansley, why are you knocking?" I asked curiously as to why she didn't just walk in, considering she was my assigned servant.

With a bit of a chipper smile on her face, she closed the door behind her and made her way toward me hesitantly. "I'm sorry to bother you, but I was told to prepare you for training."

Was she being serious right now? "Training for what?"

"Uh, I believe to go over the event. I'm not sure I was just asked to let you know," she replied, slightly uneasy by my short and clipped tone. Guilt instantly filled me with how I had spoken to her. It wasn't her fault all this shit was going on, and with a heavy sigh, I ran my hand over my face and groaned.

"I'm sorry, Ansley. I don't mean to speak to you that way. I'm just... it's been a long day. Not to mention I have a horrible migraine."

Ansley stood staring at me as if confused by my apology. Her mouth opened and closed as I moved toward the sofa, taking a seat. "Would you like a cup of tea and some aspirin? Perhaps a snack? I don't mind telling them you're not feeling well so you can rest for the rest of the day."

Rest. It sounded fucking amazing, but as much as I wanted to do what Odin and Freya said needed to be done, maybe Ansley was right. How was I supposed to do what they asked if I was overly exhausted and beyond confused?

The more I thought about it, the more frustrated I became.

"Okay... yeah, let them know I'm not up for it tonight. Maybe I do need some rest and shit."

Nodding her head, Ansley smiled. "I'll bring you something to eat and some aspirin as well. Don't worry, Cassie. Everything will be fine. You just need more time to adjust to everything."

Surprised by her sudden forwardness, I watched her quickly turn and head back out the bedroom door with her hair swaying from its ponytail behind her. The idea of having a servant was still something I was getting used to, as was all the other shit that came with my new job title. In all honesty, I felt more alone than I ever had before.

As the silence of the room consumed my thoughts, I couldn't stop myself from thinking about Lucas and the way he looked at me today on the field. How incredibly hot he was standing there under the sun, glistening in sweat. The way his dark eyes gazed upon me as if he was hungry for me but at the same time confused about how he felt.

Yet, also how angry he looked that I was once again trying to get his attention.

He wasn't the only one who was confused, though, and the more I thought about it, the more I wanted to talk to him. "Ah—what the fuck is wrong with me?"

"You know, they say talking to your sign of intelligence—"

The sound of the voice caused me to jump, and as I turned quickly, my eyes scanned the vicinity by my open bedroom door; my eyes landed upon a pair of bluish-green eyes I hadn't set sight on in weeks. My heart leaped out of my chest as I jumped from my seat, bolting across the space to the tall, broad figure of a man with chocolate brown hair.

"Silas!" I gasped out as I wrapped my arms around his neck and pulled him to my chest with tears of joy in my eyes. "Where the fuck have you been?"

Chapter Nine

Silas

"Cassie—"

Darkness filled my vision as I searched through the obsidian clouds for her body. The darkness slowly gave way to the roaring sound of chaos, and an explosion of power that illuminated the area. There upon the floor was the delicate body of a woman with pink shades within her hair and celestial blue eyes that stared blankly at me.

"Cassie... no–" What I saw before me wasn't real. Her body, lifeless upon the floor while a mirrored image of her stood ghostly before her brother's body. She was powerful and far more beautiful than I could ever imagine her being, but there was one problem.

She was no longer attainable...she was a goddess now, and far from my reach.

I'd lose her just like I lost Anna.

Flashes of the day Cassie died spun through my mind more than once since I had been gone. Watching Cassie die wasn't something I hadn't been able to handle. The moment of her death made Anna's death flash through my mind and my heart broke.

Granted, things with Anna had been different, and perhaps part of me had loved Anna–even though I knew I couldn't have her—but the problem was I cared for Cassie more than I ever did Anna.

Odin, seemed to have sensed this and sent me on an errand to appease the Fae realm.

Not something I was crazy about, but with my job done there, it was time for me to face the woman I was in love with. The one woman I wouldn't be able to have no matter how much I wanted her.

The moment I stepped into her room and heard her beautiful voice, I couldn't contain myself from making a smartass comment. I half expected her to lash out at me with anger, but instead she ran to me, throwing her arms around my neck as she hugged me.

Never had I imagined she would give me this kind of reaction, but feeling her within my arms was something I would never forget. "Silas, where have you been?"

"I'm sorry–" I whispered, "I was out of the realm on business."

As she pulled away slightly, I had the opportunity to gaze down in her beautiful celestial blue eyes once more, and though my heart clenched with hurt over my situation, I pushed a brave smile on my face. "Oh, I wasn't told that..."

"Yeah, Odin had me go take care of things. Honestly, I didn't think you would be excited about seeing me though. Maybe I should leave more often."

The deep chuckle that escaped me made her roll her eyes as she pulled away more and shook her head. "No, you're not allowed to leave anymore. I need you here with me."

As much as I wanted to believe what she was saying, I knew that wasn't possible. I couldn't allow her to need me because I wasn't going to be able to be what she wanted. That wasn't my place. I was a protector of the realm, and emissary if need be.

I wasn't someone who would ever be able to stand by her side.

However, perhaps tonight I could help her... or at least be a friend by her side... for the moment.

"Well, I'm here now. What's been going on?" Gesturing to the sofa she had once been sitting on, she followed me and sat down upon it looking more frustrated then I had ever seen her.

"I don't know what I'm doing, Silas," she replied, running her hands over her face before her fingers rushed through her hair showing the clear frustration that she felt. "I feel so out of place here."

Taking a seat upon the chair across from where she was sat I nodded. "I see. So while I was gone the past few weeks no one has really explained anything to you?"

"No," she scoffed. "They only paraded me in front of a group of people I don't know, and then told me I need to do training."

Concern filled me as I furrowed my brows in response to what she had said. I had been gone for weeks, and she wasn't any more informed than what she had been when I left. "That doesn't make any sense. I have been gone for weeks... I would have thought they would have done all that stuff quite early on."

Cassie was quite for a moment before a soft breath escaped her lips and she cast her eyes towards the floor. "I wasn't exactly myself after what happened. The powers Pollux gave me were a lot to handle, and I slept for what felt like days before I woke up."

All of which I hadn't been there for... I was a fool to have left like I did, but what Odin had me do was far more important than simply sitting by Cassie's bed when I wasn't actually welcome.

"I wish I could have been here for you when you woke up, but I'm here now and I'd be happy to answer any questions you have. The solstice games are something to look forward to."

Laughter escaped Cassie as she gave me a look of sarcastic uncertainty. "I don't know about that, Silas. The seem to be nothing but a pain in the ass and I haven't even done anything yet. Although..." she said pointedly, "I did get Odin to agree to let me help plan them."

"Oh shit. Really?" To hear Odin was willing to let Cassie help was shocking. He never let anyone help with the games as it was something he enjoyed setting up himself.

"Yeah." She shrugged. "I have no clue how they go though so it's not like I'm going to be as much help as I thought I could be."

The more she talked, the more I couldn't help but watch her. The way she pushed her hair behind her ear. How her lips moved as she told the story of how it was meeting everyone that would take part in the games. She was mesmerizing, and the more her voice floated around me, the more I realized that being even this close to her could be problematic.

Weighing my choices, I sighed, caving in to the pitiful look on Cassie's face. I had seen it before in Anna when she came here, and though Anna was a different situation I couldn't allow Cassie to have no one in her corner.

She had far more to offer this realm and others with her realistic view on the world.

"I'll help you, Cassie."

Her eyes darted up to mine with a mixture of hope and gratefulness I couldn't ignore, and with a smile crossing her plump, delicious lips, I had to reign in my beast that wanted to claim her. Cassie was extraordinary, but the godly glow that illuminated her and heightened every bit of her beautiful body made her that much more attractive.

"Are you sure? I don't want to impose on anything you currently have going on," she replied hesitantly.

"I'm sure," I retorted, adjusting myself in my seat as I cleared my throat. "Typically, the games are a mixture of strength, agility, and intelligence. So let's start with the basics. Strength."

Her eyes lit up at my words, and as she bit her bottom lip thinking about what I said I tried my hardest to look anywhere but at her. "What about sparring matches or something?"

"That's what they usually do." I chuckled before standing to my feet. The itch to move around growing inside me as I began to wander about her room looking at everything, but realizing that as pretty as this room was, it didn't reflect Cassie's personality.

"Well, what can we do to make it different?"

The question was honestly only something she could answer, and as I turned to face her, I simply gave her a small smile. "You're the designer, Cassie. Make it fit your personality."

"My personality?" She scoffed, rolling her eyes. "That wouldn't be good for anyone. No one seems to like my personality much."

Turning to face her, I shook my head. "That's not true. I like your personality."

The blush that settled over her face was something I wouldn't ever get tired of doing. She tried so hard to hide her emotions at times but the moment I complimented her, she blushed so red her ears turned pink. "You're just saying that because you're my friend."

Ouch. Friend... I forgot how much that word stung.

"Regardless of my friendship with you, it's still true," I replied, acting as if the comment she made didn't hurt, "so with that being said... what about strength do you think would be beneficial in a tournament?"

A snort of laughter escaped her as she shrugged. "Taking me on would be a good one... but I really don't know how to control this new version of me."

"Taking you on?" Raising a brow at her comment, I faced her, watching her mouth open and close slowly before a smirk crossed her lips.

"Well, yeah, I mean... before this all happened, there wasn't a single person here who could match me, but now, I guess that's different as I'm not the same person."

Every part of me wanted to clear the space between us and put her in her place but I restrained myself from doing so. "You're so confident in who you were... there isn't a reason why you shouldn't still be confident in who you will become."

Standing to her feet, she stared at me with silence as she slowly made her way towards me. "You think I'm confident... you say I'm pretty... if that's the case, why are you acting as if being around me right now is almost impossible for you to do even though you say you want to help?"

I was caught between a rock and a hard place with her comment because the look she was giving me right now made it clear that she knew something was up. "I don't know what you mean—"

"Don't do that..." she snapped as she shook her head, clearing the space between us. Her hand laid upon my chest as she looked up at me with those big celestial eyes and pouty lips.

Letting out a raspy breath, I froze at her touch. "Do what?"

"Pretend the tension between us isn't there. I know you're uncomfortable right now, and after everything we have been through, I don't understand why you're acting like this. I thought I meant more to you."

"You do," I quickly added, trying to catch my breath. Her delicious scent of lavender and honey wrapped around my heart in a way I couldn't handle. "I just have to be realistic about all of this for the both of us."

Furrowing her brows, she stared at me with confusion. "Realistic... what are you talking about?"

I didn't want to explain this to her, and the more I stood with her like this, the more I knew I had to say something. Yet, I didn't want to be the fool who assumed things when I wasn't completely sure of what this was in the first place.

Taking a deep breath, I sighed, closing my eyes. "As much as I want to be with you right now, I can't. I am a guardian of the realm, Cassie, and all I can ever be is your friend. The way I acted before was wrong."

"Wrong?" she replied, reaching up slowly to run her hand down the side of my face, "nothing about any of this has ever been wrong... but every part of it feels right."

Without warning, she leaned up on her tippy toes and pressed her lips to mine, and when she did, I lost all control of who I was. The situation may have been wrong on one hand, but Cassie was right about something... every part of this felt right.

Chapter Ten

Cassie

I wasn't sure what I was doing or what was going to happen, but something about Silas being close to me was overwhelming. Something about him staring at me the way he did drove my heart crazy. He was supposed to simply be a friend... a guy I had met on campus who happened to help me when I needed it most with Lucas.

Yet, during the time we had spent together things had changed and every part of me screamed out to be with him.

I had done it once before... and I can't resist the urge to do it again.

The moment my lips crashed upon his, a fire burnt through me that was something I hadn't experienced before, and I knew he felt it too because the heat that poured off his body told me he wanted this as much as I did.

With the lift of his arms around my body, he pulled me up higher upon his chest, my legs wrapping around his waist as he held me to him. Our tongues battled for dominance as he walked me towards the sofa, sitting down with me straddling his lap.

As much as I wanted to continue, he broke the kiss, his hands in my hair as he stared at me with darting eyes that seemed to search for answers I didn't know how to explain.

"Cassie—" he breathed out shallowly trying to catch his breath, "what are we doing?"

As much as I wanted to answer him with something serious, I couldn't. A snort of laughter escaped me as I pressed my lips gently to him again. "Kissing... don't stop–"

Attempting to kiss him again, he stopped me once more, shaking his head. "Cassie, we can't, trust me I want to but we can't."

"Why not?" I frowned in confusion at his refusal. "We have before–"

"Yes, but you're not the same as before, Cassie," he replied, cutting me off. "You're not just a celestial half-breed. You're the future of this realm, and you're meant to be paired with a mate from the games. Not someone like me."

There were no words I could say that would explain the heartache I felt, and I couldn't be angry because I could see in his own face the upset he felt in saying it. It was clear the games were more of a problem for me than I wanted to admit, and taking them seriously was something I was obviously going to have to do.

"Don't say that..." I muttered softly, shaking my head, his hands falling to my thighs as he cast his gaze to the far while breathing deeply. "Silas, don't say that... I can't lose you."

Snapping his attention back to me, he scoffed with a smile. "You will never leave me. I may not be assigned to you as your guardian, but I will always be here for you. From now... until forever, Cassie. I just can't be this that you want. You deserve to have your mate."

I hated he was refusing what we both knew we wanted, but I understood how he thought he was helping to save me from doing something that could harm my reputation or anything else for that matter. It was my life, and the fact I was being faced with all the royal bullshit and now Silas wanting to suddenly be respectable, was annoying.

Climbing off his lap, I groaned in frustration as I stood to my feet and straightened out my clothing. Here I was in the mood to have him ravish me and help me forget about all the bullshit I was going through, and instead, he stops and worries about how I would look to other people.

"Silas, I don't care what other people think about me. I will end up picking whoever I want for my mate, and that's just how it's going to be."

My comment didn't seem to sink in with him as a chuckle escaped his lips, and he stared at me with amusement in his eyes. "You don't get to pick, Cassie. That's now how this works."

Not understanding what he meant, I opened my mouth to speak but instead, hesitated as he stood to his feet. "What are you talking about?"

"I mean that you don't get to decide. Cassie, the games decide for you. You were told this, weren't you?" I couldn't lie and say I wasn't because, in a way, I sort of was. Sansa had tried to explain things to me, and I didn't really listen to certain things told to me at the gathering.

"I can change that, though..." I stuttered, shaking my head, "I won't let them tell me what I can or can't do."

Stepping forward, he shook his head with a sad glance. "Unfortunately, you don't have the power to change that."

Hearing Silas's doubts about what I was able to do was disappointing. I would have thought that by now, he would have known I was able to do anything I set my mind to unless I was a fool to believe I could. "I can do whatever I want too..."

Clenching my fists at my side, I refused to believe the man standing in front of me was saying the things he was. Only just a moment ago, we were making out, and I at least was hoping for more, and now he is standing in front of me with a nonchalant kind of glance as if what I'm saying is impossible.

I wished more than anything he wouldn't act the way he was because, besides Sansa, I really wanted him on my side. Yeah, he may have been willing to help me figure out the shit I was supposed to do... but, this was ridiculous everyone around me thought I would simply sit back and do as I was told.

"Cassie, let's not argue... this isn't what I came here for."

The calm response made me grit my teeth as I narrowed my gaze at him. "Then what are you doing here, Silas?"

He was silent for a moment as he seemed to weigh his choice of wording correctly before responding. I wasn't sure why he had come if it hadn't been to spend time with me. Then again, I had jumped to conclusions with my reactions to his arrival to begin with.

"I came to check on you and apologize for leaving," he replied politically as if suddenly he was indifferent to our interaction. Yet, even though he spoke, I knew deep down there was more to it than what he was explaining.

"I can tell there is more to what you're telling me. So why don't you spit it out and stop hiding whatever it is you're hiding."

As the corner of his lips rose into a smirk and a soft sigh left his throat, I knew my assumptions were correct. "Well, I was sincere in saying I would help you with the games, Cassie. However, I did want to let you know ahead of time that there are going to be more creatures involved than what you simply already know."

"What are you talking about?"

The cryptic message wasn't something I understood, and stepping toward me, he stared down with a sense of knowing that drove me crazy with curiosity. "Do you know much about the Fae realm?"

The question caught me completely off guard, and as I stared at him with my lips parted, completely dumbfounded, I shook my head no. "Should I be?"

"Yes, Cassie. You should be. There is more going on behind the scenes than you know, and even though you're angry at me because of what has taken place tonight... I'm not what you should worry yourself with. There are going to be people here who are going to test you, and if you're not prepared, you will fall... just like so many others have."

Silas's words were a warning, and as I watched him turn and head towards my bedroom door, I found myself left with so many questions he obviously had no interest in wanting to answer.

"Where are you going? You can't just leave things like that," I snapped angrily as I marched after him grabbing his upper arm, stopping him in his tracks.

Glancing down at me over his shoulder, he stared for a moment before pulling his arm from my grasp. "Cassie, if I stay around like I was before, I will only complicate things for you. Sansa and others are going to be able to help you more than I can."

"So you're abandoning me after you just said you weren't?" I scoffed, shaking my head, "what the hell is wrong with you? Why even come here then?"

"I came to help you... but now, I feel like I made a mistake."

Hearing him say seeing me was a mistake shifted something inside me. Anger I had never felt before bubbled deep inside my chest, and with every second that passed, I felt myself growing angrier that he was standing here saying what he was.

"So now seeing me is a mistake?" The laughter that bubbled from me made him roll his eyes.

"Stop putting words in my mouth, Cassie. That's not what I meant, and you know it."

"Do I though?" I replied, my hand reaching past him to grip the door handle as I pulled the door open and gestured with my eyes for him to leave. "Go on. That's what your good at right... leaving?"

The pain I was feeling may have been masked by the anger I was showing, but could he blame me for being angry? I had literally been on my own for the most part with all this shit, and the moment I felt hope I had him here, he shut down on me and was pulling away again.

Shaking his head he laughed once more at my comment, his hand reaching up and rubbing the back of his neck. "You can think what you want, Cassie, but you're completely wrong about that."

"Am I though?" His eyes met mine, reflecting his own irritation over the situation as I clenched my jaw, "look at us... you come back, and already we are at each other's throats."

"Yes, we are!" he yelled throwing his hands in the air, "because you're assuming shit without even taking a look at the bigger picture! You know nothing of the realm or how things are done. You're stuck in your old fucking ways, and that isn't going to fly with the shit you're required to do!"

Taken back by his outburst, I lashed out at him, shoving him towards the door in anger. My heart raced and as the adrenaline pushed through my veins,

I felt the change in my come over rather quickly. The change reflected in Silas's eyes as they widened with shock.

"Fuck you, Silas. I'm not fucking changing for anyone! Do you hear me?! I'm not changing, not that you actually fucking give a shit about me."

Shoving him again, the power behind my thrust caused him to stagger back into the wall by the door, and as it did, his hand reached out, gripping my throat as the fire burned behind his eyes. I had pushed him a little too hard, and as he stared down at me with a loose grip on my neck, I saw the confliction weighing within him.

"You have no idea what you're talking about, nor the length I would go to to make sure you're safe and happy, Cassie. You're everything to me, and it kills me I can't be what you want, but this is the life we both live and you will have to accept it the way I have had to do."

Dropping his grip on my throat, I watched him adjust his shoulders and turn to exit my room with the echoed sound of the door slamming behind him. Silas didn't leave me a chance to explain or say anything in regard to what he said before he left, and as I stood there trying to process the confession, I knew he was right.

I didn't have a single clue about anything, and if I kept acting the way I was, then I wouldn't have anyone left around me in the end.

Chapter Eleven

Cassie

The warmth of sunlight fell upon my cheek and as I slowly opened my eyes, taking in the dust particles dancing within the beams that filtered in through the open window. I realized what had happened last night with Silas wasn't a dream. I had made a stand and fucked things up like I always did and with a groan, I rubbed my hands over my face and tried to figure out how I was going to apologize for being an idiot.

The sound of footsteps upon the marbled floor caught my attention, and looking towards my bedroom door, I watched Trixie prance in wearing black knee-high boots and a black flowing summery dress that stopped at her thighs with a white belt and her hair curiously braided into two french braids.

A look that was completely different from how Trixie usually dressed, which was odd.

"Trixie? What the hell are you doing here?" I asked slightly shocked and confused as I sat up in bed, trying to process if what I was seeing was actually true.

Taking a bite of the apple in her hands, she went from wide-eyed to furrowed brows with a shrug of her shoulders. "Sansa reached out to me and told me you desperately need guidance. So, here I am."

"Wait. Sansa reached out to you?"

Unsure of what exactly was going on, I let my legs slide over the edge of the bed as I sat there in my blue cotton shorts and tank top trying to process what was going on. It wasn't like we had cell phones in this place. So for Sansa to reach out to Trixie didn't make sense.

"What the hell is wrong with you? Why do you look like you lost your puppy and don't know where to find it?" Glancing up at Trixie, I quirked a brow and laughed at her comment. She was witty with her comebacks, but half the time, they didn't make sense.

Running my hand over my face, I sighed. "I'm sorry. I just was trying to understand how she reached out to you."

"I am a witch, Cassie," Sansa's voice called out from my living room, making my eyes dart towards the open doorway and back to Trixie, who gestured towards the door, shrugging her shoulders again.

"Sansa's here too?"

"Well, yeah," Trixie said nonchalantly, "why wouldn't she be?"

It was clear something was bothering Trixie, and I wasn't sure what it was yet. But her moody comments and unwillingness to seemingly want to help were unusual behavior for her. Not that I was going to point it out.

Sliding from the bed, my feet hit the floor as I stood stretching my arms over my head. I didn't miss the way Trixie glanced at me with a smirk on her face as I padded my way toward the bathroom to brush my teeth. "So, I heard you had a visitor last night."

Groaning, I popped my toothbrush into my mouth and rolled my eyes, trying my best not to get into the topic of Silas and what had transpired between the two of us.

"Oh, come on, Cassie. Give me the details," Trixie urged as I glanced over my shoulder at her finishing my teeth with a sigh.

"There is nothing to tell. He came to visit me... we got into a heated debate, and he left."

Brushing past her, I headed towards the living room only to stop short and stare at the sight before me. Sansa sat on the floor at the coffee table with her dark curly hair pulled up into a bun on her head, papers scattered all around her, and a pencil in her mouth.

"What in the hell—" I murmured, causing Sansa to glance up at me with a smile as Trixie came from behind me and plopped herself upon the sofa.

"You know... I heard that you and Silas had more than a heated debate. That there was some shouting, and when he left, he looked more than pissed off about whatever you two talked about."

Of course, it was no surprise Trixie would know this information and want to know exactly what happened. She was a stickler for the details, and though it was one thing I loved about her, it could also be slightly irritating when it came to your personal life.

"It was nothing," I gritted out, trying to drop the subject. "Sansa, what are you doing?"

"Hmm–" she muttered absentmindedly before turning her attention to me fully. "Oh, this? It's the plans for the games, of course. I have everything mapped out for you. All you have to do is approve it."

I hadn't realized Sansa was putting so much work into this over the last day or so while I had been slacking off for the most part. She was a go-getter, and from the looks of it, she liked to plan things out as well... which would be useful in the long run.

"Oh, well, what were you thinking? Because I have no clue about what to do."

The moment I gave the floor to Sansa, her eyes beamed with excitement as she began shuffling through papers and pulling out books. I didn't realize that an event like this would take so much work to sort out, but according to the way she was acting, it must have been a really big deal.

"So, I say we keep the games as they have always been with the fighting challenges for the strength training, but what I was thinking was mixing it with the agility part. So like, maybe a course but one that they basically would fight during to break towards the end."

With my mouth partially opened in confusion, I glanced at Trixie, who sat on the sofa completely amused by what Sansa was saying. "So are we going like straight Viking then? Like the ways of Bjorn?"

The name Bjorn had come up once before in some of the stuff I had read about Anna and her lover, Bjorn. However, I had never really paid too much attention to it when I was reading it because it wasn't important at the time. Yet, as Sansa nodded her head in agreement, I found it may have been better had I read more into it.

The books, of course, I had in my room somewhere… if they were moved into the new room.

As Sansa went to open her mouth to answer Trixie, I quickly interjected, "Wait, Viking thing?"

Both girls looked at me with confusion and laughter as they furrowed their brows as if unsure of what to say to me. "Cassie, Odin is a Norse god… they are associated with that kind of lifestyle."

"Well, of course, I know that," I replied, rolling my eyes with irritation, "I'm just saying like what Viking thing are you talking about… you know, with the games. I don't get it."

"Oh," Sansa said softly, giving me an understanding smile, "sometimes I forget you haven't been here that long."

"Yeah, it's totally cool, Cassie," Trixie replied, her mood seeming to lift slightly as she leaned forward with her elbows on her knees. "Think of it like a triple cup kind of thing. So there are three events, and the winners of every event move to the next event until the last one proclaims the overall winner. Does that make sense?"

Trixie's explanation did make slight sense, but at the same time, I didn't get why Trixie had called it a Viking thing. I mean, there were tons of cultures I knew about that had done games like that over the centuries. "So what makes it Viking?"

"Well, the brutality, I guess."

Raising my brows in response to Sansa's reasoning, I sat there in shock. "Brutality?"

Glancing between the two girls in front of me, both of them nodded as if it was the most natural thing to suggest. I was a girl who came from a wolf pack and had seen sparring turn into horrible fights but thinking people would have to compete this way never really struck me as something that would happen.

If I was ever going to be able to adjust to this new life, I really had to get it together and stop doubting everything I was told. "Well, that will be interesting."

"Oh, it is... not to mention incredibly hot," Trixie replied, causing us all to laugh.

"I don't think bloodshed is hot... and you're mated to my brother, so I don't even wanna know the kind of things you two get into if you think brutality is hot."

Sansa cackled as Trixie glared at me with shock and a smile. "Oh my God, Cassie... I didn't mean like that. The guys who compete are hot... I'm not a sadist or anything."

"Well, sometimes I wonder what you're into with some of the shit you say," I replied in a teasing tone that caused her to pick up the pillow from the sofa and toss it at me, which caused me to laugh in response.

It was nice to sit here with the two of them and simply be ourselves. Especially when I didn't know exactly how long I was going to be able to continue doing this. When I was awarded the title I was, I expected some type of princess-style life, but I was slowly wondering what I was going to be going through, considering Odin wasn't like the people I read about in books.

He was in charge, but he was more sarcastic and eager to see how things unfold. I suppose like a Viking who took what he wanted, traveled often, and didn't follow any one set of rules.

"So back to the games things, why don't we do this... just draft up the ideas, put a twist on it to some of the shit you both know I like, and let Odin know. I trust you both to make it interesting."

"You sure you don't want your input?" Sansa questioned with concern in her tone, "I mean, I have no problem doing it like that, but I just want to make sure you're sure."

Letting out a heavy sigh, I nodded. "Yeah, I'm sure. Plus, they want me to take classes and learn about shit to do with heritage or something. Ansley was supposed to fill me in with that crap today."

Trixie snorted in response to what I said as she shook her head. "You mean Ansley Gray? The previous servant girl of Solina's?"

"Uh... yeah," I replied with hesitation, suddenly wondering what was wrong with the girl for Trixie to respond the way she did. It was very unusual for Trixie to be acting completely moody like this was, and the more she kept acting like this, the more I questioned what was going on.

"Be careful of that one... she seems sweet, but Solina could have her spying on you."

"Dude, what's wrong with you?" I interjected, completely ignoring what Trixie had said. "You have been incredibly moody since you got here."

"No, I'm not," she snapped under her breath as she avoided eye contact with Sansa and me.

"Actually, now that Cassie mentioned it... you are acting really weird." At Sansa's addition to what I was saying, Trixie jumped to her feet and began pacing around the room, her hand running through her hair before she started biting on her nails.

"I don't know what's wrong with me..." she finally sighed as she turned to us with tear-filled eyes.

"What do you mean... what's going on?" Trying to remain gentler in my tone so as not to upset her, I watched her take a few deep breaths as she shrugged her shoulders.

"That's the thing. There are so many things. I mean, living with your family isn't exactly easy, and then this girl Pollux used to know keeps trying to piss me off, and I'm trying to be nice. On top of that, I can't stop eating... and sleeping. I fucking sleep all the time lately."

As a smile grew on my face, I turned to Sansa, who was giving me the same look. I knew exactly what the hell was wrong with Trixie, and as she glanced between Sansa and me with confusion, I couldn't help but laugh.

"Trixie... are you pregnant?"

Chapter Twelve

Cassie

"Pregnant?!" Trixie gasped as she shook her head, "no, no, no... that's not possible."

It didn't matter that Trixie was refusing the believe she was. I could feel it. There was an heir to my family's home growing inside her, and it totally made sense she was acting the way she was. The only problem was she hadn't accepted, and no one else knew.

"I always wanted to be an aunt." Crossing my hands over my chest, I smiled at Sansa. "Best day ever."

"I'm not pregnant!" Trixie shrieked, causing Sansa and I both to laugh at the outburst she made as her eyes went wide once more, and she covered her hand over her mouth in shock. "There's no way, Cassie... I mean, it's too early."

"Trixie, it's not a big deal. You're going to be an amazing mom, and Pollux will cater to you as he was when you were here. The guy will be ecstatic."

The moment I mentioned my brother, tears filled her eyes, and I thought back to what she had said before I mentioned her being pregnant. Someone was messing with Trixie, and my brother was obviously being a fucking idiot as usual.

"Trixie, why are you crying?" Sansa asked as she stood to her feet and made her way towards Trixie wrapping her arms around her. "You don't need to be sad—"

"Whose the girl messing with you, Trixie?" I stated firmly, causing both of them to glance at me with hesitation. "It wouldn't happen to be Ashley, would it?"

Trixie nodded her head, and as she did, I almost saw red. Hearing my brother's bimbo ex was causing issues for my friend pissed me off. I had told my family to protect and guide Trixie, and it was clear there was nothing being done about Ashley.

She was a problem I should have taken care of a long time ago. I couldn't stand the girl.

"It's okay, though. I'll handle it," Trixie said, trying to reassure me. My anger did nothing to subside as I thought of the girl who had been more arrogant than was needed back in the day. She had thought because she was a she-wolf and popular at the time, that gave her the claim over my brother.

All of which vanished when he dumped her, and we came to Asgard. Yet, now with Trixie and Pollux back, she is determined it seems to make her place in my brother's life again.

"Have you talked to Pollux about this?" I asked, curious to know if my brother was aware and if he what he was doing to ensure that Ashley was put in her place again.

"Kind of... it's hard to explain." She sighed just in time for a bell to ring and my suite door to open, showing a very excited Freya standing there with her hair hanging in waves over her shoulders as her eyes scanned over the three of us.

"Good morning, ladies."

I hadn't expected a visit from Freya, and as I opened and closed my mouth, staring at her, she freely moved into my suite as if she lived there as well. What shocked me the most was the way she was dressed. The woman had skinny jeans and a white flowing halter top on as if she was a normal fucking person.

"Uh—hey, why are you dressed... normal?" I muttered just in time for Sansa and Trixie to both glance at me in shock at how I had spoken to Freya, which caused me to simply shrug my shoulders.

Glancing down at her attire, Freya smiled and shrugged her own shoulders. "I thought it was cute."

"Oh, it is cute..." Trixie replied softly, "it's just that none of us have ever seen you dress like this."

Laughter escaped Freya as she walked towards the sofa and sat down upon it next to Trixie as if she was one of the girls and had come to hang out. I didn't know what to say, and neither did my two friends, who were sitting there as lost as I was.

"Oh, come on, girls. Don't act so surprised. I saw the outfits you girls kept wearing, and I had to see what all the fuss was about," she replied in a nonchalant tone that was completely awkward.

"...and your verdict?" I asked.

Running her hands down her shirt to smooth out any potential wrinkles, her smile widened. "I love it, honestly. Jeans and those black pants you always wear...."

"Leggings..." I muttered again, causing Trixie to laugh.

"Yes! Those things... leggings. They are so comfortable."

I couldn't for the life of me believe I was having this conversation with Freya, a Norse goddess, in my suite living room. "I'm glad that you're enjoying them..."

Silence quickly fell over my friends and me as I glanced around at them. Sansa shuffled through the papers in front of her as Trixie quickly averted her gaze towards the window in my room as if something outside was more interesting than what was going on in the room.

"Oh fuck it... stop being weird, everyone," I finally snapped with a sigh, causing Freya to laugh again. "So what brings you here, Freya?"

"Well, I'm so glad you asked. I came to speak to you about the upcoming ball."

A ball... she had to fucking kidding me. "What are you talking about?"

"Well, it's kind of like a welcoming ceremony, honestly. All those who are going to be attending will be there and their families. It will be a time for all the contestants to meet you properly and have a chance to dance with you."

The fact that Freya was talking about this as if it was so natural was unsettling for me. The last thing I wanted to do was be pranced around like a prize to be won, even though that's exactly what I was. "I thought I already did that when I met the devil twins."

Freya furrowed her brows with her mouth open in confusion. "Devil twins... are you talking about Thor's children?"

Nodding my head, Freya burst into laughter. It wasn't the kind of laughter that was like a slight chuckle or a bit of amusement. She literally doubled over in laughter at my comment to the point I swore she wiped a tear from her eye.

"Why are you laughing?" Sansa muttered, causing Freya to glance at her slightly dismissive.

"Because... I'm not oblivious to their reputation, but I had never heard them described as devil children. Especially considering their heritage. I don't blame you for calling them that thought. They are very troublesome."

"That's a damn understatement," Trixie muttered, rolling her eyes.

Freya glared at Trixie, and the tension coming off her was a little too much for my liking. Quickly deciding to change the topic, I shook my head. "So why am I having to do another meet and greet. I thought that was what the thing was I went to the other day."

"Oh no," Freya smiled. "That was just to meet more of your family."

"Wait, what..." I replied, completely dumbfounded, "they are my family??"

Freya nodded her head as Trixie made a gagging noise quietly. My mind tried to wrap around what she was saying and process information all at the same time.

"What's wrong? I don't understand why you're all acting like this," Freya asked with confusion clearly spread across her face by the knitted brows and frown she was portraying.

"Maybe because the brother is participating so he can marry Cassie," Trixie finally said with a sigh of disgust. "How the heck are they related?"

That was my thoughts exactly, but the more I started thinking about it, the more it made sense and the more I felt sick to my stomach. "Oh my God... my mother and Thor are siblings..."

"Yep," Freya said with pride. "But you guys are technically like distant cousins."

"Distant?!" I shriek as I jumped to my feet, running my hand over my face. "No we are fucking cousins, Freya. That's disgusting... I'm not up for that country backwood bullshit. You have got to be kidding me right now."

There was no way in hell I would ever marry my cousin I didn't give a shit if he won or not. What got me was how casual and confused Freya seemed to be over the entire thing. It was as if something like this was normal, and that was just completely fucking weird in my opinion.

"Cassie," Freya said standing to her feet. "I don't understand why you're acting like this. It's not like he is your brother or anything."

Holding my hand up, I stopped her from saying anything else as I closed my eyes taking deep breaths as I shook my head no. "Look, I know that may sound normal to you but I can tell you right now that will never happen, Freya. Never..."

Looking at her once more, she clasped her hands in front of her and sighed with a nod. "Okay... but besides that, you do have the ball coming up, and I'm sure you will want your friends to go with you. So Ansley will show you ladies in a moment to a room for you to select your outfits. I think the dress maker did well on the dresses she came up with for each of you."

Turning on her feet, Freya quickly exited the room, leaving me standing in my pajamas staring dumbfounded at the now closed door. I couldn't believe she actually thought that shit was normal like it was something I would honestly go for.

"Dude... that was weird as shit," Sansa said with an exaggerated sigh as she picked up the papers she had scattered everywhere. "There ain't no way in hell I'd ever do that shit."

Glancing at Sansa and then to Trixie, I watched my green-eyed friend with her hand over her mouth, trying not to laugh. "It's not funny..."

"It is, though!" she replied bursting into laughter. "I mean I have heard some crazy stuff before, Cassie, but never something like that. I forget sometimes how different they live their lives from my people."

Running my hands through my hair I groaned and made my way towards my bedroom. There was no way I could deal with any of that stuff right now. The only thing I wanted was a hot shower, and to wash away the thoughts of my fucking cousin thinking he could marry me.

The realization of how different the times and traditions were with some of the people who lived here compared to the world I came from was extensive. Opening the bathroom door, I reached for the shower knob and switched the hot water on.

You would think with all this modern technology they took advantage of here in Asgard that they would come to terms with kissing cousins not being a good thing or at least not a normal thing. Yet, here I was finding out my own cousin thought he had a chance to marry me.

I'd fucking kick his ass and prevent him from ever having children if he came close to me with that notion. There was no way in hell I would give in to the idea of marrying Thor's son.

They had to be out of their fucking mind.

Chapter Thirteen

Lucas

Since my conversation with Sansa, I contemplated a lot about what she said. Every day I spent out here on the training fields working out and staying in shape to take my mind off Cassie, I found my irritation growing hearing the other guys talk about their entry into the games. Each of them thought they had a chance with her, and it made me laugh while listening to them.

Cassie was a complicated woman for sure, and the more I thought about the little time we did spend together, the more I realized I was making a mistake by not trying like she wanted. Even my beast had retreated to the depths of my soul, refusing to acknowledge me over my refusal to take my stance with her.

We weren't mated anymore, but that didn't stop my desire to have her.

She was like a breath of fresh air every time I saw her from a distance, and I wanted more than anything to be close to her, but my fear of the darkness taking over me again prevented me from doing so.

Was I a fool... perhaps?

"Lucas..." The sound of an annoying male voice I was all too familiar with caused me to tense as I turned around to see Silas striding towards me in dress pants and a green shirt rolled up to his elbows. The man looked like he had just stepped out of a photo shoot, and as much as the other men around me smiled, waving to him, I couldn't share their excitement.

Instead, I scoffed and turned back towards my stuff scattered on a bench and began shoving it back into my duffle bag. If Silas was coming to talk to me, I was planning to make it short, sweet, and to the point... I didn't want to talk to him.

"Lucas, I need to talk to you."

Slinging the bag over my shoulder, I smirked, shaking my head. "Yeah, well, I don't have shit to say to you, Silas. Go find someone else to fucking bother."

The moment I went to walk away, he snatched my arm, pulling me back to him. My eyes narrowed as I scowled at him. He had some nerve fucking touching me, and as he glared at me, all I wanted to do was fucking hit him. "I said I need to fucking talk to you, Lucas."

"Yeah, I fucking heard you," I replied, ripping my arm from his grasp, "and if you fucking touch me again, I'll knock your fucking teeth out of your mouth."

The growl that came from deep in Silas' throat was enough to make the beast in me pause for a moment in shock. I had always seen Silas as a playboy asshole who wanted everything that everyone else had and would do anything to get it.

"Look, I'm not here for casual fucking conversation, Lucas. So cut the shit and just listen to what I have to say," he replied as I rolled my eyes with irritation. I didn't want to hear what he had to say, but it was quite obvious he wasn't going to let me go if I didn't stay and listen.

"Fine–" I gritted out as I dropped my bag upon the ground and crossed my arms over my chest, "make it quick. I don't have all day."

Laughter escaped Silas as he shook his head. "Yeah because you have a lot going on lately, don't you? Working out all day... keeping to the ground... avoiding your mate."

"Fuck you, Silas," I snapped, pointing at his chest. "You have no fucking clue what you're talking about. She isn't my mate anymore, and that's for the best."

"The best for who? You?" he replied just as quickly, "don't pretend that you're doing this for anyone else but yourself."

There was no point in arguing with him over this, and it was clear he had his view on me. As much as I wanted to bust him in his mouth for speaking to me the way he was, I didn't. I stood there staring at him with a newfound hatred I never knew I could feel.

"Again, go fuck yourself, Silas. What is it you fucking want so we can end this charade?"

Silas stared at me for a moment as if he had a stick up his ass all a sudden when it came to explaining why he chose to harass me today. Yet, letting loose a deep breath, he ran his hand through his hair and gave in. "You need to enter the games... Cassie needs you."

Laughter escaped me as I bent down to pick up my bag, shaking my head. "No fucking way."

"Excuse me?" he replied quickly as I turned and made my way toward the exit of the arena, not bothering to answer his question. Sansa had already tried that shit, and now here he was, trying that shit with me. I couldn't join, no matter how much people thought I should.

"I'm not doing it, Silas," I replied from over my shoulder. "You do it."

"She's in danger, Lucas. Danger is coming, and I can only protect her so much. I need someone on the inside to help me protect her."

Silas' words stopped me in my tracks as my heart clenched. Cassie was in danger, and I didn't know what he meant by that, but I needed to know. No matter how much I want to keep my distance because of my own issues, I couldn't allow her to get hurt.

She meant too much to me.

A shadowed figure at my side caused me to glance, and staring at Silas, I took note of the serious expression on his face. He wasn't lying about Cassie. At least not from what I could tell.

"Why is she in danger?"

Glancing around the area, he looked back at me and sighed. "Let's go somewhere to talk. There are too many people around, Lucas."

Taking a moment, I thought about what he was asking, and as I let my eyes roam the area, I could see we had caught the attention of quite a few people. People who were the last ones I wanted to know any of my business. Including Bron, who was currently talking to Zia, whose scowl let me know she was still pissed off I turned her away.

It wasn't because of anything she really did before… she was materialistic and fake and desperately did want me. The problem was she wasn't Cassie, and as soon as the cloudy haze over my mind was gone, I realized how much I had fucked up.

"Fine. Let's go back to my place."

Silas gestured for me to lead the way, and turning again, we made our way through the green field outside the arena towards the front gates of the school, where I took in the sight of the students who wandered around without a care in the world doing normal shit.

Shit that I wished I could do, but unfortunately, that wasn't my life anymore.

The moment I took the steps of the palace-styled home and built with white marble and gold, I thought about Cassie and the first time she and I walked down these halls. The way she looked at me as I asked about her sharing a room with me.

I had been foolish then, and right now, I felt as if I was going to be foolish again.

Stepping into my room, I left the door wide for Silas to follow, and with the sound of the door quickly closing behind me, I knew he didn't waste a single moment of trying to get this conversation over with. Something I was pleased about.

"Let's make this quick," Silas replied flatly as I glanced over my shoulder to see him standing by the door. "Odin sent me to rally the realms for warriors for the games. On top of that, there are some characters coming that are going to be more than problematic. They don't give a shit about her and two of them I wouldn't be surprised if they tried to overthrow Cassie or have her killed as soon as the crown changes over."

Hearing there were two people who could possibly be problematic wasn't what I wanted to hear. Closing my eyes, I pinched the bridge of my nose and sighed. "Anything else I need to be told?"

"Fynnairian of the Fae realm is coming as well. The prophecy is set for their future queen, and he believes it's Cassie. However, only time will tell," Silas replied, causing me to look at him once more.

"So why do you want me to join then if that guy going to be there?"

I didn't understand why Silas wanted me there. He could protect her regardless of who is joining the games, but the way Silas was staring at me, I had a feeling he was adamant about his choice to have me go in.

"I can't, Lucas, I'm part of the guard and it's forbidden for me to join. Trust me when I say that I don't want to be here asking this of you, but there is no other way. It's better the devil I know then the devil I don't."

His reasoning made sense, and taking a moment to process everything, I sighed before nodding my head with reluctance. "Okay... but let's get one thing straight. I'm only doing this to make sure she doesn't get her ass killed."

A smile spread across Silas' face at my agreement. Pleased by my answer, he turned, opening the door to reveal a young blonde with big blue eyes and a pearly white smile holding up a black garment bag.

I didn't have the slightest clue why she was there or how long she had been there but the woman was prepared, and if she had been prepared that meant he had already known I was going to agree. "Hey, wait a second..."

Holding his hand up, he smiled at me before laying the garment bag upon the bed. "Look, I knew you wouldn't turn down the chance to protect her. The suit has been tailored for you and is for the event this weekend. It's the opening ceremony ball and is like a giant meet-and-greet. Don't be late, Lucas."

He was telling me not to be late, but I had no interest in actually going to a fucking ball. I may have agreed to go ahead and join the competition but that was it. I didn't know I had to go to all the small things in between.

"Wait a second...." I replied as Silas quickly turned and made his way towards the door, obviously leaving. "Silas, I didn't agree to go to no damn ball."

Silas stopped for about a moment, and as he glanced over his shoulder at me with a smile, he shrugged. "And I knew that you wouldn't agree to go if you did."

The man had played me. He tricked me at my own game. He got me to agree to do what I was going to do and left out the small details he knew was going to piss me off. It was well played, but it didn't mean I liked him. In fact, he just simply annoyed me even more than he had before.

The moment the door closed, I stood there staring at it. A heavy breath escaped me.

"Well, that's just fucking great."

Chapter Fourteen

Cassie

A few days had passed since I had spoken with the girls in the living room with Freya. I couldn't believe what Freya had told me. I was going to have to go to another ball and on top of that, Thor's son—my cousin—actually thought he stood the chance of being able to possibly win my hand in marriage.

The discussion of that crap was completely unsettling. I got it. They may have thought once upon a time that was a pure way to keep bloodlines and so on and so forth. But there was no way in hell my 21st-century ass was ever going to subject myself to some kind of bullshit like that.

But instead of continuing to cause a ruckus, I made myself presentable and dressed in an entire floor-length gown I was unprepared to actually go venture out. It was not the most comfortable attire I would have chosen.

The floor-length ball gown was white with a golden sheer overlay, and a corset with gold and diamond jewels on it that were enough to put royalty to shame. Of course, this type of attire was normal here in a godly realm, but it didn't stop me from staring in the mirror with a look of unease as I tried to mentally prepare myself for the shit I was about to go through.

"Come on, Cassie, Jesus Christ, woman," Sansa yelled from the living room as I stared at my reflection, not recognizing the woman staring back at me. The smokey eyes Trixie had mixed with the pale pink lipstick gave me more of an innocent look that contrasted my bright pink hair.

I wasn't sure what it was about my appearance of myself that made me think of my mother, but thinking about her longer than I desired caused an emotion to build inside me I quickly had to blink back in order to make sure my eye makeup didn't run.

With a heavy sigh of defeat, I walked towards the living room, letting my friends finally take in the completed look they both so desperately work hard to achieve, and by the smiles on their faces, I knew they approved.

"Damn, you look good," Sansa said with a low whistle that made me smile. "Trixie, I think we should start doing this shit professionally."

Trixie turned from the mirror she was looking in to give me an approving smile. She herself was dressed up as well as Sansa for the nightly event. However, she settled for a more floral dress of white, pinks, and light shades of purple. Her hair piled halfway upon her head as it fell down in ringlets over her shoulders.

She honestly looked like a fairy princess, and with Sansa decorated in a black beaded formal trimmed in silver—the three of us were prizes to be sought after.

"You look beautiful," Trixie said softly. "I wish Lux could be here right now to see you."

A pang of guilt filled me, knowing Trixie had to spend so much time away from her mate to be here with me. I hadn't meant for that to happen, but I didn't feel like I could do any of this without her and of course, she was willing to help.

No matter how much my brother pissed him off, I could tell she loved him.

"After the ball, you can head back, Trixie... I know you want to be with him."

Shrugging her shoulders, she waved the comment off as she made her way towards me, taking my hand in hers. "And leave Sansa to do all of this alone? No way. I can always travel back and forth between things. Plus, it's not like this is forever. It's just until the games are over."

"She's right, Cassie. We are going to be here by your side to see you through this. Now come on and let's go before we're later than we already are," Sansa replied, causing me to look at the clock on the way to see we were indeed almost an hour late.

"Shit... I didn't realize that was the time," I muttered as I moved towards the door, with Trixie and Sansa following behind me.

Freya had explained how important the event tonight was, but time had kind of slipped my mind. Being on time for anything in my life wasn't something I was really capable of doing.

Walking through the halls of the building, the sound of music chimed in the distance, signaling we were getting closer. I wasn't sure what it was about this whole thing that alarmed me, but the closer I got, the more my heart began to race.

"I can't do this," I whispered breathlessly as I stopped just outside the grand golden and white double doors, fear undoubtedly hiding beneath the depths of my eyes as Trixie and Sansa both came to stand in front of me.

"Cassie, deep breaths," Trixie said slowly, doing breathly regiments to get me to follow. "In through your nose and out through your mouth. It's going to be okay."

Sansa stepped forward, taking my hand as she gently pulled me forward, my feet obeying as I followed the two women into the grand ballroom. "Don't you guys leave me tonight."

The whispered demand made them both chuckle as the sight of hundreds of people filled my sight, and once again, I felt breathless in the moment. I hadn't expected this many people to be present, and the moment I entered, they all seemed to turn and stare at me.

Many of the faces in the room were guys I had seen around campus, obviously having decided to participate in the games. While others I took note of with glowing golden eyes and even some with pointed ears I had never seen before.

"There she is!" Odin bellowed with a smile on his face as I made my way towards his throne, prepared to do the proper thing—like Trixie told me—and greet him as I should.

"Grandfather," I whispered softly as I bowed my head to him in respect only to take the seat next to him as he offered for me to do. Sansa and Trixie took two smaller seats next to me that had been presented as if Odin knew they would be at my side.

"I'm pleased that you were able to join us, Cassie. I was beginning to wonder if you had gotten lost."

Opening and closing my mouth, I looked at him speechless as I tried to formulate a reason for me being late. "It took a bit longer for me to get ready then I expect... girl has to look her best."

It was a bullshit excuse because me being late had more to do with the fact I didn't want to come and did more complaining while Trixie and Sansa were trying to get me ready than actually getting fucking ready.

However, Odin seemed to believe my reasoning as his eyes gazed over me with a smile on his face. "Your friends did a very good job in preparing you. There are very important people that you will be meeting tonight."

That was what I was afraid of, and as I glanced to my friends—who were in quit conversation with each other—I didn't miss the way the eyes of so many people out on the dance floor all looked to me with more interest than I cared to see.

Standing to his feet, Odin smiled with everyone on the dance floor, who all stopped to stare at him with interest. "Thank you all for being here tonight. I know some of you traveled a very long way to be present. As you all know, my granddaughter and heir apparent, Castor, or Cassie as she likes to be called, is the prize at this years games. The winner of the event will be the one who takes place at her side."

The entire time Odin was speaking, I felt nausea seep through me. The last thing I wanted to be was a prize for everyone to desire. I wasn't like other girls who would have thought this event to be a night to remember. The idea of men competing for my hand was... nauseating.

"Tonight, Cassie will mingle with you on the dance floor... and perhaps even agree to dance with a select few. Let us all enjoy the evening for now because starting tomorrow, things will begin to be more challenging."

"Tomorrow..." I whispered glancing at Sansa and Trixie, who both seemed just as surprised as I was. I had thought the games weren't for a few weeks, but it seemed Odin had other plans, and I wasn't sure how when he said I could help with the games.

By the time he was done speaking, he took his seat back next to me and with a courageous breath, I figured it was best I found out what was going on. "What's happening tomorrow?"

He turned to me, a smiled spread from ear to ear as he picked up his horn and drank from it. "The games begin, of course. Freya gave me the information you and your friends were working on. It's brilliant, and depending on how this goes, your friend Sansa has a real future in how things work around here."

My head quickly snapped to Sansa, who heard what Odin said, and while she was shocked at that, she knew exactly why I was looking at her. "I didn't give Freya anything—"

The plans Odin was referring to were plans we hadn't even gone over so I had no fucking clue what he was talking about or if it was even something I wanted to do. The only thing I could do though was discuss with Sansa when this was all over to find out what she had written down.

With a sudden shift in the mood, I was asked to join the floor with my friends where I was reluctant to grace everyone with my presence on a more personal level. I didn't want to be around these people, and I sure as hell didn't want to dance with anyone.

However, slowly but surely, one by one men came up to me to ask for a moment to spin me around the dance floor as if that was an easy task to do. I, after all, couldn't dance to save my life.

"So you and I could be a thing," Bronn, Sansa's brother, said as he eyed me over with a hungry look on his face. He was a dark haired man whose chocolate colored skin matched the gold and white suit he was wearing very well.

Had I not known he was Sansa's brother, I would have thought he had stalked me to find out what I was wearing so he could match my attire. No doubt he overheard Sansa talking and took it upon himself to try and look the part of royalty. "Yeah... but for now, we aren't. So please keep your hand at my waist."

My murmured and narrowed response to his hand slowly traveling down my ass quickly made him stop just as the music ended to have him walk away.

For a moment, I thought perhaps I'd be able to escape the hell of this place, but just as I turned around, satisfied for putting Bronn in his place, I ran into the chest of another man with deep celestial eyes like my own, and black hair as dark as coal.

"Well, hello there, my fated… we meet at last."

Chapter Fifteen

Cassie

Fated mate?

The moment the white-haired, blue-eyed fae man with pointed ears stepped in front of me proclaiming I was his fated, I found myself completely in shock. Laughter immediately erupted from my lips, and I knew that wasn't the first impression you wanted someone to have of you, but I couldn't fucking help it. "Oh, wow, man... that's a good one. I think I need a drink."

When I said I needed a drink, it wasn't a glass of water. Pushing past the man, I made my way straight towards the bar area where Odin had many alcoholic beverages on display and grabbed the nearest one that happened to be purple with a tart taste to follow.

At this point, I didn't care what anyone had to say to me. The moment I downed one glass, I was reaching another until a firm grip on my wrist stopped me, and once again, I looked up into the Fae man's eyes which were narrowed in my direction. "I don't think you should be drinking that so fast, little one."

Little one? Was he fucking kidding me right now. "Excuse me, I don't even know you."

Taken aback by my response, he let go of my wrist and chuckled. "You are exactly how he painted you. Feisty, ill-mannered, and yet quite enjoyable."

"Ill-mannered?" I muttered, trying to process his words as I snatched the glass of whatever I was drinking from the table before he could stop me and downed it as well. "I'm not ill-mannered, for your information, and honestly, I don't know how you approach women in your world, but I have been through too much shit lately to have some random fucking man I don't know come up to me claiming that I'm his fated... get the fuck out of here with that shit. I'm not a prize to be won."

Not bothering to listen to whatever this man had to say, I stormed past him, looking for a way to escape all the men who were longing to have a moment alone with me. I didn't understand what they expected to happen by having a private conversation with me, but it sure as hell wasn't going to be me letting them sweep me off my feet or whatever the hell they imagined doing.

I was a strong independent woman... or so I kept telling myself.

"Cassie, where the hell are you going?" Stopping in my tracks, I turned to face Trixie, who stared at me with an edge of concern in her gaze. "Are you okay?"

"Yeah," I replied quickly, forcing a smile to my lips. "I just can't be in there anymore. It's been hours now, and all the faces and guys touching me is too much. None of them is the face I wanted to see, and I'm still coming to terms with that."

Nodding her head, she listened to everything I had to say about the various men I was forced to entertain in the ballroom, and at the end, she furrowed her brows with I told her about the Fae man with eyes the same color as mine.

"Uh, Cassie... did this man happen to be wearing a black suit with a blue and purple sash?"

"Blue and purple sash? I don't know, why that matter?" I asked with confusion.

Sighing, she shrugged. "Just humor me, okay... did he have one?"

"I don't know... maybe. Actually, yeah, I think he did..." I replied, trying to remember hard what exactly he looked like. The only problem was I couldn't get past the way he called me his fated... and those damn mesmerizing eyes.

Fucking snob had a lot of nerve to just proclaim me his in the middle of the damn room with all those people looking at us. Groaning in disgust, I met Trixie's gaze again and saw the ashen look on her face adorned with wide eyes and parted lips. It was clear something about what I said was wrong, and for a minute, I started to contemplate if I had fucked up.

"Trixie... what's wrong?"

Shaking her head, she took a deep breath. "Oh, Cassie... that was the fucking Prince of the Fae realm... and you just snubbed him. What the fuck were you thinking?"

Oh shit... once again, my mouth and attitude got the better of me, and as I watched her cover her mouth with her hand and she started to pace in the hallway, I realized it was worse than I thought. "So, on a scale of one to ten, how bad do you think this is?"

Turning to face me, she paused for a moment opening and closing her mouth. "Well, I mean, it could go one of two ways. One, he could be really pissed and offended and complain to Odin, and it could cause war-like issues that result in you begging on your knees in front of him for forgiveness..."

"That's not going to happen. You're out of your damn mind," I snapped quickly, causing her to laugh. "What's option two?"

Shrugging her shoulders, a smile crept across her face. "He has been known to like a good game of cat and mouse in which he would blow your mind by making you beg for him. He has been known to have two different sides, so I don't know... you did kind of go off on him in front of a room of people, so I don't expect him to take this well."

At a loss for what to say, I stood there staring at her in dismay. I had entertained a lot of people this evening, but the two people I wanted to see tonight weren't there. At least not that I could see, and that hurt more than anything.

"I guess I'll just deal with it tomorrow." I muttered with irritation. "I can't be out there right now."

Trixie stared at me for a moment before letting a breath escape her. "Okay, head back to your room. I'll let everyone know that you weren't feeling well and needed to rest. That you will see them next week for the first event."

"Next week? Odin said it starts tomorrow."

"Yeah, he did," she replied with a knowing glance, "that's where people start using their intelligence to figure out how to win."

Confused by what she meant, Trixie didn't stay around long enough to explain as I watched her swish her way back toward the ballroom, leaving me standing in the hallway alone. Defeated by everything, I sagged my shoulders and slowly turned, making my way through the various halls toward my room to only have the feeling of being watched.

The moment I turned the corner, I came face to face with my cousin Mani. My heart dropped into my stomach, I had hoped to avoid this man at all costs tonight, but from the smirk on his face, he was expecting me. Which must have been the reason why I felt like I was being followed.

"There you are, Cassie," he said as the corners of his lips formed into a smirk. "I thought I'd miss my chance to have a moment alone with you."

Dear God. The last thing I wanted was to deal with him or his sister, and yet fate hated me so much it forced me right into his path. "Unfortunately, I'm not available tonight. Perhaps you can arrange something with me another time."

Not that I would ever allow that to happen.

"I figured you may say something like that, but honesty..." he sighs, making his smile brighter, "I know that's just you playing hard to get."

Narrowing my eyes at him, I scoffed with disgust. "You're fucking insane. There is no way in hell I will ever marry you. Unfortunately, I'm not into that kind of shit."

Pushing past him, he quickly snatched me by the waist and pushed me against the wall. Mani wasn't a small man by any means and dressed up right now in this three-piece suit, I had no doubt most women drooled over him. He was very good-looking. The problem was he was my cousin, and the intimate position in which he had me pushed against the wall wasn't right.

"Get the fuck off me," I snapped at him, struggling in his arms.

"Or what?" he replied in a dark and sinister tone that made my heart race as he leaned closer to me. "What are you going to do, Cassie?"

Shoving against him again, he held me down tighter, a cry leaving my lips as his fingers dug into my arms, "you will pay for this shit. Wait until I tell Odin—"

Laughter erupted from his throat as he stared at me. "Do you think he will care? It's not like you're a virgin, Cassie. We all know that, and honestly, the reputation you have with men already makes you questionable."

The more and more Mani talked, the more I realized my situation wasn't going to end well. Mani was trying to make a point, and I was alone with him in the hallway, far away from everyone who happened to be in the ballroom enjoying themselves.

"You will never have me, and you need to learn to accept that, Mani. Let me go now and go about your business." The loud, clear tone of my voice made his eyes widen slightly as he stared at me bewildered by my comment. I tried hard to make myself seem stronger than I was. More blunt and straightforward, just as a leader should be.

Or at least I thought that was what I was doing just before he quickly gripped my throat and brought his lips closer to mine. "You can try to use that Alpha tone or goddess persona, whatever you want to call it—on me. But it will never work. I will have you on your knees with my cock shoved down your fucking throat before the games are done. I can promise you that."

A flash of black shot past the corner of my eyes as Mani's body was ripped from mine and tossed across the hallway, hitting the wall before he slumped to the floor. Panic set through me as I fell to my knees only to see a figure in front of me I hadn't expected to see.

"Lucas—" I said breathlessly as I took in the sight of his back heaving up and down as a snarl ripped from him and claws protruded from his hands. Lucas was in mid-shift and definitely not someone I would have thought would come to save me, but as I stood to my feet, it was clear Mani hadn't expected him either.

"You fucking bastard!" Mani yelled, "you dare fucking touch me!"

Standing to his feet, Mani balled his fists at his sides as anger filled his narrowed gaze. The last thing I wanted was bloodshed on my hands and as I turned to Lucas, I quickly laid my hand upon his arm, watching as he stiffened for a moment before glancing at me from the corner of his eyes.

"Lucas, not like this. Please... walk me back to my room. He isn't worth it."

"Not worth it?!" Mani yelled, "stupid bitch, you're lucky that I'm willing to marry you at all."

Another snarl from Lucas signaled his displeasure in Mani's tone, but the more I tugged on him, the more he loosened up slightly, retracting his claws as he squared his shoulders, never letting his gaze falter off of Mani. "She will not be marrying you."

"Oh, because you want her?" He laughed. "You weren't worthy of her once, and you damn sure won't be worthy of her now. You're just the bastard son of Loki… not worthy of trust."

The hate Mani was spewing was nothing but immature insults. I had expected a man of his nature to be capable of controlling himself, but it was quite obvious he wasn't at all what I had expected. He was just like the arrogant football jocks I had gone to school with on earth.

He had no control over his anger, not that I was any better.

"Enough, Mani. If you both have issues, you can handle them in the games. For now, it's time you leave," I said as I stared at him, watching the anger in his eyes grow as he quickly smoothed out his hair, turned on his heels, and disappeared around the corner.

I hadn't expected him to comply so easily, but I was glad he did.

Because now I had a chance alone with Lucas. Turning to face him, I stared up into those dark, mesmerizing eyes flecked with gold, and my breath was taken away just as it had been the first time I met him. Only when I went to open my mouth, he opened his instead.

"We need to talk, now."

Chapter Sixteen

Lucas

The moment I watched that strange man place his hands on Cassie, I lost my mind. She may not have been my mate anymore, but there was no way in hell I'd ever allow any man or creature to touch her in the wrong way. If I couldn't be with her, then I'd still lurk in the shadows as her protector.

At least then, she could live her life, and I would know that she was okay.

Making our way down the hall, I headed straight for her room. I knew where it was and made a point the day she was moved to find out its location. Even though that was something I would never admit to anyone. It was clear they didn't want me anywhere around her, and I wasn't sure how people were going to take to me being around her now.

We arrived at her room, and I pushed open the door and stepped to the side, allowing her to enter before closing it behind us. There was a lot on my mind that needed to be said, but I wasn't quite sure where to start without flying off the handle on her.

When she turned and met my gaze, my heart about stopped. Cassie looked beautiful in the golden dress she was wearing, and the way strands of her hair hung down in spiral curls around her face made her look more innocent than I knew she was. Even the plump, soft pink hue to her lips made my beast hungry to kiss her, and most importantly, when my eyes met hers, I still felt that spark between us.

The very same spark that made me want to run away for fear of hurting her again.

"What did you want to talk about?" she asked as she stared at me with such fierce intensity. My own heart began to palpitate, trying to gather as much courage as I could to answer her.

I needed to stay focused and remember exactly why I was here in front of her. Cassie had been reckless over the years, and though I myself had been reckless too, we both had to grow up, and we both had to get a hold of ourselves. Because if we didn't, if Cassie didn't, she would end up getting herself hurt or worse.

Cassie had already died once before, and though now she was embodied in an immortal goddess, it didn't mean that she was invincible. There was no such thing as mortality, no matter how much people tried to say otherwise. There was always a way to kill something, to hurt someone, no matter who they were.

Taking a deep breath, I narrowed my gaze, trying to stay focused on what I needed to say. "You need to start being more careful who you speak to the way that you do.What would have happened had I not been there? He could have hurt you. Or even worse, Cassie."

My tone and comments were obviously not what she was expecting because she quickly became defensive as she crossed her arms over her chest and narrowed her own gaze at me, glaring with such heat I myself felt slightly uncomfortable.

"Me. I didn't ask for you to save me. I was quite capable of taking care of myself."

The deep chuckle that left my throat was unintentional, but I couldn't help it. Hearing her try to be so bold and brazen was not expected, and I found it amusing she thought she could protect herself because what was going on with that man was obviously not her protecting herself.

"Is that right? Is that why you couldn't defend yourself out there against that man? And by the way, who is he? Obviously, he knows you're quite well to be able to feel he can corner you in a dark hallway all alone to have a moment of whatever was going to happen."

Eyes wide in shock, she stared at me with slightly parted lips. "Excuse me, do you actually think that I enjoyed that? You're a complete asshole. If the only thing you did was come here to cause an argument with me, feel free to fucking leave."

No matter the conflict I felt, I was slightly hesitant at that moment, wondering if I had misunderstood exactly what was going on. I knew she needed help which was clearly obvious. I could fear her heart racing and smell the uncertainty and fear coming off of her, something I doubted the other man could do. It was clear he wasn't a wolf.

"I'm not going anywhere. We have things that we need to talk about, and after all these weeks, if you're trying to talk to me, are you really saying that you finally don't want to have that conversation?" I asked her, wondering if she would finally buckle and listen to me so I could spend just a few more moments with her, even if I was afraid to do that.

"Talk to you. Do you think I want to talk to you after the way you treated me out there in that training field? I came to you to try and make amends for us to put things behind us, and all you did was the typical thing, pushed me away, and were a complete dick. So no, I don't feel like talking to you."

Running my hand over my face, I tried to clear my mind, the anger slowly building in me because of the irritation I felt with her refusal to simply just open her mouth and stop with all the dramatic nonsense.

I was tired. Tired of being in the position I was in. I was tired of being in Asgard, and more importantly, I was tired of constantly fucking arguing with Cassie.

"Will you stop?" I snapped at her, "I'm tired of this shit with you. You need to grow the fuck up, Cassie, and start listening to the people around you who actually fucking care about you. This isn't a game anymore. Shit has gotten real, and if you're not careful, your life will be over as you know it."

This was the first time I actually took the initiative to be real with her. To tell her the truth and help her to face that truth. I could tell by the gaze in her eyes and the hesitation she felt as she fidgeted with her hands that, deep down, what I was saying was true.

Gone was the defiant, bitchy side of Cassie, and slowly as it melted away, her eyes brimmed with tears as she quickly batted them away with the fluttering of her lashes. "Do you think I don't know that, Lucas?"

"I don't know... do you?" I replied, exhausted from all of the shit that had been going on between us since the moment she realized I was her mate.

Cassie

Hearing him, I couldn't contain my anger. Perhaps I was a little immature, and I did act out of anger the majority of the time—I blame that on the genetics I got from my father, though.

"Why do you care what's going on, Lucas? Why the hell are you even here?"

That was all I wanted to know. He had made it clear he wasn't interested in shit with me because of the fear he felt, and yet low and behold, he was here in front of me; a protector I hadn't asked for but so desperately needed.

"Silas asked me to be here," he replied with indifference as he stood before me, looking like the sex god he was. Even in the broody mood he portrayed with narrowed, darkened eyes and gritted teeth concealed by his rugged jawline, all I could do was think about him taking me.

"Silas?" The laughter that left me was more of disbelief. "Of course he did. He couldn't even come to see me himself. Instead, he sends someone else to do what he is supposed to do."

Lucas scoffed as his arms fell by his side. "Sorry to disappoint you. Perhaps I'll go tell him to fucking sort you out instead..."

The quick response was unexpected, but I suppose what I said was a little harsh. "I didn't mean it like that... I'm just so....fucking irritated by all of this. I feel like I'm on a merry-go-round that's never going to end."

Half expecting Lucas to lash out at me, I was surprised when I turned to find him looking at me with a softer expression. "I get it…"

"You do?" I replied, shocked and unsure of what to say.

"Yeah, I do." With a heavy sigh, he rubbed the back of his neck. "Look, this kind of shit isn't easy for me, okay. I do care about you, Cassie, I'm just not good for you… you deserve better…"

I couldn't believe what he was saying right now. He was literally using the lines every fuck boy in my school had used on one girl or another over the years I had been there. The I'm not good enough for you, it's not you, it's me, bullshit. Shaking my head, he stopped talking as a smirk crossed my face. "So I deserve someone like Silas… or maybe the fae prince who seems to believe I'm his fated…"

"Fate?" Lucas quickly said, narrowing his brows, "what the hell are you talking about? What Fae prince?"

I wasn't trying to test boundaries or upset him, but it was clear that mye revealing this little bit of information unintentionally didn't sit well with him. Not that I understood why he would get upset. What I did with my life wasn't any concern of his. He was the one who didn't want me.

Deciding to just rip the information off like a bandaid, I sighed and shrugged my shoulders. "Supposedly I'm fated to him… he staked some claim on me that I am to be his in front of everyone in the ballroom. It was the reason why I was in the hallway heading here. I kind of went off on him in front of everyone, and now Trixie is playing damage control."

Stepping towards me, Lucas clenched his hands at his side. "The only person you were fated to is me, Cassie. No fucking fae prince, or even a dragon, for that matter, will deserve you."

Watching the flash of jealousy flicker in Lucas' eyes made me smile. He literally had just said I deserved better, blah blah blah. Yet, he was suddenly acting like this when I told him someone else wanted me.

Talk about confusion.

"Why do you care, Lucas? You already made it clear you don't want me... in fact, I don't know why you're still here and not running away like you did before."

"I didn't run away," he snapped, breathing heavily before taking one step closer. "Don't fucking with me right now, Cassie. I'm not in the mood for your shit..."

"Who's playing?" The reply wasn't one he wanted, but I was being serious. I was tired, just as he had said he was. I didn't have in me to fight for a man who didn't want to commit to what he wanted. Not that fighting would help... I was destined for the winner, no matter who it was.

"Look, let's just call it a night. It's clear that you don't have anything better to do than babysit me. Not that you should be... why don't you just go, I want to get some sleep."

The moment I stepped forward to try and guide him towards the door, he quickly stopped me by grabbing my wrist. "Not until you understand where I'm coming from."

"There is nothing to understand, Lucas," I replied with a sigh, "things are pretty clear. I just need to rest. I have a lot that I need to figure out."

Lucas didn't let up on my arm as I gently tried to pull myself from his grip. Instead, he shook his head from side to side, telling me no before pulling me close to him. The strength of his body against mine was something I hadn't felt in a long time, and just when I thought things couldn't get any more unsure... his lips brushed against mine.

Chapter Seventeen

Cassie

I didn't know what to make of it when Lucas kissed me, but the moment he did, I melted into him with a soft moan that only seemed to make his actions more frenzied. Instinctively, I wrapped my arms around his neck, pulling myself up closer, helping to deepen the kiss already captivating me.

I had dreamt of this moment for so long, and now that I was finally having it once more, I didn't want it to end. I couldn't let go. Just his touch alone captivated my heart and made it soar higher than I'd ever made it felt. However, the moment I pulled closer, he quickly broke away.

"We have to stop," he whispered. He was breathless just as I was, and the sound of his voice swirled within my ears because the close proximity of us together made me shiver with anticipation.

"Why are you stopping? We don't have to stop."

Staring into his eyes, I could see the heavy confliction that weighed within part of him wanting this, but the other part, the unruly-fearing part, did not. We had only had this once before, where we had actually allowed ourselves to give in to the indulgence we wanted. After that, things became chaotic, both of us unable to move forward because of the darkness that ended up taking over Lucas's mind. Darkness I wouldn't allow to ever come back.

I loved him. Wholeheartedly, I did. But I could never tell him that, not truly. Not unless I knew he felt the same way. And with the way he looked at me now, I couldn't help but feel conflicted if my feelings were true or if I was simply being a fool.

"As much as I want to do this, Cassie, I can't. You are the prize at the end of these games, and I will admit that I am scared. I'm terrified of hurting you again. But the other part of me longs for you more than you know. So if I want to be by your side, I'm going to have to win the games just like any other contestant would."

I was shocked he was saying this, that he was going to participate in the games when Silas was the one who had asked him to come into it in the first place. He didn't come into it willingly. He came into it because he was told to, and now he was saying if he wanted this with me, he would just have to win the games.

Was that like him saying if he didn't win, it was because he didn't want to?

I was confused in that moment about how I felt. I was confused about whether or not I was going to actually allow this to happen or if I should just push him further and take advantage of a situation, which would definitely be in my character. But then again, sometimes I wondered what my character was, considering I wasn't any longer the person I used to be.

"I don't know what to say..."

It was the only truthful thing I could actually come up with. I didn't know what to say, and as he stared at me, a chuckle came from his throat. What I knew was a sense of amusement he felt at my confusion. Something that even more so infuriated me because I was confused, and he found it funny.

With a heavy sigh, Lucas placed his hands on the outer part of my arms, rubbing them up and down. He stared at me with such intent, I would never be able to forget it. "I know that all of this is confusing. But as much as I want to give in to the emotions I feel right now, I can't. It wouldn't be right."

"Since when did you become so chivalrous? This isn't the person that you are, Lucas. What happened to us being mates, to being together? If we are together, then there's no point of the games at all," I replied in desperation, trying to make him see the truth behind it. That if we did go ahead and consummate this between us, decide that we want to be together, then there would be no reason to have these games because I would already be taken.

Another heavy sigh escaped him as he shook his head from side to side. "Unfortunately, Cassie, that kind of thinking right there is what causes problems, and if both of us are ever going to make it through this with the possibility of being together, we both have to follow the rules. There are too many people who have come here from other realms, from what I can see. And the last thing that your grandfather's going to want is a war."

"A war?" I scoffed, crossing my arms over my chest. "Who in the hell would actually go to war with Odin? They would be decimated."

"It isn't just about that, Cassie. Everyone who looks at me sees the man that almost killed you, that did kill you. They see a monster, and if we break the rules of the games, they're never going to not see me like that. They will always see me like that. The games are a way for me to prove to them that I'm not that person... to prove to myself that I'm not that person. "

Lucas wasn't wrong about that. People did look at him like he was a murderer, a monstrosity that shouldn't be an Asgard, but Odin had deemed that he was to stay here under the watchful gaze of his reign and therefore stay here by me even if they didn't really want me around him.

No one under my grandfather's rule had actually come out and said they didn't like that Lucas was here, but I could see the way that some of the other gods had looked at him shortly after the entire incident had happened. When Lucas had to come before Odin and take his punishment—that was far less then what was expected , everybody was surprised, myself included.

I would never be able to forget the day I stood in the hall with everyone else that was part of Odin's reign and watched Lucas sink to his knees before Odin with his head bowed and his eyes cast to the floor, dark hair falling in front of his face as he listened to the booming words of my grandfather.

The same words that sentenced him to spend an eternity in Asgard. Not because he was granted permission, but as a punishment to keep him from leaving and going back to Earth where he could possibly cause mayhem that could destroy or even lure me or the others back there, putting us in danger.

Odin had declared this was a way for him to be able to be kept under lock and key and even though I remembered so vaguely my grandfather saying those words, I couldn't help but wonder if there was a hint of something else in his tone that day that said he had other plans.

My shoulders sagged in defeat as I nodded my head in understanding to what Lucas was saying. There was no way I was going to actually be able to get what I wanted, and that was clear. I tell myself over and over again on a continual basis that I need to grow up, that I need to get a hold of myself, I didnt know how too. I wasn't that old, and even most people at my age in the earth realm would still be immature for their age, still seeking the guidance from their parents, they wouldnt be judged for it.

Unlike me... I was judged for everything I did it seemed.

I'd have given anything to have my mother here with me right now, or even my father. I missed them dearly and more than anything, I wanted them by my side. But I knew that it would be quite some time before that happened. The only way I'd be able to see them again is when they themselves died and came to Asgard.

"Alright, Lucas, if that is what you feel you need to do, then so be it. But if you're going to do that, then we don't need to see each other again outside of the games. You wouldn't want anybody thinking that there was cheating going on, would you?"

Glancing up to meet his gaze once more, I saw something that lurked there, something that looked alot like regret.

Opening and closing his mouth, he gritted his teeth and nodded. "I need to get going. Do me a favor, though, please watch out for yourself? Don't go anywhere alone unless it's absolutely necessary. The last thing I want is for something to happen to you, and I'm not able to be there to protect you... like tonight."

There was no way I could promise him that. Especially when I was more determined than ever right now to prove to everyone I was not going to be like the others. I would grow up but I would do it like I wanted.

I would be who I wanted to be, and they either liked it or they didn't.

Nodding my head, he stepped away from me and made his way towards the door. The moment he disappeared behind it leaving me alone once more

I started to think about everything I needed to do. If they wanted me to be the royal that represented this realm then I would be. I'd be the bitch I used to be... the girl who danced to her own tune and set rules for herself.

Rules that made people fear and respect me as they should. It was obvious my cousin had no respect for me, and that wasn't going to work for me. He was the first person on my list I'd handle, the first person I'd make realize I wasn't to be messed with and if he and his sister couldn't fall in line... I'd make them cowar at me feet.

Making my way towards my closet, I slowly undid my dress and let it fall to the floor. Gazing around, I noticed my usual attire and how normal that it looked. How non-threatening it was. The first step in making myself be more than I was, was changing my attire.

If I wanted people to believe me then I needed to play the part. Towards the back of the closet laid attire Trixie had gotten for me when I first arrived in Asgard. Leather, lace, metal studs... all of it was bad bitch vibes and as a smile crossed my face I mapped out what I was going to do.

Step One... make them fear me.

Step Two... show Lucas I was a woman he wanted and didn't have to fear.

Step Three... prove to Silas and Odin I wasn't to be fucked with.

If this realm wanted a real show at the games... then I'd fucking give them one.

I'd give them all something to remember.

Chapter Eighteen

Perfection. It's a word thrown around a lot, but at the end of the day, I don't think anyone knows what the fucking word means. Instead, they throw around their own personal ideas of what they think it means and try to claim it as the only truth.

Fucking fascists.

"Cassie?" The slow, hesitant tone of Ansley caught me by surprise, and as I looked up from where I was buckling the strap on my shoe, I raised a brow in question before straightening myself, making sure I looked the part of fascist perfection.

"Good morning, Ansley. I'll be eating breakfast in the hall today. I have business to attend to."

It was unlike me to do something like this, and the fact that I was even up early made her lips part, and her eyes widen as she nodded her head. "Oh–okay. Um, I'll let them know–"

"No. Don't tell them anything."

Ansley looked more than confused, but in silence, she nodded her head and went about her usual activities of taking care of my room. I didn't abuse my status over her like so many others had, and just because I had been warned about the girl, I didn't want to believe that she was like them.

Ansley was a sweet girl... but at times, I wondered if she was actually going to be loyal to me.

Perhaps I was having my own doubts about her, but I wouldn't know until she slipped up and gave me something to be untrustworthy about. I only hoped she would prove me wrong, and that would never happen.

Satisfied with my appearance, I let a heavy breath escape me as I nodded to myself in the mirror with approval of my choice in appearance. I was prepared to go down there today and show them what kind of person I was. Not just opinionated but capable of taking them all on.

Making my way from my room with my heels tapping against the cold flooring, I headed towards the grand hall. My attire today... black dress pants, a royal blue blouse with black swirls on it, and black heels that reminded me of my Jimmy Choos I had back home.

I had worked all summer for those damn shoes, and they never made it here.

No doubt my little sister had stolen them... she was always quite the thief.

The halls of the palace were far quieter than they usually were, and the only noise I heard was coming from the open hall door that signaled everyone was in attendance and enjoying themselves. Part of me was nervous walking in there after how I had acted last night, but the other part was eager to see who was in attendance.

If I was going to pull off my new person, I was going to have to make sure my entrance was epic, and straightening my shoulders, I held my head high and stepped forward around the corner into the glimmering hall to see the two long fifty foot tables decorated with foods of all kinds... not to mention the numerous eyes of men and women who landed on me the moment I entered.

Usually, I would have been hesitant... uncomfortable even. Not this time, though.

"Cassie," Odin said with a slightly confused tone to his voice as his eyes met mine. "I didn't realize you were joining us this morning."

Moving forward, I headed straight toward him, where Solina sat at his side with her brother across from her. There was no way her brother would move, but if I was going to start somewhere, it was going to be with her.

"Well, I figured if I'm going to be the highlighted prize, Grandfather, it would only make sense that I make an appearance at all times. Plus, the people here will all one day be under my rule... correct?"

There was a twinkle of amusement in his eyes as I stopped at his side and casually leaned in to give him a small hug. The hug itself definitely shocked him as I felt him stiffen under me and gently return the favor. "Yes, I suppose you're right."

The moment he released me from the 'hug' I had given him, I cast my gaze to Solina and frowned. "I think you're in the wrong seat, Solina. That seat is reserved for the next in line... and in fact—"

I turned my gaze towards Mani and smirked. "Grandfather, shouldn't the fae prince be sitting on the other side of you, considering he is royalty?"

Mani stared at me in shock and anger. "Had you been here in time, Cassie, you—"

Odin held up his hand, silencing everyone at the table. "Cassie is right... Solina, you need to find another place to sit. As for the prince... I apologize for the confusion. Finnick, would you please take Mani's seat next to me? I don't know what I was thinking this morning."

Solina and Mani both hesitated for a moment before quickly getting up with their plates and moving further down the table. The servants made quick of placing new dishes in front of me and making sure Finnick was situated across from me.

I hadn't taken the time to properly take notice of the prince, and after the way I acted last night, I found myself feeling slightly foolish for my behavior. Something I was definitely going to have to make amends for.

Finnick didn't bother to look at me right away and instead spoke directly to Odin, giving me the chance to really take notice of him. I was definitely foolish to think less of him because, overall, he was a very attractive man. His onyx hair was pulled back into a ponytail on his head without a single strand out of place, and instead of the royal garment he wore last night, he had settled this morning for regular black dress pants and a white button-up shirt rolled at the sleeves.

As if he knew I was watching him, his eyes darted to mine, and I was met with the same mesmerizing celestial blue eyes I saw every time I looked into the mirror. The fact I had been caught watching him made me slightly blush, and clearing my throat, I quickly tried to push it away. However, it wasn't done without his notice—which only left a small smirk on his lips.

"Prince Finnick, I wanted to apologize for last night... I wasn't feeling very well." I was glad Odin's attention was on a pretty, bubbly redhead who was pouring liquid into a golden goblet for him. The sight of my grandfather groping the giggling girl was disgusting, but thankfully, I had Finnick in front of me to distract that kind of attention.

"Last night?" he replied, furrowing his brow as he lifted his fork to his mouth, savoring the meat that was on his plate. "Oh yes... you mean when you had your tantrum."

Tantrum? Was he being fucking serious right now?!

"I don't know if I would have called it that," I scoffed with a smile as I picked up my glass and lifted it to my lips, letting my eyes scan the rest of the table where various people sat eating and talking to each other. The laughter of their conversations filled the room around me.

"Oh, that's exactly what I would call it." Finnick laughed. "It was entertaining."

"I'm glad that I was able to entertain you then."

The flat response made him chuckle. "Yes... well, I'm sure you will entertain me in more ways than one in the future. Who knows... you may even enjoy it."

It was my turn to laugh, and as I did, the water I was drinking went down the wrong tube, causing me to sputter as I choked slightly, causing the poor guy next to me to turn to me with wide eyes and parted lips asking if I was okay. "I'm fine... just went down wrong."

Clearing my throat once more, I stared at my glass for a moment before meeting Finnick's gaze again. "Well, I wouldn't be so sure about that. Regardless I do hope you enjoy your stay here. I'm sure you will find someone around here to entertain you while you enjoy watching the games."

"Watching?" he replied with a small laugh. "You really don't have any idea what is going on with the games, do you?"

It was clear that Finnick knew way more than I did. As much as I wanted to reach across the table and strangle him for his smirks and clippy comments, I had to keep myself in check. One, this guy was royalty, and two, I wanted to make everyone believe I had changed.

If I didn't want to be pushed around, I had to be this different kind of person.

Just as I went to answer him, Silas caught my eye from the side doorway located on the wall behind Finnick. His hazel eyes captivated me, and as he smiled, he gestured for me to come to him. I wasn't sure what he wanted, but there was no way that I could simply get up from the table now and excuse myself.

Thinking quickly, I turned towards Odin and feigned forgetfulness. "Grandfather, I completely forgot something this morning... I was supposed to meet Sansa to go over the last details of my attire for the first day of the games. You wouldn't be angry if I left, would you?"

Odin hesitated for a moment, letting his gaze leave the girl beside him to fall on me with a split moment of confusion before a smile lined his face, and he laughed. "Of course not, go do what you need to. I did enjoy having you here this morning. So make sure you start coming more regularly."

Shit. I hadn't wanted to make it an everyday thing, but now I was fucking locked into it.

"Of course, I wouldn't miss it," I replied with a smile as I turned to Finnick and slowly stood to my feet. "Prince Finnick... it was lovely as always. Please enjoy your stay in Asgard."

A few eyes met mine as I slipped from the chair and made my way toward the doorway Silas had once been standing in moments before.

"Silas?" I whispered as I closed the doorway behind me, making my way down the white corridor until I came to a partially open door where a hand quickly reached out and pulled me into. A yelp escaped my lips until it was covered by the callused hand of a man, and looking up, I stared into Silas' eyes—the same eyes I had grown very fond of looking into.

"Did I scare you?" he chuckled as he released my mouth and stepped back with a laugh.

"You're a fucking asshole. I hope you know that…" I muttered, fixing myself as my eyes took in the large room we were standing in. White walls and navy blue accents littered the area with floor-to-ceiling bookshelves and a black desk in its center. "What is this place?"

"My office," he replied flatly, making his way toward his desk. "I wanted to speak with you about something important since no one else plans to."

"Wait… you have an office? Since when does a guardian have an office… and why am I starting to see that Asgard is run like a business instead of a godly sanctuary like we are told in the human realm?"

Sighing, Silas ran his hand over his face. "As I told you before, Cassie… humans are told what we want them to know. Everything, no matter where you go, is always about business."

This, of course, was something I was going to have to get used to. "Okay. So what do you want to speak to me about?"

Taking a moment, he leaned back in his chair and stared at me with his hand upon his rugged jawline. Silas was incredibly sexy, and I knew that the first time I met him. There was something about the way he was now that was so different from the carefree man I had known then.

"Prince Finnick is here for you," he replied calmly, catching me off guard, "he plans to make you his wife."

Chapter Nineteen

There is a point in life when you finally get tired of people telling you what you're going to do, and there is also a moment in your life when you gain clarity of how bullshit things are and you can't help but laugh. This was one of those moments, and as Silas' words rolled over in my mind I couldn't help but laugh.

"You're fucking joking, right?"

With a heavy sigh, he stared at me, "No, I'm not. Why would I joke about this?"

"Oh, I don't know. Because you find shit like this amusing," I spat, rolling my eyes. "It's ridiculous for him to think he can come here and just marry me. It's not going to happen."

"Perhaps... I mean, he does have to go through the games just like everyone else. So there is no telling what could happen," Silas replied, causing my mouth to drop open slightly. Was Finnick participating in the games with everyone else?

"He is royalty? Why the hell is he participating?"

"Uh, because it's the rules your grandfather set, Cassie. He has to abide by them like everyone else." It didn't make sense this prince I had never met before would want me, and honestly, all it did was add to the list of problems I already had. Not that I couldn't handle it. I would adjust to what I was already going to do to include Prince Finnick as well.

"Fine," I gritted out under my breath. "Is there anything else?"

Silas shook his head, clasping his hands in front of him as if he wanted to say something but wasn't exactly sure how. I hated moments like this. I missed the guy who would laugh with me and spend time with me. Since I became what I was, Silas was all business, and I didn't understand why. "No, you can go."

Standing to my feet, I made my way to the door and stopped. "Shouldn't I be the one telling you what to do?" I said calmly as I glanced over my shoulder at him.

Amusement crossed his features as he stared at me, smiling. "Do you want to boss me around?"

The thought crossed my mind for a split second, but I preferred it if he was the one in control. "I'll think about it... I have a lot on my mind lately."

"I can tell," he replied smoothly. "Don't let it get you into trouble. I know you like getting into more than you can handle."

I didn't know whether to be slightly offended by what he said or turned on by what he said but deciding against addressing it, I quickly left his office and made my way down the hall until I finally came to an open exit, allowing the fresh air of outside to filter through.

Stepping out into the cool morning air, I closed my eyes and inhaled deeply with a smile on my face. It was nice to not care about things for once and when I let everything slip from my mind, I enjoyed the sound of the realm that floated into my ears. Birds chirping, the distant sounds of running water from a nearby pond, and even the mumbled sounds of laughter from somewhere nearby were refreshing.

It made me forget I was where I was. For a moment, it took me back to my parent's home and the fact I loved spending time in the woods near my home.

A sense of longing slipped through me as I took in the fact I would never shift into my wolf again. That I would never feel my paws upon the earth and the wind in my fur as I went faster and faster. A part of me that was forever gone and would never return. It hurt, but even though it was gone physically, at least,

I'd always have the memories to remind me that once upon a time, I was normal to some degree.

"Enjoying yourself?" a voice called from my left, causing me to quickly open my eyes to find that Finnick was standing there staring at me.

"I was... until you ruined it."

"Oh." He chuckled. "Are we all done with pleasantries now?"

Rolling my eyes, I stepped forward, trying to pass him to head toward my room. I had told Ansley to let Sansa know to meet me around lunch, and I didn't want to be late for that. I had to talk to her about what was going on, and I was hoping Trixie was still around. I wanted to know more about who Finnick really was.

"Pleasantries went out the door when I found out why you were really here," I snorted, only to have him step in front of me, blocking the path I needed to take.

"Are you saying that you don't want to marry me? I figured that every woman would dream of being a queen one day."

"Yeah, not me," I muttered, trying to pass him again, only to have him block me once more. "Will you please move?"

The way he was staring at me, slightly brooding but with amusement twinkling in his gaze, made me feel slightly unsure of myself. Of course, he was incredibly gorgeous in that 'all about him' kind of way, but there was no way I was going to let him know I found him attractive. I was not interested in whatever he had to offer. Even if it was being queen.

"I think we got off to a wrong start," he finally mustered up with a small sigh as he reached up, rubbing the back of his neck. "I'm Finn."

Finn. So we were on nickname basis, were we?

"Finn." Saying his name sounded good on my tongue and by the way his smile grew as I said it, I knew he liked to hear it as well. "I hope you enjoy your stay here... if you need anything, I'm sure the staff can help you."

Distracted and slightly caught off guard by my response, I stepped around him and hastily made my way towards the door back inside. I didn't want to give him a chance to be able to stop me again, and as soon as the door closed behind me, I glanced over my shoulder to look at him once more through the glass.

Finn stood there, staring at the now closed door with an odd expression that made me wonder what it was going through his mind. Was he actually interested in getting to know me or was this man here for other motives?

The moment he turned away and seemed to speak out to someone out of sight, I turned and made my way down the hallway towards my room. Sansa would be meeting me there, and I couldn't wait to find out more about this man. As well as the other contestants. If I was going to get through this then I needed to know everything there was about Prince Finnick and the games that were about to change my life forever.

Lucas

The morning started late for me, and when I had entered the dining hall to see Cassie leaving after what looked like an entrancing conversation with the man in front of her, a twinge of jealousy filled me. Here I was trying to prove to everyone I wasn't some cold-blooded killer and she was flirting with the opposition?

I shouldn't have been surprised with the amount of men who filled the room looking to win a place next to her. The only thing I had going for me was that she wasn't going to let them win a place in her heart.

After last night, I was fairly confident she felt the same about me as I did her. The only problem was I hoped my personal feelings towards this whole situation wouldn't stand in the way. I was still a mess from the fallout, and I had tried so hard to stay away from her but for some reason fate kept pulling me back.

I loved her, and I was foolish to think I could simply let her go.

Nothing would stop me from winning that seat next to her. I didn't want it for the title or fame. I wanted it because I wanted her, and I'd gladly give everything up to prove I deserved that place next to her.

"Lucas, what are you doing here?"

Freya walked towards me as I stood near the doorway watching the others finish their breakfast and vacate the hall. Odin had been busy with some woman I hadn't recognized, and when I turned to Freya, I could see the confusion in her eyes.

She had been the only one of the gods who hadn't judged me so harshly. "I came to join, but it seems I came to late."

My eyes traveled up and down her body, taking in the more modern clothing she was wearing. A pair of jeans and a light blue button-up blouse with heels. It was normal for a woman like her to wear something like that where I had come from but to see her wearing it here, I couldn't help but smirk with amusement.

"What's so funny?"

"Nothing," I quickly replied, shaking my head. "Did Cassie rub off on you?"

She frowned with confusion as she glanced down at her attire, seeming to realize what I was talking about and smiled. "Ah, yes. I took note of her style of dress and I had to try it for myself. I have to admit that these clothing choices are rather comfortable. Not to mention, I have more free movement than I did in the dresses."

"It looks nice." The compliment made her smile widen before she cast her glance into the hall where I had turned my gaze once more.

"So, I heard that you signed up for the events. Does this mean that you have changed your mind about your situation with Cassie then?"

Freya knew very well how I felt about Cassie, and how adamant I had been to keep my distance from her. Yet, here I was going against everything I had sworn once upon a time.

With a heavy sigh, I crossed my arms over my chest and nodded. "Yes."

"Good," she said with confidence. "I was wondering how long it would take you to change your mind. I'll have to let Frigga know she owes me."

"Owes you?" Turning my gaze to her, it was my turn to be confused and as she glanced up at me she couldn't help stifle the giggle that was trying to escape.

"Yes, she owes me. We made a bet, you see... I told her you would cave before the games. She thought that you would interrupt the final results and confess your love."

Great. Even the gods are making fun of my longing to be with my mate, even if she wasn't technically my mate anymore. "That's nice to know."

"Oh, don't take it so seriously. We have to have some kind of entertainment here."

Rolling my eyes, I glanced towards the strange elf walking towards our direction with a look of determination on his face. "What's the deal with the elf?"

Freya was silent for a moment as the elf passed us, disappearing down the hallway from which I had come. My eyes instinctively followed to see where it was he had went before falling back upon Freya again.

"He wants Cassie just like the others do," she replied softly, "the difference is he has a higher claim than the others. Besides you, of course."

"Higher claim? What the hell does that mean?" My beast perked up in attention to what she had said and as I looked down the empty hall once more I found that he was long gone.

"It was foretold in a prophecy of his kind that his mate, or fated one as they call it, was here in Asgard. He believes that person is Cassie, as do many others."

There was no way I was going to let this prick try to win her over. Not when I had worked so hard to make her understand last night that I was the man who wanted her. Hesitation and uncertainty filled me as I thought over this elf trying to sweet talk Cassie into leaving with him.

"No elf is going to get Cassie."

Laughter escaped Freya as I glanced at her one more time. "He isn't an elf, Lucas. He is Fae and from the interaction I have seen between the two of them only briefly this morning, it's obvious there is something between them."

Chapter Twenty

Cassie

Storming into my room with nothing but detest rolling off me in waves, I spotted Sansa sitting on the sofa reading over a piece of parchment that looked ancient. I hadn't expected her to be here so quickly, but as her eyes gazed up at me, she seemed to sense my mood and quickly placed the paper down on her lap.

"What's wrong with you?" Her cool and collected reply made me sigh as I shook my head, trying to gather my thoughts. Sansa was a very blunt and straightforward girl but she had a sense of leadership behind her that was unspoken and something I appreciated.

"Heard of Prince Finnick?"

Laughter escaped her lips as she nodded. "Oh, yes. I heard of him and even had the pleasure of briefly meeting him last night. He is quite the... royal highness, isn't he?"

"That's a polite way to put it." I scoffed with a smile. "He thinks he has some claim on me and came to the games to try and win me. Just like every other fuckhead that's walking around here."

Sansa's smile fell slightly as her eyes brought on a kinder approach. "Look, I know that you don't like what's going on but you are luckier than you think. Most of us women can't get a man to look at her properly and if one does, they only want you for a piece of ass. Good men don't come around often. At least you have your selection of who you want."

She was partially right, I did have my selection. The only problem was if I did simply settle on one, it didn't mean I would be able to have him. I was forced into this ancient ritual bullshit at my grandfather's discretion and it was becoming a pain in my ass.

However, I didn't realize that Sansa felt this way about my situation, and part of me wondered if there was someone she wanted but wasn't able to have.

"You seem to feel that statement deeply, Sansa. What aren't you telling me?"

Sansa seemed to hesitate for a moment as if she had said more than she wanted to and quickly shook off my comment. "Don't be ridiculous. I was just simply pointing out a fact."

"Uh-huh," I muttered, "you would tell me if something was wrong wouldn't you?"

Her eyes met mine briefly before she picked up the paper in her lap again with a smile that seemed more forced than it should have been. "Of course I would. Don't be silly."

Deciding to let the conversation go for now, I thought over the situation with Finnick. He was the prince of the Fae realm, and one thing my fathers taught me growing up was if you want to know how to overcome your enemies, you have to know your enemies.

"So, what can you tell me about Prince Finnick?"

"You mean besides that he seems like an egotistical asshole?" She laughed. "There isn't much to really know. He is the Prince of a kingdom called the Kingdom of Tver in the Fae realm. He wasn't supposed to be the future ruler, but when his brother died like a hundred years ago, he ended up being the next in line..."

My eyes shot open as I turned to her. "Wait... a hundred years ago? How fucking old is he?"

It wasn't like it was new to me that some supernaturals aged differently than others, but it was still shocking to hear sometimes how old these people were. A smirk of amusement crossed Sansa's face as she gave a small laugh. "I don't know exactly... like two hundred and something."

This guy was over two hundred years old?! "Jesus Christ... cradle robber much?" I muttered in shock causing Sansa to scoff in amusement.

"In our way of life, there really isn't such a thing as that, Cassie. Some of these creatures are thousands of years old. If you want a man your age, you're going to have to go back to earth—"

The moment that she said it, she instantly closed her mouth and froze in her place her eyes wide with hesitation. "I'm so sorry, Cassie... I didn't mean to..."

"It's okay, Sansa. I'm kind of getting used to the fact that I'm not going to be going home."

It was the truth. For the most part, I was getting used to the idea I would never be going home, and though part of me yearned for the freedom I once had, I wasn't going to let it hinder my ability to get things done.

"Are you sure? I know you have been under a lot of stress lately, and I don't mean to make things more stressful," she replied as if what she was doing was stressful. Which it wasn't. I had asked her to help me, but I didn't mean for her to take over. She kind of just did that on her own, and I didn't oppose it.

With a soft smile, I nodded my head. "Yeah, I'm sure."

Sansa stared at me warily before a low groan escaped her. "So what are you going to do? By the look of you, you're trying to prove a point I'm guessing?"

Glancing down at my clothing, a small smirk crossed my face as I shrugged my shoulders. I had hoped to show everyone I was capable of being the woman they wanted me to be, and perhaps I had pulled that off initially but Finn was making it hard this morning to stay focused.

On top of that, I wanted to see Lucas, and couldn't. Not to mention Silas was acting like a weird-ass mentor right now, which was beyond ridiculous. He changed so quickly from the man he had been and I didn't know how to handle that.

"I want people to look at me differently than they have over the past few weeks. I don't want to seem like someone who doesn't know what she is doing."

"But you don't know what you're doing..." Sansa said with laughter as she smiled at me while I rolled my eyes with my own quick laughter of amusement.

"Yeah, but they don't fucking need to know that."

Shrugging her shoulders, she put away what she was doing prior to me coming in, and placed her hands on her lap with a sly grin. "Well, if you want to give them something to talk about I can help you with that... as well as Trixie. Lord knows that girl loves fashion more than anyone else I know."

"Speaking of Trixie... where the fuck is she?" I was confused as to where the girl had gone after last night.

"Probably home. After you left last night, she was all out of sorts because she missed your brother. I told her to take her emotional ass to go see him for a few days and check back in with us when she was ready."

Hearing how much Trixie loved my brother made me happy. I was glad they had each other because I cared about them both deeply. The only thing I prayed for was that Pollux's ex-girlfriend didn't give Trixie too much shit. Otherwise, I'd have to find my way back to put that stupid bitch in her place.

"Well good... I'm sure we can manage without her for a few days."

Again, the sly grin on Sansa's face grew at my words. "Oh, we can... I actually know the perfect person to call for this, but you may not like it."

The way that Sansa said what she did didn't make me feel comfortable at all. It was as if the person she was going to ask was going to be more of a complication than they were hoping. I wasn't exactly sure who it was, but I was intrigued by who she had in mind.

"Okay, then. Who is the person that you're wanting to help us?"

The side, awkward glance Sansa gave as she looked towards the door had me wondering what it was she was up to, and as if by chance, some fairy godmother had cast a spell a knock sounded at my door I wasn't expecting.

"I think you should get that," Sansa replied.Causing my mouth to drop open and my eyes to widen slightly in shock.

"How the fuck did you get someone to knock on my door?"

Again, another smile crossed her lips, and she shrugged her shoulders, looking back down at the papers sitting upon her lap, nice and neatly put away. She reopened them and pulled them out and started going over them again.

"If I told you all of my secrets, then it wouldn't really be a surprise now would it?" she replied humbly as if she knew all the secrets of the world.

Hesitation filled me before I slowly got up and made my way toward the door. My hand hesitated over the knob. I decided to push forward and opened the door, revealing Freya who stood behind it. I didn't have the slightest clue what she was doing here, and as I looked over my shoulder back at Sansa, I saw her staring at me with a wide grin on her lips, and everything suddenly made sense.

"Freya is going to be the one to help me?" The words of astonishment flowed off of me, and as they did, a scoffing sound came from Freya, who stood directly in front of me.

"Don't act so shocked that I actually know what I'm doing. Yes, I'm not supposed to get involved with certain things, but that doesn't mean that I couldn't give you a little nudge. Plus, I have money riding on you. I can't afford to have this fall through."

"You have what?!" I gasped as she pushed past me into the room and I slowly closed the door behind her. "Are you saying that you have a bet against me? And with who?"

"Bet against you? No, I have a bet on you. You're going to win all of this without issues. However, some of the people here think that you'll have a nervous breakdown before that happens and that Solina and her brother will take over instead. Of course, I know that won't happen, and I'm not supposed to get involved because, technically, that would be cheating, but it doesn't mean that. I can't exactly give you the proper advice to take whether you choose to or not."

Still dumbfounded, I struggled to try and understand what she was talking about. I was named the heir apparent. There was nothing to win. The throne was supposed to be metaphorically mine, even though we all knew that Odin would never step down, nor would he ever die, so it wouldn't ever exactly matter. But still, it was mine to hold.

So what was I supposed to be winning?

"I can't lose anything. The throne, or the title at least, is actually mine. So what are you talking about?" I asked after I had a moment to try to process what she was telling me. Hopefully, she would give me some clarity instead of the riddles that she usually threw out.

As Freya walked around the room and then casually took a seat on the chair across from where Sansa was sitting, she let her arms rest upon the arms of the chair and stared at me with nothing but amusement lingering in her eyes.

"Did you honestly think that's how this works? If for some reason you're seen as unfit and unable to take that title, Odin will be forced by our laws to give it to the next person in line, which would be Solina and her brother, and the majority of us would not like to see them there. However, those are some of the people that are betting against you, so it's best that we make sure that you do win."

Dumbfounded once more, I found this bit of information to be quite important, considering that I didn't know it and as I cast my gaze toward Sansa. It was obvious she didn't know this either. In fact, she seemed more shocked than I was at what Freya was saying.

"So in other words, I'm taking it that it's a good idea that I had called upon you to come help us."

Freya turned to Sansa with an even wider grin and nodded her head.

"I will admit, I had thought that it would be Cassie that called upon me. But having you by her side as her advisor, it was very wise of you to do so," Freya replied with still the amusement hiding within the depths of her eyes and the smile upon her face. She was a little more confident than I would have liked, and all of this information would have been nice to know ahead of time. But what got me the most was the fact she found everything amusing, something I was slowly trying to get used to, even though it annoyed me more than ever.

"I'm not an advisor," Sansa replied with a small bit of laughter. "I'm just helping my friend out."

"Oh." Her smile fell just slightly. "I'm afraid that would be a little inaccurate. You are her advisor. Slowly but surely, she's putting her team together and you're on that list, as is Trixie. She will need strong people by her side, and I thought you were already aware of this when you guys had to go to the ball together, that you are a team and those positions have been given to you. Granted, of course, she has to win her title in order for you to keep them."

If it wasn't one thing, then it was another. And as Freya continued to explain to us that there were certain ways things had to go, I realized I had more work cut out for me than I actually wanted. But this was all for the best. I was determined to show them that I could be a woman that was worth fearing, and they were going to learn their place with me one way or another.

By the time this tournament was done, three men would know exactly where they stood with me and two other people would know to cower before me.

Chapter Twenty-one

"There is absolutely no way this is going to fucking work," I said out loud as I stood before the mirror, staring at my reflection. They had expected me to go out looking like I stepped out of a dominatrix book dressed in black leather pants and a backless red halter top with no bra and bad girl vibes to a small party in the center of town.

Now, granted, I was all down for the look. It was actually something I would have picked out for myself had I been back on Earth. Stuff that I wore quite often, frequently when I was out and about. But this was not the exact look I was going for when I thought I had to impress everybody.

Turning to face Freya and Sansa, who stood behind me, watching with excitement on their faces as they too got ready, even though Freya said she wasn't actually going to go, she was going to watch and oversee how everything was going, I couldn't help but wonder if they had actually lost their minds.

"You look amazing. I don't understand what you're freaking out about," Santa replied as she put on gold lipstick and fluffing out her hair that now looked chic and full of curls, and then smoothed down the small, skimpy black dress that she was wearing as if it could get any straighter than it was.

"Isn't this the complete opposite of what I should be wearing? I mean, I thought it was supposed to impress them, not look like the old Cassie."

"Cassie," Freya replied calmly as she stepped forward. "You're trying to change who you are, and you don't need to. You need to be the person that you are, the person you've always been. The rebel with a fighter spirit, the woman who never gives up. That is the person that everyone initially fell in love with, regardless if you are mortal or not. That is who you are. Show them that strong woman because that is the woman that is going to win all of this."

Some fairy godmother Freya was trying to be. Instead, she was wanting me to hone in on my natural spirit of rebelliousness to overcome the upcoming bullshit I was bound to face. I wasn't quite sure what she was up to, and part of me wondered if she had actually bet against me, and if this was her way of making sure that I didn't win. But the other part of me deep down inside, told me she would never do something like that, that she was trying to help me.

"And what if something goes wrong tonight? What if my powers go out of control again? What if I end up hurting somebody? Are you honestly sure that going to this party and drinking is a good idea?"

Sansa and Freya stared at me with slowly nodding heads. I contemplated what I was about to do, and before I knew it, Freya was shoving me out the door with Sansa like two hookers going out for a night on the town.

Nervous didn't even touch on the way I felt as Sansa and I made our way out into the dark night of the city, down the concrete pathways towards the large gate that sat in front of the building we stayed in and out onto the cobble street roads that would lead down into the center of town where a huge soiree was being held outside under the brilliant night sky.

It was a beautiful night. In the distance, Edison lights had been hung up. People gathered around the treeline, their voices and laughter echoing down the road, through the darkness, right toward my ears.

Everyone seemed like they were having a good time, and the closer we got, the more the nervousness actually subsided. People here knew who I was, but they weren't going to make a big deal out of it. At least I hoped they weren't. And sure enough, the closer we got, the more people we passed. I noticed they didn't even look in my direction, which was pleasing because the last thing I wanted was any sort of attention.

"All right, I'm going to go see if I can find my brother and that sexy friend of his that's always hanging around. Tonight I plan on having fun..." Sansa replied as she turned to walk away, but I grabbed her wrist and quickly pulled her back.

"You're not leaving me, are you? You were supposed to be my wingman. Like, be out here with me. I mean, I don't even know what I'm doing."

"Dude, you're going to be fine." She laughed as she removed her wrist from my grasp. "Deep breaths and stop panicking. You're supposed to socialize with people. Find somebody to socialize with. These are the people you're going to be in charge of one day. You need to get to know them and their actual state of mind. Show them that you're just normal like they are."

"But I'm not fucking normal, Sansa. I'm a freak of nature. Are you kidding me?" I replied quickly. My panicked tone was making my heart race, and as I took deep breaths in and out to try and calm myself, I found that it wasn't doing any good.

"Let me tell you a little story," Sansa said calmly, "when I was learning how to swim, my mother just pushed me into the lake and either I floated and made it to the surface, or I would have drowned..."

"That's fucking horrible!" I gasped overdramatically. "What does that have to do with me though?"

Laughter erupted from Sansa as she crossed her arms over her chest. "It was brutal, but I'm going to do the same to you. You can either go mingle and have fun or have a panic attack. Honestly, I would suggest going and getting a drink because the alcohol here isn't like the alcohol back home and I'm pretty sure you'll find that you'll relax a little more with some alcohol in your system."

Before I could even say anything else, Sansa held up her finger, wagging it back and forth as if to tell me no, and then quickly turned and disappeared into the crowd of people. I was a little pissed off she had left me standing there, yes, but I couldn't blame her.

I was a grown ass woman. Not a very mature grown ass woman, but I was a grown ass woman and I could definitely do this.

Or at least that's what I kept telling myself.

With a low groan, I made my way towards the nearest bar. It wasn't much different from the other bars I had encountered in the past. The white tablecloth over a very long wooden table, a variety of crystal bowls filled with different coloured liquids, one of which I had remembered from the ball. The pinkish purple liquid swirled within the crystal bowl, waiting for me to drink it.

I didn't feel too bad when I had drank it the other night, and thinking about it for a moment, whether this was the route I really wanted to go. I gave into my weaknesses, wanting the panic attacks and anxiety to disappear, and quickly picked up a crystal goblet and filled it to the brim.

Turning to face the crowd, I placed the glass to my lips and drank down the entire contents in one go. It was then I noticed nobody else really had the pinkish purple liquid in their cups and those that did, had they been very tiny ones.

"Well, look who it is, my little rebel. I didn't just see you you drink down an entire goblet of Roslaheim, did I?" I knew that voice. I hadn't known it very long, but I knew that voice and the moment I turned to my right and saw that sexy fucking Fae man walking towards me I groaned internally.

"Why does it matter what I drank?" I replied slightly snarkier than I needed to. "I could have sworn I didn't belong to you or any man for that matter."

A chuckle left him as a smile grew upon his face. His steps brought him closer to me than I wanted but at the same time, the closeness of him made me feel slightly different. "I am no mere man, Castor."

The moment his hand reached up to brush down the side of my face, a cold chill ran through my body I wasn't expecting, and with it my heart began to race. Finn's eyes lit up with excitement at this, and part of me wondered if I had felt what I had too.

"I need to go," I muttered quickly as I pulled away from him and began pushing through the crowds to find a place to escape. All I wanted to do was find a way to fight off the anxiety rushing through me because when I lost control of myself, I lost control of my powers.

Passing a waitress with a drink full of trays, I snagged another pink glowing glass and brought it to my lips as the music flowed around me, its beat pulsating in my veins as I made my way deeper and deeper through the crowds. My eyes scanned for Sansa or anyone else I knew hoping to find someone to socialize with.

I was supposed to be socializing with the people but not one single person here actually seemed to care about what I was doing. In fact, they were too worried about hooking up with each other and the entire college party vibe going on wasn't really my thing. Even though once upon a time Melissa and I had talked about the days we would do this sort of thing.

As the music changed a hand strayed over my back, and turning, I came to face a man I didn't know. He wasn't much taller than I was, and with beady brown eyes and a scar on the left side of his jaw. "Hello, beautiful, wanna dance?"

Disgust rolled through me at his touch. "No, I don't. Thanks though..."

Pulling away from him, he narrowed his gaze at me before he grabbed at me once more pulling me close to him. The stench of ale upon his breath made my stomach turn. "You think you are better than me, bitch? You're not better than me."

Anger coursed through me slowly at the way this man was speaking to me, and the fact he thought he could touch me pissed me off even more. "Get your fucking hands off me now."

As my power slowly grew, I found myself quickly pulled away from the man as a large Fae guard stepped in between us. I wasn't sure at first what was going on but when I found a set of celestial eyes staring back at mine, I realized it was Finn who had stopped the altercation.

"Finn?" I said softly in a power induced haze, "what–"

"Don't talk... I need you to move, now," He replied sternly as he wrapped an arm around my waist and pulled me off through the crowd away from the many bodies who had been nearby.

I didn't want to go with him, but something about the entire situation had my mind spinning and with the alcohol hitting my system, my logical sense of thinking went straight out the window. "Finn, where are you taking me?"

"Away from anywhere that you could potentially hurt people..."

"Hurt people?" I stammered as we broke through the crowd as he walked me down the silent cobbled street back towards the building that I stayed in. "I wouldn't hurt anyone... let me go!"

Stopping in my tracks, I jerked myself from his grasp and stood staring at him. His eyes narrowed before he looked off only to look back at me with irritation. "The level of your power just now was enough to kill a majority of people there, Cassie... do you not know how to control yourself?"

Opening and closing my mouth,, I tried to speak but found no words at first. "I wasn't going to hurt anyone... no one saw what was going on..."

"That's because they were engrossed in the power. They were blind and clouded from it."

"Yet, you weren't affected." I scoffed, "I doubt that."

"I'm Fae, Cassie. Your powers can't hurt me... plus, I'm your soul mate. Our powers in my world don't work on each other, and from what I can see, that extends to here as well." He sighed, shaking his head before rubbing the back of his neck.

I was at a loss for words for what he was saying, and as angry as I wanted to be at him, I couldn't be. He had just stopped me from doing something horrible, and for that I had nothing but thanks for him. I didn't want to hurt anyone like I had Melissa.

"Oh... well, thank you," I muttered softly, "I'll just head back to my room."

Trying to slowly pass him, he took my hand and stopped me once more. The closeness of his body to mine was shocking and the feeling he pulled inside me stopped me again.

"One of these days, Cassie... you're going to give me a chance. And I won't stop until you do. I will win you over one way or another."

Chapter Twenty-two

Finn's words were not expected, and staring up into his eyes, I was almost sure he was going to kiss me. Yet, instead of the kiss on my lips that I expected, he leaned forward and kissed my forehead, catching me off guard before quickly stepping away. The action wasn't what I would have thought typical for a man like him, and without another word, he turned with his guard and disappeared back down the street from where we had come.

"Cassie, come with me..."

The deep voice behind me sent shivers over my spine as I realized Silas had seen the entire interaction. Turning slowly to face him, I took in the hazel eyes filled with fire as his narrowed brows loosened slightly and a heavy breath escaped his lips.

"What are you doing here?" My voice was shaky but without hesitation, he took my hand and pulled me gently behind him, back up the path from which I had come earlier on in the evening and through the doors that would eventually lead me back to my apartment.

"I felt your powers, Cassie. It seems that it isn't only your anger that triggers you..."

Gasping at his comment, I stopped dead in my tracks, causing him to stop as well. He glanced over his shoulder at me with a frown upon his lips. "You think that he caused something to happen to me? That wasn't why my powers went off, Silas."

"It doesn't matter, Cassie. It's time for you to retire."

Dismissing me the way he was pissed me off more than anything. I may have been a lot of things, but I didn't deserve to be dismissed when he was making assumptions about me that weren't true. "I was harassed by a man out there while enjoying the festivities. For your information, Finn saved me from destroying him or anyone near. Something that you should have done, but choose to ignore me instead."

Anger lurked within his gaze as I ripped my hand from his and brushed past him towards my room, barely making it past the doors to the building before I was stopped yet again by Silas' touch.

"Don't you dare walk away from me."

Staring at him dumbfounded, laughter escaped me as I shook my head. "You have got to be kidding me? You're not my husband or my partner, so you don't get to tell me what I can and can't do. You made it clear how you view me, Silas."

Snatching my hand, he dragged me down the hallway with determination as he made his way with me straight toward my room. Never had I seen such action from Silas as I did right now and as soon as my large doors came into view, he didn't hesitate to push them open, pushing me in.

"Silas... would you stop!"

The moment the door was closed, he spun and gripped my throat and pulled me close. The tension between us was overwhelming but unlike the way Lucas touched me, or even Finn, there was something about Silas that made my body want to melt against him.

"Why should I, Cassie?" he all but purred with his lips inches above mine, "isn't this what you wanted? You talk about me not doing shit and constantly give me these looks as if to say you want me but hate me at the same time. Do you know what it does to me?"

Pulling me tighter, he leaned into my ear causing me to moan softly. "Tell me..."

I was asking to be punished but in all honesty, with the way the alcohol from this place affected me, I did want to be punished. I wanted him to do things to me that only he had been able to do before. Yet as I stood there with him staring down at me, I didn't know what was going to happen.

"I don't see how you don't know how crazy you make me. How much I wish I could be by your side all the time but I can't. Why do you think I have been pushing you away, Cassie?"

I didn't know what to say to him. I hadn't really thought about any of that kind of stuff. But now that he was standing here telling me he wished he could be with me, I didn't know what to believe.

"You have a real funny way of showing people that you care."

My sarcastic comment was just enough to push him over the edge and before I knew it, I found myself caught within his grasp. His lips smashed against mine as his hands tore at my clothing, pulling it from my body bit by bit.

There was no sweet, soft passion to the way he was handling me and when my back met the cool wall, I knew I was about to be ravaged in more ways than one. He took me without hesitation, his pants had dropped to the floor, the long length of his erect shaft pushing against my core as the head dove deep inside me.

This was exactly what I wanted, and now that I had him fucking me like a bitch in heat, I wasn't about to do anything to stop it.

Gripping my hair, he yanked my head to the side, running his nose up the length of my neck as his hips continued to thrust roughly against me. His long, thick, spiked cock massaged the inside of my tight cunt causing my body to shake with pleasure. "You like this don't you, Cassie?"

"Yes—" I gasped, "please, don't stop—"

"Stop?" He laughed. "Oh, I'm going to make you scream in more ways than one."

"Prove it."

Two words were all it took for him to completely lose himself as his lips crashed upon mine with his tongue diving deep into my mouth. His fingers gripped at my thighs as he lifted me up high onto the wall, fucking me harder and harder.

It had been so long since I had slept with a man, and having Silas take me was beyond mind-blowing. The harder and faster he moved, the more I clawed at his back crying and moaning for him to give me everything. Begging and pleading for everything.

With eyes bright as gold and red as fire as if from the pits of hell, he held me tightly in place, claiming my body for himself as the ridges of his spiked cock latched inside, causing me to scream just as he tipped me over the edge and spilled himself inside of me. The moment was more than I could have asked for as we both panted, dripping in sweat as we stared at each other.

The only problem was it seemed realization had filled Silas because there was no smile on his face as there was on mine. He was silent for a moment as he looked down at our union and his eyes widened in fear as he quickly pulled out of me and let my feet hit the floor.

"We shouldn't have done that, Cassie."

"Are you fucking serious right now?" I replied in anger and shock. We had just spent an amazing moment with each other, and he was seriously telling me that we shouldn't have just done what we had done as if sleeping with me was incredibly wrong to do.

Turning to face me, confliction weighed heavily on his mind, his eyes reflecting the doubts he had and the worries that seemed to weigh upon his heart. I hadn't meant for the moment between us to happen, and it was more Silas that had caused it than me. His eyes flashed between his dragon eyes and the mundane ones that stared back at me typically.

"I can't ruin your life, Cassie. There is no future with me, and Odin will never allow us to be together. I'm but—"

"Don't say it!" I gasped loudly as I crossed the space between us placing my hand on his bare chest. The blank, ancient symbols upon the rigid muscles of his chest held some sort of story that he wouldn't tell me, but reminded me of how different we were. He hadn't had them before but seeing them now, they suited him.

A difference I didn't care about because it didn't change how much I cared about him.

"Cassie, you know what I'm saying is true. Plus, you have Lucas... and now Finnick. Those are two men you can be with."

Shaking my head, tears brimmed my eyes as I finally looked up at him again. "But what if I don't want to choose? I care for Lucas, yes, but I also care for you. I don't want to have to pick, and I can't imagine my life without either of you."

Raising his hand, he ran through my hair before his palm rested upon my cheek. His thumb brushed against the skin as I closed my eyes and pressed my face into his palm just a little bit more.

Only a minute ago, we were having a moment that I never wanted to stop, and once again I was left begging for more time, I wouldn't be able to have, because he was too worried about someone finding out. I didn't care about the rules. I wanted him to ravish me regardless of what others said, and instead he was pulling away.

Pressing his lips to my forehead, he smiled at me. "I wish that things were that easy, Cassie. I really do, but we aren't in a position for things to work like that."

"What if it could, though?"

A deep chuckle escaped him as he smiled and stepped back from me, gathering his clothing as he began to get dressed. "It can't, Cassie..."

"Yes, I'm aware of what you're saying, Silas. But just humor me for a moment. What if it could? If we could be together... would you want to be?"

Staring at him, his eyes not meeting mine, he sighed once more as he pulled the black cotton shirt over his head before turning to me once again. "Yes, Cassie. If the world was perfect, I would."

Clearing the step between us once more, he wrapped his arms around me and held me tight against him. "I wish this was a world where we could choose our own stories, Cassie, but you have to understand that unfortunately, it isn't that easy. I was given a choice once before, and I had to do what was asked of me to ensure that I was able to survive. This was the life I chose and if I had known you would be coming into my life, I would have chosen differently."

No matter what I said, it was obvious Silas was stuck in his decision. The only thing I could do was hope for stolen moments like this one. "I understand... but it doesn't mean that we can't keep seeing each other in secret."

"Is that what you want though?" he asked, narrowing his gaze. "To keep me a secret?"

"No," I replied quickly, trying to reassure him. "I'd rather have you all the time, but having you anyway is better than none at all."

"And your love for Lucas?" he asked, making me hesitate in my next words. I had never expected the idea of loving more than one man, but it wasn't like it was an impossible feat. My mother had done the same.

"I can love you both, Silas."

Love wasn't something I had expressed to Silas before, and standing before him now, the way the gold flickered within his gaze, it was obvious he hadn't been expecting me to say that either. I expected him to laugh at my admission, or perhaps shrug it off. What I didn't expect, though, was for him to look at me with such passion it made my heart want to leap from my chest.

Running his hand over my hair again, he lifted my lips to gently meet his while a frown formed upon his face. The silence killed me as I waited for him to say anything that might give me clarity as to what was going on.

"I have to go... but perhaps fate will show us what he holds in the future."

I had no clue what he was talking about. He pulled away from me and turned to leave me naked, standing in my room, watching him walk out my door. I couldn't help but feel slightly ashamed of myself and how we had acted.

My own emotions confused me as I tried to understand what had happened to bring me to where I was, and what I could do to get my life together.

Maybe I could love more than one, and perhaps my future wasn't much different from my mother's. At the end of the day, only time would tell if it was meant to be or if I was simply a fool to think I could have a happily ever after, just as my mother once had done.

Chapter Twenty-three

Silas

Storming from her room, I made my way down the hall, reeling over the events that had just transpired. Cassie wasn't like any other woman I had ever encountered in my life, and I was completely enamored by her in every way. Not only had she completely taken over my mind, she had also captured my heart. Something I had sworn I would never let another woman do after Anna had died.

"Where are you going in such a hurry," a voice softly replied, stopping me in my tracks.

"Freya, do you always lurk in the shadows?"

Turning, I spotted the bright, cheerful smile of my long-time friend. Most people didn't know that Freya and I had such a close friendship, but at the same time, I wasn't one to tell people my business, and neither was Freya. "You know I like to stay on top of the latest gossip."

"Yes, I do," I replied trying to force a smile upon my face but too flustered by what I was going to do about my attraction to Cassie to make it look normal. "Well, I need to head to bed before the first trials tomorrow. Don't get into too much trouble."

"Says the man who just left a very important woman's room," she replied as I turned to walk away. I had been caught by Freya, and I knew there was no point in denying that I had just come from Cassie's room. Freya knew everything that happened within this damn palace, and as annoying as it could be... it was also very helpful.

Turning to face her again, I sighed as I reached up rubbing the back of my neck. "It isn't what you think, Freya. Please don't make a fuss about this."

"A fuss?" She scoffed with soft laughter as she raised a brow crossing her arms over her chest. "Come on now, Silas. You of all people should know that I don't make a fuss. I simply point out the obvious, and you, my friend, are completely in love with a woman that is supposed to be off-limits to you."

"I know this, Freya. I have tried everything I can to be distant from her and stay away..." I groaned in frustration. "I just fucking can't."

"You must though, Silas. You know as well as I do that Odin will never allow you to be with her. Just as he wouldn't allow you interest in Anna. You're a guardian, and that is the only reason you have been allowed to stay here as long as you have."

Hearing her say what I already knew only made me angrier than I had already been. I knew my friend wasn't saying all of this to sway me from what I was doing, but more so like a warning to help protect me considering the consequences that would follow if I wasn't careful.

Taking a deep breath, I cast my eyes towards the ceiling, trying to think of what I could do to ease the situation, but at the end of my thought, the only thing left there was the love I had for Cassie. I wanted to be there for her, to love her in every way she deserved to be loved, and yet I was acting foolish thinking that I could be that person for her.

"What would you have me do, Freya?" I asked, setting my eyes upon the graceful woman in front of me, "Cassie isn't going to just let me go."

Freya was silent for a while as she stood there seemingly lost in her own thoughts going over everything I had just said. It wasn't like her to be this quiet, and yet as she opened her mouth, I was surprised by the advice she gave. "If it is Cassie's will, then all I can say is be careful."

"Seriously?" Shocked was an understatement at the moment. I couldn't believe this was the advice the great Freya was giving when usually she would have told me to stay clear no matter the cost of it.

Yes, she cared for Cassie because to Freya, Cassie was the future of this realm and many others. However, at the same time, she was also not someone who wanted to cross Odin. She was the smartest of any of the gods I had ever met, and I took her advice very seriously.

"Yes, seriously, Silas. Perhaps Cassie will take more after her mother than I thought."

"More after her mother?" I repeated furrowing my brows, "what do you mean?"

Laughter escaped Freya's lips as she shook her head wagging her finger from side to side. "Come on now, Silas. You know exactly what I'm talking about, and if you don't, I might have to question your intelligence."

There was no doubt in my mind as to what she was referring to but at the same time, it wasn't something I had wanted to admit in the past. I knew that Lucas was her original mate, and when her mortal form died, that mate bond had been broken. However, when I saw them interacting as of late, it was safe to assume that it was still there even though it should have been possible.

"Cassie having more than one mate would change everything. She would have to choose to select that life, and there is no way that she will. The girl doesn't even want to be in this place, and with her position... she can't have more than one consort, Freya."

"Yet, it's still a possibility," she muttered, shrugging her shoulders.

"Not with me, Freya. Cassie has to marry royalty. That's why everyone in attendance has some type of royalty in their blood."

Her eyes darted to mine with judgment at my words. "If you remember correctly... you are royalty, Silas."

"Don't speak of it," I snapped in reply. "That part of my life died with me the day I came here."

Shrugging her shoulders, Freya looked down at her nails and smirked. "All I was simply hinting at, Silas, is that anything is possible. In all honesty, I'm curious to see what is going to happen with her. I have a feeling she is going to make things extremely interesting over the next few weeks."

"What do you mean?"

Her eyes cut up to mine as she scoffed with a smile once more. "Oh, come now, Silas... you, Lucas, and now Prince Finnick... you know what they say about Finnick. When he wants something he will do anything to obtain it."

I was quite aware of that little bit of information about Finnick, and it was something that worried me completely. Tomorrow, the first game was about strength, and though they were using Viking methods to show the strength of each warrior, I wondered if Finnick would find a way to ensure he finished in the top ten.

Which was where he needed to be to continue to the next round.

Surely he wasn't a match for a shifter... he was only Fae.

"He won't pass the round tomorrow, Freya. Prince or not, I have seen the men working in those fields the past few weeks. He doesn't have half the stamina they do."

"Don't be so sure of that." She laughed. "He is Fae... crafty and intelligent are his two leading factors. Something that the majority of those in this realm lack."

True as that might have been, I also knew that Thor's children were another obstacle. "Thor's boy... what of him?"

Quiet for a moment, she seemed to glance around as if wondering if there was anyone who could be watching before she spoke. "They are going to play dirty that's for sure. However, they don't stand a chance when it comes to outwitting the Fae or Cassie."

"Cassie's judgment is all over the place, Freya. I worry that she doesn't have what it takes to get through the next few weeks. She seems confident one moment, and falling apart the next."

Freya nodded in agreement as she stepped closer to me. "Yes, I know but you have to remember... mentally she is only eighteen years old. She is still a child in some ways, and because of that, she needs people around her who can help guide her."

"No, what she needs are her parents." I scoffed, rolling my eyes, "something I can't give her."

Again, Freya was quiet for a moment as she bit upon her bottom lip thinking. "Perhaps she does, but in the meantime she needs a support system she can count on. It may be useful to suggest this to Odin when you see him tomorrow. After all, it would give you more reason to spend time with her."

She had a point, and though that also was a risk, it was one I could possibly make work. The ability to spend time with her was something I longed for but wasn't able to do. Since the moment she changed, I was forced to take my situation more seriously... I was forced to stay away from her.

It had been the only way that I'd been able to keep myself sane.

Sanity wasn't something that you wanted to lose in a place like this, and I already knew what Freya's opinion would be on that matter. "You're overthinking things, Silas."

"No, I'm not." The quick reply to her comment made her chuckle, "I'm serious."

"So am I, Silas. You need to be careful, but at the end of the day, the choice on what you do is only for you to make. I'm simply a watcher."

"Speaking of watching..." I replied, "what shady shit have you seen over the last few days."

Again, she shrugged her shoulders with a mischievous smile. "A girl can't reveal all her secrets, Silas. However, I can say that tomorrow is surely going to be interesting. Who knew that men could be so competitive."

"I could have told you that, Freya."

As the sound of laughter filtered from somewhere down the hallways in front of me, I knew that our conversation needed to be cut short. Freya had things she was doing, and honestly, I needed to get back to what I was doing. The both of us quickly sharing a look was the only goodbye we needed before we made ourselves scarce within the halls and departed quickly.

Hastily making my way down the halls I headed towards my room. The black and steel door loomed in front of me as I quickly entered and took in my lush surroundings. For hundreds of years I had been here, and every corner of the living room was covered in books and scrolls of the past.

Stuff that I had gone through over the years to find a way to make sense of what had happened in my past and the fact that Freya had brought it up in conversation, I was now stuck thinking about it. The day I came here seeking asylum was when I gave up being the man I was meant to be.

No matter how much people may have wanted me to be different, I couldn't.

The death of my past was what led to my future, and if Cassie was to be the woman that people wanted her to be, she couldn't do that with me at her side. I was nothing but a plague that would destroy her life, and I refused to be the one to see her fall because of my own failures.

Chapter Twenty-four

Cassie

The sounds of battle echoed around me within the stadium. My eyes couldn't look away from the massacre happening in front of me, and as much as I wanted to tell them to stop because this was more than brutal, I knew I couldn't. There had to have been at least fifty people on those training fields, wallowing around on the grass greener than anything I'd ever seen. Blood coated their skin as they spared each other.

Odin called these games, but in reality, it was nothing but brutal force. I couldn't understand why things weren't just done normally. Then again, I was in Asgard and Nordic traditions was the only way to go here.

"Cassie!" A voice called out to me, causing me to look down the walkway to see Sansa walking toward me with a smile and a bounce within her step. "I figured that I'd find you out here. I just was hoping that she would have waited for me."

Raising a brow in amusement, I stared at her for a moment as she sat next to me. The clothed awning protected us from the sun, the fabric billowing gently in the morning breeze. " Girl, this shit started like an hour ago. We would have been late."

"There is nothing wrong with being fashionably late," she remarked with a smirk that made my eyes roll before I turned my gaze back out onto the field.

I had awoken early this morning ready to get the first trials over with so I could return to normal life, and no matter how much I would have rather be doing anything else right now. I knew that wasn't possible. Odin wanted me here.

I was the prize these men fought for and being present was important to remind them of that.

Or at least that was what I was told.

"I can't believe they find this entertaining… this is barbaric."

Sansa's laughter floated around me as she nodded in agreement. "Yeah, but this is Asgard. You should have seen the games a few years ago. One of the poor guys lost an arm."

Snapping my attention to her with my jaw dropped, I tried to wrap my head around what she had said. "Are you fucking kidding me?"

"Nope," she muttered. "They take this shit seriously here."

Of course I had grown up around training and whatnot, but this was far more violence than was needed. They called it sparring and it was anything but that. Blood was being spilled and men were getting hurt one after another and everyone seemed to act like that was perfectly acceptable.

"It's disgusting," I replied, trying to keep a smile on my face but I had no doubt that my disgust in this was shining through.

"Girl, you think this is bad? They haven't even gotten to 'The Hunt' yet. That's when shit gets really interesting."

I didn't even want to ask what the hell that was, but I had a feeling that was the last event that Freya had tried telling me about before. I had given suggestions to small things I wanted to be added to these games but in the end, Odin said they would stick to being traditional with only minor changes.

On top of that, I was only just informed of the final task requirements this morning. The final task was I would have to entertain the last three contestants individually in the days leading up to the main event. "Oh, by the way… thanks for filling me in on my hosting responsibilities."

"Hosting?" My gaze fell to her once more, taking in the confused expression on her face hidden behind her furrowed brows. "What are you talking about?"

"Freya told me that Odin wants me to entertain the last three contestants in the days leading up to the hunt or whatever you want to call it. I'm not sure why, but I'm not looking forward to it."

By the way Sansa opened and closed her mouth, I could tell she was taken aback and confused as to what I was talking about. I began to wonder if this was something they had just made up for this particular situation. "You didn't know, did you?"

"No," she replied softly. "Honestly, I didn't. But I will admit that even though I'm surprised... I'm intrigued as to how that's going to go."

"What do you mean?"

With a smile she shook her head as she looked back onto the field. "You're not exactly the easiest person to get along with Cassie."

"Excuse me?" I replied with shock as my eyes widened and my mouth dropped open. "Yes, I am."

Chuckling she gave me a 'who are you lying to' expression as she looked me up and down. "Is that so? Because last time I checked, you had a thing for running people off."

Her words were harsh but she was accurate so I couldn't fault her for that.

"I suppose you're right," I mumbled under my breath, causing her to laugh again.

"Have you seen any of them today?"

My mind instantly went to Silas and my heart dropped. "No."

I had an amazing evening with him that completely took me by surprise, and since then, he had gone back to avoiding me again. Something that annoyed me like no other. I was tired of being avoided, and as much as I wanted to hunt him down and yell at him for acting this way again—I knew that it would do no good.

Looking out on the field, I searched for the two bodies I knew would be present today. Lucas and Finnick were both participating and as much as both men had recently irritated me, I was deeply concerned about either getting hurt.

"Are you looking for them?" Sansa asked me, causing me to sigh as I slowly nodded my head.

"Yes, but of course, I can't see shit out there. Every one of them all seem to blur together. This entire thing is exhausting."

Falling back into the lush pillow-lined chair I was reclining in, I felt like giving up on all of this. My heart and mind had been pushed to the point of breaking lately, and as much as I wanted to keep going, I didn't know how.

I needed a reprieve, and when I thought about walking out of the arena, the flash of white and black I had been searching for appeared before me like a solution. Lucas and Finnick prepared to spar against their opponents and my heart almost stopped.

"Oh my God, there they are."

My response caught Sansa's attention, and she looked in the direction I was. She chuckled. "Oh, wow, I suppose they aren't playing with opponents this year."

"What are you talking about?" I asked as I turned to look at her. "What's wrong with them?"

She raised her brows with a sigh as she pointed towards Lucas and the man he was fighting. An enormous man that stood at least a foot taller than Lucas with black and red markings all over his skin, and hair that had been buzzed to his scalp. "That's Soren. He is the future Alpha of a bear clan from Earth. They hail from the Russian territories and are known for being ruthless."

Russian... bears? You had to be fucking kidding me.

"He looks like he eats people like Lucas for breakfast!" The gasped response from me caused Sansa to laugh again as she nodded.

"Yeah, he is known to be a killer. Not sure why he isn't matched with someone in his category though. I wouldn't have thought Lucas would be ranked up there with them yet."

Again, my heart sank. "What are you talking about?"

"Well, they are ranked by skill and size. As you can see... Soren towers over Lucas in a lot of factors. Hopefully, he will be able to hold him off," she replied in a tone that sounded as if she didn't think Lucas stood a chance.

Lucas and I hadn't really spoken in the past two weeks but it didn't mean I didn't think about him often. I had just respected his wishes to let him focus on this competition and try to win me—as he called it—properly. "We have to do something."

Sansa's eyes darted in my direction as she scoffed with amusement. "aAre you fucking serious? There is nothing we can do, Cassie. It's the best of three so all we can do is just pray he wins or doesn't lose the next two."

Fuck me life… as much as I believed in Lucas, there was no way he could beat this guy.

"What about the person Finnick is with? Wait… Sansa, that's your brother!" His white hair had been pulled back into a tight bun on his head as he stood topless in front of none other than Bronn, Sansa's brother.

"Oh, for fuck sake… Bronn is about to get his ass handed to him."

I was slightly surprised by Sansa's response to her brother facing Finnick. He seemed like a very strong and intelligent character but Sansa would know him better. "Are you serious? He is way bigger than Finnick—"

"That doesn't mean shit in this situation," she sighed. "Finnick is… well I told you. He is the Fae prince–"

"Yeah, yeah I know. That doesn't mean shit though. Come on… you can't honestly think Bronn would lose so easily."

Our conversation continued for a moment before a deep bellow of laughter sounded from behind us, and as I looked up I spotted a man I didn't recognize taking up a seat on the concrete benches. "You ladies have interesting conversations."

I furrowed as I took in his deep brown eyes, shoulder length brown and gray hair. He didn't look like the others with his attire and seemed to definitely have enough of the traditional brown furs and linen attire that the Nordic communities used to wear.

"I'm sorry, who are you?"

He stared at me for a moment before a smile crossed his lips. "Balder… your uncle."

Balder... I had been learning about the gods more and more with my time here and if I remember correctly, Balder was supposed to be dead. "Aren't you supposed to be dead? Like you're allergic to Mistletoe or something..."

More laughter erupted from the man as he held his belly and bellowed, causing the attention of others to land on us as embarrassment rushed to my cheeks. "Oh my God, it isn't that funny. Will you stop people from looking at us!"

"You, dear niece, worry too much about what people will think of you. As for those stories written in books... all lies–well, mostly all lies. Since I'm sitting here in front of you it's obvious that I'm not dead."

Rolling my eyes, I frowned looking at Sansa for rebuttal but instead she sat there quietly with her eyes wide as if she was in shock of the man before us. It was clear she knew something and I would have to pick her brain on later, but for now, I'd have to deal with this man myself.

"Fair enough... so what did you find amusing about my opinion on her brother and Finnick? Seeing as that's why you initially laughed."

He took a moment as his eyes scanned out towards the field. "Prince Finnick is a dangerous man, Castor. You should be able to sense that when you're around him. He has bathed in the blood of many men far bigger than her brother, and all without breaking a sweat."

As my eyes turned back to where Finnick was sparring with Bronn, I watched him move faster than my eyes could follow and quickly toss Bronn from the ring. My eyes widenend at the display as the referee called the match won, and Finnick walked off into the crowd of men like it was nothing.

On the other hand... Lucas seemed to not be in good shape as Soren found victory in his win over Lucas. My heart broke knowing Lucas had lost but I knew he had two more chances to win. If he lost next time he would be faced with being cast out before the next round. "Shit..."

"Yes, your mate didn't seem to favor too well out there, Castor."

Spinning around to glare at Balder, I took note of the smirk upon his face. "Stop calling me that. My name is Cassie."

"You may call yourself whatever you want, but to me you will always be Castor. Now, piece of advice from one blacksheep to another... in order to win, you often need to make deals with those who are capable of winning."

I had no clue what he was on about but before I could ask, he stood and departed from where Sansa and I sat. My eyes drifted to Sansa as I gave her a 'what the fuck' kind of glare that caused her to shrug and gesture towards Balder's retreating figure.

"Don't look at me like that! Do you know who that was?!" she gasped with astonishment.

"Baldar, duh. Who cares? He is just another god."

Mouth agape, she shook her head at me. "Cassie he isn't just another god. He is the son of Odin and Frigg... he is the embodiment of immortality. Why do you think there are so many stories about him? They say the gods didn't like him? No, bitch. They envied him because he was Odin's favorite."

What she was saying didn't make any sense to me. "If that was the case, why aren't any of Odin's children... like Baldar, his so-called favorite—taking the job of heir?"

She stared at me blankly, shaking her head with astonishment. "You really haven't studied enough have you? I mean all those books—"

"Oh my God, Sansa. No, I haven't. I'm sorry I'm still working on it. Now will you just tell me what the hell I'm missing?"

Crossing her arms over her chest, she shook her head and groaned. "Baldar is the reason you are the heir. He had Odin promise that none of his children would ever succeed him as they were all blinded by power and greed and would never deserve the throne. Rumor has it Baldar is a seer, which is rare. Men are rarely ever seers, and if he has shown himself to you after being in hiding for centuries... well, he must have seen something in your future."

Chapter Twenty-five

Cassie

I wasn't quite sure what to make of what Balder had said, but the more and more I thought about it, I couldn't help but wonder if he was trying to tell me something secretly without exactly coming out and saying it, which seemed to be the usual kind of thing that happened around this place.

The moment the sparring games had finished for the day, I took my leave with Sansa and made my way down the stone steps toward the main courtyard door, eager to be able to check and see if Lucas was okay. It was clear he had taken a beating from Soren, and I felt incredibly bad that he had, especially since he was so eager to prove himself in front of everybody. And yet when he lost, it seemed like he was just ridiculed over it.

Afterward, men scattered around the area talking and hanging out after everything had finished. I followed Sansa down the corridors toward the main door and I couldn't help but stop next to the door that led to the shower areas. It must have been where Lucas had gone after everything was said and done. And as I halted there, Sansa looked over her shoulder at me with curiosity.

"What are you doing?" she asked as she stood staring at me with her brows furrowed together and a look of confusion on her face.

"I think I should go check and see if Lucas is okay."

Shaking her head from side to side, she frowned. "I don't think that's a good idea, Cassie. He is already dealing with a loss... having you go in there is only going to make things worse."

"What are you talking about?" I scoffed with annoyance, "I'm just there checking on him."

Crossing my arms over my chest, I frowned at the way she was acting. How could she think that I would make things worse? I was, at one point in time, Lucas's mate, and he cared for me greatly. He would never get upset at me for checking on him.

After a moment of the stare down, a smile crossed her face as she gestured toward the door. "Okay, then. By all means, go check on him. Just don't come complaining to me when it backfires."

Her words caused me to hesitate as I glanced toward the door and then back to her. Maybe she was right, but at the same time, I couldn't help but feel the pull to check. The image of him bleeding was imprinted in my mind, and I just had to make sure that he was safe.

In frustration, I huffed out and moved toward the door causing Sansa to groan as she turned walking away and I entered the darkened pathway. The smell of rank body odor caused me to gag as I made my way toward the lockers and searched for the dark head of hair I had grown to love over time.

"Whoa! What do we have here, men?!" The hoots and hollers of multiple men made me internally wish I had listened to Sansa. Their testosterone levels must have been through the roof because as I walked past them, they licked their lips and fucked me with their eyes.

"Get over yourselves," I snapped as I pushed past them in search of Lucas.

A tall, muscular, and well-cut wall of godliness stepped in front of me, causing me to halt in my tracks as I looked up into the eyes of none other than Soren. The man who had caused Lucas harm today. He stood in front of me completely naked with a smirk on his face and his arms over his chest like the cocky prick he was.

"What are you doing in here, Delicious? Did you decide to reward me early for my win?"

Disgust filled me. He was more self-centered than most men I had met and he only said one sentence to me.

"If you think for one moment your trashy pick-up line was going to work, you're sadly mistaken. Plus," I replied, looking him up and down thoroughly, "It doesn't seem like there's much to work with."

The roar of laughter that left the mouths of the men in that locker room was enough for anyone outside of this building to hear it—and Soren wasn't pleased with what I said. His eyes narrowed at me as he sneered at my remark. "You have a lot to say for a woman who's being passed off as a prize to please the man that wins."

Placing my hands on my hips, I refused to back down and let him see me falter. It was men like him that made me wonder if I should just be single forever. He was nothing but a prick looking to get one off and any pretty face who would entertain him.

"If that's what you think this entire thing is then I'm afraid you're wrong." Hearing me say he was wrong seemed to puzzle him, giving me the opportunity I needed to put him in his place. "You see, the winner won't win me. He will win the opportunity to please me however I see fit for the rest of his life. Granted you will have luxuries... but you will never be free again."

Silence fell over the locker rooms at my comment, and as I glanced around I watched every man in there silently question what I was saying. They had all come into this thinking that they had a chance to bag themselves a princess as some may say. Yet, never stopped to think that perhaps that wasn't the case.

"You're lying," he muttered.

Turning to him again my smile widened. "Am I?"

It only took a moment for him to step aside and storm off without another word. He didn't like what I had to say, and I didn't care if he didn't like it. It was the truth. I would never let a man think that just because he won the tournament, I was his property to do with as he pleased.

I was no one's property, and if that was what people thought my future was going to be, they were sadly mistaken. Moving through the lockers, I turned every corner until my eyes landed upon the dark hair of Lucas, his dark eyes connected with mine. "Cassie?"

"Lucas, I found you," I muttered as I wrapped my arms around his neck and pulled him close to me. There were cuts and bruises all over his body and I knew that with time, they would heal but it didn't stop me from worrying about him.

The comforting moment only lasted a moment before he pulled back from me with a frown. "What are you doing in here, Cassie?"

"I came to make sure you were okay... aren't you glad to see me?"

He seemed taken back that I was there, and for a moment, I thought I saw pleasure in his eyes upon seeing me but it quickly disappeared and was replaced by something else that I didn't understand. "Cassie, you can't be here. You need to leave."

I opened and closed my mouth to respond, but nothing came out. I had thought he would have been happy to see him considering it had been so long but instead of happiness, he was frowning and telling me to leave.

"I'm not leaving," I replied flatly with my hand on my hip as I stared at him in disbelief. "I came to check on you. It was brutal out there, and I wanted to make sure you were safe."

Agitation and annoyance flowed off him as somewhere within the locker room laughter echoed, and I realized that there must have been people listening to our exchange which only made him even more upset that I was here. "I'm not a fucking two-year-old, Cassie. I don't need you to come check on me. You being here makes me look weak, and complicates everything I'm trying to do."

"What are you talking about?" I gasped trying to understand what was so wrong with me being here. "Girls do it all the time..."

"Yes! Exactly! Girls, Cassie... fucking girls. You're still mentally eighteen, Cassie. You may be twenty on earth, but you're not on earth anymore. Not to mention twenty year olds don't do shit like this and your immature behavior is really starting to make me wonder if you're even ready for the future you're supposed to have. Now leave, and don't do this shit again."

My heart ached at his words as he grabbed his white shirt from the bench and pulled it over his head. He was still just as gorgeous as I remembered, and yet I couldn't understand why he seemed so cold toward me. I guess he had a point but at the same time I hadn't meant to act immature. I was genuinely worried for him, and he was scolding me like I was a child.

Stepping closer to him, I lowered my voice into a whisper. "Tell me you're only acting like this to throw them off. You don't mean that..."

He paused for a moment before his brows knitted together and a heavy breath escaped him. "I'm being serious, Cassie. I know what you're looking for, but I already told you where I stood with things. I am participating in this contest like everyone else, and if I don't win, then I'm not worthy of you. End of story. Now fucking leave and don't come back."

"Lovers quarrel—" a mischievous and annoying voice commented behind me. "Here I thought this competition was going to be fair."

Turning around, I took in my cousin, who stared at me with a lust-filled gaze I hadn't wanted to see. His body leaned up against the far wall as he used a towel to wipe off his hands while he raked his eyes up and down my body. "Cousin... I don't know what you're referring to."

"Oh, don't play coy with me, Cassie. I am aware of what he is to you."

Before I could address his comment, Lucas stepped forward with his fists clenched at his side. "I can assure you there is nothing going on. I was just telling Cassie it wasn't appropriate for her to be here and that she didn't need to come back."

The tone of his voice was demanding and cold, and as I stared between the two men, I had to hold back tears of anger that threatened to fall down my face from the way Lucas had spoken to me, and in the end, all I could do was lash out in anger. "You can both go fuck yourselves."

I didn't bother to hear anything else they had to say as I stormed past them back through the locker room and out the door back into the cool fresh air. I was a fool to think going in there to check on Lucas was a good idea. I had allowed myself to be made fun of and ridiculed and all for what? To have a man I care about speak to me as if I was nothing?

Sansa had been right, and there was no way she was going to let me live this down.

I walked forward toward the city from the outskirts where the arena lay. My mind reeled over what had just happened as my heart clenched knowing that things had indeed changed between Lucas and me. I had hoped that he would still make exceptions to come see me even though he was in the contest, but of course, that had only been wishful thinking.

The moment my feet hit the cobbled steps leading toward my building the tears of frustration that I had been holding back slowly began to leak through. I may have been immortal but I still had mortal feelings. "God, how could I be so stupid..."

"Talking to yourself again?" a familiar voice asked from within the garden walls of wildflowers marble statues. Looking around, I quickly wiped the loose tears from my eyes until Finnick came into sight.

"Are you following me?" I snapped without meaning to sound as harsh as I did. "I'm really not in the mood to play games, Finn."

The tall, godly figure of Finn came properly into view as he strode forward in loose white and blue linen clothing that was more ornate than what I was accustomed to seeing. His white hair was partially up, and loosely hung down around his face is waves highlighting his chiseled jaw and piercing eyes. Even with his clothing that seemed so simple but clung to him in certain areas, accenting the rigid well built muscles of his body made me mentally pause in my steps to admire him.

He was gorgeous, but something about him still made me wary.

"Cassie, what's wrong?" There was a seriousness of concern in his voice as he stepped toward me. His hand reached out to wipe a stray tear from my cheek as he stared into my eyes with the same celestial glowing hues I was so accustomed to seeing in my own reflection.

"Nothing, I'm fine. It's just been a very long day..." I replied trying to avoid having an awkward conversation with him. Typically, I wouldn't want to speak with him at all, but right now his presence was honestly comforting.

"Cassie, I can tell something is wrong with you. Let's go to my room... I'll have them make some tea and we can talk about things."

Shaking my head, I tried to refuse him, but he took my hand nonetheless and pulled me forward. I wasn't sure what to expect, but no matter how much I found myself uncertain about what he was asking of me I couldn't help but wonder why it also felt right.

Chapter Twenty-six

Lucas

Guilt filled me once more at the way I had just disregarded Cassie like I did, but the moment she left I was faced with an evil I didn't want to address. Mani stood there staring at me with a wicked grin on his face as if he had something to say. Not that I cared about what he had to address with me. He had become nothing but a problem this entire time.

From his ridiculous comments to the boosting remarks of how he would make Cassie bend her knee to him. All I wanted to do was beat the living shit out of this man, but I knew that would get me nowhere. It was more than likely exactly what he was looking for and I couldn't allow him to win one over on me.

Grabbing my things I pushed past him, bumping his shoulder causing him to laugh.

"Jesus, Vega. I know you are sweet on that girl but come on, man. You and I both know you don't stand a chance with her. You had one and fucking blew it instead of being a real man."

Spinning around on my feet, I narrowed my eyes at him with anger. He had no idea what I had been through with Cassie and the fact he thought he knew only pissed me off further. His amused and sadistic gaze let me know this was exactly the reaction he wanted. I decided to stay a step ahead of him and simply smiled. "If you want my seconds, all you have to do is ask."

"Seconds? To me, it seems like she has you sucking on her tit like a babe to its mother."

Clenching my fists at my side I stepped forward, watching Mani straighten himself as if he was preparing to square off with me. I wanted more than anything to beat the shit out of Mani considering he had been nothing but a pain in my ass lately. However, if I did that there was a chance that I'd be thrown out of the games, and that was the last thing that I wanted to happen.

"You have a lot to say for someone who will never get the chance at the throne," I replied watching the grin on Mani's face fall. "How does it feel to be passed up as heir, Mani?"

"You little shit," he snarled before the laughter of other men echoed down the halls. People were coming, and Mani cared very much about his image. There was no way that he was going to allow something to happen that could ruin his image. Not that I was worried.

"That's what I thought." I chuckled shaking my head. "Why don't you just keep your fucking mouth closed when it comes to Cassie. If there is anyone who doesn't deserve her, it's you."

Turning my back on Mani with confidence, I made my way out of the locker room. I wasn't worried about what Mani would do. There was nothing he could do to me that would make any of this shit worse than it already was.

Slamming my hands against the door, I watched it swing open as I stepped out into the cool afternoon air. One thing about this place I loved is that it never really got hot. Letting out a heavy breath, I tried to re-examine what it was that had transpired today.

I had lost my first round in the strength and agility games. There were two more that would take place different from the first, and I couldn't afford to lose either. Losing another match would mean losing my chance with Cassie, and while she was sometimes a pain in the ass, she was my pain in the ass.

Perhaps I was hard on her, but it was only because I didn't want her to think I couldn't do this. I loved Cassie more than anything, and if that meant being tough on her then so be it.

Turning towards the city, I made my way back home to try and cool off and figure out my next plan of action. The other men all had people to help coach them and prepare for this shit, but I was on my own. Not a single soul would help me considering what I had done to Cassie before.

They believed me to be evil. The whole like-father,like-son concept.

I was nothing like my father, and if I won this, I could show them how much I wasn't. I'd stand by Cassie's side and help her to rule this place if it came down to it. I'd father her children and spend every waking moment of every day making things up to her. She deserved the best, and I would be the best... but only for her.

Giving up wasn't an option; eventually, I hoped she could forgive me.

Cassie

When Finnick asked me to come with him I didn't feel like I had a choice. My emotional state made me feel hollow. Once again I acted immature as Lucas called it, and I had thought by being bold and straightforward forward I was showing these people that I could be the ruler they wanted.

But of course, I just fucked that up like everything else around me.

"You're deep in thoughts, little one. Care to share what's on your mind?" Finnick asked as we walked down the hallway towards his room. There was a calmness about Finnick I hadn't noticed before and as much as I didn't want to share my personal thoughts, I couldn't help but feel comfortable around him. So much so that I did want to share.

"I wouldn't even know where to start," I mumbled as we turned the corner of the hallway and came to the navy blue double doors of Finnick's room. I had never been to this part of the palace and standing here beside Finnick, I wondered why I hadn't. I had assumed I'd seen this entire place before Finnick ever came here, but I suppose I was wrong.

Stepping into his room, I was instantly blown away by its appearance. The room was base white yes, but there were open windows everywhere lined with colored curtains in a variety of colors. From oranges and blues to yellows and reds. I literally felt like I had stepped into India or Morocco with the beautiful array of vibrant colors. Even his bed, which sat far off in the corner, was round and decorated with tons of pillows of all shapes and blankets that seemed to go on for days.

It was definitely not what I had been expecting and from my open-mouthed expression, Finnick seemed to notice as well. "You like it?"

Did I like it? I honestly didn't even know what to say.

"Yes," I muttered glancing at him once more. "It's beautiful."

His celestial eyes glanced around the room once more before turning back to me with amusement dancing within them. "I suppose it is."

"I take it you live like this all the time?"

Shaking his head, he chuckled before heading towards a small wet bar that was on the far left side of his room near another door that I was assuming was his bathroom. Slowly, I moved forward checking out the variety of trinkets and photos he had displayed. I hadn't taken Finnick to be a man who was sentimental, but from the looks of what I'm guessing was family portraits, he was. "Is this your family?"

Glancing at him, he looked over his shoulder at me and smiled. "Yes. That is my mother and father and my siblings."

"Oh," the muttered reply was barely audible as I continued my slow stroll around his room. It was the clink of crystal that caught my attention once more, and as I turned, I found Finnick lounging upon an oddly shaped chair that reminded me of a bean bag.

"So, back to what's on your mind. Why don't you sit down and talk to me."

Finnick had initially come off as an arrogant man who seemed to hold his position in high regard, but right now he was showing me a side of him that I was curious to know if most people saw. "Why are you so interested in what's on my mind?"

"Because I find you intriguing," he replied with a hum of amusement that made my eyes roll before I took a seat on an oversized white fur chair across from him.

"Intriguing... I'm not sure if that's a term most people would refer to me as."

"Is that so?" he replied softly, "what would most people call you?"

There were so many things that most people would call me, and for some reason him asking this caused the anger from my conversation with Lucas slowly began to bubble up. "Oh, I don't know... a bitch, stubborn, self-centered, and immature."

Venom laced that last word and with a low whistle, Finnick laughed. "Immature... you said that word as if it was fresh in your mind. Did you have an argument with someone?"

"It doesn't matter." The quick response made his brow raise as a smirk crossed his lips that made me huff with irritation. He asked me here to talk and all he seemed to want to do was find amusement in me. "Did you just bring me here for your entertainment because if that's the case, I'm not interested."

"Is that what you think this is?" he asked, his smirk turning into a frown as he sipped upon the lilac colored liquid in his glass. "If I wanted amusement, I'd have a whore brought to me."

"Oh, you're one of those kinds of men."

Finnick frowned, his eyes slightly narrowing as a scoff left his lips. "No. I'm not."

The tension and silence that filled the space between us was unsettling for a moment, and the thought to leave crossed my mind more than once. I hadn't meant to sound bitchy when I asked what I did but the questions he was asking were more than annoying.

"I'm sorry, for snapping at you," I finally sighed as I ran my hand over my face. "There's just so much going on right now and it's so overwhelming. I feel like everything I do is wrong, and when I think I'm helping I'm not."

"So stop helping." The answer he gave sounded so simple, but at the same time complicated. I didn't even know I was really trying to help until it happened and by that time it was too late.

With a heavy breath, I cast my eyes away from him as I fiddled with my hands. "I wish I knew how to quit helping. It seems like I just keep doing it no matter how much I try to keep to myself."

As my eyes met his again, a look of understanding seemed to pass between us I hadn't been expecting. I wasn't sure why he stared at me the way he did but I felt comfortable with him. "Perhaps you simply need a break from this place for a few days."

"Yeah, that could happen." I laughed, "Asgard is the only place I'm allowed to go, didn't you know?

My comment didn't seem to amuse him as he furrowed his brows at me in confusion. "I don't understand. Why can't you go anywhere else? Are you a prisoner to this realm?"

I opened and closed my mouth to say something but didn't have an answer as to why I couldn't. No one had ever really said that I couldn't leave this place per say. Just that I couldn't ever live on earth again, or something like that. "No, I guess not. I just am immortal or something."

"Or something?" He laughed, "Cassie, you're not a prisoner to this place. I don't see why you can't go somewhere."

"Tell that to Odin... he acts like I can't. I mean, I went and saw my family on earth a few months ago and I didn't even get twenty-four hours before I was forcefully brought back here."

Making a face he wrinkled his nose with a frown. "Because that's not toxic."

A small burst of laughter escaped me and I quickly covered my mouth to stop it. The reaction made a grin appear across Finnick's lips as a twinkle lit his eyes. "I like hearing you laugh, you should do it more often."

Again I rolled my eyes with my own smirk before I stood to my feet smoothing out my blouse, preparing to leave. "I think I should be going, Finn."

"Are you sure? You only just got here," he replied, placing his glass down as he stood as well.

The situation went from comfortable to slightly uncomfortable really fast and I wasn't sure exactly why. Perhaps it was because of the hungry gaze that Finnick gave me as his eyes traveled over my body or maybe it was because I enjoyed his presence so much that it slightly frightened me. "I'm sure..."

Nodding, he stepped closer to me with a small sigh. "Before you go can I ask you one more thing?"

"Yeah," I replied softly. His hand reached up to gently brush down over my arm causing a shiver to run down my spine I hadn't been expecting. "Ask what you want..."

"If you could go anywhere right now, where would it be?"

No one had asked me what I wanted in a while. Of course others had asked me things that pertained to the games but it was never about what I truly wanted. Taking a moment to think about what he asked, I gazed down at my feet with hesitation.

"If I could go anywhere... I'd love to go home."

"Home?" He questioned with a hint of surprise in his tone, "why there?"

Shrugging my shoulders, I gazed at him once more thinking about my family and how much I missed them. They were everything to me, and being separated from them was taking a toll on me more than I wanted to admit.

"I miss them, Finn. Family is everything, and being here—I don't honestly have that."

There was a sad expression on his face as he stared at me, and taking my hand within his he said four words I wasn't expecting. "I can fix that."

Chapter Twenty-seven

Finnick

In my entire life, I had never met a woman who puzzled me as much as Cassie did. Watching her leave my room I couldn't help but want to figure out every last thing about her. The problem was that while I was here, I was having to share her attention with two other men that I knew she had deep relationships with. Something that I wasn't privy to obtain yet.

For days my mind had been going over how I could get closer to her. The games were only a cover for being here. Today when I faced my opponent, I didn't even need to move to know that I would win. The man I faced was nothing but a boy and the moment he launched himself forward, I took him down with ease.

I was hundreds of years older than they were, and my skills far surpassed anything that any of them would ever have. I may not have been a god, but I was godly in other ways.

Turning back towards my wet bar, I poured another glass of the lilac concoction into my glass and chased it back with a sigh. Cassie had made it clear that she missed her family and wasn't able to see them. I hadn't known it was impossible for an immortal to travel to other realms but perhaps that is simply what they had told her to keep her here in Asgard.

If that was the case... it was fucked up.

A new determination set into my heart as a smile crossed my face. If she wanted to go home then I could take her, and I would be her chaperone, which would give me time to get to know who the real Cassie was.

There was no game to what I was doing. Cassie was my mate, and the woman I was destined to be with. I had foreseen her coming for so long and now that I had my eyes on her, there was no way that I was going to let her go.

As I placed my glass down, I quickly exited my quarters and made my way down the hallway in search of one person who could help me with what I wanted. As much as I would normally have just taken her wherever she wanted to go, I wasn't in my realm. Odin would have my head if I simply let her go where she wanted.

So that meant I needed his permission.

Aro, my guard and oldest friend, matched my footsteps in silence as he followed me toward the main courtyard where Odin frequented this time of day. Since the moment I arrived in Asgard, I had Aro follow and keep track of every single person here of importance. No matter what my father had said about this place being safe, or Odin being his oldest friend—I didn't trust it.

"Are you sure that you want to do this, Finn?" he asked, causing my gaze to turn to him, taking in his tall muscular stature and long shoulder-length black hair that was pulled back into half updo with silver pieces woven in. It was different seeing him out of his usual armor and not with his sword but I was pleased to have him with me regardless.

"Why do you think I shouldn't?"

The question made him scoff as we turned a corner, the courtyard door coming into view as the sound of Odin's cheerful bellowing voice and laughter sauntered towards us through the air. "I think that you are infatuated with the woman, and are grasping at straws... Your Highness."

One thing about Aro that I loved was his straightforward responses and boldness. Deep laughter of my own escaped me as I glanced at him once more, shaking my head. "My dear man, this is the fun part of courting. Who knows, maybe if you're lucky you can see the dangerous side.

Aro was obviously not amused by what I was saying but his silence let me know that he was going along with my plan, for now.

Stepping out into the courtyard, I took in Odin's figure laid upon a lounge chair with Frigga and a few other women and men. Curtains billowed in the breeze as they ate and drank their way into happiness. However, as Odin's eyes met mine I saw a twinkle of surprise and a smile that made me hopeful that he would agree to what I was asking.

"Prince Finnick, how are you today?"

"My lord Odin, I'm well. I was wondering if I could borrow a moment of your time," I replied with a smile as I made my way towards him only to have him embrace me before gesturing towards a fur-lined seating area on the ground.

"Of course, of course." His eyes connected with the other figures around and quickly they departed. "Come sit and tell me what's on your mind."

I didn't hesitate when I moved forward, taking my seat upon the thick lush blankets and oversized chairs that littered the area underneath the awning. Speaking to Odin was important because it was the only way that I was going to be able to get what I wanted. Something that of course, everybody else might have a problem with but for me, I had a special degree of importance and in Odin's eye, I was the son of his oldest friend and the alliance that he had with my kingdom was important.

"I wanted to see if I could speak to you about Cassie," I replied as I looked at him, watching as his facial expression turned from one of happiness to slight concern. His brows furrowed slightly as a soft breath escaped him that almost sounded like a sigh.

"What has she done now? I know that she's been quite difficult lately but I was hoping that she would have adjusted by now."

Hearing him ask what she had done came as a surprise because as far as I was aware, there were too many issues that Cassie had been a part of unwillingly for her to be a problem. She may have been immature in the way she acted on certain things but she was new to the way we lived.

Perhaps Odin didn't quite see that. "She hasn't done anything wrong. On the contrary, I noticed that she was a little out of sorts lately, and appeared to be stressed. I had a solution that might perhaps help her... adjust to her new role."

His brows raised as a look of understanding crossed his face, a smile picking the corner of his lips as he nodded. "By all means, if you have any suggestions, I'm all ears."

"Well, from the little that I know about your granddaughter, she's slightly uncomfortable being here. Given the circumstances of her arrival, it's only understandable that she would feel out of place. She wasn't raised the way we were and though her parents are the Alpha's of their pack... Earth packs aren't like the old traditional packs; the hierarchy is a bit freelanced, if you will. Which would be the reason why she doesn't have the same etiquette values that the rest of us do. Something that I am sure even Freya wouldn't be able to address with her. Perhaps having her go back to her roots and grasp a better understanding of what happened to her there would make things better."

It pained me to say what I did to Odin, but I had to make him believe that Cassie needed help. I had to make him believe that there was a need for her to improve and that I could help her. My little mate was an amazing woman, and in my opinion I didn't think she realized just the amount of potential she had and if this was what I had to do to help her then so be it.

I was going to let others bring her down when I had hope I could help her be who she was destined to be.

Odin sat silent for a moment as if pondering over what I was saying. His mouth opened and closed before he looked off into the distance and nodded once more. "So you think that she has some underlying issues that need to be addressed in order for her to be able to act more properly in her position."

"Essentially, yes. I think that everything that had happened with her family and from what I understand, her friend... caused a lot of issues originally not seen. She did say that when she went back before she wasn't allowed to stay long enough."

"Yes, that is true. She wasn't but it was just timing with the trilogy games. Not to mention, I didn't want her to get comfortable with the idea of being able to stay," he replied in a manner that made it seem there was more on his mind than just simply it being the games.

"Is that why she thinks she can't go back?" I asked with curiosity, watching the mischievous gaze in his eyes turn towards his cup with a smile.

"Perhaps, I shouldn't have told her that but I have to protect the future of this realm. She was chosen to be what she is… I can't have things off balance. You of all people know the importance of preserving the lineage."

I did know what he meant, but what I didn't understand was why Cassie. He had many other children and grandchildren who should have been in line for the throne before her. Yet, for some reason, he dismissed all of them to put her in place.

Something that didn't make sense.

"I do understand what you mean, but I don't think she will. I mean no offense by this, but if we want her to be compliant, we need to treat her as the woman she is supposed to be. Let her take more of a stance in what you do on a regular basis. Let her know more about the other realms. Right now, the only thing she was slightly allowed to do was the games, and that is just a minor task." Odin's demeanor turned dismissive as he stared at the drink in his hand without responding to me right away.

I wasn't trying to tell him how to run his realm, but he had to know that I had a point. If he wanted Cassie to stop from acting out and making immature choices, then he had to treat her in a way that would force her to grow up. Hard truths bring better understanding. Lying to her was going to do nothing to help her grow up.

"If I were to say that you were accurate in what you are saying, what would be your suggestion for fixing things? You seem to know more about this than I do." Odin's comment was slightly sarcastic, and when his eyes met mine I could tell he wasn't exactly pleased with the conversation we were having. Yet, instead of lashing out in anger, he was giving me a chance to properly give a suggestion to his problems.

"Well, for one I would have a conversation with her explaining that she isn't bound to this realm." I replied, watching Oding laugh as if my suggestion was amusing.

"Out of the question. Until I can know for sure that she isn't going to run, I can't afford to have that happen, and Cassie is known to run when things get hard."

It was clear that Odin wasn't going to be easily persuaded, and his decision honestly irritated me. I was all for keeping things in line, but to lie to her was ridiculous. And from the whispers of that lingered the halls from the servants, this wasn't the first time he had done such—which honestly made me question his judgment as a ruler.

I nodded. "Well, perhaps letting her have a break from things to spend time on earth with her family. It could let her accept what happened to her and grow from her past. I'd have no problem accompanying her there as her chaperone."

"You?" He laughed at the wrinkles at the corner of his eyes creasing with the amusement he found in my statement. "You would travel to earth with her? Have you ever been there?"

In all reality, I hadn't, but I had studied much about it growing up and had no doubts I could maneuver around it easily. "No, but I am well versed in their ways."

A deep bellow escaped Odin that irritated me. He cackled like a hyena over the conversation and hearing his obvious self-doubt that I knew what I was doing was insulting. "I'll tell you what, Finnick. We have two weeks before the next trials... I will let you venture there with her, but I will send my best guard with you as well. Just to make sure no issues arise with her returning... she is known to be a handful."

"I'm sure I can handle her—" I replied only to have Odin hold his hand up dismissing what I was going to say as that same mischievous glint reappeared in his eyes.

"Don't be so sure about that, Finnick. You don't know Cassie as I do. It may not seem that I know my granddaughter, but I can promise you that I do." Standing to his feet, I followed the same action. His eyes left mine as he gestured to a small blonde-haired woman with large brown eyes and a soft smile. "This is Grace, tell her what you need and she will ensure it is ready for your trip."

"Thank you, Odin. I assure you by the time Castor comes back, she will be a changed woman."

Or at least I was counting that she would.

Chapter Twenty-eight

Cassie

When Ansley informed me that I was to pack a bag and would be traveling without any information, I hadn't expected that it was going to be with Finn. In fact, I was shocked to see him standing outside the portal gates with an overly excited expression on his face. I didn't have a clue where I was going, but it was clear wherever it was, I wasn't going anywhere alone.

"What's going on?" I asked as I approached Finn with a confused and furrowed expression. I glanced around taking note of the dark-haired man that had been Finn's shadow since the moment he got here.

"We're going on a trip," he replied cheerfully, "aren't you excited?"

Stopping in my tracks, I raised a brow as a smile of amusement crossed my lips. "With you? Are you messing with me?"

"No, I'm not. We're going somewhere you're going to like."

There was no way that Odin was allowing this, and I had suddenly become very hesitant about this entire situation. What if Finn was trying to get me into some kind of trouble and roped Ansley into getting me to go without approval? A wave of unease flowed over me until I spotted a familiar figure walking down the marble steps of the building heading straight for me.

"Silas, what are you doing here?" Silas didn't seem to be in the mood for idle chit-chat as he grunted in disapproval of whatever was going on and made his way toward the portal without a single word. "Alrighty then…"

"Silas, I wasn't aware that you were coming along?" Finnick said aloud, causing me to wonder if even he wasn't aware of the golden dragon's presence in whatever outing this was.

Seemingly annoyed by all the questions, his shoulders sagged as the portal opened and as he turned to face us, his eyes darted between mine and Finn's figure. "Odin told you a guard would be going, and unfortunately, I drew the short straw. Now, can we get going?"

I didn't understand why Silas had such a bad attitude about everything. He seemed irritated that he was having to go with us and when I turned to Finn, he didn't seem pleased by it either. I still didn't have the slightest clue as to where we were going, but considering the tension in the air between the two men, I decided not to press and just simply follow their lead.

Silas being there, however, did make me feel slightly more comfortable about the situation. Because Silas was going, that did indeed mean that Odin had given permission. I highly doubted that Silas would accompany Finn and try to take me somewhere without Odin's permission.

We stepped through the portal and I was once again transported to another realm, a place I had no clue existed until the moment we stepped through the other side and I realized that I indeed did know this place. Once again, everything looked completely different, the overgrowth more so prominent. However, new structures and the distance made me realize that my pack had been busy.

As my feet moved me forward onto the grassy green area between the woodland and the pack's actual property, I couldn't help it turn and look over my shoulder. "You brought me home?"

"I did, Cassie. I figured that you could use a little bit of separation from everything going on with the games and that perhaps visiting your family would do you some good." Finn was quick to step forward and take responsibility for the whole idea, but I couldn't help but wonder why Odin, my grandfather, would allow something when he was so adamant that I couldn't stay longer than I had before.

Something felt slightly off about the entire situation, but instead of dwelling on what was actually going on, I ignored both men and started running as fast as my legs could carry me straight to where the pack house was. To see my family again was something I had dreamed of and I couldn't wait till I ran into my father's arms.

The howling sound of wolves echoed through the night air as the stars above me twinkled and the moon sat high and full within the sky. They knew that I was here, and though I couldn't hear them anymore, I ran harder and faster, only to be stopped dead in my tracks by three wolves who growled at me.

I didn't understand why they were growling at me. I was the daughter of the Alpha's. There was no way that they didn't recognize me. I stood there utterly confused, watching them slowly crouch towards me with their ears back and their teeth bared, I suddenly became very uneasy about the entire situation.

I didn't have to worry, though, because Silas's body was quickly in front of me, and as he bared a sword in his hand. The wolves prepared to launch at him, my throat constricting, enabling me to scream at them before the sound of my brother echoed through the distance.

"Enough!" I couldn't see him, but the wolves quickly backed away, their ears returning to their normal position before they turned darting off into the woods to my left. I couldn't understand why they had acted that way towards me, considering I was my brother's sister and they acted as if I was an enemy on their land.

Silas quickly put away the sword at his side, sheathing it once more as he turned to me with a furrowed expression that seemed slightly angry, but also concerned for my well-being. There wasn't time to question him as a shadowed figure slowly came over the hill and I realized it was my brother standing before me. As soon as his eyes landed on me, a look of excitement washed over his face before he ran towards me, throwing his arms around my waist as he lifted me into the air and spun me in a circle.

"Cassie, what are you doing here?"

Shrugging my shoulders, I didn't honestly know what to tell him. "I don't know. They told me that I was able to come and see you guys and God, I've missed you so much. There's so much that has happened and I've been so lost without you guys."

Tears brimmed my eyes as thin came to stand by my side. "Hello, Pollux. My name is Prince Finnick of the Fae realm." He held out his hand towards my brother, who quickly stepped away from me and looked between him and Silas with slight confusion before his eyes fell on me once more.

"Are you with both of them, or should I be concerned that there's something that's going on I'm not quite getting yet?" he asked me and instantly I knew what he meant.

"Oh my God, no, I'm not with them both. Are you kidding me?" I stated quite quickly, with astonishment in my tone, feeling absolutely shocked that he would insinuate I was with both men.

"Well, I mean, you could take after our mother, so it's always best to ask instead of assuming."

The chuckle that left his lips was reciprocated by Finnick, who stared at me with absolute amusement, dancing within his eyes. However, Silas did not seem amused by the comment whatsoever. "I think we should get Cassie inside, where she can be reunited with her parents."

Pollux nodded his head and gestured for us to follow. I, of course, quickly fell into step with my brother, who began telling me about the different arrangements that they had made the pack and that his child was doing well. Which completely took me by surprise, considering Trixie had only been gone a week or so.

"That doesn't make sense. There's no way she had the baby. I just saw her over a week ago."

"Cassie, you forget the time works differently between our realms. To you, it's only been a week. For us, it has been a year," he replied, making me realize that time indeed was different. In Asgard, I was still 18. But here, I was far younger than my brother. Though he looked his age, I did not.

"How are our siblings?" I asked, eager to see them again. "Are they doing okay? It's been so long since I've seen them."

My brother stayed quiet as he looked at me and then the house that lay in front of us, seemingly so different from how I had remembered it being. I knew there had been changes before the last time I was here, but now I could tell that Pollux and Trixie had to put their touches upon the home and it looked magnificent. "Think that it's best you wait and speak to our mother about that. She can fill you in more as she keeps tabs on them better than I do."

There was something in the way that he spoke that made me wonder if there were things going on that I hadn't been privy to. But again, it wasn't like communication was easy between our realms. Instead, I was constantly left wondering what was going on and how everybody was. And as time grew on, everybody on Earth grew older—with me back on Asgard, remaining the same.

The moment that I walked through the door, I had anticipated everybody running to greet me, but instead the house was quiet and as I moved towards the living room, I realized that so much of this place was different.

The crackling of the fire coming from the living room drew my attention, and sitting on a gray corner sofa was Trixie, whose hair was no longer the vibrant blue I remembered but instead it had dulled to reflect the age that had caught up with her.

Her green eyes turned to me, and I realized that she was much older than I had remembered her a week ago. Instead, it looked as if years had been put upon her instead of a girl of eighteen. I remembered she looked like she was in her mid to late twenties, as if stress and time had worn her down. "Oh my god... Cassie."

Trixie jumped to her feet, throwing down the book she had been reading and wrapped her arms around me pulling me into a hug. I was stunned by the situation, and as I hugged her back, I realized that I really was missing out on everything.

"Trixie... I have been so worried about you."

She stared at me for a moment with a somber expression as she nodded her head, turning her gaze to my brother. "I'm sorry I have been away so long. So much has happened since I last saw you."

"It honestly hasn't been that long, Trixie. It's only been a week," I replied trying to find a polite way to tell her what's been going on and realizing quickly that no matter what I said, the way we once lived together in Asgard wasn't going to reflect how things were here.

"A week?" she whispered with a frown as her brows knitted together and she rubbed her hand across her face. "I almost forgot that times were different... I take it the games aren't over yet?"

Shaking my head, I sighed heavily. "No, they aren't. I brought people with me though."

Turning, I looked over my shoulder towards Silas before looking back at Trixie. "My guard came with me."

Trixie broke into laughter at my comment before going to hug Silas. "It's good to see you, Silas. I have to say I don't think I ever imagined you coming to this realm again."

Silas frowned at her comment with an irritated expression. "Trust me... I never wanted to, but I didn't exactly have a choice."

Trixie looked back at me once more with a question glance as I rolled my eyes. "Finnick wanted to bring me back here to spend time with my family. The only way I was allowed to go from what I'm guessing is with a guard, and Silas as he said 'drew the short straw'."

The moment I said Finnick's name, Trixie went pale as her eyes darted towards the vacant area behind Silas. "Do you mean—" she whispered as Finn's body came into view. A shocked eek noise left Trixie's throat as she dropped to her knees before him. "Prince Finnick, my apologies. I didn't know you were coming."

It wasn't like a Luna to bow before anyone and the low growl that left my brother's throat showed he wasn't pleased by what she was doing. Finn quickly realized this as he stooped down to Trixie with his hand upon her arm forcing her to stand. "Please, Trixie. You're the Luna of this pack. You do not need to bow to me or use formalities."

"Yeah, this is just a normal visit." I quickly added, stepping towards my brother, who looked more angry and confused than anything. "Finn is the prince of the Fae realm, Pollux... it's Trixie's royalty."

Realization crossed his face as his temper simmered down and he quickly wrapped an arm around Trixie's waist pulling her towards him. "I see. My apologies, it isn't customary for a Luna to bow to anyone."

Finn quickly waved him off with a smile, not seeming to care about what happened. "It's okay, don't worry about it. I probably should have warned you ahead of time, but it didn't cross my mind that Trixie would react to seeing me the way she did. It's my fault for not saying something sooner."

To hear him admit that this was his fault was shocking. I didn't take him for a man that would act that way and by the look on Trixies face, she didn't either.

"What are you guys doing here anyway? I didn't think Odin would allow you to come back."

With an open mouth, I looked to Silas and Finn for answers before closing it shrugging my shoulders. "Honestly, I'm just as surprised by all of this as you. But I'm not going to complain. I miss this place, and it's exactly what I needed after everything that's happened lately."

"Oh, my," Trixie said as she pried herself from my brother's arms. "Why don't I show you all to the spare rooms and in the morning, we will have a long talk just the two of us."

Nodding my head, I started to follow Trixie before I stopped realizing I still hadn't seen my parent's, who should have been here. Looking over my shoulder at Pollux once more, I frowned with confusion. "Lux... where are our parents if they aren't here?"

His face fell for a moment before he cleared his throat. "A lot has changed since you left last time, Cassie. You will see them soon, but for now... rest."

There was something cryptic about his message that didn't settle well with me, but instead of prying, I nodded my head and continued with the others towards the staircase. An uneasy feeling in the lower of my belly that made me wonder if I wasn't going to like what he had to say.

I had only just arrived and already I felt like I had hit a brick wall.

One, I was an aunt now, and knowing that I missed out on the child's first year was heartbreaking. Two, my parents weren't here to great me, and the feeling that something was wrong lingered through me like an a serpent wrapping around its prey. I wanted to know what was going on, but I also knew I had to be patient.

Patience was the only way I'd get anything from this situation, and all I wanted was answers.

Chapter Twenty-nine

Cassie

Waking early the next morning, I had anticipated my mother being there the moment that my eyes opened, but instead, when I awoke I was simply greeted by the dim lighting of the sun shining through the room. Things were definitely different here and as much as I wanted to remember them as they were the day that I had left. I knew the time had passed so much in the years that I was gone here.

Even though it only felt like weeks to me.

It honestly made sense the reason why the wolves had greeted me the way they did. The moment that I had died in Asgard, my connection to this pack was severed and every single wolf that was within it felt my life force go. People thought wolves were monsters. Uncontrollable wild animals that would kill you in a heartbeat.

But nobody knew the depth of how our family worked, how connected we really were. It had always bothered me growing up knowing that while we held deeper family values than most humans did, we were the ones that were seen as predatory.

Sliding from my bed I padded my way toward the connecting bathroom to my room. Though I had usually stayed in bed longer in the mornings because I dreaded going to be social with people in Asgard, I was looking forward to what lay ahead for the day.

I wanted to see the pack, talk with Trixie, and find out everything that I had missed.

My arrival wasn't as I had expected it to be, and I knew that with time people would adjust to me being here, but until then I would have to deal with being the outsider. The girl who had died and stepped foot back into a realm that hadn't seen me in so long.

Half an hour later and ready for the day, I made my way downstairs to hear the soft words of Silas and my brother in the kitchen. I wasn't sure what they were talking about but the moment I stepped into the kitchen their eyes turned toward me, their conversation stopped.

"Good morning, you two," I replied with a curious gaze as I spotted the coffee pot on the counter and felt the urge to cry having missed the coffee on earth. The shit they had in Asgard was okay, but the moment I found out it was mushroom-based, I lost all hope of real coffee.

Grabbing a cup from the rack next to the pot, I eagerly poured some from the glass carafe and put it to my lips moaning with pleasure as I inhaled the familiar aroma, teasing my taste bud until the moment I placed my lips upon the cup and savored its contents.

"Jesus, Cass... did you not have coffee this entire time?" Pollux asked me with a chuckle that I refused to allow to ruin my moment.

"You tell me... if you had found out that all the coffee you had been drinking was mushroom-based, would you miss this?"

Wrinkling his nose, he glanced towards Silas, who shrugged his shoulders indifferently, "I suppose, I would. Did you sleep well?"

"Yeah," I replied with a nod. "I do like what you have done with the pack house. The rooms are very nice."

"They're not as nice as the ones in Asgard. Trust me... I have tried to find a mattress to match the bed I had there and it doesn't exist here on earth."

Raising a brow, a smile crossed my lips. "Well, maybe the mattress fairy can bring you one."

"Would that be the royal that's with you?" he replied, causing me to choke as I thought of Finn with wings and a tiara delivering mattresses.

"I resent that comment," a voice said from the doorway causing both Pollux and me to turn to stare at Finn, who looked absolutely gorgeous in normal clothing. Dark wash jeans, a black fitted t-shirt, and a man bun. I was in utter shock.

"Why would that be, Finnick?" Silas said coldly, causing me to wonder if the two of those men had issues they needed to desperately work out.

"Because I am Fae... I'm not a fucking fairy."

His statement didn't make sense, and as I went to open my mouth, another body entered the room carrying a small child, who I had been all too eager to meet. "Oh my god!" I squealed with excitement. "Is this her?"

The golden blonde hair and large blue eyes of the child captured my attention right away. She was beautiful and looked like the spitting image of her mother—for the most part.

"Yes," Trixie smiled as she kissed the side of her daughter's face. "This is Evelyn."

"She's beautiful," I replied in awe over how delicate the child looked. A smile crossed the little girl's face as she hid within the crook of her mother's neck. "I can't believe she is one already."

Trixie chuckled, staring at the child, "I know I say the same thing everyday."

Doing the calculations in my head, I tried to understand how long I had been away, and then when Trixie visited me. The numbers weren't adding up right and the more I thought about it, the more confused I became. "I would have thought she was older..."

Laughter escaped Trixie, but my brother must have understood where my mind was going and he was anything but amused. "I'll explain everything, Cassie. Don't worry. In the meantime, Pollux, sweetie, why don't you show both of the men around the pack? Cassie and I have a lot to catch up on."

There was silence as the three men looked at each other, seemingly not pleased with what Trixie said, probably because they didn't want to be around each other more than they had to be. But as Pollux sighed and Silas stood to his feet, I realized they weren't going to argue with her. She was the Luna of this pack, which meant that she deserved respect.

Clearing his throat, my brother looked at both men with an uncomfortable expression upon his face. "Gentlemen, if you will follow me this way."

It was so strange to see that Trixie literally had my brother's balls in a vise by the way he followed her orders. But I was glad to see that the young dickish man he once was now was replaced with what seemed to be an Alpha our people respected.

"Come on, Cassie… let's go to the sunroom. I'll have Gia bring us tea."

"Who's Gia?" I muttered as Trixie headed from the kitchen with me trailing behind her. The entire house was breathtaking, and I could tell that the floral and greenery that lined everything was nothing but touches of Trixie. It was clear that she missed certain aspects of her previous life and brought what she could here to the pack.

The moment that we cleared one room, I followed her out a white doo rway.The sun shined through glass windows that formed the walls of a large greenhouse I got a really clear view of how Trixie was doing. My mouth dropped open in shock at the size of the greenhouse. Floor to ceiling ivy climbed the pillars and the walls accented by vibrant colors of flowers that I honestly didn't know existed.

"Trixie, did you take flowers from Asgard?" I muttered as I turned my eyes towards her in concern. A sheepish grin crossed her face as she sat little Evelyn down within her play area.

"Not exactly, and don't worry. It's all concealed within this garden. Only a handful of people are allowed in here, and I take care of maintenance. It gives me something to do."

I wasn't sure how much I trusted that statement but taking a seat upon the white antique loveseat that was adorned with throw pillows and accompanied by two white chairs, I started to understand why she didn't come back.

"You never planned to come back to Asgard, did you?" I asked softly, catching her attention as she turned from speaking to a very short red haired girl with green eyes.

"I did…" she replied with hesitation as she opened and closed her mouth, "but then when I came back here, everything changed."

"What do you mean?"

I could tell by the look in her eyes that she was holding back something she wasn't quite ready to share. Something that seemed to conflict her green eyes that had dulled over the years, leaving a woman who had experienced too much. "When I came back, chaos had consumed this place, and I knew that I couldn't leave. Not to mention I was pregnant with Evelyn all that time I was away... almost two years had passed with me being gone, Cassie."

"You were pregnant for two years?" I gasped, not sure how that was possible.

Trixie laughed as Gia brought the tea back while setting the tray upon the small white wicker table in front of us. "Well, not technically. See, when I went to Asgard, I was the right timeframe, however when I came back and because Earth time moves faster than Asgard, it had been so long."

Realization kicked in as I stared at her wide-eyed and in shock. "Oh, Jesus, I take it my brother wasn't pleased you had been gone that long. Trixie, I'm sorry, I didn't realize—"

"Oh, Cassie, stop," she said softly with a smile on her lips as she waved off my apology. "It isn't your fault. I chose to stay and help you in Asgard. I'm just sorry I hadn't told you I wasn't coming back."

"It's okay, Trix. Your place is here with my brother and your family. I'm just glad that I could see you again. You seem so different, and to me it hasn't been that long."

Trixie scoffed slightly with a smile that didn't quite reach her eyes like it used to. There was something about the way that she looked down at the teacup in her hand that made me wonder what exactly had happened to change her. When I first met her, she was bright and bubbly and so full of life, and now she seemed so drained and worn down.

It broke my heart to see my friend this way and when our eyes met mine once more, I could see the tears that brimmed them. "You have no idea how much I've missed you as well, and how much I wished you had been here through everything that has happened over the past few years."

Quickly, I was to my feet, making my way across the small space between us. My hands found hers and as I pulled her and my embrace, giving her a warm hug, I tried to imagine what she had gone through. "Trixie, I'm here now. Tell me anything that you need to. I'm here for you no matter what."

Her soft giggle of laughter seemed almost sarcastic and forced as I pulled away and looked down into her eyes, watching her stare at me as if I wasn't really here. She furrowed her brows, wrinkling her nose before shrugging her shoulders, casually brushing me off to move.

The whole movement was awkward, and as she quickly stood to her feet, putting down the teacup, her eyes scanning towards her child before looking back at me. I knew something terrible must have really happened. "Cassie, I've waited for this moment for so long to tell you everything that has happened, but now that it's here, I don't even know where to begin."

"Well, just start from the top," I replied in a very nonchalant kind of way waiting for her to express to me what she had gone through. Whoever it was, I was here to help her handle it, to help her get through everything. The only problem was when she opened her mouth, I wasn't expecting what she would say next.

"Well, for starters, the moment that I left, I came back to find out that Ashley, your brother's ex, was trying to move her away into things. And on top of that, your mother was doing her best to make things work, but Hale refused to hand over the full title of Alpha until I had come back because he wasn't sure that Pollux was in his right mind. I suppose from what I've been told, he was slightly going crazy, lashing out at everybody. Oh, and then just to make things even better, Damien contracted a weird disease and is sick."

I could tell immediately the last part of that sentence she didn't mean to say by the way that her eyes went wide and her hand quickly flew to her mouth. I was at a loss for words, trying to understand what she meant, that my father was sick. I mean, I knew I was an Asgardian, but they could send me messages or something. There wasn't a way that they would keep something like this from me, was there?

"Wait a second. What do you mean my dad is sick? He can't be sick."

"I'm sorry. I didn't mean to tell you that. I promise. I'm so sorry," she said over and over again, apologizing as she came towards me but I held my hand up, stopping her in her tracks as I stood to my feet and anger began to bubble through me.

"Why didn't my brother tell me this the moment that he saw me? Why didn't anybody try to send me a message about what was going on?" My questions were valid and she seemed speechless.

"I wasn't supposed to tell you. Your mother said she wanted to be the one to tell you and your brother. He made me promise not to say anything, and now that I have, I know it's going to cause complications. I just. I was so angry and I... I didn't mean for it to come out."

Trixie was completely sincere in her words, and she must have said something to my brother through their mindlink which was odd because she was a pixie, and I had thought only those with the gene could do that. But before I knew it, my brothers bombarding figure came through the open doorway, causing me to look over my shoulder to see him, Silas and Finnick standing there, staring at me with concern on their face.

There wasn't much that my brother could say to me right now that wouldn't make me want to strangle him. Not only was he my brother, he was my twin, and he didn't even have the common courtesy to let me know that my father was sick. Taking a moment before I opened my mouth, I closed my eyes, patting my hands together as I tried to find the right words to say to him without screaming obscenities at him.

"Please tell me right now that you planned on informing me of my father's illness." When I opened my eyes, I saw Finn and Silas staring at me, wide eyed and absolutely speechless, as was my brother, who quickly darted his gaze towards Trixie with a frowned expression. I waved him, catching his attention once more as I wagged my finger from side to side. "Don't look at her. You look at me. Answer my question."

"It isn't that easy—" That was the wrong answer, and I didn't bother to let him finish before I was across the room with my hand around his neck and his body pressed against the wall. He may have been an alpha, but I was a fucking God, and if he thought for one moment that he could keep secrets from me, he was sadly mistaken.

Chapter Thirty

Cassie

"Cassie, no!" The scream that left Trixie's mouth went partially unnoticed by the anger that coursed through me. My hand was gripped around my brother's throat as I stared into his eyes, watching his wolf crawl to the forefront snarling like the beast he was. No one in their right mind would ever act like this towards an Alpha, but then again I wasn't "no one".

"Castor, that's enough."

The cold sound of my father brought me back to the present and snapped me out of the anger I was in. My hand instinctively released my brother as I turned to look at my father Hale from over my shoulder. "Daddy?"

A concerned expression marred his face as he let a heavy breath escape his lips. My feet couldn't carry me fast enough as I threw my arms around his neck and hugged him. I had missed my parents terribly and the fact they hadn't been present when I arrived had unsettled me for reasons I didn't understand.

"Castor–" he said softly, "what are you doing?"

Looking up to him I frowned with confusion, "I–I just–"

"You just lost your fucking mind!" Pollux growled, causing my father Hale to growl back at him in return.

"Enough, son. I understand that you're upset right now, but you're Alpha now. You need to control your wolf and remember that she isn't used to our world anymore."

Turning towards my brother, I stared at him with a wide-eyed apologetic expression. "Pollux, I'm sorry... I wasn't thinking."

He huffed with irritation, his hand rubbing his throat as he turned towards Trixie, who now stood holding her daughter. "Take her upstairs. This is too much excitement for her."

Trixie didn't argue as she gave me a sad look without another word and brushed past me back into the house. I wanted to call out to her, but I knew right now that was pointless. Even Silas and Finnick, who stood there staring at me with shocked gazes, said nothing. I had fucked up royally and had only just arrived.

"Castor, I think we need to talk," Hale said, catching me by surprise, but without arguing, I nodded. "Your mother is inside. I'm glad that I came out here instead of her."

He didn't wait for me to reply to him as he glanced once more at Pollux with a heavy sigh before he turned and made his way inside the house past Silas and Finnick. Neither man dared say anything to him about the situation, but the moment I passed them, they followed behind me.

I had done many things in my life, but disrespecting an Alpha—that was something unforgivable. Yet, I crossed the line without thinking. I was testing limits left and right and I knew it. Once again, I wasn't thinking before I acted and the words of Freya and Sansa told me echoed in my mind.

When I turned the corner into the living room, my eyes found my mother's and though her face was aged more than I had remembered, I still saw the kind eyes I had seen once before.

"Cassie–" she whispered, wrapping me into her embrace. "I've missed you so much."

"I've missed you too, Mama."

I didn't realize I was crying until she pulled away from me and wiped the tears from my cheeks. I had only been a girl when I left. Barely eighteen and experiencing life. My freedom wasn't earned and though I had been through so much in such a short period of time, I couldn't help but wonder what my life would have been like had I stayed.

"I know something happened outside… tell me what it was." The stern look she gave me reminded me of the look she gave me as a child, and I knew full well there was no way that I was going to be able to lie to her. Especially as I looked around and saw my fathers James, Talon, and Damian giving me the same look.

"Pollux and I just had a disagreement," I replied softly. "It's over."

"Over?" Pollux scoffed from behind me as he brushed past me, bumping my shoulder to take a seat in a red armchair on the far side of the living room. "Cassie attacked me."

My eyes darted towards Pollux, wide as I glared at him, "I didn't mean–"

"Cassie?" my mother whispered, "why would you do that?"

I was at a loss for words as I glanced around at everyone in the room trying to find the words I needed to explain the way I had acted. Yet, no matter how many times I opened and closed my mouth to tell them what happened, I couldn't. Nothing sounded right.

"I was angry… why didn't anyone tell me dad was sick?" Turning my gaze to Damian, I watched his expression change as it became understanding, a small smile on his face that didn't reach his eyes as his shoulders slumped in defeat.

He looked twenty times older than he should have. His dark hair graying as his eyes seemed so dull compared to the man I knew growing up. "Oh, Cassie," he whispered, shaking his head as he gestured for me to come to him. "I'm sorry you had to find out this way."

I wanted to go to him. Hell, I wanted to curl up in his lap like I used to do when I was a little girl, but I couldn't. I couldn't because I was too hurt to find out how I did. "Why didn't anyone try to tell me?"

"How would we have done that, Cassie?" Pollux replied, causing the others in the room to look at him with slight irritation. "It isn't like there is a phone that will allow us to communicate, Cassie. You're in a realm only accessible by death."

Pollux was being a little dramatic over his last statement. You didn't have to die to go there.

"Trixie could have come to tell me…"

"No!" He growled, slamming his fist down on the arm of the sofa. "I almost lost her once... I went years without her because of your selfish bullshit. I'm not going to let her go again."

It suddenly dawned on me what he meant. He went years without her and didn't know how to get to her, which must have driven his wolf mad with hatred for me. My own brother sat here before me with hatred in his eyes, and instead of trying to understand, I attacked him.

"Pollux," I whispered, stepping towards him. "I'm sorry. I didn't mean—"

It seemed it didn't matter what I had to say, because the moment that I tried to apologize, he rolled his eyes in anger and stood to his feet leaving the room. Not that I had done much to remain welcome in this place, even if it was my childhood home.

"Give him some time. It will be okay."

My mothers words weren't as comforting as I would have liked them to be, but I didn't bother to argue with her. I had made a mess of things and I needed to stop before it got worse. The best thing I could do was keep my mouth closed and try to make the most of the time I had here.

Making my way towards the sofa, I took a seat next to Damian. "I don't understand what's wrong with me. Why do I keep acting the way I do? You would think I'd have learned by now."

Small chuckles left the lips of James and my mother. I didn't miss the gaze they gave each other before they glanced at me once more. "Cassie, you don't need to blame yourself for this stuff. You're still young. You will make mistakes no matter what you do."

"I'm supposed to be Odin's heir. I shouldn't be making mistakes," I retorted with annoyance, "I'm supposed to set examples."

My mother strode towards me with a sad smile upon her face before taking a seat next to me, pulling me against her so that my head laid against her shoulder. "Oh, sweet girl, you have so much to still learn about ruling. Don't be so harsh on yourself."

Tears brimmed my eyes at her words. I hadn't realized that I would be so emotional seeing my family again, but the fact that I had missed them terribly did nothing to help me control myself.

"I don't have time to learn though. They expect me to do everything."

It was at this that a small noise to the doorway reminded me that Finnick and Silas were still present and again I felt foolish in how I was acting. I wasn't supposed to get emotional like this, and my mother seemed to understand my sudden uncomfortable posture as she turned to both of them.

"Gentleman, why don't you head to the kitchen and find Gia. She can get you something to eat why we talk and then perhaps we can go take a walk after."

I had expected them both to oppose the idea, but Finnick was quick to bow his head at her words and grab Silas's arm to pull him along. "Of course, that sounds wonderful. Please take all the time that you need."

There was a look of confusion on Silas' face as he glanced at me and then Finnick, who gave him a wide-eyed silent look that finally made him follow Finnick out of view before Hale closed the double doors to the room we were in.

""You didn't have to do that," I muttered under my breath, causing my mother to smile at me with a twinkle of amusement in her eyes.

"No she didn't," Talon replied as he stood by James with his arms crossed over his chest and a steely expression that showed his brooding side hadn't disappeared over the years. "Yet, I agree with her choice to have them leave. It seems we need to have a heart to heart with you."

Hearing Talon say we all needed to have a heart to heart was shocking. Talon had never been a man to take up such conversations. "Okay..."

"As I was saying, Cassie, you still have a lot to learn. It took me years to know my place here within this pack. But having your fathers by my side helped me grow into my position."

I never considered the fact that my mother hadn't known everything right from the start. I had grown up with her already being in the prime of her position, and to not think differently wasn't odd for me. Yet, staring at her right now, I could see the sincerity in her eyes.

There was a lot I was missing, and as Hale proceeded to tell me about how life with them really was before I was born, I found myself realizing that I didn't know everything I had thought I did. My perception of life was completely wrong, and sitting here with my parents made me feel different.

As if I was complete... which maybe was what I needed to get through what lie ahead.

Chapter Thirty-one

Cassie

After the long morning I had, I was quick to accept my mother's invitation to take a walk with her around the property. When I first got here, I didn't have the chance to really take things in and enjoy it.

"Things have changed a lot since you were here last."

My mother's words caused a grin to cross my lips as I looked around. "Yeah, I can see that. You guys have been busy."

With new buildings of various sizes, and the landscaping in the area well maintained and not overgrown, I could see that Trixie had been working hard to make this place just as much her own as it was my family's. It was just one more thing about this place that reminded me it wasn't my home anymore.

That I wasn't part of this world, and never would be.

"I can see something is troubling you, Cassie," my mother said calmly as we walked along cobbled paths lined by green grass that looked soft enough to sleep on. "Your fathers may have filled you in on how things used to be, but at the end of the day, the only way you will figure out who YOU need to be is by asking the questions you need to ask."

I had never known my mom to be some type of philosopher, but walking beside her in our homeland made me see things differently. All this time in Asgard, I assumed I had to do everything on my own and leave my old life behind, and it seemed that my old life perhaps was the salvation to my new one.

"I know, Mama. I'm starting to realize that perhaps I had been taking the hard way all along. Especially when the easy way was simply calling me home."

The chuckle that escaped us both was warming especially when she wrapped her arm around my shoulder and pulled me closer to her. The scent of her perfume wrapped around me like a warm hug that I didn't want to ever let me go.

"I'm glad you're home, sweetheart. The sunshine around here is a little brighter with you near me."

Glancing up at her I sighed, wishing I could feel the heat upon my skin. Yet, the moment I stepped foot in this place, it was as if nothing about the way this world worked affected me in the way it used to. Which was strange but not important enough for me to find out why.

"I'm glad I'm home as well." The shadowed figure beneath the canopy of trees to my right caught my attention. I focused my gaze and took in the sight of Silas' rippled body standing there, staring at me with his hands crossed over his shoulders and Talon's back to me as he obviously engaged in conversation with Silas.

"So, are you going to tell me about the two men you're here with?" my mother asked, causing me to glance at her. I opened and closed my mouth, trying to find the words to express the answer she was obviously seeking. "Don't act surprised, Cassie. I could tell the moment I laid eyes on them that there is something going on with you three."

My mother was clearly very perceptive, and I should have remembered that from when I was growing up. She always knew when something was going on, and though I used to get annoyed by it when I was younger, I was sort of glad she did point it out. Because I really wanted someone to talk to about everything.

"Well, Mama." I sighed, taking a seat on the cast iron bench beneath the limbs of a large oak tree. "I don't even know where to start when it comes to dealing with that issue."

Slight laughter escaped her as she took a seat next to me. Her blue eyes stared out at the green rolling fields in front of us where children ran around and flew kites within the sky. "Why don't you start from the beginning. Who are these two men?"

"Well, the brooding one talking to Talon is Silas." I finally fessed up. Starting with Silas seemed easier even though out of the three men, he was the one I was so unsure of. "He is a guardian of Asgard. Odin sent him with us to keep an eye on me."

"Oh, is he?" The tone my mother took was one that made me wonder if she was plotting something. A twinkle in her eye that turned her straight smile into one of mischievousness.

"Yeah..."

"I think he is here because he wants to be." I wasn't sure why my mother thought that but the more we seemed to speak on this, the more I saw her enjoying the topic of conversation. "In fact, I bet that he is here because he wants to make sure he doesn't lose you."

"...lose me?" Laughter erupted from my lips at her remark, "he doesn't want me."

"So you haven't slept with him?"

"Oh my god, Mom!" Shocked filled me at her question as I sat there staring at her with wide-eyes. I couldn't believe she was being so forward with my love life, but she sat laughing at me as if what she had asked was just natural for a mother to ask her daughter.

"Oh stop it, Cassie. You're not a little girl anymore. Don't be so dramatic."

It wasn't that I was being dramatic. I just found it weird for my mother to have the conversation she was having, but at the end of the day if there was anyone I could talk to about this, at least it was her and not one of my fathers.

Letting out a heavy sigh of uncomfortableness, I cast my gaze towards the ground and fiddled with my hands. "Yes, I have... on a few occasions."

"I figured as much." Looking at her once more, I watched a confident smile cross her lips. "He isn't a wolf, I know that much for sure... what is he?"

"A dragon..." I muttered as she looked at me with surprise.

"Dragon? But I thought they were extinct?"

Shrugging my shoulders, I didn't know what to tell her. I didn't even know they had existed until I met Silas so at least she knew they did even though she thought they were extinct. "Yeah, well, there he is in all his brooding glory."

"I take it that things aren't great with the two of you by the way you're acting." Once again, her awareness of our situation was a little disturbing, but I didn't bother to deny what she was saying.

"Yeah, he says it can't be and blah blah blah... it's all really annoying."

Nudging me, she caused me to smile as she nodded her head. "Men typically are, Cassie. I can't tell you how many times the four of mine pissed me off so bad I was half tempted to smother them in their sleep. But at the end of the day, the heart wants what the heart wants and he won't be able to fight it forever. Just let him do what he wants... it won't last."

Amusement filled me with her confidence over the situation. She didn't know Silas like I did. There was no way that he would give in again. Ever since the last time, he had done his best to avoid me, and if he could have it, I guarantee he would leave Asgard and move somewhere else to avoid me. "If you say so..."

There was silence for a moment as she continued to look out over the fields. I'd have given anything to be able to read my mother's thoughts. To know what it was that made her keep going day after day even though she had been through so much. She had a strength that I could only hope to achieve.

"So, tell me about the other one... the elf prince?"

The uncomfortable way she said elf prince caused me to chuckle as I thought about Finn. "Honestly, Mama, I don't even know what to say about that one. He is cocky and doesn't really know the meaning of personal space but ... there is something about him that makes me want to be around him."

"He does seem to be an odd one."

For her to call him odd wasn't the term I was expecting, and laughter filled the space between us at her description. "Oh god, what did he do that makes you think he is odd?"

"Wel,l when you first arrived, he was out there talking to the plants out front. I thought perhaps he was a little crazy, but when he and Silas introduced themselves to us with your brother, I realized otherwise. Still seems odd to know that elves are real. I mean... I knew a lot of things were, but I don't know, it just feels foreign on my tongue when I say it."

"Elves seem foreign? Mom, we're werewolves... come on now. I think odd shit is the least of our worries anymore," I replied, causing my mom to smirk.

As much as I was enjoying the conversation, I knew it wasn't meant to last forever when she got this frozen look on her face and her smile fell slightly. Something was wrong, and as she stood to her feet I stood to mine as well.

"We need to head back to the house."

"Why? What's wrong?" I asked as we both started making our way back rather quickly. A sense of urgency in her the way she was acting had me on alert, but before we reached the door she stopped and turned to me with hesitation.

"I will go ahead and tell you this now before we go inside. Your father... Damian. What's wrong with him isn't curable, Cassie. He is going to die, eventually... we just don't know how much time he has left."

The happy moment I had with her was gone, and once again the seriousness of the situation was back to the forefront. I didn't want to think about anyone that I loved dying, but it was a natural part of life. I just had expected he would have more time as shifters typically lived long lives. Much longer than those who were mundane.

"How? I don't understand why he is as sick as he is. The five of you were once immortal... I mean you still have—"

"It's because we no longer are that he is." Her comment didn't make sense to me, and the more I thought about it, the more confused I was. I knew the story of my parents. How they fell in love, and how they saved my father once before. But it just didn't make sense to me.

"I don't understand, Mama."

A heavy sigh escaped her as she looked down at the ground and then back towards the house before meeting my eyes once more. "The day we took our immortality and gave it to Damian, to bring him back to life, he was cursed in a way. The thing about fate is that no matter how much you try to change it, the universe will find a way to correct itself. So, though we saved him, Cassie... all it was, was borrowed time."

Her words were powerful, and I knew what she meant.

They brought him back, but it was only for a short time. Fate was still going to take his life in the long run because that was the order of things, and my father being alive right now shouldn't have been possible. "I hate seeing him like this."

"I do too, sweetheart, but you being here has actually made him smile for the first time in a long time. Eventually, he will be in Asgard with you and there the two of you can catch up on so much lost time."

The idea of him going to Asgard put a thought into my head that I decided to keep to myself. Damian was on the verge of death and in pain, but perhaps there was something I could end up doing for him in the long run.

"I know... Mom, go ahead and go to him. I know you want to make sure he is okay. I'm just going to walk around for a while and take everything in."

"Are you sure?" she asked furrowing her brows as she took my hand, "I don't want to cut our time short."

Nodding my head, I smiled. "We have plenty of time to spend together before I leave. Go... have fun, and we can catch up later."

My mother didn't need to be told twice for her to quickly disappear inside the house, leaving me standing alone on the front doorstep. She loved my fathers with everything in her just as she loved her children. They had given up so much for us and wanted more than anything to give back to them.

Which perhaps I would be able to.

For now, I had to get myself together, and a lot of what she said made sense.

If I wanted things to go right, I was going to have to stop fighting what fate wanted to happen.

Chapter Thirty-two

Cassie

Standing in silence staring at the space my mother once stood, I contemplated some of the things she told me. Everything took time and time wasn't something I had given a chance. It was instead something I fought against and hoped I wouldn't have to face. Since the moment I stepped into Asgard, I never really gave it a chance, and because of that, I fucked up at every corner.

I wasn't the only one that had been thrown into a life they weren't ready for. My mother was a prime example of what I was going through, and if she was able to make it one in one piece and come out on top then why couldn't I?

Trekking back down the sidewalk that she and I had come from, I took in the pack and admired all the hard work my family had put into this place in order for it to grow with the ages. I was merely a thought—or memory, within the pack territory.

A person who had once been a big part of life and left to be more.

"Cassie." Finn's voice caught me slightly off guard as I rounded the corner of the public garden and came face to face with his celestial eyes that reminded me of my own. Everytime that I looked at him, I was shocked by the gaze that looked back at me, but yet I couldn't pull away.

"Finn—what are you doing here?"

He shrugged his shoulders, looking around at the beautiful array of colored flowers and greenier. Something that I was certain was Trixie's doing as she loved nature more than anyone I knew.

"Just taking a walk around your pack. It's beautiful here... though I have to admit my own gardens back home are twice the size of what is here." Of course he would one up it, but then again, did I honestly expect less from him?

"I'm sure they are, but because I have never seen them, I'll just take your word for it."

"You know you could," he replied with a smirk.

"I could what?" I missed the hint he was giving and when I asked what, I did he chuckled in response.

"You could come see them. In fact, if I win, you could live amongst them."

Live amongst them... something about his offer made me slightly uncomfortable. I had just gotten settled in Asgard after being pulled from the only home I had ever known and now he was suggesting I move to his land if he wins? I wasn't too sure about that.

However, there was no way that I was going to let him know that I was uncomfortable. "You mean, if you win. I have seen the competition out there Finn, and even though you beat the last guy, I don't think you can take all of them."

He flinched with a smile as he dramatically expressed his hurt in what I said. "Ouch, princess... you wound me with your words."

His sarcastic comment made me smile even though I didn't want to. Everytime I thought that I was able to get away from smiling and flirting with him, he dragged me back in. Something about his charismatic ways made me curious to know who he really was. Considering he seemed to be all rainbows and sunshine, I knew damn well there was no way that he could be that happy all the time.

"What are you saying... that you can take them on?" I asked as I flirtatiously gazed at him from over my shoulder. I walked around the rose bushes and wisteria that grew around the white archways of the garden paths.

He followed me, his eyes never leaving mine and though I turned away from him, I could still feel the heat of his gaze as a low chuckle escaped his breath. "I can take them, and you, my dear."

Dear. A word of endearment that I hadn't expected to hear caused me to pause in my place as I thought back to Lucas, who had been the last one to call me that. The brooding silence from him was deafening. Not that he probably even realized I was gone.

No matter the situation, there was no reason to think over what I couldn't change. Lucas would be Lucas no matter what and in the meantime, I was possibly passing up on something—someone who might make me happy.

Turning to face Finn, I realized that he was closer to me than I had expected and as I slowly gazed up at him from beneath darkened lashes, I felt my breath catch in my throat. "Perhaps one day you will be able to prove that."

"Oh, I hope that I can."

It was a promise that deep down I was hoping he would keep.

Silas

From the moment that we arrived at this place, I couldn't help but feel uncomfortable. I didn't want to be here but no matter what, I was stuck in a situation I had to make the most of. Odin had given me an order, and I was glad for it. Because knowing that she was coming here with Finn and no other chaperone wasn't something I wanted for her.

There was something about Finn that didn't settle well with me, and yet there was something about him that felt so familiar.

"You have been standing here watching her for a while." The sound of Pollux walking up beside me caused me to sigh. I had already dealt with entertaining Cassie's father Talon for a while as he told me about the warriors he had around his pack and the training he did for others.

It was obviously something he was proud of and to ensure I wasn't rude to the man that could potentially cause me issues with Cassie if I was, I entertained him.

"Yes, well that is my job," I replied in a flat monotone kind of way, clearly showing my enthusiasm for my task.

"Man, she's safe here." He chuckled. "Why don't you take a load off and get a drink with me."

Glancing at him from the corner of my eye, I contemplated what he was offering. We were in his pack. A pack that belonged to Cassie as well and from research that I had done was one of the safest packs in North America. What did I have to worry about?

"Very well... I suppose you're right." I agreed to his offer but deep down a feeling of uncertainty rolled through my gut, making me wondering if I was making the right choice.

"I am right. I'm the Alpha."

Cocky as ever, I continued to follow Pollux further and further from Cassie. My mind screamed at me to turn around and go back to her, but my gut told me she needed the space. There was something about being in this place that felt calming, yet I was on alert.

For a man in my position, that wasn't an easy mix of feelings to have. I was a warrior... a guard of Asgard and instead I was acting like a frat boy on vacation by going to drink with the Alpha who was five times younger than I was.

The moment that we exited off the beaten path and rounded the back of the pack house to a small guest house that sat alone near the woodline, I realized I hadn't seen this place before. It was quaint and had a charm to it that screamed feminine energy. "What is this place?"

"Oh, this place?" He chuckled, glancing around the room. "It was my mother's a long time ago. Now, I simply use it as a place to clear my mind when I need to get away from things."

The small, white cottage looked like it needed a small touch up but the moment he opened the door and we stepped inside, I could tell it had been recently renovated. The smell of paint lingered in the air and as I gazed around at the minimalist decor that consisted of a couple photos on the wall, a sofa and a tv with a small kitchen, I could tell that no one had been here in quite some time.

"It's... charming. As your sister would say," I replied as my gaze fell back onto Pollux, who pulled a bottle of whiskey from a cupboard and two coffee cups.

"Speaking of my sister..." He sighed, pouring the whiskey into the glasses before he turned to hand me one. "I was thinking that it may be best if she had her own privacy out here. Away from things while she worked on gaining a better understanding of who she is."

Hearing that Pollux wanted his sister out of the main house wasn't what I had expected. In fact, I was taken aback by the idea that he would want her away considering she had been gone for so many years. Then again, the little outburst between the two of them earlier on could be the reason. Perhaps that closeness that they both once had wasn't as lasting as one might have thought.

"Why would you want her out here?" I finally asked, watching him turn to stare out the window with a determined yet lost sort of gaze.

"It's complicated."

"Complicated... you haven't seen your sister in years. So, why push her away now? Why force her away from her family, Pollux?" He turned to stare at me with a frown marring his lips before he brought the glass to his mouth once more and down its contents.

"She's a liability, Silas." It was an answer that I had expected but as he walked back towards the counter, I had a feeling that he wasn't finished. "I had hoped her coming back here would be welcoming, but she showed earlier that she can't control her powers."

"She had a minor outburst," I replied in anger, "she is still your sister—your family."

"And this is my pack!" he shouted in return, catching me slightly off guard. I would tolerate him raising his voice right now, and I can understand his anger but at the end of the day, I was raised that family was everything. "What would you do if you were in my situation?"

Shaking my head, I thought over what he was saying. First off, I couldn't imagine myself in his situation, but right now, staring at the man in front of me, I saw his hurt, his anger and frustration, and I knew that he was simply being an Alpha trying to protect his pack, his own family.

Chasing back my drink, I set the glass down upon the small table and turned towards the door. I didn't want to give him the answer he was looking for but when he called my name, I stopped in my tracks and sighed looking over my shoulder at him again.

"Please... just answer my question. If you were in my place, what would you do?"

Staring back at the man in front of me filled with so much desperation I tried to place myself in his shoes. "I'd be wary, but I still wouldn't throw my sister under the bus. Instead, I'd get to know her and find out why she is the way she is."

Chapter Thirty-three

Cassie

The afternoon spent with Finnick wasn't one I had expected. We walked around and talked about a variety of different topics from the way his realm worked to whom his family members were. The way Finn acted was completely different from the type of person I had thought him to be, but I was still on my guard.

From the garden through the fields that surrounded the various pack houses and by the new elementary school, Finn and I ended up at a path that led through the forest back towards the backside of the pack house.

We walked side by side as if there was no care in the world and more than once this man at my side had me laughing at the stories he told. Finn was far different from Silas and Lucas. He wasn't brooding like the other two, and he didn't have an attitude as if he was pissed off at the world—which was refreshing.

"A penny for your thoughts?" Finn's words pulled me from the thoughts drifting around my mind like a gentle breeze. Looking up to him, I smiled softly before I shrugged my shoulders.

"There is nothing but darkness and confusion there. Not sure you really would be interested in what's in my mind."

"You'd be surprised," he replied, causing me to laugh, "plus, I've never been afraid of the dark."

Stopping in my tracks, I turned to face him. The shadows of the forest cast around us under the canopies as the moon slowly began to rise up into the sky. Most would call this a romantic situation but I found it comforting.

The darkness was nothing but a safety net I had ignored for years.

"You should be."

"And why is that, Cassie? Why should I be afraid?" he replied, stepping closer towards me.

My breath hitched in the back of my throat at the close proximity of Finn. Everytime he was close to me like this, I couldn't think straight. I knew he called me his fated and though I refused to believe it, part of me wondered if it was true.

Was he really my mate? Was I following in my mother's footsteps with my mate bonds?

"Because I'm not..."

"You're not what?" he muttered, his hand reaching up to cup my cheek as I closed my eyes, relishing in the feeling of his skin upon mine. As much as part of me wanted to pull away from him, I couldn't and because of that, I allowed myself to feel things I didn't know I could.

"Normal..." I whispered softly before he leaned forward, his lips brushing against mine as he kissed me softly. The swipe of his tongue crossed my lips, begging for entrance. I parted them and let him in. Allowing him to deepen a kiss I hadn't expected but was glad for.

The soft moan that escaped me as he pulled my body tight against his was only the start of what would more than likely be an eventful evening. Or that was what I thought until low whistling in the distance quickly ripped us apart.

"Get a room!" The unknown voice called out as others whistled and hollered at the interaction between Finn and I. My cheeks instantly turned red as I tried to hide my face, biting my bottom lip only to have him grip my chin with his thumb and forefinger with a smile on his face.

"I didn't take you for being shy."

"I'm not... typically." I smirked before pulling away from him, walking further down the path towards the pack house. I didn't have to worry about him not following because the moment I got ten feet away from him, his footsteps resonated behind me, and I knew he would quickly catch up.

Kissing Finn was fun, and though Lucas and Silas were exhilarating and full of fury when I spent time with them, with Finn it was different.

The dimly lit lampposts at the end of the trail came into view and as I approached them, a firm grip on my arm stopped me in my tracks, leaving me once again to look into the eyes of Finn. Something about the way that he was looking at me made me wonder what he was thinking.

I had many men look at me with hunger in their eyes before. I wasn't naive to the idea of sex and love, but the way that he was looking at me was something much more. As if he had waited his entire life to stand before me.

"What is it that you're hoping for, Finn?" I asked him, hoping he could shed light on why he was so adamant in being around me. Why he looked at me with such an intensity made me unsure of myself.

"I'm hoping to get to know you more, Cassie. That's why I brought you here."

Brought me here?

I didn't understand what he was talking about. I had thought that my grandfather had allowed me to come home but now he is telling me it was him that had brought me here. Puzzled for a moment with a dumbfounded look on my face, I processed what he was saying.

"You talked to Odin and asked him to let me come?"

"Yes," he replied with a small smile. "I did."

"But why? Why would you go against Odin's wishes and discuss with him letting me come back here?" I watched as he opened and closed his mouth. Finn was thinking over his next words carefully and as much as I wanted him to just spit out the truth, I also wanted him to be completely honest.

"Because I want you to be who you were always meant to be, Cassie. No one properly explained how these things work. Nor did anyone take into consideration that you needed proper guidance to reach your potential. They just threw you into something you weren't ready for and it wasn't fair. I figured coming back here could give you clarity."

Shocked by the honesty from him, I stood there with my lips parted, staring at him for what felt like an eternity. No one had ever been as forthcoming to me about their agenda as Finn was, and I didn't understand why he was being so truthful.

"You're honest…" I muttered, giving him a peculiar glance as a small frown crossed my lips.

"I'm Fae, Cassie. We have no need to lie. We may embellish on the truth from time to time, but we don't lie outright. If we are asked a question, we tell the truth."

He was literally telling me trade Fae secrets, or at least I would assume they were, as if it was no big deal. "Seriously?"

"Yes, I am being serious. You doubt me?"

Shrugging my shoulders, I rolled my eyes and scoffed. "Well, I mean yeah, who just tells someone something like that?"

Laughter escaped him as he crossed his arms over his chest and continued to stare at me with what seemed like disbelief. "You act like it's hard to believe someone would be honest with you?"

"Well, we can just say I haven't had many people who would choose to be honest with me."

"That's a shame," he quickly replied. "Honesty is the only way to create a bond with someone."

The way he said it made me wonder if there was more behind his words that he was saying. The tone in which he said it made me hesitant and curious as to whether or not he knew something that I didn't. "Is that why you're so honest with me? Because I'm your fated?"

"Yes… are you saying you finally believe me?"

Shaking my head, I quirked a brow as a smirk crested the corner of my lips. "Not that easily, hot shot. You have a lot more to prove before I'll accept that."

Not bothering to let him reply, I continued off the path back into the open grass area behind the pack house. The lights glittered against the quickly approaching night and within it I saw the shadows of my family.

Curious as to what they were getting up to, I continued on my way until I was stepping through the back door and straight into chaos. My brother yelled at Talon and Hale, trying to make sense of things with my mother, who seemed to be caught in the middle of it as Trixie tried to control Pollux.

"What in the hell is going on?" I gasped as I stepped into the kitchen where they were with Finn at my heel, my eyes connecting with Silas, who stood on the other side of the room leaning against the doorframe with a stern glare upon his face.

Pollux's eyes met mine as he sneered in anger. "You need to leave, Cassie. Your presence here is causing issues."

"What? How am I causing issues?"

"Because!" he snapped, "you can't control yourself, and I won't put my family or my pack in jeopardy because of the magic that runs through your veins."

His words were like a slap to my face as I stared at him in complete and utter shock. I may have been a lot of things but a danger to my family or this pack wasn't one of them. What he was saying broke my heart. He was my brother and for him to think that I was going to hurt someone didn't make any sense.

"Pollux, I would never hurt anyone here."

My mother quickly was across the room and at my side as she pulled me close to her and turned her narrowed gaze on my brother. "This is your sister, Pollux. You of all people should know the kind of person she is."

"I don't know her at all!" he yelled once more. "My sister died years ago. The girl before me is not the same."

Again, my heart ached at his hateful words. When he left Asgard we were fine, and even when I first arrived here, things were fine. So for him to suddenly feel this way didn't make sense to me.

Why would he turn on me so easily?

"Pollux, it doesn't matter what you want, we can not leave right now. The portal is closed for another few days," Silas finally pipped in. It wasn't the truth, and I knew that. Silas could open the portal at any time, but for some reason, he was lying to my brother, which had me curious as to why.

Pollux looked between Silas and me as if pissed off that what he was saying was true. The anger boiling within him was easily sensed as I felt it radiate off him like a bomb ready to explode. Slowly, he paced back and forth in the kitchen as silence fell over us all, and as I looked to my mother, I saw her glancing at my fathers with concern in her eyes.

Something was definitely wrong, but I didn't know what.

"Fine... you can stay until the portal opens, but I don't want you anywhere near my family. You will stay out in the cottage with the two that came with you, Cassie, and if I so much as get a whiff that something has happened to anyone in my pack, I will end you."

Storming from the kitchen, I was left standing there in utter shock as Trixie mirrored my own gaze with tears in her eyes. "I'm sorry," she whispered, biting her bottom lip before she turned and quickly followed him out.

My mind froze with thoughts as to what had caused his sudden change in attitude.

Turning to my fathers and my mother, my lips parted as I let out a breath that I hadn't realized I had been holding. "What the fuck just happened, and why does he think I'm a threat?"

I wasn't sure what happened, but now I was dead determined to find out what was going on.

Chapter Thirty-four

Cassie

Left in the kitchen, I stood there with everybody trying to figure out exactly what it was I was going to do, and that was the moment I felt the air in the room shift. Lo and behold, Sam, my brother's best friend, came walking around the corner towards me with a solemn expression upon his face. One that told me I wasn't going to like what he had to say.

I should have known that after all these years, Sam would have ended up becoming my brother's beta, but I had never really taken it into consideration as my life from here had ended long ago. Asgard was the 0nly realm I was meant to focus on, and while there, it never occurred to me I would forget the importance of family... among other things.

"Sam, I see that you've taken up your position next to my brother, as I had always expected you to." He chuckled before his laughter quickly died. His eyes softened on me as if he had so many things to say, but wasn't exactly sure how to say them.

"I'm sorry that all of this is going on. Things have been a little strained lately, but on a positive note, I have gotten your brother to agree to at least let you stay near the pack house. He said that the cottage outback is where you can stay, and of course, you can still have your meals and everything here in the main house. That way you can spend time with your family."

"Are you serious, Sam?" I gasped, not believing my warm welcome home was completely gone and I was left to live with this.

"I'm sorry, Cassie. He hasn't been himself lately."

That was an understatement.

I knew exactly what cottage they were talking about. It was the one that my mother used to live in a very long time ago, and since then it had stayed abandoned for the most part, except for the occasional guest that came to visit—I knew there wasn't going to be much there.

Not that I would complain. I wanted more time with my family, and if I had to stay out there then so be it. All I wanted was to make him see I wasn't a danger to anyone. I was his sister no matter the changes that had happened with me.

"That's fine. I've noticed that my brother isn't himself. I thought maybe it had something to do with the altercation he and I got into this morning. I hadn't meant to upset him the way I did, but for him to act the way he is—"

My words cut off as I cast my glance around the room, trying to understand exactly what it was that it had happened. Even though I had acted the way I did, nothing that I had did showed any real kind of violence. I had only pinned my brother against the wall out of anger and frustration that he had kept something from me.

It wasn't like I had viciously attacked him or that he had gotten seriously injured, or that anybody else did for that matter. Yet I could see why he would be upset, considering his wife and his child were in the same room when this had happened.

Shrugging his shoulders, Sam looked at me giving me a weak smile as if trying to reassure me, but it did nothing but cause the void inside me to grow just a little bit more. "Come on, let's go ahead and take you down there so you can get settled in."

"What about Silas and Finn? Will they be allowed to stay in the house?" I was concerned for the guys, but as Finn went to protest Sam chuckled again shaking his head.

"Oh, no. The two guys are supposed to stay with you as well."

My eyes widened with shock, there was no way that he was serious. The cottage only had one bedroom, which meant the two guys were gonna have to sleep in the living room, if anything, and that was a little unnerving, knowing I was going to have them sleeping so close to me.

I mean, yeah, I had sex with Silas and what not... but still that was on my own terms.

Groaning internally, I stopped my childish thoughts and went to reply with understanding but was quickly cut off by my mother, who was pissed beyond belief.

"This is ridiculous. I'm going to go talk to my son," my mother exclaimed as she let out a heavy breath and stormed off down the same direction my brother had gone. Even my fathers looked between each other, a little concerned for what had happened.

"Cassie, just stay out there tonight. We'll have things fixed and in the morning, it'll go back to normal. I'm sorry the three of you are having to go through this," Hale replied as he stepped towards me, placing a hand on my shoulder, giving it a gentle squeeze.

Hale was always the more composed one out of the four of my dads. He had, from what I understood, taken over the position of alpha of the pack under uncertain circumstances regarding Damian. I had heard various stories growing up about what happened, but from the distant look in Damian's eyes, I could see he didn't like what was happening.

He sensed what was wrong, and even though he had his own internal battles at one point in time, he managed to be a man everyone respected.

I decided not to waste anymore time feeling completely embarrassed of the situation that had occurred. Silas and Finn looked at each other with uncomfortable expressions. I'm sure this wasn't what they were expecting when they thought coming here was a good idea. However, as their gazes met mine, I felt a wave of comfort flow from them into me giving me the reassurance I needed.

"Goodnight everyone, I'm going to get settled in." Bidding everyone goodnight, I turned quickly and made my way back through the kitchen door I had come through earlier. The sound of the guys coming through the door behind me echoed in my ears.

"Cassie, wait. Don't act like this. Don't let your brother get to you," Finn replied as he came down the trail, following me towards the cottage. I didn't have words for him. He had no clue what my family dynamic was, and the only thing he knew were the small bits of information that were public knowledge, or things that I had also told him.

"I'm not going to let my brother get to me, but I will tell you that this is not his normal behavior. Something is wrong, and perhaps coming back wasn't just beneficial for me, but also beneficial to figure out what issues are lurking beneath the surface of my brother's skin."

Silence consumed us as the sounds of Finn and Silas' footsteps echoed on the path behind me, and the moment I approached the cottage, I stopped in my tracks, staring in disbelief that this was going to be where I was staying.

Not just by myself, but with two men who did nothing but confuse me at every turn I made.

How was I supposed to continue staying here under pretenses that were more hostile than inviting and be able to realize what I needed to do to be the person I needed to be?

The cottage sat ahead of me as it once had when I was a child. The white walls, brown roof, and black trimmed windows were familiar, but the greenery that grew around it and up the walls wrapping it tight within its grasps was new.

Pushing forward, I opened the door to the cottage and stepped inside, taking in the very minimalistic aspects of it that were within it. Which was anything but inviting.

Not bothering to look around, I made my way straight towards the bedroom where a queen size bed was. White comforters with a white headboard sat next to a window, overlooking the thick grassy area where the moon was high in the sky.

Sleep, that was what I needed. A long day of spending time with both my mother and Finn was wonderful. But the arguments with my brother were absolutely draining, and it seemed nothing I could do would change the way that he saw me.

At least not right now.

He may have seen me as a monster, but I was not the monster he thought I was. I was an asset to him. I was his sister, his twin. His blood. Though something was clouding his mind, I knew that over time, I would possibly be able to fix that.

That is if time was actually on my side. Lately fate seemed to have other plans for me.

Odin may have given me quite some time to be here, but already I was itching to go home. As if an invisible tether called at me telling me my time on earth was coming to an end. That it was my time to take my place where I belonged.

"So, how do we want to manage these sleeping accommodations?" Finn chuckled from the living room, causing me to turn at the doorway to glance over my shoulder at him with a raised eyebrow.

"I think that's something that you and Silas need to figure out. I'm claiming the bedroom. The two of you can figure something out here, I suppose. Perhaps the sofa is a pull out couch. You guys can each share it."

Silas, ever brooding, stared at me with his arms crossed over his chest and a huff leaving his lips over his distaste for what I had said. But Finn on the other hand stared at me wide eyed, glancing over at Silas before glancing back at me in utter disgust.

"There's no way that I'm sharing anything with him. You, on the other hand, I wouldn't mind accompanying you to bed..."

"Of course you would," Silas snorted, rolling his eyes.

Finn sneered at Silas' outburst before continuing, "As I was saying, we don't have to do anything but sleep. Unless, of course, you ask nicely."

There he went, straight back to being the cocky fucking asshole I knew he could be. And though his offer was appetizing, because part of me really wanted to make Silas feel slightly jealous for the way that he had been acting lately, I made sure to stand my ground.

There was no way I was going to allow something to happen between us. I seriously just wanted to sleep and sometimes being around these guys was just too much to handle.

"As inviting as that sounds, Finn. I'm going to have to decline. I'm tired, and I don't know what this all is with you two and me and then Lucas back home. I don't want anything sexual or whatever right now... I just want to sleep and try to find out what the hell is going on in my pack."

Both men seemed slightly taken back by what I said, and I wasn't surprised. It wasn't like me to turn this kind of offer down, but sex was the least important thing right now. What was important was for me to get rest so I had a clear mind, and then of course, meet with my mother to ask what the hell had happened to my twin.

Something was going on and as I shut the bedroom door, disappearing from both Silas and Finn's view, I stood there thinking over what could have happened while I was away.

Whatever it was, I was going to get to the bottom of it. My family deserved peace and if that was all I could give my brother and Trixie, then you better believe I was going to.

Chapter Thirty-five

The all consuming darkness wasn't something new to me, and no matter what I tried to do with my life, I was plagued by visions that filtered through my mind, reminding me of everything I didn't want to be. I wasn't supposed to be a queen, princess, or even an ascending heir. I was simply supposed to be me, and as the shadows of danger filtered through my mind, I stepped forward seeking a way towards the light.

I wasn't a monster like everyone suggested, and every step I took forward through the darkness I kept telling myself that. The words whispered of my lips over and over were a reminder of the truth. That I was not the person they sought to fear.

"What are you doing, child?" the dark sultry voice of feminine beauty swirled around me in the darkness, causing me to stand still in fear, unsure of whether or not I had finally lost my mind.

"Who's there?"

My voice sounded off, and though I knew the words had left my lips, I couldn't help notice how they didn't sound like me.

The chuckling laughter of a woman swirled around me and as it did, the apparition of a woman I had seen so many times before appeared in front of me as if she was just as alive as I was. "Anna? This isn't real..."

Her kind eyes stared back at me as her hair swirled around her as if blown by its own breeze. A breeze that didn't quite touch my own skin but made me wonder if she had power as I did. "Don't seem so surprised, child. This visit is long overdue."

Panic filled me as I tried to rationalize what was going on. It wasn't possible for her to be here so the only way was if... if I was dreaming. That was it... I was dreaming. I instantly felt stupid as I glanced at her once more and sighed.

"I really am losing it. I'm so stressed and off beat, I'm dreaming about you, Anna. My brain is trying to help me process."

Anna stared at me with an odd expression as if not understanding why I was acting the way I was. The lavender dress she wore flowed around her as her hair slowly calmed to lay upon one side. "You are not just dreaming, child. This is real, we are speaking."

"If that's the case then why are you here?" I asked with amusement, deciding to humor her in this conversation.

"To warn you, Cassie."

Warn me. Warn me about what? The statement made my mouth open and close with hesitation as she stared at me with an indifferent expression. "What do you mean?"

The moment the question left my throat, the swirling breeze that surrounded her picked up becoming a little more forceful. My heart raced at the idea that something was about to happen and with it came fear. A fear that penetrated my mind and body and no matter what I did I couldn't control it.

"Let me show you," she whispered as a scene unfolded before me, and I was tossed onto a battlefield of chaos and fire. The screams of the innocent filled my heart, and I doubled over, covering my ears to try to muffle them out.

"What are you doing?!" I shouted at her, searching the area around me for her figure, but my eyes were unable to find her shadows. Instead, her voice filled my head and with it, the sense of impending doom.

"This is the future your brother is projected if the darkness isn't cast from his pack. His mind is clouded, and nothing his mate does will protect him."

My brother?! This was about Pollux?

I was confused even more upon hearing her, and as I tried to find a way from where I was, I quickly found myself cemented to the spot. Unable to move as a scream ripped from my throat at the panic that filled my mind. "Let me go from here!"

"No!" she yelled as her face appeared inches from my own in almost a ghostly state. "You're not a child anymore, Cassie. This is a gift I bestowed upon you. Your future was set in stone long ago, and fate helped me to make you see what needed to be seen to save the future of our worlds."

"What are you talking about?!"

Grasping my face, she jerked it back towards the field of blood and fire. "Look, Cassie. For once, open your mind and look. You're a goddess with more power than Odin, but you will never be able to reach your potential unless you stop your childish behavior and accept who you are so the people you love can be safe."

The war before me shimmered slowly as the fires of hell seemed to dim down. I wasn't sure if I was seeing like Anna wanted me to, but as I continued to look, I realized the scene around me was changing. Instead, darkness filled my vision once more but above me were stars. Millions of stars that twinkled like diamonds.

"It's changed..." I muttered as Anna slowly let go of my chin.

"Yes, because you're finally looking. Tell me, Cassie, what can you see?"

As I gazed around, a warm feeling rushed over me. A sense of ease and calmness as I watched the trees appear before my eyes. Leaves blowing gently through the evening breeze and the familiar feeling that I knew exactly where I was. "This is near the secret lake Pollux and I used to go to as kids."

I didn't wait to hear what she had to say as I found myself once again able to move. My feet were not hitting the floor as I realized that instead of walking, I sort of glided. It wasn't until I was about to break through the brush towards the water that a noise filled my ears, and I halted to see my brother break through the clearing to face a woman I was all too familiar with—Ashley.

"What the hell—" Anna's finger pressed against my lips, shushing me as she stared at me with a stern expression and then pointed slowly to my brother and Ashley, who stood in soft whispers.

"Do it again—" he asked her. A smug expression on her face let me know that she was up to no good. Which didn't surprise me because she had always been a snake in the grass.

"I don't know, Pollux." She sighed in a very dramatic way. "Giving you power like this... I feel like you're using me."

He quickly grabbed her wrist as he shook his head. "I'm not, Ashley. I never used you... please, I feel it draining, and I can't. I have to be the best, and because of that, I need your help."

Ashley hesitated for a moment before nodding and as she did, he kneeled before her, placing his forehead against her stomach. She placed her hands on either side of his head. I had no clue what the hell was happening but the moment she started chanting, I saw red.

"She's fucking using magic on my brother?!" I roared as my eyes darted towards Anna with anger. I couldn't believe what I was seeing and the way the magic felt—it was wrong.

"I told you that you are needed, Cassie. Most can not feel what she is doing, and the magic she has is very dark and very old. However, your powers allow you to see what others are hiding. Your brother thinks this is helping him, but she only has him fooled. She is turning him dark, and if she isn't stopped, your family will fall and those you love will die."

With a wave of her hand the scene changed once more and the flames and chaos once again lit my vision. I finally understood what she was telling me and before me were the bodies of my family and a dark mass that surrounded a woman who had just taken her revenge. It wasn't until I almost tripped over something that I looked down and realized that Trixie laid dead at my feet with a small child in her arms.

It was then that the scream of pain and agony ripped through me.

It was then that I felt determination as I pulled them both into my arms and cried.

"Cassie!" a voice came loud and clear through my mind as I cried and slowly opening my eyes, I found Finn's familiar gaze staring back at me. Confusion clouded my judgment before I quickly realized where I was and what had happened.

It was just a dream... wasn't it?

"What are you doing in my room?" I finally muttered as I slowly sat up and realized that Finn was almost naked and Silas was shirtless, both men staring at me wide-eyed and slightly confused.

"Are you fucking serious right now?" Silas snapped as he narrowed his gaze. "You gave us a fucking heart attack, Cassie."

Dumbfounded, my dream slowly started coming back to me and as it did, I realized that what had happened was a warning, no matter how strange it was. I just didn't know what to tell Finn and Silas—although part of me knew I had to tell them something.

"I'm sorry..." I whispered as I slowly turned to face them, crossing my legs upon the bed as my hair fell loosely down over my shoulders. "Was I being loud?"

"Were you being loud?" Silas snorted as Finn quickly shot him a glare.

"I think what Silas means is yes, Cassie, you were screaming, and it didn't matter how many times I tried to wake you, I couldn't. Even the tears coming down your face were scaring me. What happened?"

Tears? Lifting my hand to my cheek, I felt the wet touch of the tears he was speaking about and sighed. "Again, I'm sorry. I had a bad dream, or well... a warning from Anna."

"Anna?" Her name came off Silas' lips quite quickly and instantly, I felt a pain of jealousy in my chest from the way he had said it. It wasn't like he was mine, but the stories he had of her and their relationship reminded me that while I had a few sexual encounters with Silas, there was still so much that I didn't know about him.

"Yeah." I sighed, casting my eyes towards my hands as I fidgeted. "It was weird as if she was like a ghost or something in my mind, and the way she spoke to me..."

Finn stepped forward, taking a seat on the bed next to me as his hands reached for mine, taking it gently within his grasp. "Take your time, Cassie. This kind of thing isn't strange to me. I have people where I come from that can see the future—"

"Of course you do," Silas snorted. "Let's cut the shit, Finn. She isn't a baby and her family has been dealing with shit like this for a long time."

"What is your problem?" I snapped at him trying to understand why he was acting the way he was. "Ever since we got here, you have been acting like an asshole. If you don't want to be here, you're free to leave."

We held each other's gaze for a moment before he finally caved in with a sigh. "I'm sorry. It just seems like it's always something with you, Cassie. I didn't want to be here, but if you think for one moment I'd let you come back here and not be protect—"

"I am protected, Silas," I retorted, cutting him off. "Finn is a great warrior and can protect me."

Laughter exploded from his throat as he looked towards Finn. "He may be, but hate to break it to you both... he doesn't know a fucking thing about being in this realm."

I looked towards Finn, who simply sighed and shrugged his shoulders. "He is right, Cassie. I can protect you but this realm is completely new to me."

I didn't want to accept what they were saying and in frustration, I jumped to my feet with my hands on my hips as a heavy breath escaped me. "Look, I'm sorry that I'm a pain in the ass, guys. I didn't ask for any of this. I'm just trying to understand what's going on as much as you guys are."

They were both silent at my words and exchanged a look that made me slightly uncomfortable. I wasn't sure I could handle the silence or anything else going on for that matter, but when Silas opened his mouth next, I was surprised by what he had to say.

"Start from the top and tell me what happened. We can figure this out together."

"Really?" I asked in shock, my lips parted and eyes wide.

Silas rolled his eyes as a groan escaped him. "Yes, really."

Glancing at Finn, he nodded in return, and I sat there for a moment trying to figure out where I was to begin. While things were fresh in my mind, they were also very confusing. "She was warning me that something was wrong with Pollux. That I needed to stop what was going on."

"Your brother? Anna was trying to warn you about Pollux?" Silas asked in a tone that radiated confusion.

"Yeah, she was. She showed me an area that we used to frequent... Pollux and I." My mind seemed scattered for a moment as I opened and closed my mouth. My eyes drifted off, out towards the window as I looked up at the stars in the sky. "A woman was there and she was using very dark magic... old magic on my brother."

"Did you know this woman, Cassie?" Finn asked, causing me to glance at him with a new found determination.

"Yes, her name is Ashley and I'm going to kill that fucking bitch."

Chapter Thirty-six

Cassie

All night I stayed up thinking about everything Anna had warned me about. I wasn't sure what I was going to do, but I knew that my warning was clear. Ashley was poisoning my brother's mind, and it didn't matter what anybody else said... I was going to be the one to have to stop it.

The only problem was trying to figure out what she was. Anna had told me to open my mind to my powers, and let it come to me. So, that was what I was going to have to do. I was going to have to get to the bottom of what was going on at any cost.

First though, was breakfast with my mother. A way I hoped could shed light on why Ashley had such influence over my brother. Or if she even knew he was still seeing her.

The sun shone brightly in the sky as I made my way across the grass towards the veranda where I was meeting my mother. This time of year was beautiful in my opinion. It wasn't cold outside, but it wasn't hot. Instead, the breeze blew gently through the air creating a peaceful environment, which was what I desperately needed for the conversation about to take place.

Step by step, I made my way towards her. Her eyes gazed up to meet mine as a smile spread from ear to ear as she lifted her delicate hand to wave at me. I had never seen her so happy, so carefree. I had always remembered her being this stressed out, strict woman, trying to raise all her children, while still trying to be the Luna of the pack.

I had never seen any other side to her before, but I was glad that I could now.

"Good morning, sweetie. I'm glad that you could make it," my mother said softly as she stood to greet me, wrapping her arms around my body as she pulled me into a hug before I sat down.

"I wouldn't miss this with you, mom." Taking a seat across from her, I lifted the glass of orange juice to my lips and gazed down at the array of fruits and pastries she had provided. It reminded me of when I was a kid and her and James would make Sunday morning breakfast this special.

Except it usually had tons of protein for all the growing men she was feeding. "How did you sleep?"

I hesitated for a moment as I reached for a strawberry, bringing it to my lips as I took a bite. "I slept okay. Can't say it was as well as the night before though."

"Yeah, I'm sure," she muttered softly. "I didn't get to talk to your brother properly about everything yet. He was so angry last night, Damien said I should just let him calm down, but I promise I'll talk to him about it today."

A scoff of laughter escaped me as I glanced at her with a smile. "It's okay, Mom, honestly. I'll make do in the guest house."

"Yes, I suppose you will," she replied with her own soft laughter. "Thankfully, we put in a brand new extra large bed in there for you, so it's big enough for the three of you temporarily."

Laughter erupted from my throat at the thought of them actually sharing a bed with me, or that my mother thought that they would. "The bed was very comfortable, however, I don't know if the guys would say the same thing. They didn't sleep in it."

"What?" she muttered softly as she bit into a pastry covered in chocolate, staring at me in utter confusion. "What do you mean they didn't share a bed with you? They're your mates."

"No, that's where you're wrong. They are not mated to me. They're two men that I like and, well, one of them says he's fated to me, but it's not official. Not to mention, I'm not sure I actually believe it. Therefore, they got to enjoy the sofa bed."

My mother did not find amusement like I did at what I said, and though I laughed, she stared at me, absolutely shocked with her eyes wide as a dumbfounded expression across her face. She couldn't believe I had allowed them to sleep on a pull out sofa.

Granted, they may have came with me and we may have fucked around a little bit in the past, but there was no way in hell I was going to allow them to share my bed... at least not until they earned it. I mean, there were a few things I wouldn't mind them doing for me, one situation in particular involved them both being on their knees, but that's besides the point.

"Sweetheart, please don't give them a hard time. They both seem to be very sweet, caring young men. I want you to be happy." She sighed running her hand through her hair as she stared at me with the same motherly look she had given me for years when she was trying to get me to understand what she was talking about.

I wanted to agree with her, but this was my life and my sex life had to be put on the back burner. I couldn't focus on that right now when my brother needed desperate guidance.

"I'll take it into consideration, but for now let's talk about something else."

Rolling her eyes, a smirk crossed her lips as she shrugged her shoulders. "Fine, fine. What would you like to talk about?"

"Well, actually, since I can't properly talk to Trixie right now, I was hoping you could tell me what happened with the entire Ashley situation. Last time I saw Trixie in Asgard, she was upset about Ashley trying to take Pollux, but now it seems everything is better?"

The ghostly look that crossed my mothers face as her smile fell let me know that things in fact were not fine. There was definitely something going on, and as much as I wanted to force her to tell me everything, I couldn't. She was my mother and it was clear this topic was upsetting for her.

"Oh, goodness," she said with an uncomfortable laugh. "I don't even know where to start with that topic. The girl was always so troubled. You remember how she used to fawn all over your brother when you guys were in school."

"Yes, I do." I nodded as I leaned back in my chair watching her with a raised brow as she seemed to stumble over her words in an unusual manner. "So, what's going on?"

"It's hard to explain, Cassie. Ashley was trying to push her way in, and I could tell something was different about her. I mean, after you guys left she disappeared for months. Her parents were worried, and no one knew where she went."

"She disappeared?" I questioned, "did she ever say where she went?"

Shaking her head, my mother's frown deepened. "No, but I spoke to her mother not long after she returned, and they thought maybe she went to find her birth parents."

"Whoa whoa, birth parents? Those aren't her real parents?"

"No... did you not know that Ashley was adopted?" my mother asked me quite surprised. Not that I was sure why she was. If that was public knowledge back in the day, everyone would have known. She was the popular girl.

"No, Mom. I had no idea, and I don't think that most people knew that," I replied with a bit of shock to my tone. It made sense now how Ashley would have powers. If she wasn't a purebred wolf and perhaps a half breed, then maybe there was more I needed to figure out then I thought.

"Yeah, the poor girl was adopted when she was a baby. I was there when her parents brought her home. Of course they had to have mine and your fathers permission to do so because we were the leaders of the pack—"

"So, do you know what she is then?" My question cut her off and seemed to catch her completely off guard as her open mouth slowly closed.

"If you mean do I know that she is a halfling, then yes, I do. She isn't a pure wolf but she is pack no matter what. Even if she doesn't live here anymore."

Hearing that Ashley was no longer in our pack surprised me as well. Then again, if her grasp wasn't that strong on my brother before, I could see her being cast out since she had caused issues for Trixie, who was the rightful new Luna of the pack. "Where did she go?"

Before my mother could answer, a soft voice caught my attention and looking back over my left shoulder, I saw Trixie standing there staring at me with a sense of desperation on her face. "Trixie... what are you doing here?" I glanced around to see if I could see my brother.

The last thing I wanted was more drama and with the way he had been acting I'm sure I'd get it.

"Can we talk? It's important," she replied, glancing around herself.

"Uh, yeah, sure."

An uncomfortable expression crossed her face as she gestured with her head for me to follow her. "Not here. Let's take a walk."

Glancing at my mother, I watched her nod for me to go, and quickly I stood making my way down a small path from the veranda following Trixie further into her garden where the bushes stood far above my head providing the protection we needed from prying eyes.

The moment she spun around to face me, I could see the panic in her eyes as she fidgeted for a moment with her hands. "I need your help."

"Oh–okay," I replied, slightly caught off guard. "What do you need help with?"

"I know you have seen that something is going on with your brother, Cassie. Don't pretend you didn't notice it the morning that you guys got into it."

Her stating the obvious wasn't something I had expected, but slowly I nodded my head admitting that yes, I had noticed something was going on. "That morning wasn't the most pleasant. I mean, I am shocked though that he went off on me the other night."

"Exactly!" she gasped running her hand through her hair. "He is losing it. It's been going on for the past year now. I don't know what's going on with him, and as soon as I think he starts to get better something happens, and he is—"

"Losing himself again?" I said finishing her sentence as she sighed in defeat.

"Yes, exactly." Tears filled her eyes as she crossed her arms over her chest. "Cassie, I don't know what to do. I thought I could handle this, but I can't..."

"Have you tried using your powers—"

"Oh, God no!" she exclaimed, shaking her head. "I couldn't do that... plus... my magic hasn't been exactly normal lately."

The last part of her words were muttered softly, and I couldn't believe what she was saying. "How is that even possible? What do you mean it's not normal?"

Trixie looked sad for a moment before she straightened her shoulders and lifted her chin up in the air. She was the Luna of the pack after all, and she couldn't be seen having moments of weakness, or at least I knew that's what she would end up saying.

She wasn't someone to just break down and lose control. I had known Trixie for a little while now, and she always seemed so composed, carefree, and happy.

Yet, right now she wasn't.

"Since I came to earth, I have been slowly losing parts of myself. I have been talking to Finn about it, and he wants me to go to the Fae realm to recharge, but—"

"But what?" I asked with confusion not understanding why she wasn't accepting the offer to go. "You should take his offer and go."

"I can't, Cassie. I can't ever go home. I can't leave my family."

It wasn't a matter of losing her family, and the fact that she thought that angered me even more. Something was seriously going on, and I knew deep down who was behind it. The problem was figuring out what to do to stop it, and right now, the only two people who could help me were Finn and Silas.

"Look, I can help you. Let me figure this out okay," I replied, watching as she nodded.

"Okay, but we have to do something soon, Cassie. The Silvermoon pack is coming for the gathering, and we have to be prepared."

Frowning, I tried to understand why she had such a sense of urgency about getting this done quickly. "What's with the Silvermoon pack? Why do they matter?"

"Because it's Ashley's new home, and that means she will be attending."

Chapter Thirty-seven

Cassie

After leaving Trixie I wasn't sure what to do. I hadn't realized things were as bad as they were but after seeing her the way she was, I realized she was in a bad situation. Trixie refused to go further into detail about what all had been going on, but I could see by the shaken look of her that the exhaustion I had noticed when I first arrived was only the cover she used to show people she was okay.

My mind reeled over and over the information as I made my way back towards the cottage, where I had assumed Finn and Silas would be waiting for me. They were both gone early this morning when I had left.

A roar of anger in the distance caught my attention the moment I approached the cottage and as I turned looking off towards the house, I saw Pollus arguing with Sam about something. The anger that filled his voice was unrecognizable. It was clear that the way he was acting was far from him being in control, and that wasn't good for anyone.

An Alpha was expected to remain in control, and though I wasn't part of their pack anymore I still knew that. I could only imagine the anger he was pushing through the pack link right now. To know that he was acting this way was heartbreaking because it wasn't who he was.

Seeing Hale and Talon approach him calmed the ache in my chest a bit as I turned and made my way inside the cabin, trying not to let the scene get to me.

"Cassie, I was wondering where you were," Finn replied, coming from the bedroom half-naked towel drying his hair. "Did you have a good morning with your mother?"

My mind short circuited a moment as I took in Finn's well sculpted muscles and the defined six pack on his stomach. He had a body that would make anyone clench their thighs and right now, I was one of those women. "Uh, yeah—it was good."

"Are you okay?" he replied with a smirk as he dropped the towel to the sofa and strode towards me. His pants hung low and loose upon his hips and the way his "V" line dipped towards a trail of curled blonde hair made me curious about the monster within his pants.

I couldn't let myself get distracted though.

"Uh, yeah. I'm fine. Just a lot going on right now, and my brother is losing his shit outside... I actually needed to talk to you and Silas about something."

"Talk to us about what?" Silas' voice resonated from the front door as he closed it with a little more force than I would have expected.

Letting a heavy breath escape me, I gestured for him to sit on the sofa. "You guys may wanna sit down for this because it's a lot of information."

Finn didn't hesitate to take a seat, but per usual Silas narrowed his gaze and me and curled a brow as he crossed his arms over his chest. "I'm fine. Start talking."

Dick...

"Alrighty then... So, I was having breakfast with my mother and Trixie ended up showing up, which of course, was completely unexpected—"

"Trixie showed up?" Finn frowned. "I'm surprised your brother allowed that after what happened the other day."

"Well... he didn't." I frowned, shrugging my shoulders. "She snuck away to talk to me. She said that he has been acting weird for a long time now. She is really worried, and on top of that her magic is depleting."

Finn's eyes turned to Silas, who stared at me unmoving. "Yeah, she told me that, and it doesn't make sense because being in this realm shouldn't cause those issues."

This was news to me. I thought maybe being here was causing the problem with her magic but Finn would know that for certain. Which also didn't make sense because then why would he tell her otherwise. "You didn't tell her that though."

He was silent for a moment as he slowly nodded his head. "Yes, but that was because I didn't want to alarm her and let her know it was probably someone stealing her power."

"Is that even possible?" Finn and I both glanced at Silas, who seemed suddenly concerned as he dropped his arms and began pacing back and forth. "If that's going on, that means there is someone who is intentionally trying to bring down your family."

"Again..." I muttered before I realized both men were looking at me crazy. "Years ago, when I was born, my parents had their first run in with Loki... that's why I said again."

It was hard to talk about what had happened back then, because Damian had died. Even though he was brought back, it was at the cost of my parents giving up themselves to do so. Which didn't seem to work well because now time had caught up with him, and he was dying.

"I see. So you think that has something to do with your brother now?" Silas questioned, making me wonder why I was explaining all of this to him. The most important aspect I had to remember was that I needed their help in order to solve what was going on.

I could see clearly that he wasn't sure about what I was saying. It didn't make sense for an Alpha to be in this position, but I knew what I did was real. My brother was seriously messed up and Anna had sent me the warning for a reason. "Yes, Silas, I do."

Silence fell between us for a moment as both men sat there contemplating what it was I had told them. It wasn't every day you come to a different realm to help improve something and then other shit happens. Then again, this was me we were talking about.

Chaos seemed to follow me everywhere.

"Okay, okay," Silas finally replied. "Tell me what you know, and I'll see what I can find out."

"Really?" Shock filled me that he was taking this so easily. I had expected Silas to put up more of a fight, but he wasn't. Even the calm demeanor in which Finn was laid back on the sofa watching the conversation with me unfold seemed way too casual considering everything.

"Yes, Cassie. Really."

A sigh of relief washed over me in the moment as I tried to quickly collect my thoughts so I could finish explaining to them what I knew. "Okay, well like I said, Trixie said that something has been off with Pollux, and I think it has something to do with a girl named Ashley."

"Who is this girl?" Finn asked curiously. "Who is she in your pack?"

"Well, years ago. when we were in school... well. I mean years ago here when we were in school... she was my brother's girlfriend, I guess you could say. She wanted to be Luna of the pack but of course my brother was adamant he only wanted his mate. Then of course when we went to Asgard, he found Trixie."

"Ah, I see. So, she is a jealous ex-girlfriend wanting the throne," Silas replied, rolling his eyes. "What does that have to do with the way you're acting?"

"Because when I spoke to my mother today, it turns out that Ashley isn't pure blood like the rest of us. She is a halfling and adopted. Not to mention, she caused issues before for Trixie and Pollux's relationship, and the vision Anna showed me had Ashley using magic on my brother."

There was no way for Silas to disclaim what I was saying. He knew that the information I had given him pointed clearly to there being an issue and running his hand over his face, he nodded before turning to Finn. "Keep her here and stay put. Let me go find out what I can from Hale and I'll be back shortly."

"Hale? Why are you going to talk to my dad?" I gasped, taking a step forward only to find that Silas was quick and out the door before answering my question.

Turning to Finn with a wicked smile on his face, he shrugged his shoulders before standing and making his way towards the small kitchen where he pulled a clear bottle of liquor from a cabinet and turning to me with a smile. "Well, since Silas gave us orders to stay here, perhaps we should have a drink."

"Seriously... I'm trying to find a way to save my brother and my pack, and you want to drink?"

Laughter escaped him as he held up his finger and smiled. "Correction... your brother's pack. You're not a wolf anymore, remember."

The jab was a strike to my heart that made me sneer. The last thing I wanted for him to do was to remind me of that. Everyday I felt the urge to touch my wolf and let her run through the trees feeling the wind across my fur but then I remembered that she died the day I did, and my soul cried to touch her once more.

Holding back tears that threatened to fall, Finn seemed to realize that he upset me. Because before I knew it, the bottle was placed down upon the table and his arms wrapped around me pulling me close. "I'm sorry, Cassie."

"It's okay, don't worry about it."

"No, I crossed the line there. It wasn't right for me to say that to you," he replied, holding me tight against him. "I don't want to be an asshole or anything like that."

Kind of late for that. However, even if I wanted to stay mad at him, I couldn't. The smell of Finn wrapped around me like a blanket, and as I inhaled, all I could do was close my eyes and relish in the way he made me feel.

"It's okay," I muttered before pulling away from him. "Maybe you're right. Maybe I do need a drink. There isn't any point in carrying on like I have been until I have all my information correct."

"Touche," he replied as he picked up the bottle and handed it to me. "You're a smart woman, Cassie. I have no doubt you will figure this out."

"Is that right?" Taking the bottle, I unscrewed the cap and tossed back some of the liquid, letting the burn run down my throat and into my stomach. The horrible liquid wasn't pleasant and instead tasted like I was drinking gasoline. "I think you're just trying to get me drunk."

He chuckled as I handed him the bottle, watching as he swigged it back as if downing the liquid didn't bother him one bit. There was so much to Finn that I didn't know and as he pulled the bottle back setting it down on the table, I realized I wanted to know more about him.

"Do you think I'm a crazy fuck up, Finn?"

My question caught him off guard as his eyes widened and he closed his mouth. "No, I don't."

Pleased that he didn't think I was a fuck up, I nodded in understanding. Trying to understand how someone like him wouldn't think so. "So, what do you think about me?"

"I think you're sweet," he said with a smile that caused me to roll my eyes.

"Come on, I'm being serious... you and I both know I'm not nice."

Tilting his head from side to side, he moved closer to me once more. His hands reached out to graze my hips as he quickly jerked me closer to him. "Why don't you show me how mean and naughty you can be?"

The whispered response set goosebumps over my skin as he slowly leaned forward, nipping at my lips as I tried to process what he wanted. The irrational part of me would have said no at one point, but this other part of me. The primal part of me wanted to submit to him in ways that didn't register normally.

Leaning up I let my primal nature take over and as my lips brushed against his listening to the soft gasps escape him I nipped at his bottom lip earning a groan of approval before his mouth was on mine.

The raw desire that pressed through us both was much needed, and if he wanted to fuck me into the morning sun, I'd let him.

Chapter Thirty-eight

Cassie

The moment he kissed me, a feeling inside my soul erupted like fireworks soaring across my skin. I had felt things with Silas and Lucas but this was different. Finn was different. His hands roamed my body as we pulled at the fabric that concealed us. Every single negative thought I had before vanished as I let him take control of me.

I wanted it. Every single thing he had to offer me.

"There is no going back after this," he whispered against my lips as his eyes looked deep into mine. The celestial blue I was so used to looking at in the mirror captivated me in a way I couldn't explain, and I knew what he was saying was true.

There was no going back.

Nipping at his bottom lip, I smiled. "Then what are you waiting for?"

The deep chuckle that escaped him was the last sound I heard as his lips crashed upon mine once more. One fisted in my hair as the other wrapped around my waist, holding me close to him. The movements between us were second nature, and as he reached down grabbing the back of my thighs, I was lifted into the air never once breaking the tongue-tied, twister game we were playing.

That was until my back found the lush comfort of the blanket upon my bed, and I found myself staring up at him. The shirt he once wore was ripped from its buttons, letting sun that peaked through the window to ripple off the well defined ridges of his muscles.

His hands slid over my body as his fingers worked at my clothing. One button at a time, he removed my jeans, sliding them off my body taking my white cotton panties with them. The delicate touches he provided me sent a sensation to my core that made me ache for the things he was going to do, and though I thought he would take what he wanted with force, he didn't.

Instead he let me feel everything he was doing slowly, and on purpose.

The wicked smile on his face was laced with mischievousness. This clearly was pure enjoyment to him. "Tell me what you want, Castor. Tell me how you want me to please you."

"Taste me," I replied. "Taste how much I want you."

The words seemed almost foreign to me but the flow of power I felt burning beneath my skin made me crave more of what he had to offer.

Slow to his knees, I watched Finn sink until he grasped my thighs, pulling me to the edge of the bed as he took his time kissing up the inside of my thighs. My breaths came in slow pants as I let my eyes raise to the ceiling, letting my mind focus solely on the sensations he was creating.

If this was going to be slow, I was going to remember every bit of it.

"Please," I begged. "I need more."

Like a whore craving what he was going to give me, I begged for it. It was all he needed to dive between my thighs, his mouth attaching to my aching cunt with a hunger I hadn't expected. The gasp left my throat with a short cry and made my back arch, and I couldn't help but grind myself against his face, wanting more.

With everything that had been going on lately, this was the escape I had been craving.

"I see that I can't leave you two alone for a moment, can I?" Silas' voice caused my eyes to dart towards the door, where he stood watching what was going on.

Part of me wanted to pull away and cover myself, but Finn didn't let up on what he was doing and from the dark hungry gaze in Silas' eyes, he wasn't angry by what he saw.

Confusion filled me and as Finn came up for air. He chuckled, licking his lips as I looked between both men. "She tastes just as divine as you had said."

What?! They had talked about me?

I didn't know what to say or think at that moment but the way both men seemed to smile with a common sense of knowing had me worried. They had discussed this moment before it happened, and now that I was splayed upon the bed like a buffet waiting to be devoured I was unsure of how I felt.

"Don't let me stop you, Finn," Silas said with a smirk. "I enjoy watching her come undone."

Holy shit! "What?" I gasped only to have Finn's mouth back at my core, causing me to cry out in pleasure once more. I didn't know how to feel about Silas watching but he stood there by the door with a hungry gaze that turned me on more then I realized it would.

"Finn–" I cried out as the swirl of his tongue against my clit had me coming undone with a shudder I hadn't felt in some time. My eyes rolled in the back of my head as I tried to calm my racing heart.

Finn was far from done with me, and as he came up, gripping my hips to pull me to him, I gazed down, watching the long rigid cock he had concealed within his pants spring free with its bulging head that wanted every single part of me.

He was huge, and though Silas and Lucas were big as well, this man's beautiful cock curved in a way I was sure to bring more pleasure then you would think he could provide. I was hungry for him, and before I could say anything, a fist in my hair stopped me.

It was Silas, and as I looked up at him, he held my hair tight with a smirk at the corner of his lips that made my heart beat faster. "Do you think you get him that fast?"

Shock filled me with his statement. "Please Silas... I need it."

He made a tsk-tsk noise as he shook his head. "On your knees, Cassie. I want to watch you please him before he fucks you senseless."

There was no asking in his statement. He demanded me to my knees, which I did without a second thought. The idea of taking Finn into my mouth as Silas watched was a huge turn on and with Silas still having a hold of my hair, I gently grasped Finn's long erection. Looking up into his eyes, watching as his lips parted in enjoyment.

The moment that Silas allowed me to lean forward, my tongue flicked out to run across the slit of Finn's cock. I heard a low moan escape from him that made my thighs clench together. Who knew that hearing a man's excitement over the pleasure I could bring him would be this enjoyable, and as I slid the length of his shaft into my mouth, the sounds of his pleasure grew.

Over and over I let the length of his shaft slide in and out of my mouth. My tongue swirled around it as my hand moved over the length in smooth motions with my lips. The faster I seemed to go, the more he seemed to groan, and the harder and thicker his cock seemed to get.

I was overtaken by the pleasure and with Silas using my hair to guide me in Finn's pleasure, I had a feeling that he was enjoying this too.

With a loud pop, my lips retreated from Finn's cock, only for Silas to let loose of my hair gripping the back of my neck to force me to my feet. "Are you ready to be fucked like the bad girl you are?" he whispered in my ear.

"Yes," I gasped only to find myself tossed onto the bed, my stomach flush with the blanket as Finn gripped my hips pulling me towards him.

I displayed for him my ass high in the air and my pussy dripping as he ran his finger over my lips, which made my aching cunt clench with excitement. "God, you're fucking perfect."

Finn's murmured words were the encouragement I needed when the feeling of his thick erection was pressed against my entrance, making me wonder how he was going to fit the massive head of his cock inside me.

I had only had sex a handful of times, and right now with Silas and Finn in this room with me, I had a feeling that this moment would make me forget about all the other times. This time I would be forever ruined for any other men because I would crave the attention they were both giving me.

In one swift motion Finn thrusted his full length inside me, causing me to scream out at the pain and pleasure. The way his cock hooked upwards caused friction in all the right places and the more that he moved, the closer he brought me to the edge.

There was something about the way that Finn and Silas manhandled me that made me crave more, and thoughts of them both fucking me at the same time thrilled me to no end. However, Silas wasn't giving me that right now. This was all about Finn pleasing me while he watched.

One, two, three times, and I was seeing stars before my eyes. My throat dry from screaming in pleasure and when I thought it wasn't going to end, Finn seemed to finally reach the brink as his fingers dug into my hips and he groaned in pleasure. The feeling of his pulsating cock inside me as he emptied himself a welcoming feeling.

Leaning his forehead against mine, he sighed with a smile across his lips before gently kissing the corner of my mouth. "My little mate... you are absolute perfection," he whispered.

For the first time in a long time, I couldn't stifle the giggle that escaped me as he pulled me close to him nuzzling into my neck. My eyes turned to find Silas' but to my surprise he was gone.

"Where did Silas go?" I asked, turning to Finn with a furrowed expression.

Finn looked up towards the open doorway, the sound of the front door closing catching me by surprise as he sighed shaking his head. "I'm not sure... would you like for me to go find out?"

His question made me hesitant. We had just had amazing sex, and I didn't want him to think bad because I was thinking of Silas but as I bit my bottom lip without saying anything, he chuckled and kissed me cheek.

"It's okay, Cassie. I don't mind," he whispered, unwrapping himself from me as he slid from the bed, his sculpted ass a perfect sight I wanted to continuously see as he slid on his pants and walked towards the door. "Stay in bed, I'll be back in just a moment."

It wasn't a request for him, but more of a demand.

A demand that I was all happy to obey, because if this was how things could possibly be if I followed my mothers footsteps... then I was definitely interested to see what could happen.

Chapter Thirty-nine

Silas

What the hell was I thinking?!

The moment I entered the small cottage and saw Finn pleasing Cassie, I was overcome with the urge to watch her passion unfold. I didn't want to turn away and even mustered the courage to be able to help participate.

The way her body gave in to him, and the way she so willingly pleased him while I guided her head allowing her to only have what I wanted her to have... it made my cock harder than it had ever been before.

Of course, I was a dragon and it was typical for creatures like me to end up taking multiple mates but there was no way in hell that Cassie was my mate. There was no way in hell that any of this was fucking possible. Yet, when she came and he filled her, it took everything in me not to claim her myself and mix my seed with his to ensure she carried a child.

It took everything in me to also make sure he knew she was mine, and only got her when I said he could have her. Dragons were possessive creatures, and it was only because of her I let him taste her to begin with.

Anger boiled through me as I stormed out of the cottage and out into the evening air. My hand ran through my hair as I tried to calm the raging inferno inside me. Never had I been denied anything, and yet I denied myself the pleasure of Cassie.

I let another man take what was rightfully mine.

Thrashing out, my fist connected with a nearby tree and the splintering of wood echoed through the forest near the cottage. I promised Pollux I was going to control my anger, and that I wouldn't shift here because of the humans that lived nearby, but at this moment I was finding it difficult for me to keep the promise I made.

"Silas!" The sound of Finn's voice was the last thing that I wanted to hear. However, I expected it after everything that just happened.

"Leave me alone," I snapped, refusing to look at him. "Go back to Cassie's side where you belong."

Laughter escaped Finn, causing me to spin around in anger as I spotted him standing outside the closed door of the cottage with his arms crossed over his chest and a smug expression on his face as if what had happened was everything he had ever wanted. "Why are you acting like this, Silas? We talked about her before."

He wasn't wrong on that front. Not long after we had arrived here and she was spending time with her mother, Finn pulled me aside and explained to me why he had wanted to bring her here. That he was looking to get close to her because she was the one he was fated to, and he needed her to realize that.

That she needed to realize she was his queen.

The thought now irritated me. I didn't want them to be together, but then at the same time, part of me did. The conflict weighed heavily on my soul and thought I was trying my hardest to be supportive. It was a challenge. "I'm not acting like anything."

"Oh come on, anyone around can see that you're pissed. So, why don't you just tell me what is wrong so that we can move past this, and I can go back in there to my woman."

"Your woman?" Clenching my fists at my side, I narrowed my gaze further and sneered, "You think sleeping with her like you just did makes her yours? That is an amusing assumption."

"Jealousy isn't becoming of you, Silas, Prince of Draconia."

Shock filled me hearing him call me by a title no one should have known. Draconia was a name I hadn't heard in hundreds of years and the fact that Finn knew that bit of information put me on alert. I had been through a lot of things in my time, and hiding away from the title I once held was something I didn't want to go through again.

"How do you know that name?" I snapped, taking a step towards him, "no one knows that name."

Finn didn't even flinch nor did he seem surprised by the fact I was irate he had known my true title. Instead, he stood there staring at me as he was before but with a brow raised and amusement lingering in his eyes. "It's my job to know things, Silas. Did you really think when you came to my kingdom I wouldn't find out who you really were? Odin may have thought he was smart sending you as an ambassador, but it wasn't."

"What do you mean?"

He scoffed, letting out a heavy breath as he shook his head. "Fae know everything. Plus, I have contacts that do their job very well at keeping me informed."

Again, the irritation in me grew. He had purposely sought out to know who I was, but I wasn't sure why he would go to such lengths. "What reason would you have to know who I was?"

"The scent and aura of my fate lingered over you and intertwined with your soul. I guess in simpler terms, I was checking out my competition. Though that is irrelevant now that I am quite aware of how this situation will play out."

Standing there absolutely dumbfounded by what he was saying, I tried to understand how he would even know something like that. He was Fae yes, and I knew that their people had powers that the majority of realms couldn't even begin to comprehend, but for him to know about my interactions with Cassie shouldn't have been possible.

"You seem speechless," Finn replied after the silence that filled the space between us. "Look, I know that you're not pleased by everything going on, but it isn't about you. We all care for her. Even Lucas, no matter how he tries to act like he isn't deserving."

"Yeah, because he fucking killed her once," I scoffed in a bitter tone that made Finn's lips turn into a smirk once more as he raised a brow in my direction.

"Bitterness isn't a quality a dragon such as yourself should have. Everyone makes mistakes, Silas. At the end of the day, it's not about what we do or who we were. It's about what we are willing to do now to correct ourselves and be who we are meant to be."

I should have known that Finn would end up coming at me with this kind of conversation. The Fae were known to be wise as they were known to be mischievous. Their whole lives revolved around knowledge, which made sense as to how he knew about me.

"It's not easy to trust someone who committed a crime like he did," I finally replied, watching Finn step forward. His look of amusement shifted into one that reminded me of a scornful parent.

"Yet, Anna forgave you in the endn didn't she? Afterall, you were the main reason her mate had been killed—"

"That was not the same!" I bellowed as rage filled me and the fires of my anger bubbled to the surface. "How dare you speak on something you know nothing about!"

I had expected Finn to back down. To take back what he said. Instead a dark force seemed to cloud his eyes as black lines slowly crept over his face and the celestial blue of his eyes burned like a blue flame.

The evil side of Fae, full of rage and yet still composed, ready to strike.

I feared this side of him. Though I would never admit it.

"Do not deny it, Silas. I know the truth about what happened, and I agree with the choices you made. Bjorn was out of control and would have condemned the human realm to chaos had he not been stopped. If Odin was able to forgive you as Anna did, then you need to be able to forgive Lucas. You are mated to Cassie, and though you deny it now, you can't for long."

Gritting my teeth, I continued to sneer as I shook my head. "I am not the man she needs to be with. I can do nothing to make her happy. All I will do in the end is bring her pain."

"Fate!" Finn snapped, "has made up its mind already, Silas. You must fulfill the destiny and stand at her side as Lucas and I must do. This is the reason that Anna has come back. She and Cassie are one, and in order for Cassie to fulfill her destiny, this is what must happen."

"Don't say that," I replied breathlessly. The thought that what he was saying about Anna and Cassie being true was too much for me to handle. Granted, I had considered it so many times before, I just didn't want to accept it.

I had loved Anna with a passion so fierce it broke me when she was gone. I had wanted her to be mine, and though rejection was the only fate I had obtained in regards to Anna, it didn't stop me from loving her.

Cassie reminded me so much of Anna. The same fierce determination flowed through Cassie that I had seen so many times in Anna's eyes and with it, it constantly brought me back to memories I had tried to bury away for a hundred years.

"It's time to stop playing games, Silas. She needs you and with us working together, she will finally be able to be the person that she is meant to be."

Lashing out at him was pointless when I knew that he was right.

Letting out a heavy breath, I ran my hand through my hair and over my face trying to collect my thoughts as to what I was going to do. I couldn't deny helping Cassie, when not only was she my charge, but the woman I felt bonded to. The place we were in, her home, was full of negative energy and perhaps that was why fate had ensured we came back.

Not just because Finn had wanted to, but because we weren't meant to.

"Fine," I replied firmly. "I'm not going to say that I believe in fate or anything else because I don't. Fate has done nothing but bring me pain over the years."

"Hey... you're making a step in the right direction," Finn replied cheerfully, making me scrunch my nose in disgust at how quickly he went from irritated to bright and chipper in no time.

"Don't start that shit. I'm not agreeing to the mate shit with Cassie and don't you dare tell her who I am."

Holding his hands up, Finn laughed nodding his head. "Okay, okay. I won't tell her, but we do need to help her. This place is all wrong, and I trust in the visions she is having..."

Rolling my eyes I groaned. "Don't call them that."

"Don't call them what?"

"Visions, Finn. Don't—you know what, never mind." I sighed as I slowly began to walk back and forth. "Look, I went out and looked around the area. There is definitely a negative force, but it isn't celestial. There is a witch in the area, and I have a feeling she is what is messing with Pollux."

Quiet for a moment Finn seemed to contemplate what I was saying as he looked off towards the main house and then back towards the cottage. "We need to tell Cassie. Perhaps this girl that she mentioned before has something to do with it. I mean it would make sense. Bitter ex-girlfriend happens to be part witch looking to take revenge. It's kind of cliché but women tend to be complicated creatures."

"Fine, let's talk to her," I muttered as I made my way past him only to have him stop me before I reached the door with an arm slung over my shoulder.

"Whoa, let's not do it right now. It can wait till morning, Silas. No point in ruining an amazing evening." Finn chuckled, causing me to shrug off his arm and turn to him with a glare.

"Touch me again, and I'll break your arm."

Laughter echoed from behind me as I made my way back into the cottage. Finn found this all amusing, and though I wanted to burn him alive because he annoyed me more than anything, it wasn't an option. Cassie liked Finn, and there was no way I'd be able to do anything to make her unhappy. Even if I wanted to... my heart wouldn't allow it.

Cassie had me wrapped around her finger, and she didn't even know it.

Chapter Forty

Cassie

The dim lighting from the sun filtered through the cottage window as a cool breeze brushed against my skin. I hadn't remembered sleeping as well as I did last night in a long time, and as the memories of what had happened with Finn and Silas filtered through my mind, I couldn't stop the blush that crossed my face.

Finn had pleased me in a way I couldn't even begin to explain, and Silas had been a part of that.

Even if he hadn't actually touched me sexually.

My eyes drifted around the room, my body partially covered by the white sheets upon the bed, and as I took in my surroundings, I realized that Finn and Silas were nowhere within the room.

Did they please me and then leave? Was it just a quick fuck?

The thought that I had perhaps fucked up by sleeping with Finn last night made me cringe internally. I didn't regret it at all, but I wasn't looking forward to the awkward conversation that could follow.

Slowly moving around in the bed, I sat up holding the white sheet to my chest when the bedroom door opened and Finn came in carrying a tray with food on it, and a very unhappy Silas behind him. "Good morning, Cassie."

"Uh–morning," I replied hesitantly, "breakfast in bed?"

"Yes," he replied sweetly as I got myself comfortable and he sat the tray upon my lap. The array of colored fruits, juice, coffee, and toast was a welcome sight. I wasn't sure why they were being sweet like they were as they had never done anything like this before, but I wasn't opposed to being waited on.

At least for right now, anyway.

"So..." I muttered, lifting the coffee to my lips, "about last night."

Finn stopped dead in his tracks as a smile spread from ear to ear. "What about it?"

"I hope it's not going to make things weird between us..."

There was a slight pause before Finn glanced at Silas, who stood brooding as always, and he laughed. I felt foolish for having said something, but Finn, as always, seemed to understand how I was feeling and leaned over, kissing the top of my head gently.

"Don't worry," he muttered softly, running his hand over my hair. "There is no reason for things to be weird. That won't be the last time we spend a night together, you can be sure of that."

Well, he is overly confident.

The smugness of this man was both irritating and slightly a turn on. Something about his confidence made my heart swell and a small smile to cross my lips as I let my gaze slide from him to Silas. "What's wrong with you?"

Silas let his gaze meet mine with a heavy sigh as he seemed to ponder his words carefully before he spoke. "Nothing is wrong with me. I'm simply here to help figure out what you want to do."

"Do?" I questioned, unsure of what he meant. "Do with what?"

The blank expression across his face was riddled with annoyance before he loosened up a bit letting his arms fall at his sides. "Your brother..."

"Oh!" I exclaimed with soft laughter. "Sorry... I'm not really a morning person. Still trying to wake up."

It was true in all honesty. I wasn't a morning person, never had been. So for me to wake up and have conversation thrown at me, I wasn't always coherent. Silas didn't comment on what I said, but Finn made a snort that sounded like a chuckle before gesturing towards the tray.

"Eat up, Cassie. You need to replenish yourself, and in the meantime, we can explain what we have found out about everything."

It wasn't really a suggestion, as it was a demand for me to eat. Typically, I would have settled for simply coffee but seeing the determination in Finn's gaze for me to do as I was told, I did. They both stood watching me until they seemed content with me picking up one of the pieces of toast and placing it into my mouth.

"Wonderful. Now where were we?" Finn hummed before turning to Silas with a smile. "Do you want to explain, or do you want me to?"

Rolling his eyes, Silas snorted. "I'm a grown man, Finn. I can do shit on my own."

"Yes," Finn nodded. "However, sometimes you leave me to wonder."

It was clear that the two of them weren't getting along as well as I would have hoped. I had fallen asleep last night before Finn had come back from checking on Silas. I wasn't sure if Silas was upset about what had happened last night or if maybe he was upset at Finn. Regardless, something was definitely wrong with him, and I wanted to know what it was.

"I went and checked out a few things yesterday around the perimeter of this place—"

"Which isn't guarded as it should be," Finn said slowly, cutting Silas off, who glared at him with irritation.

"As I was saying...." Silas gritted out. "What I did find out is there are traces of magical residue to the north. There is a lake up there, and it was the strongest there. I tried to track where it was coming from, but I lost it about three miles west of the location. It ended in a small town, and once there, it wasn't traceable anymore."

"So someone is using magic on him..." I muttered. "Do we have an idea on what kind?"

Glancing between both men, I could see that they knew something they weren't sure they wanted to share with me. I hated secrets, and I had kept many over my lifetime. But I wanted them to be honest with me. The feeling of their uncertainty seemed to flow through my veins, making me question what it was that Silas had found.

"It wasn't Celestial." Silas finally replied.

"It would seem, my dear, that your family has a witch problem." Finn finally piped up.

Witch? That wasn't possible.

I was confused as to why a witch would want to cause issues with us. If in fact Ashley was a hybrid and Wiccan was the blood she shared with her wolf gene, it would make sense. Yet, it would also mean that she hasn't taken a coven or tried to be part of her Wiccan heritage.

My family had been at peace with the Wiccans for a long time. We worked together to make both of our communities thrive, and my father actually had been in business with a coven down in California. "That doesn't make sense… if that's the case, then we have a bigger problem."

"Why do you mean we have a bigger problem?" Silas questioned as I sat the tray aside and quickly climbed from the bed naked and fully aware that both men were eyeing me up and down like desert ready for the taking.

"I have to talk to my father," I replied absently as I grabbed my shorts and slid them on as well as my sports bra and white t-shirt.

"Cassie, can you stop for a moment—"

Finn was trying to get me to halt at what I was doing, but I didn't have time for that. If we didn't speak with the coven leader down there quickly, it was possible that more problems would arise from me handling Ashley than I wanted. "I don't have time to talk, Finn. I need my father."

"Which one, Cassie… because you have four… which father are you going to see?"

Silas' snarky comment pissed me off. Yes, I had four, but I only had two that I shared blood with.

"I'm going to pretend that you didn't just make that comment, Silas," I replied calmly, not wanting to have an argument with him that I knew he would only regret later. The morning had been peaceful and if that's what needs to happen to ensure that things got done without tension, then so be it.

Making my way from the bedroom, I headed out the front door of the cottage and down towards the training field where I knew that I would find them both. Talon and Hale were identical twins, and both biologically my father.

They were twins and though we will never honestly know which helped create Pollux and I, it was pretty easy to tell. I was reckless, like Talon, had his temper and personality traits. Pollux, though at times temperamental, was more like Hale. He kept himself composed, was extremely smart—a natural born leader.

And when you got down to DNA... they were identical. Which meant that they were both biologically mine and Pollux's father. Regardless of which actually fertilized my mother's egg.

No matter how weird that was, to think about it.

As I ran across the green, hilly fields that lined the outside of the training area, I saw the men fighting in the distance. My fathers both stood side by side with their backs towards me as they watched the sparring. It was weird, in a way, to see them like this as it had been so long, and though for me, it didn't seem too long ago.

The way that time changed since I had been gone still tripped me up. Both of the men standing there looked far older than I remembered.

Talon turned first to meet my gaze as I approached, a smile spreading from ear to ear as he opened his arms wide, to which I quickly jumped into them, wrapping my arms around his neck as he spun me around. "There's my girl..."

"Hey. Are they looking good out there?" I asked as he placed me on my feet. Hale ruffled my hair a bit as he pulled me close, kissing the top of my head.

"They are okay..." Talon muttered with a sigh, "nothing like you were though."

Laughter escaped me and Hale snorted, giving me the side eye and a small smirk in regards to Talon's comment. "I had a good teacher. Unfortunately, not everyone listens to what they are told."

"That's for damn sure," Talon muttered, shaking his head at the poor performance the guys on the training field were giving.

I was surprised by how much both of my fathers had changed over the years. No longer were they as strict as they once were, and Talon did have much more patience than he once did. Which was good for the newcomers, because he wasn't always the easiest trainer to have.

Deciding not to prolong the reason why I came out to see them, I let out a heavy breath that caught both of their attention and bit my bottom lip. "There is actually a reason I came to talk to you both, and it's going to seem weird, but I really need you both to be open-minded."

"Okay," Hale replied with a raised brow. "What's wrong?"

"I know what's wrong with Pollux, and I need your help to fix him."

The looks that both men gave each other was one I had been hoping for. They knew that Pollux needed help. Hell, I was almost certain that my parents had been talking about it for quite some time because there was no way this was a new issue, especially after what Trixie said.

"Explain," Talon replied, staring at me with a narrowed gaze. "What do you mean?"

With a heavy breath, I nodded. "Someone is controlling him with magic. I had a vision, and Silas sensed the power near the secret lake Pollux and I used to go to as kids. It isn't Celestial, it's a witch, and I know who the witch is."

The look of understanding that crossed Hale's face was hard to miss. He knew exactly what I was hinting at when I said that it was a witch. There was a lot at stake, politically, and in order to handle this, he would have to make a few calls.

"I see. Who's the witch, Cassie?" Hale finally replied as Talon seemed to be lost in his mindlink, a distant gaze in his eyes more than likely talking to my mother.

"That's the problem, Dad. It's Ashley, and I have a feeling she has something big planned for the upcoming event. Something that could risk our pack all together."

Chapter Forty-one

Twenty-four hours later and so much with preparations, I stood in front of the long mirror in the bedroom I had been staying in, checking out the sleek black dress I was wearing to tonight's event. My brother had tried multiple times to say that I couldn't come, but after much discussion with my mother, she had changed his mind.

It didn't matter what I was, I was still family.

There was no doubt in my mind that Ashley had convinced my brother that I was here to take everything from him. That I had come back now after so many years to try and destroy everything he had built. I mean, he was already convinced that I had tried to take Trixie from him, and that was far from the truth.

"Are you almost ready?" Finn's voice caught my attention and pulled me from the thoughts floating around in my mind all afternoon. Thoughts of what would transpire this evening at the gathering, thoughts of what Hale had planned. He hadn't kept me in the loop with it entirely, but if I knew my dad, he was going to have surprise guests joining tonight.

"Yeah," I replied with a soft smile as I turned to catch his gaze. My eyes scanned up and down his body with shock as I took in the attire he was wearing. "Did you raid my dad's closet?"

The three-piece navy blue suit he wore was paired with a light blue shirt and two-toned navy and silver tie; a great statement piece. Honestly, the last thing I had expected him to wear. Finn was a prince, yes, but his normal attire was more traditional than where he had come from.

"James lent me a suit," he replied, holding up his arms to admire the outfit. "Do you not like it? I thought I pulled it off well."

Chuckling softly, I stepped towards him, running my hand over the material as I stared up into his eyes. "I like it. Just never expected to see you in something like this."

"Well, if I'm going to fit in with the people around me, I should probably start dressing like them. At least for the time being."

"Touche." The smirk that crossed me as I glanced over Finn's shoulders to where Silas stood looking over a sheet of parchment drew my curiosity. "Everything okay, Silas?"

His eyes quickly glanced up to meet mine with a look of concern. "Yeah, everything is fine. I was just checking a few things out for your mother."

To know that my mother had gone to Silas for information piqued my curiosity. It was obvious by the way Silas quickly shoved the paper into his pocket. He didn't plan on sharing it with me right now, but at the end of the day, he wouldn't be able to hide it from me forever.

"Okay..."

The tension in the room grew as I turned away from Finn, and Silas and continued getting ready. The black heels I was wearing tonight were simple, and the decision to not wear jewelry made me feel more confident in my attire. I didn't want to come off as being flashy, even if I was royalty. All I wanted to do is get to the bottom of what was going on before I had to leave.

That way I would leave knowing my family was safe and the future would be protected. There was no telling when I would ever get to come back. The next time I could potentially see them would be when they arrive at the gates of Asgard… though that was something I didn't want any time soon.

Regardless of what people may have thought about me when I was growing up, I cared about my family greatly. I would do anything for them, and tonight was going to prove that. My brother and I hadn't been close in quite some time, and no matter the hatred he may have felt for me, I couldn't let someone control him like they were.

I'd kill Ashley before that was allowed to continue.

"People are beginning to arrive," Silas finally said, breaking the silence between us, "it's time to go."

Remember to stay on course…

The sound of a voice whispering at the back of my mind caught my attention and stopped me in my tracks. I had never felt a sensation like that and though one may have found it alerting to hear voices in your mind, I found it comforting.

How? I asked it hoping for guidance.

Remember who you are, Castor. Be the light your people need. Don't hide from your destiny, embrace it and be free.

Anna. It had to have been Anna and, knowing that, my lips turned up into a smile.

"Everything okay?" Finn asked, my eyes lifting to meet his as I nodded.

"Yep, everything is perfect. Shall we go meet the guests?"

Finn offered his arm as I took steps towards him, my eyes meeting Silas' and for the first time in a long time, he smiled at me. The warmth of that smile traveled over my skin and right to my heart. "You look beautiful, Cassie."

"You don't look too bad yourself, Silas," I replied as he opened the front door for us to walk out. This was the first time I'd been attending something with the two of them, and in that moment, my mind drifted to Lucas and what he was probably doing at that moment.

I missed him just as I would if it were Silas or Finn. I wished he had been able to attend, but it wasn't like we knew this was going to happen. All of this was the last thing that we had expected to happen, but I was glad I had Silas and Finn at my side.

Walking towards the back of the pack house, I anticipated what awaited me, and I wasn't surprised when the back door opened and Sam stepped out with a straight face. It was clear that before going in, my brother had sent him to set ground rules and though it was ridiculous—I'd cooperate... for now.

"Sam..." The warm tone of my voice caused him to sigh and I knew right then that whatever he was about to tell me he didn't want to. "Is everything okay? Shouldn't you be inside?"

"Yes, but I was told to come talk to you first."

Glancing at Finn and Silas, I could see they weren't pleased with being stopped before going in, but they also knew better than to intervene when it wasn't needed. "Okay, well, what is it?"

"Pollux wanted me to tell you to be on your best behavior. Don't speak unless spoken to, and to stay away from the guests unless they address you. You're also not allowed to tell anyone what you are. As far as they know, you have been away because of bad behavior and have only just come home."

Are you fucking kidding me?! Bad behavior?! I internally screamed.

Calm yourself, Cassie. Remember who you are.

The voice inside me calmed my soul as it spoke. A warm blanket cooling the anger that threatened to expose itself. "I see. Well, I suppose that is the story we will have to go with tonight."

A smile grew on Sam's face, hearing me oblige to the requests that were made. "Awesome. Why don't we go inside then?"

"I do want to point out, though, Sam. I will not lie if I am asked a direct question. So it's best that my brother keeps the guests in check if he doesn't want them knowing the truth."

Turning slowly to me, I watched his smile fall and though he wanted to say something, perhaps plead with me to behave... he didn't. "Alright, I will let him know."

An hour later and having enjoyed dinner with those sitting around the table, I could still feel the glare of my brother's stare upon my skin. He wasn't happy that I was here nor was he happy that I said hello to Trixie and my niece the moment I came into the home. They were family, and no matter how much he may have wanted me to stay away from them, it wasn't going to happen.

The grand dining hall was filled with people, most of which I didn't recognize, but one face in particular I knew made Trixie very uncomfortable. Ashley sat to the side of some young pack leader from the west and according to him, they were in love.

I doubted that, of course.

I wouldn't have actually been surprised if she had him under some kind of spell as well, because the way she kept looking at my brother with fluttering lashes and pouty lips didn't speak to a girl who had actually met her mate like the young Alpha proclaimed.

"We are hoping to have a pup soon if the stars align," Alpha Carlos replied as he looked at Ashley. "Aren't we dear?"

She quickly sipped on her wine, nodding her head with wide eyes as she tried to get out of answering the question. She didn't want to have children with him, she wanted the position Trixie held, and seeing Ashley act the way she did made me want to rip her throat out.

"Trixie, dinner was absolutely lovely." My mother finally spoke up to which everyone, even Carlos, agreed. All except Ashley, who rolled her eyes in annoyance before plastering on a fake smile.

"Yes, my mate out did herself again," Pollux chirped up taking her hand. "Why don't we all head all head into the next room? The staff have prepared more drinks, a nice fire and some wonderful music. The night is still young and we still have so much to discuss."

"I think that's a lovely idea, brother."

I spoke up, breaking one of the rules he gave me. All eyes, including his angry ones, turned towards me where I had sat during dinner quietly. I hadn't said one word the entire night and now that I had said something, I had gained attention he didn't want me to have.

Nonetheless, we all stood from the table and one by one headed towards the next room where soft elegant sofas of dark wood sat near the fireplace and a piano played softly. It was where things would eventually spiral out of control for my brother, but before that happened, I was going to give Ashley a chance to fix her mistakes.

"Cassie, what do you think you're doing?" my brother snapped, gripping my arm tightly as he pulled me back while the others went into the next room.

"I am playing the sweet sister and behaving as you requested. Now, let go of my arm."

His eyes were full of so much hate, and it broke my heart to see that he looked at me this way now. All I could do was try to remind myself that this wasn't him. That he wasn't the monster he had become, and Ashley was behind all of this.

"Don't you dare tell me what to do—"

"Alpha or not, I will put you on your ass if you don't remove your grip from her arm," Silas replied from behind me, cutting Pollux off. I wasn't sure what he looked like staring at my brother, but as my brother released my arm, I saw a small twinkle of fear in his eyes.

It wasn't every day you pissed off a dragon, and I had no doubt that Silas looked fierce.

"Keep her on a leash, Silas, and I won't have to put her in her place."

Stalking off, I felt Silas try to brush past me, but gently, I grabbed his wrist and stopped him. His eyes met mine as I gently shook my head with a smile. "It isn't worth it, Silas. Remember, he isn't thinking clearly and will be more than sorry when he realizes what's going on."

Sneering, he glanced at where Pollux had disappeared before letting out a heavy breath, returning his gaze to me once more. "Fine, but you better hurry with your plan. Otherwise, I can't promise I won't kill him if he touches you again."

Laughter escaped me as I nodded, looping my arm through his as I rested my head against his shoulder. "You know... it's sexy watching you act like this. Perhaps the demanding side of you should put me in my place a lot more often."

A low groan escaped his lips as we made our way into a room. "If you're extra naughty tonight, perhaps I will show you how demanding I can be."

His words were a promise I was looking forward to because, in just a moment, I was going to turn this room upside down and leave everyone in shock.

Chapter Forty-two

Evil comes in all shapes and sizes.

The thought crossed my mind more than once as I stared at the figures within the room. There was no telling who Ashley had her claws into, and the more I stood there evaluating what was going on, the more I had a feeling my brother and Alpha Carlos weren't the only ones. Which of course, was problematic. I had to be more careful with what I did.

Otherwise, there was a chance things could backfire on me.

Looking across the room, I caught Hale's gaze, waiting for the moment that he would give me the okay to handle what needed to be handled. Yet, his acknowledgment never came. Instead, he raised his brow and shook his head no.

"Are you okay?" Finn asked me as he approached. "You look like something is wrong."

Keeping my voice low, I sighed. "I'm not sure. Hale is telling me no, but I don't understand why. Something has happened..."

My father must have sensed my confusion because before I knew it, he was crossing the floor towards us with a smile on his face as the rest of the people in the room talked amongst themselves. No one here in this room reeked of magic but Ashley. It was clear she had been using for a while, and if no one else could sense that, I didn't know how to explain to them that she was the cause of all their problems.

"Walk with me," Hale muttered softly, keeping a smile on his face as he passed through the doorway behind me, back out into the hall. Knitting my brows together, I looked to Silas and Finn, who matched my confusion, but both nodded for me to go with him.

The moment I stepped out of the room with Hale and the doors closed behind us, I had a feeling he was going to tell me something was terribly wrong. The look upon his face gave way to the concerns he must have felt about this entire situation. I hadn't spoken with him since we had talked the day before, so I didn't have a single clue as to what he had found out when it came to the coven of the Wiccan.

"What's wrong?" I asked with hesitation, making sure to keep my voice low so that it didn't draw attention to where we were standing. The last thing I wanted was anybody in that room to overhear the conversation my father and I were about to have, especially if it was going to be about Ashley.

"I spoke with the Council and they are supposed to come out here, but the problem is they said that Ashley doesn't belong to their coven."

His words stunned me, but only for a moment. But it actually was a good thing she didn't belong to them because if I retaliated against her, then it would mean that things wouldn't go up in smoke when it came to the main coven of the Wiccan and our pack.

"Well, that's good. That means I can handle her..."

My father shook his head at my comment, causing me to stop in mid-excitement. I didn't understand why he was saying I couldn't handle her if the coven had nothing to do with her.

Nothing made sense, and I was tired of waiting on others to take care of business.

"It isn't that easy. Ashley is a part of something else, something that they too want to find out. They had been getting calls all over the coast saying that there was magic in the air. That occurrences were happening and they couldn't figure out what was linked to. But I told him the situation with Pollux, and they think she may be behind those other attacks. So they want to come here and take her away."

My world felt like it was falling apart. I wanted to destroy her. Perhaps that was the vengeful side of me, but I just couldn't stand the fact of her getting away with what she was doing. There was no telling if she was actually going to be punished, and there was no telling if Alpha Carlos was going to allow them to take her. She was, after all, part of his pack now.

"Dad, we have to break the connection she has with Alpha Carlos and Pollux. It's the only way to ensure that they are free. Alpha Carlos doesn't look like the kind of man who's going to just let his supposed mate go." There was a moment of clarity that registered in my father's eyes as he realized what I was saying.

If the coven came in here and took Ashley from Carlos, it could cause big problems for us. Carlos would think we had set all of this up, and that could start an unnecessary war between our packs that we didn't need. Even if we, technically, did set it up, if he wasn't in the right frame of mind, he wouldn't know the truth.

"I don't know, kiddo. I'm really at a loss right now at what we should do." My father looked absolutely defeated about the entire situation, and I could understand that, but for some reason, I didn't feel the same defeat that he did. Instead, I felt a clarity; a calm, warming, buzzing feeling that floated over my skin, telling me exactly what I needed to do.

Lifting my hand, I placed it gently on my father's arm and gave him a warm, reassuring smile. "Everything is going to be okay." I may not have belonged to this pack anymore in the sense that I wasn't a wolf. But no matter what had happened in the past, they were still my family. Every single pack member was still part of my heart, regardless if the connection was there or not.

I wasn't going to allow this woman and her magical abilities to come in and destroy everything that my family had worked so hard for. I also wasn't going to allow her to find a seat on a throne that she didn't deserve. Alpha Carlos's mate was out there somewhere, if Ashley hadn't killed her, and he deserved to be happy.

We all deserved to be happy.

"Sometimes, Dad, you have to learn to stand aside and let somebody else take care of things for you." I didn't know where the confidence came from, but it felt right in the moment.

"You have grown up so much, Cassie," he replied, cupping my check with a warm smile. "No matter what, your insecurities are when it comes to the position that you have been given. You are far more ready for this than you realize. I'm so proud of you, sweetheart."

Tears brimmed my eyes as I batted them back. The last thing I needed was to get emotional and as both of us softly chuckled, I quickly wiped a stray tear from the corner of my eyes and adjusted myself.

"Look at me getting all emotional," I laughed. "There isn't time for me to be like this, I've got bonds to break. Now, why don't we go where you join the party?"

Nodding his head, he offered me his arm and turning, the two of us made our way back into the room. The doors opened slowly as the eyes of those in the room moved our way. Hale and I had come to a small understanding, and the main thing was to sever Ashley from the two men so that when the Coven came, they could handle her.

The only problem was I was working on a clock that wasn't entirely in my favor.

I couldn't completely destroy her the way I wanted to. But I could sever the bonds she had with my brother and Carlos to ensure that when the coven came to take her, her hold would no longer be upon them.

Quietly, I took my place once again by Silas and Finn. The comfort of being around them put me at ease, and as Finn leaned in kissing the side of my head, I didn't miss the way Ashley stared at me. Ashley, from what I had noticed, had not stopped looking at Silas and Finn the entire night. I had no doubt in my mind she knew for a fact that they were far different from the other men in the room.

She had always been one to seek power placement and above all else. She was the embodiment of a gold digger; a woman scorned and rejected, only ever taking materialistic things and positions to make herself feel better about who she was. Never someone's first choice, but always tried to make sure she is their only choice in the end.

"Everything okay?" Finn whispered into my ear, causing me to smile.

"Mhmm..." It was the only reply I could give him right now as I stood watching Ashley from the other side of the room. My mind swirled with the possibilities of how to handle our current situation. "Just waiting for the right moment."

Silas wrapped his protective arm around my waist as he pulled me close to him. "One wrong move from anyone in a negative way, and I can't promise I won't hurt someone."

The low comment was made just for me, but Finn chuckled upon also hearing Silas. "For once, I agree with you, Silas."

"Everything is going to be fine... patience, you two."

There was something about the way Finn and Silas acted that made my body warm and fuzzy. I had never anticipated both of them could make me feel as safe as I was right now, and I was thankful they were here by my side when things were about to get heated.

Letting my eyes settle once again upon Ashley, who had her own look of disgust settled on her face, I knew she didn't like the attention I was getting. They were two men she would never be able to touch, and even the thought of her trying made something shift within me.

Something that let me know that these two men at my side were my mates, no matter how much I wanted to refuse in believing that could be true. They were mine.

As for Ashley? Well, she had a mate, one that she had selected when she was rejected by my brother, and though she had her hooks in two of those men, if she came anywhere near Finn or Silas, I'd rip her throat out and deliver it to the Coven on a silver fucking platter.

Chapter Forty-three

"Cassie, I never got to say how lovely it is to see you again. It's been years and you still look exactly the same as you did in high school." The taunting jab Ashley had thrown my way, I suppose, was to upset me. However, this woman was far stupider than she looked if she thought that was going to work.

Ashley, with her perfectly styled blond hair and glittering gold dress, had sauntered her way towards Finn, Silas, and I after our little stare down in the room. Pollux and Carlos had been laughing and discussing god knows what when she left their side. Something I was grateful for considering what was about to unfold.

"I suppose you could say that looks are everything after all. As for you though..." I let my comment slowly slide off and linger as I glanced at her from head to toe, taking in her appearance. "It's clear age didn't choose to settle well with you... you know they make anti-wrinkle creams to hide that kind of stuff."

Touching the corner of my eyes, I let her register that I was talking about the crows feet she had sported. Perhaps if she stopped giving people dirty looks all the time, she would have aged better and people would have liked her more.

Silence filled the room at my comment, though. I had just insulted Alpha Carlos' supposed mate in front of a room full of people, some who weren't paying attention, but some who were. I absolutely gave zero fucks about what she had to say on that matter, and I could see with her mouth open and her eyes wide with shock, she had not expected me to speak to her that way.

"Excuse me, I am a guest of your brothers." She gasped, feigning shock and disgust over what I said as she placed her hand upon her chest like the poor, pitiful little victim she was.

"Your point?" I question with a smirk on my lips as Silas tensed beside me.

"What is the meaning of this?" Alpha Carlos bellowed as he stormed next to his supposed mate. My brother and Trixie, not far beyond. "Did you just disrespect my mate?"

"No, I gave her a piece of advice. The same that she gave to me."

"You little bitch!" he snapped as he took a step forward only for Silas to let out a low growl that stopped the man in his tracks. His eyes looked past me to Silas, who I knew would tear the Alpha apart without a second thought.

Glancing to Trixie, I gestured towards the door. There weren't words that needed to pass between us for her to understand I was telling her to leave the room with her child. My mother followed Trixie as she, too, left quite quickly.

My fathers remained to ensure my brother and I didn't end up killing each other. Not that I'd ever let myself lose control again like I had before. Their eyes remained on us as they sipped upon their whiskey glasses and seemed to be having internal conversations within their mind link.

"I'm sorry. Did I not speak clearly? Your mate decided she was going to insult the fact I look so young, considering how much time has gone by since she had seen me last. So, I simply repaid the favor by explaining to her that while yes, I may be young and beautiful because time works differently, where I come from, it didn't do her well."

The snickering snort from Sam and one of my fathers caused Pollux's face to turn red with anger. He was not pleased with the fact I had verbally insulted a woman he thought so highly of, but only because she was using her magic to affect him.

"Cassie, that's enough," Pollux snapped. "I've had enough of you, and enough of this bullshit. You will not insult my guests."

His deadly remark was laced with venom and made me internally laugh. There was no way in hell I was intimidated by him, but I found it cute he thought I was. "You know, brother. You're right. I shouldn't insult your guests. However, there are some truths I think that you and alpha Carlos would love to hear. Some things that might be enlightening."

"This is ridiculous," Ashley quickly piped up, looking to her fake mate for a resolution to all of this. "There doesn't need to be arguing, Carlos. Perhaps we should just go. I can't blame Cassie for acting the way she is. She's always been jealous of me. Even in high school, she was always jealous of me."

Laughter erupted from my throat as she lied to Carlos about me being jealous of her. I had never been jealous of her. In fact, she was jealous of me. I had more attention than she did, and the only attention she got was because she was with my brother.

"I'm sorry. I think you have me confused with someone else. I had no reason to be jealous of you in high school, Ashley. I am the princess of this pack. You were only popular by association, or did you forget that little bit?"

Again, Ashley's eyes slid to mine, and I saw the burning fire of hatred within them as her lip curled into a sneer. She was trying to control herself, trying to keep her magic at bay, but she was failing miserably. And the angrier she got, the angrier Carlos and my brother got.

Which was exactly what I needed to know... how deep was their connection.

Stop toying with them, girl. Handle the problem and get rid of the witch.

Anna's voice echoed through my mind, clearly annoyed I was enjoying this instead of taking care of business. Could she really blame me though? Ashley had always been a nightmare and for the first time in a long time, I was enjoying toying with this woman as I watched her squirm.

"Very well," I muttered to myself, knowing that Anna was right. I needed to take care of business and quickly before the coven leader got here to stop what I was about to do.

"What was that? What did you say?" my brother snapped his teeth bared as he and Carlos looked ready to rip me apart.

"Brother, I think it'd be wise that you calm yourself, and that goes for you as well, Alpha Carlos," I said very clearly, letting my eyes slide between the two men. "As you can see, if you look around this room, we are not the only ones here. In fact, we are far from being alone, and the force behind the men in this room aren't going to let you do anything."

Alpha Carlos and my brother slowly looked around, realizing that what I was saying was true. The only people in the room overreacting were the two of them and that was it. "What is going on? Somebody better start talking because this is my pack and I am the Alpha—"

"Whoa, whoa, whoa with the power trip, Brother. We know you're the Alpha. Just like we know Alpha Carlos is an Alpha. The problem is, the woman in between the two of you is not the woman you think she is. In fact, she's a witch, and the only reason that she feels compelled to be here is because you denied her the throne and title of Luna, brother, and Alpha Carlos was the next best choice."

The angry roar that came from both my brother and Alpha Carlos over what I said was expected, from me at least. However, the two men that stood behind me were ready to rip them both apart if they even laid a finger on me. Call them over protective bodyguards if you want, but I did feel safer with them around.

Although, I had a feeling that they would both punish me later, and if the testosterone floating off of them kept swirling around me like the wind on a warm summer breeze, well, let's just say I'd probably be naked before we even got back to the cottage.

Not that sex should be on my mind at a time like this.

"How dare you throw that insult at my mate, you little bitch!" Alpha Carlos roared, but only before Finn had him pinned against a nearby wall, held up by the grip he had on the man's throat. Finn may have been Fae, but he was far stronger than most probably realized.

"Alpha Carlos, I'd be careful what you say about my woman. She is here for a reason, to help you. And though you may feel that you are far more superior than she is, I want to remind you that you're not. You're in the presence of something far more powerful than your world has ever seen, and if you disrespect her again, I will not hesitate to kill you."

Something about Finn asserting his dominance was rather sexy. It made me want to play out this little scene after all this was done. The sight of his muscles flexing beneath the suit he was wearing while he dominated this man was a huge turn on.

"You know, you do look rather sexy standing there with him against the wall. Maybe this is something we should try later..."

The comment was meant to be internal, but when Silas snorted in amusement, I realized I had actually vocalized where everyone could hear me.

"Behave, my lady, there is plenty of time for that later," Finn replied, glancing over his shoulder with a smirk on the corner of his lips before returning his eyes to Carlos, who struggled before him.

"Cassie, call off Finn or so help me God, I will make your life miserable."

Pollux had threatened me before, and though I had dismissed it, something about his threat right now pissed me off. His eyes were cold and the distant look in them let me know this wasn't really him speaking, but instead, it was Ashley.

"Enough of this, Ashley," I finally said, turning my gaze to her, "release them both and I won't kill you."

Silence fell over the room as all eyes turned toward her. A smile littered her lips before she slowly began to clap her hands together as if intrigued by everything that was going on. "Bravo, Cassie. How did you know that it was me?"

"Seriously?" I scoffed, rolling my eyes. "You're sloppy, and the magic you use leaves traces everywhere. Now do as I said, because we don't have much time before your keepers come to take you away."

The smile on her face slowly fell as she narrowed her eyes. "What are you talking about?"

"You will see... don't make me ask you again."

"I think you will find that you're far out of the loop over these past few years, Cassie," she replied, taking steps toward me. Silas tensed at my side again, but placing my hand on his arm, I calmed him before taking a step forward to meet her toe to toe.

"Is that so? Why would you think that?"

Raising a brow, she smirked as I felt her power slowly start to build. "I'm not the girl you knew back in high school, Cassie. I'm far more dangerous, and you're no match for me."

No match, huh? Internally, I was buzzing with excitement.

"Is that so?"

"Yep," she said, letting her cherry red lips pop as she spoke. "I could kill you and everyone here. Just with a snap of my fingers."

Enough of the games, Cassie. Take care of her. They are almost here.

Anna's words caused me to hesitate for a moment, and sure enough, I could sense the approaching vehicles. Though, I suspected Hale knew because out of the corner of my eye, I watched him slowly retreat towards the door, which thankfully Ashley seemed oblivious to.

"Alright then." I sighed, speaking to Anna but watching as Ashley seemed to think that I was talking to her. "Let's put that to a test."

Snapping my fingers, the power within me surged as I watched Ashley's eyes widen with the realization she had seriously misjudged who I was and what I was going to do to her. The sound of her heart racing as the panic swelled within her body was a joyous sensation, and doing as Anna had said before, I welcomed the darkness, letting it slowly take over me.

Down to her knees, Ashley dropped as if a force was holding her down in place while I slowly began to walk around her. "You thought that you were in charge here, but I think you will find that it is me who is in charge."

The moment I stood in front of her, I reached out touching her forehead as her head shot back, her eyes staring up at the ceiling with nothing but whites lingering within her eyes. The feeling of her connection to my brother and Alpha Carlos laid there within the white void, a tether that I sought to break.

As I reached into her mind, I snapped the connection she had built. The sound of two bodies hitting the floor echoed in my ears, but I didn't bother to look at them. Instead, I watched as Ashley's eyes returned to normal, and she stared at me with fear. "What are you?"

"What am I?" I chuckled. "I'm a goddess, Ashley. One that will remember what you did to my family when it is your turn to be judged."

The sound of the wooden doors opening behind me let me know that the coven was here to take Ashley, and slowly I turned looking into the eyes of two men and a woman who looked shocked to see the sight before them. "Welcome, I believe she belongs to you?"

"You're.. You're..." the blue-eyed gray haired man stuttered while staring at me. "You're not human."

Raising a brow to Hale, who seemed to find what the man was saying amusing, I sighed. "Well, I suppose that determines your definition of human. None of us are human."

"And the man there... he isn't like the rest of them..." the red-haired witch replied softly, staring at Silas with lust and intrigue. Something I found odd, and glancing at Silas, I watched him roll his eyes before the touch of Finn at my side made me smile while I leaned into him.

"Apologies for the lack of introduction," I smiled. "My name is Cassie, and these two are Silas and Finn."

"She means I'm Fae and this brooding hulk of a man is a dragon," Finn chirped up, his comment causing Silas to groan with irritation.

"Are we done here?" Silas finally started, causing the three newcomers to quickly come out of their stupor. "Take the woman and go. The bond she had with the two Alpha's has been broken, and she is yours to do with as you please. I would suggest killing her though because if she becomes a problem again, I will come back and kill her and anyone that stands in my way."

And there goes the brooding dragon once again.

"Such the people pleaser, aren't you, Silas?" I replied mockingly with a smile as I watched the two men pass me, snatching Ashley by the arms and slowly dragging her out. I hadn't got to have the fun I wanted with her, because honestly torturing her sounded more pleasing.

But I was pretty proud of myself that I handled the situation a lot better than I would have before. Maybe listening to the voice inside my head was a good thing, as long as I didn't tell anyone. Last thing I needed was for people to think I was crazy.

Chapter Forty-four

The next two days played out as they should have. My brother finally returned to normal and Trixie had the mate back she had longed for her entire life. Seeing them together and back to how they were supposed to have been was a touching sight. I was glad that they had each other, and for once, I could see that Trixie was beginning to look like her normal self, which also pleased me.

The only thing I didn't care for was the fact that no matter how much I tried to find a way to help Damian, it wasn't going to happen. Instead, I watched him grow sicker by the minute, trying to spend whatever time he could with his granddaughter. While hoping and praying that things wouldn't have to end the way they were.

Standing by the back door of the main house, I looked out across the grassy field, watching Damian, who I had never truly been close with, play with my niece. Even my mother, who stood nearby laughing cheerfully with James as she too watched them, seemed to act as if Damian wasn't dying.

As if everything was normal.

I didn't understand how they could be so calm about everything, while I stood here in fear of what the future was going to hold.

"He looks good right now, doesn't he?" Talon replied as he came to my side, wrapping an arm around my shoulder as he pulled me close, kissing the top of my head.

"I don't understand how you can all be so calm about everything. He's dying and everyone just acts like it's a normal day."

"Would you rather us be moping around and mourning the fact that he was going to be passing instead of letting him enjoy the last days that he has?" he asked me, causing me to pull away and look at him with confusion.

He had a point, but no matter how much he was right about what he was saying, I couldn't help but feel regret. Regret that I was so hard on him when I was growing up. Regret that I pushed him away, and acted as if he was weak for doing what he did all those years ago. He gave up being Alpha, and I had always looked at him differently for that.

Even though, when I was growing up, I didn't know the truth.

Truth that I now understand... though it was too late to fix how I acted in the past.

"It just isn't fair," I said softly, my eyes brimming with tears as I glanced back at Damian, "He is still so young, he shouldn't be dying."

"Do not let yourself be full of regret, Cassie. He has lived his life and he understands that with every gift there are consequences. Fate gave him a second chance of life, and it's obvious that fate now believes he is needed elsewhere. Who knows, perhaps he is needed with you in Asgard."

Turning back to Talon, I furrowed my brows in confusion. "What are you talking about?"

Instead of replying, he simply shrugged his shoulders and gave me a wide grin. "I recently had a conversation with Silas and Finn..." he said, pausing for a moment before carrying on. "Your time here has come to an end, and when you leave tonight to go back to Asgard, you will be taking him with you."

"What?" I gasped, shaking my head in disbelief. "No... it isn't his time. It doesn't work like that. I can't just take him with me—"

"Yes, you can. I've already cleared it with Silas, and it will be happening. Damian has suffered too long with his illness. It's time for him to find peace, Cassie. He is needed in Asgard with you. And if fate did not want that to happen, he wouldn't allow it. So, all we can do is wait and see what fate deems to be possible."

"I don't think that I'm ready to go, though. I don't think I'll ever be ready to go back," I whispered under my breath. "If I go back, there's no telling if I will ever see you again."

Talon chuckled as he stared at me. "Well, of course we'll see each other again. This isn't the end, Cassie. We will all end up in Asgard with you, just at different times. Remember, time there moves slower. You never know when we will show up, but I'm sure when we do, you will be there to welcome us with open arms."

I knew what my father was saying was true. Even if deep down I didn't want to accept the fact that he was right. I had missed out so much on my time with my family having gone to Asgard that the thought of them dying broke a part of me.

"Daddy, I don't know if I can do this... I don't know if I can be the person they want me to be."

For the first time in a long time, I cried harder than I ever had. Talon wrapped his arms around me, pulling me to his chest as he smoothed down my hair, hushing me like I had when I was a child. "It's okay, Castor. You're so much stronger than you realize. It's why I trained you as hard as I did, I knew this day would come."

"What are you talking about? How could you know I would be where I am?" I sniffled as I buried my face against his chest, taking in the earthy smell of my father. A scent that I never wanted to forget. If I was ever to be a daddy's girl, I was glad Talon filled the role of my father.

He was the one I had bonded to the most.

"Sweetheart, I know that I have always come off as harsh, blunt, and a little unorthodox for most. However, before you were born, I had a dream that showed me what you would become. Now, I wasn't one to believe in those kinds of things, but over time, I realized that it was the fate's way of showing me what I needed to do. It was fates way of showing me what I needed to live for."

Pulling away from him slightly, I looked up into his eyes with confusion, and saw his own tears lingering on the corners of his eyes. "What do you mean you needed to live for?"

"That doesn't matter..." He chuckled, wiping his face. "The point is that you were always meant to be who you are, and I'm so proud to have been able to be a part of your life, Cassie. One day, when I arrive in Asgard, you will have to show me everything you have worked so hard to accomplish."

To me it seemed like he was trying to tell me goodbye. Which I suppose was fitting, considering I was leaving to go back to Asgard in a few hours, but it didn't stop me from feeling like there was something else. Something important that I was missing.

"What if something happens after I leave? I need to be here with your guys."

"What?" He laughed. "Cassie, we have been taking care of this pack long before you were born. The pack isn't your responsibility, nor is it protecting us."

"You say that, but look what happened to Pollux," I replied, watching him sigh because he knew I was right. I hadn't been here and an issue with Pollux happened.

How was I supposed to just leave and believe everything would be fine?

"Cassie, this isn't up for discussion. You have to go back tonight... we will manage everything here, and I'm sure now that he is back to normal, Trixie isn't going to let him out of her sight."

It was true that since he had been back to his old self, Trixie hadn't left his side. In fact, I wouldn't doubt that they were trying to create more nieces and nephews for me right now.

A thought that made me cringe in disgust thinking about it.

"I guess you're right..." I muttered. "Still, doesn't mean that I like how this is going."

The tension that had been there between us only a short while before had started to dissipate. I felt the pressure less within my gut when it came to the thought of leaving, and turning to look over my shoulder, I spotted Silas and Finn and realized why.

They were calming me... they were the reason why my heart felt less heavy.

"I also approve of your mates, Cassie," Talon whispered in my ear, causing me to blush as I realized my father was insinuating that I belonged to both men.

"Thank you, Talon. I appreciate that you approve of me," Finn said confidently. He stood there next to Silas with his chest puffed out and a proud smile on his face. While Silas glanced at him before rolling his eyes with a huff.

It was clear that the men might not have seen eye to eye with each other, but they had come together to stand by my side, and more than once the last two nights they had my toes curling and my body melting at their touch.

Something that I would never be able to get used to.

Without another word said, Talon kissed the side of my head as he turned, making his way down towards where my mother, Damian, and James sat upon the grass. They looked happier than I had ever seen them and though I wasn't ready to let sights like this go, I knew I would have to.

"Are you okay?" Silas asked me as he came to stand by my side.

"No," I sniffled, wiping away a loose tear. "But I will have to be. Talon said that he talked to you about Damian coming with us."

"Yeah, he did."

Turning to him, I shook my head. "Is it even possible?"

His reddish golden eyes turned to me with a look of amusement as a smile slowly crept across his lips. "Cassie, you're Odin's heir. Asgard is yours. That means that you can deem whatever you want to happen and no one can stand against you."

The thought that no one could stand against me caused me to laugh. He was talking as if I was all mighty and powerful. Both of which weren't true. "I'm just me, Silas. I'm not some almighty being or anything like that."

"The fact that you think that proves why you are the best thing that has ever happened to Asgard. You don't let the idea of power get to your head, and instead, think of the people around you before thinking of yourself."

I hadn't considered that, but after coming back here and dealing with everything like I had, I could admit that I felt different. I felt as if things were starting to make sense and the confusion that I had felt before was slowly slipping away.

Maybe that had to deal with me partially getting closer, or maybe it had to deal with me finally coming to grips about my situation with Silas and Finn.

I wasn't sure of either, but I was sure that as long as I had them by my side, anything would be possible.

I just had to remain positive, and let Fate decide my future.

Chapter Forty-five

Night fell across the pack and with it came the illuminated lights of its people making their way towards the treeline I had once stepped through with Silas and Finn. When I had imagined what it would be like when I left, I hadn't expected that the entire pack would come to say goodbye to me. The eyes of so many of my people were a sight to behold.

After so much time they still cared about who I was—even though I was no longer a wolf.

"I can't believe that everybody came today."

"Are you seriously that surprised that they would want to come and see the Princess leave?" Finn asked me with surprise, lacing his tone. Something that I knew he probably wouldn't understand, considering royalty was a specific avenue of normalcy in the Fae realm where he came from.

"You don't understand them like I do, Finn. They never saw me as a Princess or royalty or anything. I was the spoiled daughter of the Alphas and Luna of this pack for so long, and the way things were back then... It was completely different to how I am now."

Glancing up to meet his gaze, his celestial eyes stared back at me while wisps of his white hair fluttered around him. I couldn't understand how I got so lucky to have him. Even when he smiled he was able to calm me, and though I didn't understand that, I was glad I had him. "Things have changed, Cassie. You have changed, and it's time to just accept that."

He was right. I did have to accept that. My future was going to be different, and I was going to be different. Which isn't necessarily a negative thing. It was positive in so many ways.

"Very well. We should get going, shouldn't we?"

Finn let his eyes float from me to over his shoulder where Silas stood, opening the portal. The only people who could go through were those of us who were meant to be there, and as my mother said goodbye to Damian, I felt like I wanted to cry.

There were no tears lingering in their eyes that I could see, but every part of me could feel the grief coming off every person who had come in attendance tonight. Damian was the original Alpha of this pack, and though he passed that title onto Hale, I couldn't help but feel that the pack still saw him as the Alpha he was before the war.

"Stop being so nervous. Everything is going to be okay," Finn whispered in my ear as he pulled me close to him, kissing my cheek gently. "If Silas didn't know if this was possible, he wouldn't allow it to happen."

Again, Finn was right, something I was going to have to get used to. He never really lied. He was actually very honest and though sometimes his honesty was too blunt, I also knew that he had a tendency to leave out details that were often needed.

"You say that, but I keep feeling like something is wrong."

Before he could say anything, Damian turned to me. His eyes seemed settled as if there was no fear lingering within his soul. "I'm ready to go when you are, sweetheart."

Of course you are, daddy, I said to myself, trying to keep my composure together.

Holding back the tears that threatened to fall, I nodded my head, pushing a smile to my face. "Let me just say goodbye to Mama and we can go."

"Of course, sweetie. I'll go see if Silas needs anything."

Silence filled the area as I walked past him, straight towards my mother, who I wrapped her arms around me. "You be safe now, you hear me? You take care of your father and let him take care of you."

For me, I was losing a father, but for my mother, she was losing her mate. The moment that he crossed over with us to Asgard and his life ceased to exist here on Earth, she would feel the connection with him break. Their bond would quickly shatter, and it would crush her entirely.

I hated that she would go through so much pain. But I was also strong and knowing that my other fathers would be there to take care of her?

"Don't worry, Mama. We'll take care of each other. You just stay strong here for everybody else and I'll see you soon. It's never goodbye. It's always see you later."

She chuckled. I had just said what she had said to me so many times throughout history and it meant a lot to her because this wasn't goodbye. We were just saying goodbye for a short period of time, then we would be with each other once more.

Talon tried to tell me multiple times. Time in Asgard moves slowly. Before I knew it, my entire family would be with me, which I wasn't sure if it was a good thing or a bad thing, but regardless of that, we would be together again, eventually.

After standing with my mother for just a few more moments, I finally pulled away. Taking a few steps back, I turned, making my way towards where Silas and Finn stood with Damien next to the portal.

I wasn't sure how this was supposed to go, but on instinct, I grabbed Damien's hand, lacing my fingers through his as I looked up at him with a smile. "Let's go home, Daddy."

And as he nodded, we didn't look back at the others who stood behind us. Instead, the two of us kept our eyes forward as we stepped into the portal. The white clouds of mist swirled around us until the green grass of Asgard once again came into view.

It was good to be home. But at the same time, the longing I had for my family would always linger in my heart.

Lucas

Twenty-four hours without Cassie anywhere in sight, and I was panicking. The last thing I heard was that Silas and Finn had taken her off on some adventure back to Earth. I couldn't believe it when I heard it. But it was Freya who told me what was going on.

She said that Cassie was allowed to spend up to two weeks on Earth, which was only a day or two here in our realm, but it still didn't matter. I was pissed beyond belief.

How was it possible that they would be stupid enough to let her go back?

What if something happened to her?

What if I wasn't able to be there to protect her?

Or better yet, what if Finn used this to try and win the competition, to try to steal her away from me, to secure a place with her so that I wouldn't be able to prove to everybody what I was trying to do?

The stench of betrayal filled me that she would entertain other men and go off on an adventure with them on Earth, while I was stuck here training day and night to prove to her that I loved her, and I wanted to be with her. To prove that I deserved that place beside her.

I didn't know whether to be angry or to cry because I hurt that much. All I wanted to do was prove to her I was the one she was meant to be with. Once upon a time, fate had picked me for her, and I was repaid for all my hard work by losing her.

That wasn't going to sit well with me in the long run. I would do whatever it took to keep her.

Shaking my head, I curled my fist as tight as I could and swung at the punching bag once more, the sound of the chains rattling as the crack of the bag echoed through the room. I had been at it for hours, going over and over everything that I needed to do, and yet I couldn't stop thinking about her.

"You're still here? Why am I surprised?" The sound of Sansa behind me registered in my ears and with a narrowed expression. I glanced at her from over my shoulder before letting a scoff escape me as I turned my eyes back to the punching bag that was quickly coming towards me.

"What the fuck do you want?" I snapped in irritation.

Moving towards me, she laughed until she came into view. "I came to let you know that Cassie's back and she's not alone."

Hearing this news, it stopped me in my tracks and as I grabbed the punching bag to stop it from swinging, I turned to Sansa once more with a furrowed expression of confusion. "What are you talking about? She's back, but not alone. Who's with her?"

Sansa was a beautiful woman. Her light honey brown skin, beautiful curly hair, deep chocolate brown eyes and unwavering attitude, ready to snap you into place if you fucked up was quite attractive. Though she wasn't the type of woman I'd end up with. Instead, she was more like the sister I never realized I wanted around.

And like a sister... we often had meetings like this where I wanted to strangle her.

Crossing her arms over her chest, she raised a brow with an unimpressed expression upon her face and shook her head. "You know you're a real asshole when you want to be, Lucas. I have been here trying to help you realize that you're a fucking idiot and all you can do is get an attitude about everything... sometimes I wonder why I waste my time."

"Jesus Christ, Sansa, are you just here to bitch at me or are you going to tell me who the fuck came with Cassie?" I groaned, not wanting to hear her bullshit anymore. She had been at it for the past two days, since the moment I found out that Cassie was gone and I went to her about all of this. All she has done is lectured me over and over again.

"Don't get an attitude with me, okay? You're the one that fucked up multiple times, and you're the one that's being an idiot thinking that you can just push her away until you win this competition. You do realize that you're not going to fucking win, right?"

"Again, Sansa, stop with the fucking bullshit. I don't have time for it, nor do I want to hear your negativity. Who came with Cassie through the portal?" I snapped at her once more, hoping that she would see how serious I was about my question. I was tired of the drama. Every time she came here, it was always a lecture about something.

And I didn't have time for that.

All I wanted to know was who had come with Cassie through the portal. That was it. Then she could go about her merry way. I would never understand why women had to be so difficult about everything.

After a moment of silence and her standing there staring at me with nothing but irritation lingering in her eyes, she finally sighed and gave in. "Well, if you must know, it's her father, Damien. It seemed that he was not well in the Earth realm, and she brought him back permanently."

I didn't understand or comprehend what the hell she was talking about. I didn't know that it was possible to bring people from Earth here. Though if he were here and he was dying there, doesn't that mean that he's a ghost?

My thoughts rolled through my mind with so many different scenarios taking place that I found it hard to focus. "So, she brought a dead guy to Asgard. Does that make him like a God now, or how does that work?"

"You know, Lucas, for somebody who has been through as much shit as you have, you really are the most ignorant person I have ever met. But regardless of tha,t and the fact that I don't have time to deal with your attitude today, we'll just say that he is a permanent resident within Asgard. Not a ghost, not an Angel or whatever other shit you wanna try and call it. He is just a permanent resident of Asgard, and it has been a long time since one has been here. He is here to stay, so be prepared for questioning."

Questioning? I didn't have a chance to fully ask her what she meant by that before she escaped out the door, and I was left there to comprehend all of the information that she had just placed into my lap.

Damian, Cassie's father, who never liked me from the moment that I stepped into the pack and started going to school with Pollux and Cassie was here in Asgard.

"Great." Either someone's playing a sick joke on me, or fate really has it in for trying to make my life as difficult as possible.

Regardless, I planned on trying to stay as far away from that man as possible. I had seen what he had done to other men who had hurt Cassie. And though she may not have known all the stories, I was not trying to be one of those statistics here in Asgard.

That man was deadly when he wanted to be.

Chapter Forty-six

Cassie

The moment we arrived we were greeted by the guard, Odin, and Freya. My grandfather's eyes stared at me with surprise and curiosity I wasn't used to seeing. It was as if he was looking at me in a new light—like I wasn't the same girl who had left.

"Welcome home, Cassie." His deep and hearty voice made me smile as he opened his arms wide, and I embraced him into a hug. "I see that you brought someone back with you."

Pulling away from him, I glanced over my shoulder towards Damian. "Yes, I did. It was his time to come home to the garden and fate has deemed he is needed here."

Odin was quiet for a moment, and with his silence I glanced back at him to see him staring at Damian with complete indifference. Part of me felt like there was a problem, but the other part of me knew deep down that this was meant to happen.

Moving past me, Odin made his way towards Damian without saying a word. The uncomfortable silence that seemed to pass between all of us. I looked towards Finn and Silas, slightly worried for a moment but before I could address anything, Damian spoke up.

"Odin, it's a pleasure to meet you again."

"Yes, it is," Odin replied before opening his arms and embracing Damian into a hug. A sigh of relief escaped me as a smile returned to my face. "Welcome to Asgard, Damian. Let's show you to your room and then tonight, we will dine and you can tell me all about how my family is doing on earth."

Watching the two of them walk away towards the open doorway of the portal garden was a sight I would never get over. I had spent the last twelve hours worried sick about what was going to happen, about whether or not he would be accepted and it turned out that I had worried for no reason at all.

I was pleased he had been accepted here because the idea of having him around comforted me. "Let's go inside..." Silas said as he came to stand beside me.

"Okay." I reached out to wrap my fingers through his and was taken back when he moved away, not allowing me to seek the comfort of him that I had on Earth. It was as if he suddenly refused to show the affection he once had with me and that was more confusing than anything.

"It's okay," Finn said as he took the place Silas once had at my side. "He has a lot running through his mind right now, and none of it is because of you."

Turning to Finn, I furrowed my brows in confusion. "What are you talking about?"

Finn hesitated for a moment before he gestured his head towards the doorway. "Come on... I'll explain everything to you. First we need food and a drink."

****

Ten minutes later, I found myself sitting in Finn's room as I once had before, surrounded by the flowing colors of the fabrics he had hanging around his room. To imagine what it would be like in his realm was something I had done often lately. Thoughts of how beautiful it must have been, and what his people were like made me curiouser by the minute.

However, looking at Finn, who took bites of fruit and cheeses drinking from a silver goblet as if he had no cares in the world was another sight I wouldn't get used to. Finn was a prince of one of the oldest realms in the universe and for someone in his position, you would think him to be a man who was stressed and not easily able to converse.

Instead though, he was a man full of life. A man who didn't take anything for granted and cherished every moment that he made.

"I will say, Cassie... the Earth realm is quite remarkable. Your family definitely has done well for themselves there."

Small laughter escaped me as I lifted my own silver goblet to my lips. "Yeah, I guess."

His celestial eyes looked to me with intrigue as he made his way to where I was sitting. "What's wrong, Cassie? You were happy when we arrived, what changed?"

A heavy breath escaped me as I tried to find the words to express how I was feeling. Between having to leave my family again, Damian dying—even though he was with me—and of course Silas acting the way he was, I didn't know where to start.

"I suppose I'm just confused by the way Silas was acting."

"Ah." He smiled as he settled in closer to me. "Well, I can tell you a secret, Cassie, but you have to promise to keep it between us until it's absolutely necessary to use it."

"What do you mean?" I questioned, our faces only inches apart as he lifted his hand, running it down the side of my face. The deep celestial blue of his eyes were memorizing and though I found myself easily lost within them, I knew the conversation had to be finished before we lost each other in the flesh of our bodies.

"Silas isn't just a dragon. Nor is he just a guard," he started, causing my smile to fall slightly as I tried to understand what he meant. "He is far older than that and when he came here, he was running from a past that sought to destroy him."

"Who would want to destroy him?" I whispered, his lips getting closer to mine.

"The man who wanted to steal his rightful title, a creature that wanted to steal his throne."

The realization of what he was saying slowly began to settle in as his lips brushed against mine, setting my body on fire. Silas wasn't just a dragon who sought comfort in Asgard. He was royalty that sought asylum from those who wanted to kill him.

Which honestly just complicated things a hell of alot more.

Silas

Walking away from Cassie like I did killed me. I didn't want to brush her off the way I did but now that we were back in Asgard, my duties resumed and I was no longer able to be free with her like I wanted. Odin had made his sentiments clear on that front, I was a guard and nothing more.

However, it didn't stop the ache in my chest from the hurt leaving her created.

"Silas, how did things go?" Freya asked, coming to meet me in the hallway as I made my way towards my room, needing a reprieve from everything going on.

"I don't feel like talking right now, Freya."

My cold and brushed-off tone only made her smile more as she fell in step with me. A smile was upon her face as if she knew exactly what happened and only had wanted me to clarify it.

"Come on, don't act like that. I can sense her all over you, Silas. She is your mate and your dragon has claimed her as his, hasn't he?" she asked, causing me to stop in my tracks as I turned to face her with a narrowed expression.

"It doesn't matter," I snapped in a low tone. "Odin made it clear what my job was here. My dragon will have to obey as I do, regardless of what it may claim."

Just saying that made my beast claw at the surface of my skin, angry I was rejecting the idea of being with the woman fated for us. Dragons were known to be possessive creatures and never shared anything. It already shocked me that he was quite fine with sharing Cassie with Finn, and possibly Lucas.

If Lucas was even still in the picture.

"It doesn't matter what Odin says, Silas," Freya replied, crossing her arms over her chest with a smug expression. "The rules of the tournament apply no matter the ruler. Tomorrow, Finn, Lucas, and Mani are going to be competing against each other in the last stage of the tournament. The winner will get to decide what happens to Cassie."

"Mani isn't going to win," I gritted out, knowing exactly what it would mean if he did. The man would submit Cassie to the gallows if he was allowed. He would ensure she stayed under lock and key and would force himself upon her to create an heir and secure his claim to the throne.

"You don't know that, Silas. Time is running out, and more than ever right now, you three men need to band together under some kind of agreement."

Scoffing, I shook my head in disgust. "Agreement? She isn't a contract, Freya. She deserves so much more than that, and I won't be the one to force her into something she doesn't want."

"And how do you know what she wants when you haven't even discussed it with her."

Touche.

She had a point. I had avoided talking to Cassie about any of this and the discussions that Finn and I had never really went anywhere. Other than we agreed she belonged to both of us.

"Look Silas, just think about it. Though, don't think too long. In the morning, the three men will compete to the end to claim Cassie. Her future hangs in the hand of what choice you make. Guardian or prince... that's for you to decide."

Freya didn't bother to let me address what she said before she was disappearing back down the hallway from where she came. Over the years that I had known her, I had seen the woman get into some crazy shit, but never has she ever been so invested in something as she has been with Cassie.

Standing in the hallway, I ran my hand through my hair as irritation and anger built within me. My mind raced over what Freya said, which caused me to turn and punch the wall with a roar escaping my throat. "Fuck!"

How could I have let myself fall so deep?

Turning, I made my way in the opposite direction from my room. I needed to see Finn about tomorrow before it was too late. If we were going to make things work then he was going to have to step up to the plate and ensure that he won.

The closer and closer I got to his room, the more I sensed Cassie within. She was here with him privately and with his guard standing by the door, I wasn't sure I'd be welcomed. Just because things were kosher between us on earth didn't mean that he would feel the same way here.

"He isn't taking visitors." His guard stated clearly with an indifferent expression. "He is resting for the evening. You will have to wait until tomorrow."

"I don't have time to wait," I snapped trying to calm myself. "I need him now. Step aside or go get him. Either way, I will be speaking with him."

The man's eyes narrowed as he stared at me. "I don't think—"

"Calm down," the sound of Finn's voice filled with amusement was a welcome sound. The last thing I wanted to do was put his guard in his place, but I would in order to speak with Finn about Cassie. "Silas, Cassie just left only a moment ago... did you want to join us?"

"No," I sighed, though glad Cassie wasn't still here. "I need to talk to you about something important."

"Of course, Silas. Come in... my home is your home."

Unsure of how I felt about that comment, I followed Finn into his room, prepared to discuss with him what needed to take place at tomorrow's event, and I was sure he wouldn't be overly pleased with what I was going to suggest.

Chapter Forty-seven

Finn

"What do you mean you want me to talk to Lucas?!"

When Silas showed up at my doorstep wanting to talk, I figured it had something to do with us sharing Cassie. I didn't even consider the idea of him coming here to discuss with me about the event that would be taking place in just twelve hours. The only problem was he wanted me to convince Lucas to join in with our plan, and then we would share her.

"Finn, it's the only way to make this work," Silas exclaimed, trying to make me see his side of the situation. "Without Lucas on our side, it only complicates things further. We need you to win tomorrow."

"Your faith in my skills is comforting, Silas," I muttered, lifting the goblet to my lips as I rolled my eyes and made my way towards the lush piling of pillows that sat within a corner of the room.

"It isn't that I don't have faith in your skills, Finn. We just need to make sure nothing bad happens," he replied confidently.

I didn't understand why Silas suddenly felt the need to handle things considering how he had acted earlier and how he had been so off with the idea of keeping Cassie before. The man was beyond confusing even for me, but I could see the desperation in his eyes. A desperation that cried for help to keep a woman that he loved.

"Okay. I'll talk to Lucas, but I can't make any promises that it will work, Silas. The kid doesn't even know me and seems to have a very self-centered perception of who he is."

Nodding his head, a smile crept over Silas' face. "That's okay. All I ask is that you try."

As Silas turned toward the door, obviously done with our conversation, I felt the need to know what was really going on through his head. "Before you go... what suddenly changed your mind?"

He stopped dead in his tracks, his shoulders sagging a bit as he let a heavy breath escape him before turning to face me once more. "What do you mean?"

"You know exactly what I mean, Silas. Why is it that you suddenly changed your mind about wanting to be part of Cassie's life? I understand that we all copulated back on earth, that you indulged yourself in the love that she wanted, the attention that she wanted. But the moment she got back here, you fell directly back into your guard duties. Why is it that you suddenly have come to terms with the fact that you want to fix this situation?"

He stood there staring at me for a moment as if he wasn't quite sure exactly what answer to give me. And I could respect that because, it was a hard decision. To know the choice between right and wrong, desire and need. It was complicated for anybody who would have been in his position, but it was important for me to know the true answer behind this.

Because if I was going to stick my neck out there to make things work, instead of keeping Cassie for myself, I want to know that the men that were planning to stand by her side would also stand by mine.

"You know why I want this, Finn?" he replied calmly, his eyes trying to look anywhere but at me. "I am in love with Cassie, just as you are. And because of my position, I am going against orders from the main god of this realm. It isn't easy for me to make things work, but you... you have that chance. As the winner of the games, you could make what we want a reality."

For the first time in a long time, I was looking at a man with sincerity written all over his face, stating that he was hopeless in this situation. I could make everything that everybody wanted come true. I did hold the key to all of this, the way for us all to be able to be together without anyone stopping us. But it still made me wonder why he would trust me when he barely knew me.

"Very well," I muttered, nodding my head as I watched him turn and continue leaving the room. I would do as he asked. I would go and talk to Lucas and try to find a solution to all of this. I couldn't promise that Lucas would do this willingly because he didn't seem like the kind of man to easily back down. But I would do what I needed to in order to make sure that Cassie was happy.

Now the problem was I had to figure out where Lucas was and make sure that I could have this conversation before the competition began.

Lucas

There was no time to simply go to sleep tonight and "get good rest" like Odin had told us to do. If I was going to win this thing, I was going to have to spend every waking moment training to ensure that I could beat Mani. I knew I wasn't any match for Finn, but Mani... I had a bone to pick with that one.

Since the moment that I decided to join in the competition, Mani had made it his purpose to piss me off at every turn. It didn't matter how much I tried to stay out of his way if he wasn't the one that bothering me, it was one of his goons. That was the last thing that I needed right now. I needed uninterrupted training where I could focus and plan my revenge against him.

Mani wanted to hurt Cassie, and I had heard from so many different people talking exactly what he was planning to do to her, how he was going to bend her to her knees. How he was going to breed her to no end and when he finally was done with her, he would make sure that she stayed within a cell, never seeing the light of day again until she either took her life or he decided to take it for her.

Of course, she was a celestial and she couldn't die. But I was sure that he could make her wish that she was, which was something that I wasn't going to allow to happen.

Away from my room, I quietly edged out towards the garden. I was planning on going to the training arena, but the moment that I stepped outside, I ran into a figure that I had been hoping to avoid. "Lucas, I was hoping to finally see you."

Damian stood before me clad in a purple robe, staring up at the sky when I initially had walked out, but his eyes fell on me quite quickly as soon as he heard the noise wrestling behind him. To say that he was the last person I was hoping to see would be an accurate statement. I mean, I would have rather had ran into Mani than Damien.

"Damien, what are you doing out here?" I asked, halting in my step, wondering if I should run because he was going to try and kill me, or if I needed to stay in place and face him like a man, which would have been the more obvious thing to do. I just wasn't quite sure what kind of mood this man was in.

He definitely looked a lot older than I remembered.

"I could ask you the same question. Shouldn't you be inside resting, preparing for the event tomorrow?" There was a look of amusement in his eyes that allowed the tension growing within me to die down.

"I couldn't sleep. So I decided to get a last training session in."

"This late at night?" Damian questioned me, shaking his head. "No, Lucas. You're going to go to bed. Even the best of warriors know when it's best to call it a day."

"Excuse me?" I muttered, shocked that Damian actually thought he could tell me what to do. He wasn't my father and he definitely wasn't my keeper. It wasn't his place to tell me what I could and couldn't do.

"You heard me, Lucas."

Shaking my head, laughter escaped my lips as I dropped my bag on the ground and crossed my arms over my chest in a show of defiance. "We aren't on earth anymore, Damian. You can't tell me what to do."

Never once did Damian waiver in his expression. His smile held and instead he stared at me with intrigue before his eyes fell to the bag on the floor and back up to me once more. "What is it that you feel you need to train for, Lucas?"

Dumbfounded by his question, I opened and closed my mouth before gritting my teeth. "I need to be as strong as possible to defeat Mani tomorrow."

"I see," he replied, nodding his head. "You're not worried about Finnick then?"

Of course I was, but there was no point in worrying about Finn. He was faster, smarter, and way stronger than I was. I had confidence in myself to an extent, but I wasn't going to be unrealistic. It didn't matter how much I wanted to beat Finn, I doubted I could.

"He is extremely good at what he does. My target is beating Mani."

"Well, if that's the case, Lucas, then you should already be ready. Strength means nothing in war, however, what does matter is the mind of the warrior. If your mind isn't at its best, then you will lose whatever battle you're walking into. The weakest of men can come out victors if they use their brain and not the body."

I didn't understand what it was Damian was playing at but he passed me on the garden path headed for the door as if he no longer cared what I was going to do. "Where are you going?"

"To bed, Lucas. Like you should be."

"So, you're just going to leave me out here to do what I want?" Of course the question was stupid, but I was so taken back by how Damian—the Alpha of Alpha's—was just leaving from a conversation without a care in the world.

As I watched him, he stopped at the door and turned to look at me from over his shoulder with a smile on his face. "You're a grown man, Lucas. At the end of the day you have to decide what kind of warrior you want to be. No one can tell you the answer to that... only you can decide."

What the fuck...

I didn't have the slightest clue what had just happened, but the moment he was gone, I was left standing there trying to decide who it was I wanted to be. Never once in my life did I really even consider that I needed to make this choice, but if the same cold Alpha I once knew could change, then perhaps there was hope for me in the future after all.

Bending down, I picked up my bag, and turned heading back towards my room.

Damian was right, if I wanted to beat Mani... I'd need all the rest I could get.

Chapter Forty-eight

Cassie

Thinking back on my past, I couldn't remember the first time I rode a bike or my first day of school. I also could no longer remember what it was like the first time I had shifted, but standing on the balcony terrace within my room, I could remember the first time I came to Asgard. It was the first time I felt like I had somewhere where I belonged, and today was the day my future would be determined.

"Cassie, did you hear me calling you?" Sansa came over bright and early to help me prepare for the day's events, and though I had felt like it was ages since I had seen her, I knew for her it had been a lot less.

Letting a smile fall across my lips, a bit of laughter escaped me as I turned from the balcony. "You seem more excited about getting out there than I am."

For the first time in a long time, I saw a sight of Sansa I hadn't seen in quite a while. Her look was more relaxed. She wore her skinny jeans and a loose, flowing yellow shirt that complemented her skin color quite well. Her hair was pulled back and styled into a beautiful high ponytail with loose curls that hung around her face.

Even her makeup was more on the natural side.

This was the normality of her I enjoyed seeing. The one thing I hated more than anything were people who tried to pretend they were something they were not and with Sansa, I always knew that when it came to her, she would always be honest and up forth with me.

"You're damn right that I'm ready to get out there. You know how many hot guys are probably waiting on the sidelines to talk to sweet girls? I mean, come on, you may be claimed, but I definitely am not, and it's been a while since I've been laid, so excuse me if I want to go check out the competition."

There was nothing but amusement laced within her tone and her comment caused me to laugh. Sansa, the party girl, was also extremely intelligent, and she loved men and loved watching them. She also had a good head on her shoulders and she knew exactly what life expected of her. She had high expectations and it would take one remarkable man to be able to capture her attention.

"Whatever you say," I muttered teasingly. "So, what monstrosity are you throwing me into today?" I asked eagerly as I glanced around the room, half expecting there be some gown on a mannequin set forth for me, ready for me to put on and parade around like the royalty I was supposed to be.

Sansa's eye met mine as she gave me a dumbfounded expression and shrugged her shoulders. "I don't fucking know. Go look in your closet and find something."

"Wait, are you telling me that I finally get to pick out my own outfit, and I don't have you or Freya trying to tell me what I need to wear?"

The shock in my words caused Sansa to laugh as Ansley came into the room, looking slightly confused with what was going on. "Is everything okay?"

Turning to Ansley, I nodded. "Yeah, everything's okay. Sansa was just letting me know that I actually got to pick out my own clothes today."

Opening and closing her mouth, Ansley stood quietly as if she wanted to say something.

"Ansley, I can see that you want to say something. Do you want to offer your opinion? If so, by all means, go ahead and offer it. There's no reason for you to be shy here." I was still trying to get used to how this girl operated. I knew that she had issues with her previous matron, Solina.

But she should have known by now that I was completely different.

"I was simply going to suggest the black and red dress at the back of the closet that you fell in love with when you first came here. You never got to wear it, perhaps you should wear it today. I mean, it is a statement piece or whatever it is that you and Sansa call it.... I just figured since you get to pick your own clothes, maybe you would want to wear that."

Her reply was timid but it made the smile upon my face grow wider. I was proud of her for sticking up and saying what was on her mind, and honestly, her opinion and suggestion were fucking fantastic. The idea of wearing that dress today sent goosebumps over my skin as I wondered what the guys would say when they saw me in it.

"I love that idea," I replied excitedly as I turned and made my way towards the closet, ready to sift through the fabric to get ready for the day.

"Does this mean that I need to get changed if you're gonna be looking like a hooker today?" Sansa called out after me, causing both of us to laugh as I shook my head and lifted the gown from its hanger. I admired the material, eager to put it on and show everybody exactly who I was.

****

Lucas.

After last night's conversation with Damian, I made sure to take myself back to my room and get plenty of rest. And I appreciated his suggestion because I definitely needed it. The moment I had gotten back to my room last night, I crashed easily but woke up feeling more refreshed than I had in weeks.

With my bag packed, I made my way down towards the arena. A new found determination in me that I hadn't yet felt before. Yes, I had always been determined to prove myself to everybody else and to prove myself to Cassie that I deserved her. But this was the first time that I wanted to prove to somebody else that I was worth it.

I had fucked up tremendously when it came to Cassie's family. Having been the cause for her to lash out and kill her best friend Melissa, and also the fact that I had killed her here in Asgard so she never was able to return home. I felt the weight of what I had done constantly.

It was holding me back from being able to be who I needed to be.

So being able to prove to Damian today that I was remorseful over what had happened and that I could work hard enough to win her meant everything to me. I wanted to prove to him that I wasn't the demonic asshole everybody assumed that I was.

Perhaps if I'm able to prove to Damian I am worth it, then maybe the others would think that I'm worth it too.

The moment my feet hit the grassy field that lay between the living quarters and the training fields, I heard my name being called in the distance. I turned, looking over my shoulder to find Finn jogging to catch up with me. "Finn?"

His celestial blue eyes reflected that of Cassie's and constantly caught me off guard every time I had a conversation with the man, which wasn't very often. Today, he had his hair pulled straight up into a high ponytail. He was shirtless, revealing tribal marks all over his skin that looked to be made of some type of paint, something that must have been Elven tradition before they went into battle.

Even the pants he wore fit snugly at his hips. But did nothing to hide the view of the defined cut he had that would leave nothing to the imagination of the women that would most certainly gawk over him.

"Hey, Lucas, I wanted to actually talk to you before the event started today. There's something important that we need to discuss."

"I don't know what can be important. We're getting ready to battle for Cassie's hand. Anything you have to say can wait until afterwards," I replied, not wanting to have a deep conversation or a chance for Finn to fuck with my head before we actually went out there on the training fields.

The moment I went to step away though, he grabbed my arm and stopped me in my tracks again, giving me a look of concern to show he was very serious about what he wanted to say to me.

"Look, I've spoken to Silas. There's something that you need to understand and we need to come to terms on this to ensure that Mani doesn't win today."

"What are you talking about?" I asked, confused as to why he was telling me he was having conversations with Silas.

I could give two fucks less about Silas, and Silas didn't really care for me either. So the fact that Finn had been talking with Silas and came up with some agreement and they wanted to bring me in on it didn't sit well with me.

"It's about Cassie. There's no way that you're going to win this battle today. I understand that you want to prove a point to Mani that you're better than him, but we need to work together to take him down to ensure he doesn't win."

"Look, I don't need your fucking help to be able to beat Mani. I've been training for a while for this. I can do this," I exclaimed in frustration. "I don't need you babysitting me out there and what the hell does this have to do with Cassie anyways? Of course we don't want Mani to win, but what does that mean that you and I need to work together? No."

The anger within me began to grow. I could feel my beast lurking beneath my skin, wanting to lash out at Finn for even suggesting we would need his help. I wasn't a weak pup that needed protecting.

"Look, there's no reason for you to be arrogant right now. Cassie is like her mother. She has more than one mate. We need to ensure that Mani doesn't win today. Silas, me, and yourself are all destined to be mated into Cassie. She loves each of us. Therefore, we need to work together in order to make her happy—"

"Enough," I scoffed, not wanting to listen to anymore bullshit he was trying to spew. I should have known this elf would have tried to get into my head, tried to fuck with me, to deter me off the path that I had chosen. That would make it easier for him to win.

Perhaps in reality he wasn't as good as I thought he was.

Perhaps this was his way of making sure that he did win because he was threatened by me.

I wasn't entirely sure what his game plan was, but staring at him with the narrowed expression of hatred, I shook my head and turned around and walked off. I didn't want to hear what he had to say, and the closer the training arena came into view, the more I felt that determination to prove myself.

I didn't need anybody's fucking help to win this shit. I was going to do what needed to be done to ensure that Cassie and I ended up together in the end.

She could have been with Silas and Finn as many times as she wanted, and though that thought slightly disgusted me, it didn't change the fact that I loved her.

I absolutely and unequivocally loved Cassie.

Nothing was going to stop me from proving that.

Even if I had to kill both Finn and Mani to make sure that I did.

The idea of bathing in their blood and watching the light leave their eyes fed the beast within me. He was hungry. Ravenous for revenge, and I was ensuring that I would give it to him.

Chapter Forty-nine

The cool, crisp morning air left white puffs of clouds coming from my breath as I stood on the starting line waiting for the starting gun to go off. After the conversation with Finn, I made sure to put his words far from my mind. He stood to my left. With Mani at my right.

Both men wore the markings of their people and though the hungry determination in their eyes would make most people fear them, it didn't bother me.

I didn't even bother to look back to see if Cassie was in the stands. While the other two were distracted by whatever they saw, I couldn't be. I had to stay strong. I had to make sure that my mind was clear and focused—otherwise I'd fall.

"Get ready!" The announcer bellowed out through the arena, causing us each to take our marks, the dark wooded forest laid ahead, its shadows calling me home. There was no stopping me from getting what I wanted. I was ready to take both Finn and Mani on—no matter the cost.

With the blasting sound of a horn the three of us took off as fast as we could to the treeline. It was under the shadowed canopies that our bodies became out of sight to those who waited patiently for the winner to come back through.

It was impossible to cheat and skip the line. We had to make our way through the trails fighting one another only to have a talisman at the other end that was needed to bring across the finish line to win. Yet, this was always where bloodshed became possible and often people didn't return across the finish line at all.

I wasn't as fast as Mani or Finn, and quickly their figures disappeared from view.

I had to pace myself though. I couldn't allow myself to get winded. That was how I would end up losing this race, and as I continued in a slow jog down the path the eeriness of the forest slowly got to me, my beast on full alert.

Something or someone was out there, slowly stalking me.

Finn and Mani didn't pose the only threats out here in these woods. In fact, these were the same woods that I had once visited because of Inanna. Within them were dark beasts that laid in wait to prey on those who ventured too far off the path.

Steady was the only way forward. Keeping my heart calm and steady.

One wrong move, and everything I had worked so hard for would be over. My life would be over.

A flash of light blinded me for a split second as a direct hit to my side caused me to tumble. I hadn't seen the blow coming, and by the time I got my bearings and spun around to take in the creature or person who had caught me off guard—all I saw was the amusing smirk of Mani.

"Did you really think that I would allow you to continue to the finish line, traitor?"

I would never understand why it was this man thought to piss me off at every turn. He had no reason to act the way he did or better yet be jealous of me—if that was why he acted like a dick.

"This isn't a road you want to go down. Turn around and continue on your way." To my surprise I didn't threaten him like I thought I would. I didn't even try to rip his head off. Instead I saw him for the weak and insecure man he was. If he was smart... he'd walk away.

Laughter escaped from Mani as he stared at me shaking his head, "are you fucking serious right now? You have a lot of fucking balls kid."

"Kid?" I scoffed, "who the hell do you think you're talking too?"

The tension in the air between the two of us was electrified and not in a good way. Mani bulked up huffed like a raving lunatic while I… felt the beast beneath my skin as I always did. As much as I wanted to let it out and let it loose on Mani, I knew I couldn't. If it got out there was no telling what the hell would happen or if I would ever control it again.

He lunged towards me moving swiftly to attack me. Dodging to the left I missed his punch but not bouncing back quick enough I took another hit to my right. Back and forth the fists swung between us. His grasp on my arm tossing me through the air, my body connect with a nearby tree before slumping to the ground.

Mani may have looked weak, but the strength he had was remarkable. As long as I was able to dodge him—I was safe. Unfortunately, I was wearing down and there for, more easily attainable.

"Did you really think you could beat me?!" Mani laughed maniacally. "I'm descend from Thor! No one can beat me!"

Lifting my head I spit out the metallic taste of blood that was in my mouth. My eyes slowly sliding up to meet Mani's gaze before I spit towards his feet. "Yeah, and her cousin you sick fuck."

The rough kick of his book to my stomach made me cough again, and just as I tensed ready for another I watched Mani drop to his knees clutching his neck with a wide-eyed expression. Whatever happened was to quick for me to take notice of until Mani fell completely and I realized that Finn was standing behind him holding a thing branch.

"Now do you understand what I mean, Lucas?" He asked me with a narrowed gaze, "there is no way for you to win this. Though I could have left you to die and only have to share her with Silas… I'm saving you, though I'll never understand why."

"What do you mean you'll never understand?" I snapped completely confused as to what the fuck just happened.

Straightening his shoulders he crossed her arms over his chest, raising a brow at me as he scoffed. "You seriously don't see why you would be questionable… when it comes to mating with Cassie? You're… less than appropriate for her."

Still I wasn't sure what the fuck he was talking about, even though I was pretty sure he was insulting me. Regardless of my confusion—Finn, a man who barely knew me, saved my life all because the woman he loved desired me.

That on it's own was interesting.

"I supposed a thank you is in order," I stated slowly as I climbed to my feet. "However, I don't understand why you would save me and not think I'd still try to beat you to win."

"If I thought you were that stupid Lucas I would have let Mani kill you. Yet, I didn't. So let's try not to be fucking stupid right now."

The statement was tempting to defy. However, he was right. There was no need to be stupid. It was clear that Finn was more than able to kill me without a moment's notice if he really wanted too. He was willingly let me live for Cassie, and I appreciated it.

Maybe he was exactly what she needed in life. He could be a lover and a protector.

"Fine... go get our girl."

My response, though not fully thought through, was clear for Finn. I was accepting the offer and that was exactly what he wanted to hear. "Good, but how about we go get her together."

*****

Cassie

Dread filled me the moment that the gun shot off into the air and the guys took off running down the field until the tree line swallowed them whole. There was no telling which of them would win, but the fact that Mani was even an option made me sick to my stomach.

I didn't miss the way he looked at me before the race started. The eagerness, and desire not be with me but prove that he was right. He wanted to prove that I wasn't able to do anything and by winning me he wont the title he wanted. He could give a shit less who he was bound too.

"What happens if neither of them come out..." I muttered softly my eyes refusing to glance away from where they had disappeared, but seeking Sansa's confidence that they would be okay.

"Cassie, did no one explain to you what typically happens in the race?" Sansa replied softly finally causing my eyes to slide her way.

The fact that she was asking me this filled me full of dread. Of course, no one bothered to tell me what happens during this race. One I had been gone, and two people seem to automatically think I know everything about this place.

Granted, I was far more confident now then before I had gone to visit my parents.

"Cassie—" my father Damian's calming voice wrapped around me as he leaned forward over the back of my seat to give me a soft squeeze before kissing the top of my head. "Stop worrying."

"How can you say that? You barely know either of them." I replied to him before turning back to Sansa. "Tell me what can happen."

She was reluctant, but finally caving in I felt like I was going to explode. "Well, it's a free for all. People usually don't often come out alive. They have been known to kill each other... the forest is dark and there has always been something wrong with is."

Oh my god! They are going to die because of me!

The anxiety that washed over me was unexpected. Heavy breaths coming and and out of my mouth, slowly at first but them picking up quickly. "They... they can't. I—I can't lose them."

The low blow of an airhorn resonated through the air causing my heart to lurch from its place. I wasn't sure what the airhorn was for, but whatever it was had the crows of people who had come to watch cheering.

"Damn, they move fast." Sansa laughed. "Either one of them works quick, and took out the others—"

"Sansa!" My father snapped sternly. "There's no need for that type of conversation, especially now."

Sansa stared at him, mouth wide open. She couldn't believe that my father would speak like that to her. But it was something she would have to get used to. Damian was very old fashioned, or should I say just old. When it comes to how things are done. The last thing he would settle for was negative talks about death or anything else.

Turning my eyes towards the field I slowly saw the figures of two men escaping the treeline making their way towards the finish line near where I sat. My heart leaped to see that the two faces of the men I cared about were both okay, though Lucas seemed to have seen better days.

"There alive—" I gasped with a smile on my face. "Sansa, they're alive!"

I watched as Finn turned to Lucas a moment of silence seeming to pass between them as Lucas waved for Finn to continue. Something I didn't expect, but as I looked over my shoulder at my father I saw the twinkle in his eye and the smile on his lips he usually got when he knew something no one else did.

Lucas was going to let Finn win, and though I didn't understand why—part of me was glad for it.

The moment that Finn crossed the finish line the crowds erupted into cheers. The games were finally over, and the Prince of the Fae realm won my hand in marriage. Something, if you had said it to me years ago, I would never have believed it.

"It would seem that you have your match, sweetie." My father whispered causing me to look at him once more with curiosity.

"You knew though..."

Nodding he scoffed with laughter, "of course I did. It was the best choice Lucas could make."

"Why do you say that?" I asked trying to understand what he knew that I hadn't been privy too.

Standing to his feet he looked down at me with gaze in his eyes I had seen so many times growing up. It was the look of understanding that he had often given my mother and my other fathers. A look that showed he knew more than he was telling, and though I'd never understand it completely it made me trust the process a little more.

Whatever was going on was planned, and I would have to follow the process and see it through.

Chapter Fifty

Cassie

I wasn't sure what to expect when it came to the games being over, but one thing was for sure, my grandfather didn't disappoint when it came to a coronation party. Stepping into the grand hall, I was greeted by the aroma of freshly cooked meats, breads, and the lingering smell of flowers. It was by far the most elegant event that I had ever seen, which was saying a lot considering the parties here never seemed to end.

"Welcome, all!" Odin's voice echoed through the grand hall with a force that caused everyone to turn their eyes to where we were. Odin stood on his feet with his throne behind him, me at his left, sitting, waiting for my future husband to arrive.

Nervousness filled my body at the thought I was going to be married or mated, as some would say. In my mind, I was too young, still searching for fun and adventure. Although, on the other hand, I also knew that fun and adventure weren't a luxury I was allowed to have.

Scanning the crowds in front of me, my eyes connected with that of Solina, and I saw the hatred she bore for me. She was pissed, and after what I heard the servants whispering about, I'm not surprised. They said that his body was body beaten with a blade having gone through it. On top of that, the creatures of the forest quickly ate him.

Not really a service you would have for a dying celestial, though I didn't understand how he died. He was a celestial, just like me, and it shouldn't have been possible.

Something that I was going to have to ask Silas about later.

"As you all know, the past few weeks have been trying. Many of the men who competed did their best, but in the end, only one person could win it all..."

The crowds in the grand hall cheered again before slowly parting to make way for the victor. A victor that I was pleased to see. Finn had changed and now stood there at the end of the hall, slowly making his way towards me, dressed in his royal attire of blues, purples, and gold. His hair was perfectly pulled back and tied at the nape of his neck with a blue ribbon as his celestial eyes stared deeply into mine.

He was a man on a mission, and the fact he was making his way towards me was enough to make my thighs press together with an anticipation of what he had in store for me later.

"Thank you, Odin. It's a great honor to have won the games, and also to take your granddaughter as my fated," Finn replied loudly, with nothing but confidence in his tone.

"Please, Finnick, come up here and take your place next to your betrothed."

Odin gestured to the empty throne next to me, and Finn didn't hesitate to take a step forward. However, instead of proceeding, I watched him glance at me with a twinkle of what seemed to be mischievousness in his eyes before he stopped once more.

"Odin, if I may... can I ask you something first?" Finn asked, in a very political manner.

My eyes quickly cast towards Odin, who stood there in silence with a confused expression on his face before he nodded. "Of course, you are the winner and therefore you can ask anything."

"Wonderful," Finn replied, continuing his steps until he was upon the throne's perch, turning towards my grandfather and the crowd. "As the winner of the games, I would like to request a change in circumstances."

Gasps echoed through the hall as I saw in silence. I was beyond confused, and for a moment, I turned to Damian, who stood just below me on the hall floor, staring at Finn with a smile on his face. Something was definitely going on, but I wasn't entirely sure what it was.

"A change in circumstance?" Odin repeated, more to himself than anyone else. "Well, by our laws, you are the winner, so in this situation you can do as you please. What are these changes that you want to make?"

"Well, as you know, I am the prince of my realm. I can't rule two kingdoms, therefore I would like to have someone who stands in my place here and at Cassie's side."

"You can't do that!"

"This is an outrage! Why did you compete!"

The comments thrown towards Finn kept coming from the crowd, but not once did Finn back down from his decision. Instead, he stared at Odin with an indifferent look that showed this wasn't something he was backing down from.

"Silence!" Odin finally yelled, quieting the crowd. "As the winner by our laws, Prince Finnick is allowed to make any requests that he wants. Now... who is it that you want to stand in your place?"

Moving slowly to the edge of my seat, I was ready to hear what he had to say. I too wanted to know exactly who he was putting in his place because, as far as I was aware, there were only two people that I would accept. Two who no one would ever allow.

"Prince Silas, the true heir to Draconia, will sit at her side on the throne. Lucas... the scored Lycan, will head the royal guard, and as for me, well, I will act as ambassador, which will allow me to come and go, taking Cassie as I please while also ruling my realm."

The roar of angry protests that erupted in the grand hall was unlike anything I had ever seen before. Both those who resided in Asgard and a few Demi gods were pissed beyond belief that Finn had actually suggested this. Not only that, it seemed that Odin was actually considering it.

Though as he turned to look at Silas, I could see he wasn't at all surprised.

"Is this what you want, Silas? Do you want to sit at her side and rule Asgard?"

Silas didn't bother to even glance in my direction as he squared his shoulders and nodded. "I will, if it is what Cassie wants."

"Even if we accept Silas, there is no way the Lycan who killed her should be allowed to protect our realm!" This time it was Solina who spoke up. The anger over her brother's death wasn't the only rage I watched linger in her eyes.

She was pissed, just like so many others, and for a moment, I wondered if Lucas—who stood by quietly—would even be allowed after the treason he had committed.

"This is true..." Odin replied softly as he turned towards me. "He knows nothing of how the realm works, Cassie. Are you really sure you trust him to take on this role after what he did to you?"

All eyes turned to me as I glanced from Finn to Silas to Lucas. My heart already gave me my answer, but at the same time, I couldn't deny the reality that he wasn't ready for the position. He was far from ready to have those responsibilities. Just as I was far from ready to rule.

Although, deep in my heart, I knew that he would. "Yes, I trust him. I believe that with the right teacher, he would benefit from this realm greatly. And I know that he will protect me with his life."

My confession seemed to silence the angry protests as Odin glanced from me to Lucas. There was truth behind Lucas needing training, and my grandfather seemed to be deep in thought over this. He had given Finn his word that whatever changes Finn wanted to make, he could.

"Who here will train Lucas for this role?" he finally asked, and just as I expected, the room was silent. That was until the one person I never expected to accept him did.

"I will," Damian announced. "Regardless of what he has done, I will train him, and if I can forgive him for his past discretions, then I expect everyone else here to do the same."

"You would really take this on, Damian?" Odin asked. "What changed your mind from our conversation the other day?"

I had no clue what Odin was talking about, and neither did Finn nor Silas, who both looked at each other, confused. Needless though, my father smiled at Odin before turning his eyes to me.

"I was given another chance by my daughter to do right in my life. She was the reason that Ivy and my brothers were able to bring me back. Her powers that were gifted from you are enough to change the world as we know it, and now, being here, I am able to be the man I was always meant to be and help to create a home for my family, and your daughter, when they arrive."

Odin slowly took steps down the staircase towards my father with a smile on his face before placing his hand upon his shoulder. "I'm proud of you, son. If anyone can teach Lucas to be the man he was always meant to be, I know it's you."

It was those words that brought tears to my eyes as I watched him then turn to Lucas, who was standing near my father, and pull him into a hug. My father knew what it was like to be outcasted. To feel as if he wasn't worthy of love or anything else, and he wasn't going to let Lucas fall into the same mistakes he made.

He was going to help Lucas be the man he was always meant to be, and because of that, Lucas would forever be at my side as well.

Wiping the tears from my eyes, I watched Odin gesture for Lucas to take his place upon the stage with Finn and Silas. He was hesitant at first, but after a moment, he made his way towards me with confidence in his aura, with a confidence I hadn't seen since before the situation with Inanna had occurred.

"Silas, Finn, and Lucas... Do you three promise to protect this realm together?"

"Yes," they replied.

"Do you plan to stand by Cassie as her mates for all eternity?" My heart felt as if it was going to leap out of my chest at Odin's words, but sitting quietly, I waited for their reply.

"Yes," they said in unison.

"Then let it be known that Prince Silas will take the throne beside Cassie in Asgard, Prince Finnick, the Royal Ambassador and future king of his realm, and Lucas Vega... the head of the Royal Guard. No one within my realm will stand against this, and those who try to will be condemned for treason."

Odin's words were law and one by one, I watched those within the grand hall kneel before the four of us. Silas, Finn, and Lucas rose to their feet before the three of them turned towards me. It was my chance now to stand beside them in acceptance and while I was nervous as hell, I couldn't imagine this any other way.

I had fought for so long to prove my love to Silas and Lucas. I imagined time and time again that they were playing with me or hated me, and in reality, it was the farthest from the truth. All three of them had planned for this to happen, and by the time I made my way towards them, I realized just honestly how much I was truly loved.

Fate didn't mean for me to have only one mate. It would take three men standing at my side for me to accomplish who I was meant to be. Something that now no longer scared me.

With Silas, Finn, and Lucas at my side—I felt invincible.

Chapter Fifty-one

Cassie

Had anyone told me I would be where I was right now a few months ago, I would have laughed at them. Never in my life could I have imagined I would have been ruling an entire realm. Nor did I imagine I would have three men who wanted nothing more than to please me in any way I could imagine.

It was weird for me to accept that Silas, Finn, and Lucas were all my mates.

Two of them had done everything they could to stay away from me, and Finn... well, he had always been persistent. He was the one who surprised me the most because where I thought he would have been an egotistical asshole who thought highly of himself, he wasn't.

"Are you disappointed?" The party was in full swing, and with Silas sitting at the throne at my side, I watched Finn and Lucas talking to party goers in the distance. My heart swelled with pride and excitement.

"No, not at all," I replied, turning to Silas with a smile spread from ear to ear. "Just shocked."

He chuckled at me, nodding as he reached over and took my hand. "I'm sorry I didn't tell you."

"Tell me about what?" Confused as to what he was referring to, I watched him point to the top of his head, making a circle motion to signify a crown or what one would think was a halo.

"Oh..."

"Yeah, oh." The laughter that left him was comforting, and as he lifted my hand to his lips, kissing the backs of my knuckles gently, I felt the butterflies within my stomach flutter.

"It's okay, Silas. I'm sure you had your reasons. What matters most is that now, we are all together and will be for all eternity."

The sound of music filled the hall as many began to dance, and though I contemplated joining them, I found my attention directed elsewhere. Finn made his way towards me with a look of determination in his eyes. He gestured to Silas with his head to somewhere off the stage area.

The silent communication with the two of them was irritating at times, but with Silas holding my hand, I found myself on my feet before Finn even reached me.

"What's going on?" I asked with furrowed brows of confusion.

"We have a surprise for you," Finn replied as Silas led me off the stage.

Not one single person seemed to notice we were leaving. The party was continuing as it always did and as I stepped through the side door, I found myself being led the other way, down one hallway and through another.

I wasn't keen on surprises, but after everything that had transpired, I wasn't going to ruin whatever these three men had in mind. After all, like Finn had told me many times, I'll enjoy it.

The moment I realized we were going to my suite, I felt a twinge of excitement wondering if they were planning to mark me or mate with me or something. I had no idea how this worked with me as a celestial because I wasn't a shifter anymore.

I stepped into the room and was taken back by the sight. Candles and flower petals were scattered everywhere and within the center of the room stood Lucas. He and I hadn't had a moment to speak the entire evening, nor had we really had any proper conversation since the games had started.

Realizing that Silas and Finn had brought me to him was unexpected. Turning to look at them both, a frown fell over my face before I turned back to Lucas in confusion. "What's going on?"

Taking a deep breath, Lucas stepped toward me with determination in his eyes. "I know that things have never been great between us, Cassie. But I want to fix that. When Silas and Finn told me the plan for all of us to be together, I couldn't understand it—"

He was breathless as he spoke, his steps slow until he was right in front of me.

"I understand now, Cassie," he whispered, his hand lifting to brush against the side of my face as he stared down at me with those same dark eyes I looked into the night I found out we were destined to be mates. "I may not feel the wolf's bond anymore, but I do still feel a connection with you that I will never understand."

"Does this mean you won't leave me again?" My question was completely random, but for some reason, it was the only thing that came to mind at that moment. Deep down, I was terrified he was going to leave me again. That I would wake up one morning, and all this had been just a dream, a fantasy I was simply living out in my head.

The corner of his lips turned up into a smirk as he shook his head. "No, I won't ever be leaving you again, Cassie. I love you too much to ever leave you."

Hearing him say he loved me made tears brim my eyes. I had wanted to hear it for so long, and between us both being stubborn and all the other shit that had happened in our time in Asgard, I didn't realize how much it would mean to me to hear it.

"You do?"

"Yes," he whispered again. "I will always love you."

Closing the space between us, he wrapped one arm around my waist and pulled me flush against his chest before pressing his lips against mine. The kiss took my breath away. He deepened it, kissing me as if he had never kissed me before. The heat of his touch upon my skin crept over me and down between my thighs.

Everything about this moment was exactly as I had once imagined it and now that it was happening, I didn't want it to stop.

Before I knew what was going on, his grip on me loosened and the touch of another caught me completely off guard. Breaking our kiss I looked to my left and was met with celestial blue eyes, and on my right, the reddish toned ones I had grown so familiar with.

Both Silas and Finn had come to join them and the thought of them all taking me together was something I couldn't fathom.

"So, how are we going to do this gentleman?" Finn asked, causing Silas to chuckle.

"Well, since you won the tournament and made all this possible, it's only fair she carries for you first," Lucas' statement made me turn to him in shock. I had never considered the fact that I would be having children anytime soon, and now hearing the possibility, I wasn't sure that I was completely ready for that.

"Don't look so worried," Silas replied as he gripped my chin lightly and pulled it towards him. "If you're not ready to have children, you don't have to right now."

"It's not that I'm completely unsure, I have just never considered it."

My admission was hard to make because I didn't want to disappoint anyone in the room, but to my surprise all three of them seemed to understand.

"If that's what you wish for, my queen, then I will make sure to not let that happen. However, we weren't exactly careful any other time we had sex." Finn wasn't wrong there. We weren't careful and realizing that made my heart race. There was no going back now, and no reason to completely panic. That was my fault for never having considered it before. "Very true, I suppose if it happens... it happens."

Grabbing the side of Finn's face, I pulled him towards me, planting my lips upon his with a hunger I didn't know I had. He didn't hesitate one bit to put the same amount of hunger and aggression into his response. He reached up towards the hair clip in my hair, removing it so my hair fell down in waves over my shoulders.

"We're going to make you feel amazing things, Cassie," he practically purred against my lips. Silas undid the buttons on the back of my dress, the cool hair hitting my bare skin as a low rumble echoed from Silas' throat behind me.

"She is completely naked beneath this dress," he replied as the gown dropped to the floor and each of the men got to feast upon my naked body.

"I am." My cocky remark followed by a smirk was enough for Finn to snatch me up, toss me over his shoulder and make his way towards the separate room where my bed laid. A swift smack to my ass caused a sting that made warmth pool between my legs.

No more words passed between us after my response. My body was tossed upon the soft cotton blankets and sheets of my bed, my eyes staring up into three sets of hungry gazes as each of my mates began to undress.

They were unique in their own way and all mine. Ripped abs, tattoos, flawless skin, and black, blue, and reddish-golden eyes. A blend of lean muscle and bulked demi-gods. They were absolutely perfect. However, when they dropped their pants to reveal the beasts between their legs, I knew I was in for one hell of a ride.

"Are you ready to play with all three of us?" Lucas said in a teasing manner.

Raising my brow, I smirked. "What, are you saying you know how to share?"

Finn didn't bother to hide his laughter as he climbed on the bed towards me. "Oh, you little minx, you have no idea what we're capable of."

Gripping my thighs, he jerked them apart and dove face first between my legs. His mouth attached to my core like a hungry lion as his tongue did circles around my clit that had my back arching in pleasure. The sensations he created in me were a thing of dreams. No man had ever ate me out the way he did and I loved it.

"Oh, fuck," I moaned as Silas and Lucas came to either side of me.

"While he fucks you with his tongue, little one, your going to please both Lucas and I with your mouth." Demanding as always, Silas climbed on the bed to one side of my head while Lucas followed suit on the other both of them stroking the lengths of their rigid cocks, waiting for me to taste them.

I was hungry to have them in my mouth. Turning to Lucas first, I leaned my head over, running my tongue over the slit of his cock before slowly lowering my lips over it.

Deep throating his dick, one, two, three times, I swapped and gave Silas his turn. His spikey rigid cock waiting for me to embrace him. My fingers gently stroking over the length feeling the soft touch of his spikes, even though they looked like they would hurt

Over and over again I switched until I was gagging on Lucas' cock as Finn caused me to spiral out of control. My eyes rolled into the back of my head as Lucas' cock popped from my mouth; a scream ripping from my throat as I came undone.

"I think it's time to see how much she can really handle," Finn said, wiping his mouth as Silas moved, and Finn came to lay on the bed next to me. "Climb up here and show them how well you can ride me."

Taking a breath, I giggled but did as I was told. My legs came to rest on either side of his thighs as I lowered my aching pussy down his long thick erection. Finn filled me to the brink, and as he did, I gestured for Silas to come close. "I want to suck you off as I fuck him."

"Is that right?" he murmured coming closer. "What if Lucas played with your ass at the same time? Would you like that too?"

The idea was overwhelming, but I couldn't refuse. I wanted to know what it was like to have them all touching me, pleasing me, pushing me to the brink and then beyond.

"Yes..." I gasped. "Please, I want it."

With Finn inside me, Silas' standing off to my right side with his cock in my mouth, and Lucas using his finger against my ass, I could barely contain my pleasure. All of this was more than I could take. Eventually, Lucas gripped my hips, stopping the fast motions I took on Finn's cock before slowly pressing his dick into my puckered hole.

Inch by inch, he slid into my ass, the fullness of Finn and Lucas causing me to gasp out as I tried to relax myself against them. Only when I nodded at Finn did he begin to move again. Slowly at first and then faster and faster, his fast movements with Lucas' slow ones tipped me over the edge as I gagged on Silas' erection—screaming as I came undone.

Lucas pulled out first, the feeling of his cum spraying upon my ass as a groan escaped his lips was a tantalizing combination. Silas didn't back down as he shot his load down my throat at the same time Finn thrusted up one last time hard, before stilling inside me.

The three of us found our release, only for me to collapse upon Finn's chest trying to find my breath. "Jesus Christ…"

Moving from the bed, Silas disappeared with Lucas towards the bathroom. Both men came back a moment later looking slightly cleaned up with Lucas carrying a warm rag. "Don't tell me you're already worn out, Cassie. We still have all night ahead of us—"

"And tomorrow," Silas replied, finishing off Lucas' sentence.

Laughter escaped us all as Lucas helped to clean me up before I rolled over onto the bed, my body spent and a new feeling of happiness filling my soul. All I had ever wanted to do was to be happy, and have someone to love me. Now, I have three men to do that.

"I do have to leave in a few days to go back to my realm, Cassie," Finn said, catching me off guard. My eyes met his as I watched him stand at the edge of the bed, slipping back on his pants. "I was hoping you may accompany me for a week or two. It will give Silas and Lucas time to take care of things here while you get a much needed vacation."

"I mean, I'm fine with that, if everyone else is."

Silas plopped onto the bed next to me, his lips finding the side of his head as he smiled. "We already discussed how everything is going to work, and Lucas and I do have a lot we need to do over the next few weeks. So, if you want to go, then it's okay with us."

"Really?" I asked, turning my eyes to Lucas only to see him nod in approval.

"I'm down with it. Your dad has a lot for me to do over the next few months."

"I bet he does," I laughed, before turning back to Finn. "Okay, I guess I'm off to live with the fairies for a while."

Finn deadpanned as Silas and Lucas both began to laugh at my response. I had no idea what was so funny, but when Finn ran a hand down his face and crawled back on the bed next to me with a smile, I realized it must have been what I had said.

"We aren't fairies like Tinker, what's her name, Cassie. We're Fae... and you, my love, are their new Queen."

To my darling readers...

Did you really think this journey was over? Haha haha.

Not even close.

There are at least seven more books in this series to be released... this year.

However, this time we are going on a wild journey that will take us to realms we have never seen before and destinations that will blow your minds.

Sex isn't the only thing that the Celestials have to offer. There are far more sinister things lurking within the darkness, waiting to devour you whole.

Check the following pages for a sneak peek on the next book in the series, as well as the first book in my new series.

LILLITH CARRIE

THE TEMPTRESS OF ELDER HALLOW

Chapter One

Salem, Massachusetts.

More than a city known for the fanatics who came in search of supernatural adventures, Salem was a place that held history and power within it. A place supernaturals of all kinds flocked to regularly to find solace in something magical and enchanting. Not that I could complain about something like that, I had done the same thing.

The only difference between me and the fanatics... I wasn't exactly human.

Too many times I ventured out at night in order to sate my hunger, and just like always, I found my victim willingly. It wasn't like I had a choice. It wasn't who I was, but instead, what I was.

A predator.

A predator constantly hunting, seeking my next fill for desire, which coursed through the veins of any man who crossed my path.

Years of practice had led me to control my urges more than others like me, which also got me classified as tame. But even if I was more tame than others, I still had trouble controlling myself sometimes.

Though I made sure that I never killed them. I refused to be like my mother in that aspect.

Tonight had been no different. I had left work with every intention of just going home, but instead the urge to feed took over, and I was forced to give in. So under the slowly darkening sky, I had made my way towards the nearest night club in search of my next fix.

A fix that gave me what I needed and made me feel a hell of a lot more powerful afterwards.

Pulling my keys from my pocket, I placed them in the lock of my front door and turned the knob. The smell of lavender and patchouli from the incense burners invaded my senses, welcoming me home.

My home wasn't much, but after the shit I had been through over the past few years, it was mine.

Walking into my small but spacious one-bedroom apartment, I smiled, happy to finally return home after a long day. Work had been agonizing, and though I hadn't expected to feed tonight, the offer that presented itself was too good to pass up.

"You're getting sloppy," a cool sweet voice said from the shadows of my living room. I wasn't unfamiliar with the voice and as she turned on the lamp on the table next to her, the dim yellow light filled the space around us. I let my smile fall.

"Sloppy, Claire?" I chuckled, setting my keys and purse down on the table next to the front door. "Never. I just finished up work."

The soft green eyes of my sister narrowed as a smirk settled on her perfectly red lips. "Is that right? So, who was the delicious emo-kid with multiple ear piercings you feasted on earlier?"

I shouldn't have been surprised she was spying on me. My sister had a thing for watching me so she could run back to our mother and tell her everything that I was doing that didn't fit with the "code" of how we were supposed to live. Rolling my eyes, I moved away from the table by the front door and further into the living room.

"He is like... twenty-four. I'd hardly call him a kid. Plus, I didn't kill him like you would have. I left him slightly... coherent."

The jab I made caused her to purse her lips with annoyance as she crossed one of her legs over the other, laying her hands delicately on her lap. "Yeah, in an alley with his dick out. Not very classy, Taylor."

"Perhaps, but in the end, we both got pleasure in some sort of way."

With a sneer on her lips, she stared at me with disgust. "Doesn't change the fact that you left him the way you did."

Her description of him made me chuckle. It wasn't entirely my fault the guy ended up that way.

"Oh, stop being such a prude. He enjoyed it... mostly," I replied, thinking about the cocky guy who claimed he could make me scream his name in four languages. In the end, it turned out he was the one who ended up screaming right before he passed out.

My sweet sister Claire, as my mother would call her, was the last person I had wanted to see this evening. Ever since we were kids, she had been a pain in my ass and did everything she could to point out my flaws to make herself look better.

Like kissing Mommy Dearest's ass on the regular.

Something I wouldn't do.

"This has to stop—"

"If you came to lecture me, I'm not in the mood for it," I stated coldly, cutting her off mid-sentence, "so why don't you tell me why you're here instead, and make it quick."

I wasn't a stranger to her random visits. Every year she liked to pop up and surprise me with her antagonizing remarks, delivering messages to me from my mother that I ignored, unless delivered in person. In fact, the last time she came round, I ended up with a bullet hole in my thigh.

A story for another day.

"The warm welcome you give is always joyous," she replied with sarcasm in her tone.

I ignored her melodrama and walked towards my room. The sound of her heels echoing against my hardwood floors let me know she was following me. I wanted to protest her following me, but it was pointless. Claire always did what Claire wanted to do. "Mother wants you to move back home. It isn't safe out here on your own, and I agree."

Home. That wasn't something I had thought about in quite some time. The dull, asphyxiating feeling of being back at my childhood home was more like a nightmare than a dream. "No, thanks."

"Taylor, this is serious," she snapped.

"So is my shower, Claire." I called back as I turned to jump in.

"Damn it, Taylor!" she exclaimed, snatching my arm as I tried to step into my beautifully-tiled shower I had spent a fortune installing. I wasn't typically one to be nostalgic, but when I designed this bathroom, I did it to replicate the Elder Hallow baths of my home. It was the only place that I had ever felt solace in when I lived with my mother and the only part of my childhood I allowed to follow me. "The hunters are closing in, and the only way we are safe is together."

Glancing down at her grip on my arm, I narrowed my eyes in anger as my lip curled to show her my irritation. Sister or not, she knew I hated being manhandled. "Move your hand, now."

She hesitated for a split second until it sunk in what she had done. The rapid haste in which she moved her arm would make one question whether or not my skin had burnt her. However, it was simply because she knew what happened to the last person who had touched me without my consent.

I'd torn him limb from limb and played in his blood, just like the monster they claimed me to be.

"I'm sorry. Just, please... come home." She finally sighed. "It would make everyone feel better if we knew that you were actually safe."

Desperation was clear in her eyes, and rolling mine, I decided to entertain her. "Fine.. I'll think about it."

It wasn't a yes, but I would take it into consideration as long as it meant she would drop the subject and leave me alone. The only thing I wanted to do was enjoy my shower in peace without the irritation of my sister trying to convince me to go home.

"That's all I ask," she exclaimed, excited by the prospect of me agreeing to what my mother wanted. After all, it wasn't often I said I would consider it. "I'll go. Enjoy your shower."

***

Twenty minutes later and freshly dressed in leggings and a tank top, I walked out into the living room with a glass of red wine on my mind. When I turned the corner, my sister's face came into view.

"I thought you would have gone by now," I admitted, passing where she sat headed towards the kitchen.

"Wow, hoping to get rid of me?"

"Well, that was the hope, Claire. Why are you still here?" I replied with irritation.

Grabbing a goblet from the nearest cupboard, I tried to ignore her presence. Perhaps if I was cold enough, she would finally get the hint. Then again, that was always wishful thinking.

"I need to make sure you come back with me. Mom's words, not mine."

Snapping my gaze to Claire, I pulled the cork from the already opened bottle and frowned. "I said I would consider it. I'm damn sure not going right now, and you can't stay here."

The pout that appeared on her lips grated on my last nerve. She tried to pout her way out of everything and it may have worked on my mother, but it wouldn't work on me. Giving her a pointed, indifferent glare, she crossed her arms over her chest. "Fine, but I'll be back in two weeks. I have to go take care of some stuff in New York anyways. Make sure you're ready."

Taken aback by her comment, I glared at her. "If you have to go there, why the hell did you come here? This conversation could have been a phone call or better yet, a text."

Standing, she fixed her designer clothes as if she had to look perfect everywhere she went. If we didn't look similar, there was no way anyone would ever know we were related. She and I were complete opposites. "Two weeks, Taylor."

Two weeks, my ass... I wasn't going.

"Yep. Call first before you come back."

The sound of the front door closing was a blessing. I wasn't sure how she had gotten in since she didn't have a key, but I wouldn't be surprised if she hadn't charmed the building manager at some point.

Pouring my wine to the rim, I sipped it as I headed towards my lush gray sofa. The white, furry throw blanket called my name as I made myself comfortable and picked up the remote. Late night binge watching of my favorite shows was on the top of my to do list, and as I flipped on the TV, the news came on, causing me to frown.

First, she breaks into my place, and then she fucks with my TV.

I never watched the news, and the fact it was on meant my sister had purposely made sure to put it on this channel. In an attempt to ignore it, I went to hit the guide button, only to stop when they started talking about a string of murders in Salem.

Salem was the closest major town to where I lived—Marblehead—and my hunting grounds. I chose the opportunity to work in Salem while living outside so as to not draw attention to myself. The small book and alchemy shop I owned was a cute attraction for the tourists who flocked to Salem every year for its witchy atmosphere.

Their desire to obtain a special remedy for illnesses, or broken hearts, was endless.

It was also something I loved. I was gifted in making herbal remedies and the art of alchemy. My remedies have helped so many people since I had moved here—even if it was slightly tainted with real magic, something most of the tourists wished they had.

I had made a few friends here, but none of them knew what I was, and that's how I stayed safe. Stay mysterious and sweet and never let anyone in.

Was it lonely?

Sometimes.

I made do as I always did.

But being low key was how I had been able to stay hidden for so long. As the news anchor kept talking about the many men killed over the past year, I kept listening. They hadn't been able to connect the murders in the past, but after the latest one, they finally had clues to close in on the killer.

I wasn't sure what supernatural creature had done this, but it wasn't good. The last thing I wanted was this kind of attention being drawn to the area I fed. There was no way the mundane law enforcement would be able to find this creature. As much as I liked to stay to myself, it dawned on me I was going to have to help them in the long run.

I couldn't lose the only thing allowing me to stay in one place.

With a groan, I pulled out my phone and texted my sister. "It wasn't me."

It didn't take but a moment for her to reply, and her text made my brows knit together in confusion. "Are you sure? Keep watching."

"Keep watching? The hell is her problem—"

The last thing I expected was for a picture of the guy I had fed from tonight to pop up on the screen. It was labeled as the last murder victim of this pristine serial killer, and my heart sank. When I left him, he had been alive and the fact he was dead shocked me.

"It wasn't me... he was alive when I left him," I replied with frustration, trying to understand how this happened. "Someone is framing me."

The bubbles showed my sister was typing a long message, which made me worry even more. She wasn't usually one with a lot to say unless she was in your face. Dealing with her in this kind of situation made things more complicated. She was playing the middleman between my mother and I, and this latest stunt would make it even easier for my mother to get me home.

"I'm not sure what to tell you, but Mother has seen this and we are both concerned. You're making a mess of things and getting sloppy. If this isn't a wake up call to come home, then you're more delusional than I thought."

Fuck... if I didn't figure out what the hell was going on—my future here was done.

A DARK EROTIC ROMANCE

HIS
LONELY
REIGN

DARK HEART SERIES

LILITH CARRIE

CHAPTER ONE

You can do this... I mentally told myself. *No distractions.*

Gazing up at the dark, looming building in front of me, I admired the white and black letters: Solv Logistics. The building was no different from any other skyscraper in New York City, but somehow it seemed more intimidating—more menacing.

Like a giant towering over the ant-like figures walking the sidewalks, it cast shadows across the city with no care in the world other than to stand out amongst the sky. The sleek black walls were made up of windows that seemed to ward off the sunlight rather than reflect it. My anxiety was currently through the roof, I took a deep breath and pressed forward in my Mary Jane pumps to the glass double doors that waited for me ahead.

Solv Logistics was a reputable company headquartered in NYC for decades. They specialized in transportation of anything, and had been globally known for helping in humanitarian situations. So when new intel came into my father's company, Elite Humanity, there was more under the surface, well, it took everyone by surprise. I drew the short end of the stick, forced to investigate what was actually going on behind the high-rise walls of regalia.

When I stepped inside the building, I was taken back by how beautiful it was. Gazing around at the dark velvet seating, and the coffee center brewing the most delicious aromas, I realized I wasn't in Kansas anymore. The designers had outdone themselves, and though the black, gold, and white toned decor were simple, it really gave way to how serious they took themselves.

Or how much this company prided itself on being the best in its industry.

"Damn," I breathed out softly.

"Miss, did you need something?" The voice of a man pulled me back to the present. I turned my attention to the main reception area and found a huge, burly looking security guard with dark eyes and an annoyed expression.

At least he's human.

"Yes, I actually have an interview this morning."

Raising a brow, his eyes drifted up and down my attire with curiosity. "The secretary position... yes. Mr. Grey told me a young woman would be coming. What's your name?"

"Sydney," I replied, trying to keep my composure. Something about this man just seemed off, and the way he was staring at me creeped me out.

"Does Sydney have a last name?" he asked flatly.

Nodding, I cleared my throat. "Yeah...sorry. It's Adams."

Typing away at the computer, he picked up a card and ran it through a card reader before holding it out to me. When I went to take it, he held onto it and stared at me just a bit longer. "You look familiar. Do I know you from somewhere?"

Shit. Shit. Shit.

"No," I replied, shaking my head slowly. "I'm new around here so I doubt it. I just moved here from California."

"California? It says on the paperwork you're from Iowa."

I had almost forgotten that little bit of information. I did put that I was from Iowa and, thinking quickly, I smiled at him. "Yep, that's where I was born. I went to school out west and lived there for a few years. That is until I landed the chance at moving to the Big Apple."

The security guard seemed hesitant for a moment before reluctantly releasing the card. "Very well. Go straight through this checkpoint and scan your card. Then take the elevator up to your floor. You only have access to the fourteenth floor."

I didn't bother to wait around to have him question me further. Bidding him a thank you and goodbye, I quickly made my way past the checkpoint scanner and straight towards the elevators, where a few others waited patiently to enter.

All my years of training I hadn't been scared of much, but today I couldn't shake this dreadful feeling in my stomach, I was taking on more than I could handle. Wiping my sweaty palms on my skirt, my eyes stared at the numbers above the elevator, watching them count down until the doors had finally opened.

"After you," a woman said, causing me to snap my gaze towards my left, coming face to face with the true form of Succubus. Her curved horns shimmered blue as the scaled markings on the side of her face contrasted with her golden green eyes. I had never seen a succubus in person before, and I tried my best not to stare, but damn it—I couldn't help it.

"Are you okay, dear?" she asked, snapping me out of my daze with a furrowed brow of confusion. "Do you need help?"

"Oh, I'm sorry," I replied, shaking my head. "My mind is all over the place. I have my first interview today with the CEO, and I will admit I'm really nervous."

It wasn't entirely a lie, but I was trying to save face, so this woman didn't notice I knew she wasn't human. After a moment, her face softened as she nodded in what seemed to be understanding. "Oh, I get it. Don't worry yourself, sweetie. He isn't that bad at all."

"Thank you, I hope he likes me. I really want this job."

The conversation died as we piled into the elevator. Almost half of the people in the elevator with me were supernatural. Their glamor might have fooled normal humans, but not me. My great-great-grandfather had fixed that minor problem with some chemistry and a quick pinch of a needle long ago. All of us were given what we called the X-vac—a shot that allowed us to see these monsters for what they truly were.

Because of that, I had a new nifty gift that allowed me to do my job a lot better.

Still, I couldn't help but shiver as I kept my eyes forward. The human beside me was completely oblivious, flicking through a file of papers as she muttered to herself. I wish I could tell her to run. To leave the company and never come back, but that would just give me away. I had to act normal.

Besides, New York City was supposed to be a neutral territory. I wasn't allowed to do anything, even if I wanted to.

It seemed like every floor we hit, the elevator stopped and the doors would open, letting people off until finally, I was the only one remaining. The doors swished open, revealing a smaller version of the lobby downstairs, minus the coffee, which I wished I had gotten before I'd come up.

More velvet chairs surrounded a sleek couch set to my right. The company's name hung on the wall to my left in gold, bright against the black background. Ahead of me was a secretary's desk, also black, but the only part of her I could see was the top of her head.

"Excuse me?" I said clearly, forcing myself to walk up to that desk, another fake smile plastered on my face as I tried to seem as natural as possible.

The woman's head snapped up, human eyes meeting mine, giving me an internal sigh of relief.

"Take a seat. Mr. Grey will be with you in a moment."

Taken aback by the woman's brash response, I thanked her again before doing just that. Perched at the end of the couch, I glance around. Most of the offices around where I was sitting had their doors closed, and though I couldn't hear them talking on their phones, I was able to see them through the blinds in their windows.

Creatures of all sizes, and species; from Fae to Harpies, Succubus to Shifters, even a Nymph in the distance pouring coffee in what seemed to be a break room carried on as if everything was normal. Then again, I suppose for those here it was.

I just couldn't believe the amount of humans working alongside shifters, who had absolutely no clue what kind of danger they were in. Something my father would be eager to know once I was done with this interview.

Not that I was looking forward to that conversation. The man may have been my father, but he wasn't a very likable person and his confidence in me was minimal. I was only here because it was what my grandfather wanted. Nothing more, nothing less.

"Ms. Adams?" a voice called out as the most gorgeous man I had ever seen stepped through the glass doors around the corner. He was tall and slim, his tailored, three-piece suit clearly more expensive than the rent on my downtown apartment. Even the rigid way he stood made him appear to have definitely come from the upper class. I doubted that the faint lines carved into the skin around his eyes and lips were because the man smiled a lot.

On top of his freakishly gorgeous looks, it only took a moment for me to realize he was a fucking vampire.

No wonder you're gorgeous. You're a blood-sucking killer.

Pulling myself together, I jumped to my feet holding out my hand. "Hello, I'm Sydney Adams."

He eyed me as if I were the monster. The tips of his fangs peeked out beneath his upper lip as they formed a sneer. Dragging my eyes up, I hoped he hadn't noticed my slip-up when I was gawking at his teeth, but I couldn't help it. I'd never actually shook the hand of a vampire before. I'd only killed one.

"You can follow me," he replied flatly, ignoring my offer of a handshake as he quickly turned around and began walking back the way he had come.

Aren't you a ray of fucking sunshine... I muttered to myself as I followed him down a long hallway that wrapped around the building, with offices lined up on either side. People scurried between them, doors opening and closing, stacks of papers being carried or rolled out on trolleys. I weaved through the slight crowd, trying to follow who I assumed was Mr. Grey.

"This floor is for inventory management and data collection," Mr. Grey explained, speed-walking down the hallway. Well, I guess it was a normal speed for him—speed-walking for me. "You'll be Mr. Solvmane's personal assistant, so you'll need to know what each floor and department does and the usual ins and outs."

"Oh." Was this an interview or fucking orientation? And I knew absolutely nothing about what a logistics company actually did. Maybe my cover as a new-to-town college graduate wasn't well thought out. "Alright."

"Your resume did say you were a fast learner." Mr. Grey glanced over his shoulder at me with his eyes narrowed.

"I am," I reassured him, perking up. My smile didn't seem to affect him at all. Instead, he curled his lip with a look of disgust as he slid his eyes away from me and pushed open another door. I stopped short when I realized we were right back in the lobby. Mr. Grey was unfazed, already pressing the button for the elevators as if he couldn't wait for all of this to be over, and when they opened, I had to rush to jump in next to him, otherwise I was certain he would have left me behind.

It was like that for the next thirty minutes as we went to each floor, speed-walking around the halls as he quickly explained what each department did. I tried to keep up. I really did. By the end of this tour, my mind was just as exhausted as my feet.

And there was no way I remembered half of what he told me.

So much for just a simple interview.

"And that's about it." Mr. Grey stepped out of the elevator—hopefully for the last time. We had gone all the way up to the last floor and it took a moment for me to realize this must have been the big man's office. I could see out the windows across the small lobby, overlooking Manhattan. It was a gorgeous view, but unfortunately, Mr. Grey didn't give me long to admire it before he was calling my name again.

"Ms. Adams?" Mr. Grey's slender eyebrow rose as he gave me a disdainful look.

"Coming." Ducking my head, I hurried after him, feet protesting the entire way. I mean, if I knew I was going to walk this much just for an interview, I wouldn't have worn platforms. Instead, I would have come more relaxed and with a notebook to take notes so I could actually remember everything he was telling me.

There was no doubt if I wandered off on my own that I would get lost. I needed a map to get through this damn place.

"And this will be your desk," Mr. Grey said, stopping just beside the office door. "Do you think you can manage to remember all this or do you need me to make you notes?"

"You have notes—"

He scoffed at my comment, and I quickly realized he was being sarcastic. Why in the hell would he want to make me notes? "I've got it. I don't need notes... it's all stored away in my head."

Curling his lip again, he rolled his eyes. "Yes, I suppose we will see how true that really is, won't we?"

Fucking dick.

My eyes swept over the desk he had gestured to moments before. There was nothing special about it. Just a desktop computer, a laptop, a few pens, a notepad and a black, stocky swivel chair.

"Mr. Grey."

I nearly jumped out of my skin as I whipped to the left. The door of the office was open and a man I didn't recognize stood just inside the doorway staring at me. He was handsome—no, scratch that—the man was downright sinful. He towered over me, broad shoulders barely contained by his jacket or blue suit. His black hair was slicked back and shaved on the sides. The tips of black ink upon his skin barely poked out beneath his collar.

When my eyes caught the silvery gray of his, I thought my heart stopped.

Not just because of his looks, but because of what he was.

It took everything in me not to recoil as he studied me. It took everything not to run right out those damn doors. My dad had said there might be a supernatural running the company here. That it would lead us to what we were actually looking for—whatever that was.

However, he said nothing about the CEO being a Lycan.

Coming May of 2023

Celestial Series Book 5: Temptress of Elder Hallow

Dark Heart Series Book 1: His Lonely Reign

Dark Heart Series Book 2: Lawbreaker

Coming June of 2023

Celestial Series Book 6: Taming Pandora

Dark Heart Series Book 3: Tempting Australia

Coming July of 2023

Celestial Series Book 7: Secrets of Thorn Hollow

Shattered Obsessions